JUNGLE TREASURE

LOUISE FURLEY

Jungle Treasure

ISBN- 978-1-7357712-6-7 (Paperback)
ISBN- 978-1-7357712-5-0 (eBook)

Cover design by Pixel Mischief Design

The characters and events portrayed in this book are fictitious. Any similarity to real persons, living or dead, is coincidental and not intended by the author.

iii

JUNGLE TREASURE

Chapter One

*W*ishing she could turn into a vapor and float away, Tirsa Auret imagined there was a red K dripping blood down the middle of her forehead. K for killer.

Afraid she stood out like a sore thumb, she hung back a few feet from the other college interns, praying no one could see her body quaking like a darn tuning fork.

The other interns on the research ship, two young men and two young women, were excited. Bubbly and nervous they chattered over each other like discordant parrots.

As if she thought they could read her terrified mind, Tirsa tugged her knit hat down further all the way to the dark tinted glasses. Struggling to block out the guilty thoughts of her furtive mission, she tried to focus on what one of the interns, Dia, was babbling on and on about.

Grouped with the five interns, there were also five new seamen gathered in the dayroom for the mini reception.

In the furthest corner of the room, the chief mate on the trip to New Guinea, Jancarlo Mercury, casually leaned a tapered hip against the wall, crossed bulked arms over his chest, and observed the scene as unobtrusively as possible. Although he was only a few years older than the interns, they were already giving him a headache. These young, barely twenty-somethings' endless jabbering made his ears ring.

He had studied the manifest of all of the new seamen added for this venture as well as the interns. Running their backgrounds, he'd memorized who was who.

Everyone seemed to fit, relatively, except, his eyes narrowed at the plain girl with the knit hat that covered virtually all of her hair, tinted glasses that hid her face and the color of her eyes, and the over-sized clothes.

There was something fishy about her. Something not right. He would speak with the colonel later about his suspicions.

All heads turned as the professor entered the room. The great wad of messy black hair and full fuzzy beard matched the boisterous voice. Dressed in a rumpled tweed suit, suspenders and a crooked bow tie, he called out a common New Guinea greeting cheerfully, "Happy noon, everyone!"

He nodded to the five newly hired seamen in the back of the room. In return they briefly bowed their heads in respect to him.

The interns immediately broke apart and hurried over to meet their sponsor. Even though the professor was disheveled and clownish, the young people fought over each other for his attention. They gathered around him throwing out question after question.

Dia Lopez moved in close, flapping her Latina eyelashes at him. "Oh, Professor Robinson, I couldn't wait to meet you! This expedition is the only thing I've been able to think about for weeks!"

Full figured at 5'8 with a big fluff of shoulder length dark hair, she was hard to ignore. She reached out a fairly square hand for a girl, and set her fingers on his arm.

A shorter, thin to the edge of anorexia, young woman with long strawberry red hair elbowed the pushy brunette out of the way. "Professor Robinson, this trek is *so amazing*," the redhead gushed, further nudging Dia aside.

"A trip to New Guinea to search for the lost book is too fantastical to imagine!" She pointed at her nametag, "I'm Lindsey Lanahan, I can't wait-"

"Quit hogging him, freckle-face, he's here to meet all of us." A lithe young man pranced up on muscular but wiry legs like a dancer's and pushed her away with his arm. "Professor, I am Max Kovsky at your service." He shook the professor's hand with vigor. "Sir, will we be seeing the Hindenburg Wall?"

The other male intern, tall and strongly built, name tag indicated, Raine Kepper, pushed his baseball cap back off his dark auburn hair and announced, "That would be so cool. It's a giant rocky wall where unique patterns of air movement have sculpted the surface."

"*Ja*, young man," the professor nodded. "Very dramatic panorama, also, highly dangerous. *Neen*, we won't be going there."

The four interns all talked at the same time vying louder and louder for the professor's attention. The five new seamen, Owen, Stav, Bruno, Lil Dam, and Ji, stood outside the clamoring circle of interns waiting for their moment to meet their new boss.

Hovering behind them hoping to avoid attention, petite and nondescript, Tirsa hunched her slender shoulders and stuffed her hands in her pockets.

Jancarlo Mercury had as much as he could take of the obnoxious yammering. Sliding out the door behind him, he went outside and made his way up top deck to the bridge where he'd wait until his boss was ready.

The air was refreshingly cool. A clipped breeze ruffled his long sleeved t-shirt, the dark hair was trimmed too short to stir. Pulling his phone out he sent a quick text. Absently rubbing the cell against his close-trimmed bearded jaw, he clicked it off and stuffed it in his jean's pocket.

He fished out a pack of skinny European cigars from his pocket, shook one out, lit it, sucked deeply then exhaled a cloud of smoke and rested his forearms on the railing.

Cigar between his thumb and finger, he gazed out over the vast sea, anxious to get a move on. Still anchored in a port above Cairns, the sea was choppy but the 120-foot research vessel buzzing with activity barely rocked in the Australian bay.

Docked miles away from coral reefs, it had taken all day to load the ship with supplies and equipment. Departure wasn't until tomorrow morning. Finishing the cigar, Jancarlo headed to the bridge.

Back in the dayroom, everyone gathered in a loose bunch to hear the Professor's itinerary and instructions. This was the first any of them had seen or met Professor Russell Robinson, the man running the show, and the ship.

His glasses so thick, Robinson started talking to a large plastic plant until very importantly, intern Raine carefully maneuvered the professor so that he was facing the group.

Robinson pushed his glasses further up his nose and smiled at the people. "Welcome everyone to the Mediatrix Expedition." He waited while they clapped. "*Dank u*, thank you, thank you. I am sure you have carefully reviewed the itinerary. I will state quickly in a nutshell what is to progress."

Max leaned sideways slightly and whispered in Dia's ear, "He speaks so precisely and plodding, so very carefully, his thick accent is strange, like he pronounces thank as thoonk."

Dia nodded then whispered back, "He sounds kinda like Norwegian or Russian."

Max shrugged. He leaned over again and said, "With a name like Russell Robinson? Hmmm, maybe he's just a little slow or-"

Lindsey's red hair swung around as she snapped a sharp, "Shh!"

Robinson held up his list of information in front of him squinting at it. He moved the paper closer then further, peering through the inch-thick lenses.

He started, "The expedition is built on our very strong evidence that a second Bible, ahh," he ran his fingers through his wild curly hair, then tugged at blue suspenders over the red shirt that gave him a tweedy American Flag look.

"Well, not exactly a Bible, but um, papers, probably actually papyrus and tablets, written after the resurrection by Jesus Christ himself. Also there are words from his executioner, Pontius Pilate, who recorded notes of conversations he had later with the risen Christ.

"Additionally, more writings dictated to a scribe by the released criminal Barabbas, who may have actually been a freedom fighter in the Jewish resistance to the Romans, told about what he and Jesus talked about whilst on the cross, and again when they met weeks later."

Robinson wiped a hand on his wrinkled jacket and then coughed into the hand. "Uh, um, thus, I know as you all are archeological students of that time era, you must be quite enthused about this project."

Prattling on, he talked about the ancient time for a while, the seamen started swaying and shifting, intern Max barely stifled a yawn.

"So, ah," Robinson continued, "we leave at dawn tomorrow on this great vessel, it carries a small speedboat, therefore-"

Someone coughed stopping his diatribe. He cleared his throat and continued on, "Ahem, I digress, anyway, our basic course is to head out to the Coral Sea, head north skirting Moa Island, cruise across the straits past Daru and eventually into the Fly River. We'll be going slowly through the sea, no more than 3 or 4 knots."

Adjusting his glasses, he reviewed his notes again. "*Ja*, so, once we get to the river we will leave this ship and go on a smaller live-aboard whilst travelling upstream."

He pulled at his beard, slowly enunciating every word, "I'm sure everyone has read that New Guinea has more than 1,000 different ethnic groups, and somewhat of 280 different dialects, although pidgin is the most commonly spoken."

Lindsey cooed, "I hope we see as many diverse peoples as possible, it's so amazing to have this opportunity."

The professor bowed slightly to Lindsey. "*Ja*, young lady, it will be amazing. So, we will go a ways up the river and then we will stop for a period of time and stay on land to get our bearings and such, review our maps, etcetera, etcetera. Then we will undertake the rest of the journey to search on foot."

Raine said somewhat nervously, "I hope I brought the right attire for traveling the fiercely rugged interior of New Guinea. I've read that we will be in majestic forests, expansive open savannas and mucky swamps, but the terrain can be considerably hazardous."

"Well, duh," Seaman Bruno mocked with a slight Spanish accent. "It is a primeval jungle with unpredictable weather, un-contacted possibly treacherous natives, and lethal reptiles and insects."

Max grimaced. "Yeah, and all those inoculations were a pain, huh?"

Seaman Ji Wook stated robotic like a Wikipedia, "In the first few months of 2013 an estimated 6000 Iranians arrived in Indonesia and Australia by boat this year."

The others eyed him oddly wondering why he offered this information. "No offense, bro," Seaman Owen cut in yawning, "but who cares, ya know?"

Ji glared at him. "Just saying, *yo*."

Bouncing back and forth on strong athletic legs, Max asked, "Professor Robinson, isn't it illegal for anyone to enter New Guinea through the Torres Straights except natives of the islands?"

The professor opened his mouth but Max added quickly, "Plus don't we need a Surat Keterangan Jalan?"

His hands clasped behind his back, the professor nodded seriously at the handsome intern with wavy dark hair and neatly cropped goatee. "We have squared all of this away, the travel permits and approval to cross and enter past the straits. We're going in at the Fly River. As long as you all have your VISA's and passports we have everything else handled."

Raine raised his hand. The professor squinted at him then nodded. "*Ja*, uh, young man,"

"Raine Kepper, sir," the good-looking intern offered. Like a pitcher, he moved his baseball cap around on his auburn head without actually taking it off. "How are we, how do you know, where, um, where to go, where this book, or these papers are?"

Robinson peered at Raine. Blinking behind the bug-eyed lenses, his hands still clasped behind his back, he teetered forward and back on his feet, his front shirttail draped sloppily out of the side of his trousers.

"Well there young Raymond, I have maps, information that has been passed down to me that I have gone to painstaking lengths to verify." He still spoke carefully, pronouncing every word slowly, so slowly his audience strained mentally to help him push out the words.

"That's uh, Raine, sir, not Ray-"

"So, sir," tall, and stringy with long arms and legs, one of the five new seaman interrupted Raine. "Owen Windlebee, sir." He bent his round head in slight deference; sand colored, mop-like hair flopped in a bowl cut around his head. Looking like a beige lollipop, he said, "Will we-"

Piercing whistles drowned him out. Robinson immediately headed for a doorway. "That's three bells, people, everyone off to bed now, we will leave at dawn. More of your questions can be answered on the way. Good night all." He tripped over a footstool, awkwardly danced around a table and stumbled out the door.

The group stood in shocked silence, then, they started yakking all at once again, even the new seamen. "Would you get a load of- how did he get to- do you think he knows what he's doing-"

While the flummoxed people pondered the odd professor, some giggling, Tirsa stole away to a set of stairs in the back of the room that led to the upper deck.

Emerging on the top deck, the wind had picked up; it hit her full in the face. She didn't mind; she needed something to slap at her, push away the frightening thoughts, and build up the courage she needed for what she had to do tonight. She made her way to the rail.

Clutching the cold wood and metal railing to steady her hands, Tirsa looked out at the darkening sky and sea like Jancarlo Mercury had earlier.

She turned her attention to the shore. She had no plans to be on this ship when it sailed for New Guinea. Her mission was to be completed tonight and she was to get off, unseen, before anyone knew what she'd done.

Breathing deeply to quell her roiling stomach, she dashed at falling tears with the heels of her hands then turned to go to the cabin she shared with the other two female interns.

Hours later, it seemed forever before Tirsa heard Lindsey's gentle snoring and Dia's bear-like snorts and grunts take over the quiet room. She slipped off the narrow berth and trod silently to the door.

She'd slept in her clothes, the hat, and even her shoes. Pulling the tinted glasses out of her pocket she slipped them on in case she ran into anyone. Quietly closing the door behind her, she crept down the dark hall.

As she passed the other cabins she could hear a cacophony of snores, whistles and grunts. She continued down the dimly lit hall to the end where she knew the professor's cabin was, last door on the left.

She hesitated outside his door to make sure no one was coming. It appeared everyone was asleep, only the wash of the sea lapping at the hull and the snores broke the still of the night. Her shadow the only thing moving in the hall, Tirsa carefully turned the knob with sweating hands, the door was unlocked.

Holding her breath, she opened the door slowly and crept inside. Waiting a few banging heartbeats, she tiptoed to the bed and looked down to make sure it was the professor. The only light came from the window but even in the faint light she could make out the unkempt, curly dark hair and furry beard. His arms were flung out over the sheet, his breathing low and steady.

Her hand shaking like a blade of grass in a monsoon, Tirsa pulled the knife out of her pocket. For a moment she couldn't move at all, couldn't breathe, couldn't think. But she prodded herself, she had to do it, she had to do it for Meggie.

Closing her eyes, she turned her head away, held her breath. Her palms slick with sweat, she lifted the knife with both hands and brought it down she hoped right in the center of the professor's chest.

But- something hard stopped her hands in midair. Her eyes flew open, the professor was awake and holding her wrists with one very large, very strong hand.

"Hello Miss Auret," he said quite calmly. Then, in one lightning movement he rolled, pulling her with him until she was lying on her back on the bed, and he was on top of her holding her wrist with the knife still in her hand, but now the knife was at her throat.

Chapter Two

*T*aking the knife from her frozen fingers, the professor braced himself on his left forearm. Holding the blade at her neck with his left hand, he pulled off her glasses with his free hand and studied them.

"As I thought, plain tinted glass." He tossed them on the table next to the bed. Her frantic gaze followed his movements then flew to his face.

His face, obscured by the thick beard was only a few inches from hers. In a deeply masculine, heavily accented voice, he demanded, "Tell me why you broke into my cabin in the middle of the night to kill me?"

One dark eyebrow over an eye so dark it appeared black, rose in question at her. He looked down at her small quivering hands splayed against his strapping bare chest, ineffectively trying to push his big body off her.

Face as white as a sheet, Tirsa's breath had left her, she just blinked at him with petrified blue eyes and pushed at his chest as hard as she could.

When she didn't respond to his question, bracing his weight on his muscular forearm, Robinson kept his body just slightly touching hers enough to pin her to the bed, the knife still at her neck, he said calmly, "Perhaps you don't fully understand your position, Miss Auret. Let me recap, you broke into my room in the dead of night and attempted to kill me. The evidence as you see is in my hand."

Her body trembled so violently she vibrated against him. Even though it was obviously futile, he was twice her size and weight, she continued to push at him, it was like a kitten pushing at an ox.

He made a slight movement pressing the blade against her throat. "This is my ship and you are in my bed. Since you tried to kill me and are therefore a criminal, I have the right to do whatever I want with you and you will have no way of complaint. Now, tell me who sent you here."

When she still said nothing, just gaped at him, he took a different tact. "The fact that you are in my room unbidden indicates you are offering yourself to me sexually, and therefore anything I do now would be considered consensual."

Tirsa's gasp widened, her eyes struck with breathtaking terror. Tears teemed quickly, blurring the blue irises. Her chest rose and fell rapidly as deeper panic set in. She tried to squirm out from under him, but he pressed more of his weight on her, completely immobilizing her.

His eyes swept the length of her body then back to her face, clearly establishing his threat of rape. No trace of the bumbling professor's slow studied speech was present, but there was still an accent.

To emphasize his point, the knife still on her neck, he pushed his legs between hers. His stiffening erection pressing on her demonstrated he was quite capable of carrying out his threat.

Helpless to move at all to fight him, Tirsa cried breathlessly, "Please, you can't…" tears spilled, her throat closed, she couldn't speak.

"Oh but I can, and I will if you don't tell me right now who sent you here and why you tried to kill me." His voice devoid of emotion, cold dark eyes glittered down at her.

All semblance of the silly professor except for the hair and beard had vanished into harsh eyes and a hard body. He was wearing only loose pajama bottoms and was bare-chested. Black hair shadowed his surprisingly huge, heavily muscled chest.

The dim light made him all that more frightening, like a deadly brigand. Tirsa's lips parted but she still didn't make a sound except for cutting gasping breaths. Tears streamed down her cheeks with her sobs.

When she still didn't respond, he changed positions, moving up to straddle her. Stuffing the knife in the back of the waistband of his pajamas, he wrapped his long fingers around both of her wrists. Holding them together over her head with one huge hand, he reached down and unbuttoned the top button of her oversized shirt and demanded, "Tell me who sent you."

She cried out hoarsely, "Stop, stop or I'll..." her terrified voice shook, she could hardly speak above a whisper her throat was so constricted in fear. "I'll scream," she choked out. He unbuttoned the next button, "*Please*," she begged, squirming frantically under him.

Opening a third button, he said, "Go ahead and scream. You're in my cabin. Believe me, unless it's me screaming no one will do a thing. Tell me who sent you here." He undid a fourth button then as she still didn't answer him, he opened the last one.

Her lips pressed tremulously together as if trying to keep the words in.

He pulled apart the lapels of her shirt exposing a pink lacey bra. "Well, well, my little intern," he muttered, gazing

13

at her breasts, "you *have* been hiding a nice little package, just as Jancarlo suspected." Still holding her hands over her head, his erection now a thick hard ridge bearing down on her, he moved his hand towards her chest.

She writhed against the mattress and cried, "Please, please, I beg you! I can't, I can't tell, please don't," her eyelids glued closed, she broke into tormented sobs.

The professor sat back on his heels and regarded the hysterically distraught young woman under him acting very un-murderess-like. Holding her hands letting them rest on her stomach, he said blithely, "You could at least apologize."

He waited but she said nothing. Lying on a strange man's bed in the dark with him as big as an angry bear, half-naked, hovering over her and holding her captive, she was too terrified to even open her eyes.

Sighing, he said, "I find I'm not in the mood for rape, assassins are generally not my type." He adjusted his erection off her. "So, I've decided instead, if you don't tell me who sent you, I'm just going to rip out your insides and throw your body over the side of the ship. The sharks will take care of the rest."

Still holding her wrists he pulled the knife back out and held it as if about to plunge it into her gut. Turning her head, she clamped her eyes shut harder, her lips moving in soundless prayer, her chest shook and jerked with silent sobs.

The professor sighed, perplexed. He let go of her hands and lowered the knife. "I don't understand, woman, what is so much more terrifying to you than your own death that you refuse to tell me who sent you and why?" He waited, but she only covered her face with her hands and wept.

He stuck the knife back in his waistband and rolled off the bed. Padding in bare feet to the dresser, he plucked some tissues out of a box and returned to the bed. Handing the tissues to her, he said coolly, "Dry your face, we're going up top." He went back to the dresser, opened a drawer and pulled out a t-shirt.

She sat up, wiped her eyes with trembling hands and watched him warily as he pulled the shirt over his head, tugging it down over the hard slabs of muscles. The pajama bottoms hung low on his taut lean hips.

Standing beside the bed he suddenly grabbed one of her upper arms and picked her up, pulled her off and to her feet.

Her eyes bugged out, the silly professor had lifted her right up off the bed with one hand. She stared at him stunned.

Well over 6 feet with bulging arms like a boxer, he walked to the door, opened it and ordered, "Come with me." Scared out of her mind that he was about to make good on his threat to throw her overboard, she balked.

He said tersely, "Don't make me carry you, Tirsa, if that's your real name, because I have no problem dragging you out of here and tossing you over my shoulder, but it'll be easier, and less embarrassing for you if you do it on your own steam."

Chapter Three

*P*rofessor Robinson stood in the doorway watching her, waiting. Taking a shuddering breath, Tirsa wiped her eyes again, dropped the tissues in a wastebasket and went to the door. He stepped aside for her to cross the threshold.

Turning almost sideways to avoid coming in contact with his body, she slipped quickly past him.

Closing the door behind them, he took ahold of her arm, walked her down the narrow hallway and up the stairs to the bridge. When they reached the bridge, he opened the door and pulled her inside closing the door behind them.

His team of seasoned seamen, Third Mate Johnson Brown was at the helm. Chief Mate Jancarlo Mercury, and Second Mate Knox Adams were there too, they all looked like they had been expecting them.

All three men stared at Tirsa's open shirt. Johnson Brown set his hefty hands on solid hips and grinned at Jancarlo, "*Broed*, you were right, she's packing a damned fine rack."

His face all hard angles, Jancarlo's impassive expression didn't change and he didn't respond to the comment.

16

Scowling at Tirsa as if it was her fault she was exposed, Robinson snapped, "Cover yourself, woman!"

Her cheeks flaming, Tirsa tried to button her shirt but her hands were shaking so badly she couldn't hold a button. The professor stood in front of her, his wall of shoulders deliberately blocking the view of the leering men.

Tirsa's face flushed beet red as he pushed her useless hands aside, his knuckles lightly brushing her breasts while he buttoned her shirt for her.

Seeing her plump flesh rounding over the lacy bra, and his fingers inadvertently touching them was setting off a reaction in his pants, again. Robinson needed to quickly step away from her before he embarrassed himself.

When he was done, he suddenly yanked off the knit hat that covered her head and threw it on the floor.

Bright blonde hair tumbled out and down, soft fat curls waved over her shoulders and down half her back. Unconsciously, with a purely feminine move she tried to stop her hair from falling. The tinted glasses were back in the professor's cabin, her disguise was gone.

His dusky brown skin gleaming, Third Mate Johnson exclaimed, "Whoa." Dragging a huge palm over his shaved head, his astonished eyes on Tirsa, he said to Knox Adams, "She beats you out in the knit hat category."

A permanent scowl etched on his narrow face, long, lean Knox's expression was as impassive as Jancarlo's but his eyes widened.

The girl in the oversized clothes, knit hat and dark glasses had morphed from a plain, nondescript looking female into a stunning bombshell. His gaze sweeping her body, making no comment, Knox pushed his own dark blue wool hat back, and pulled at his full tapered beard with elongated fingers.

The professor pointed to a chair over on the far side of the bridge, he said to the girl, "Go sit there." This time she hurried to do what he said. They all watched her stride away, staring at the natural soft sway of her hips. She sat down on the chair, petrified as to what the four men planned to do to her.

The men stared at her, their expressions, except for Johnson's blatant admiring gaze were unreadable. Then the seamen turned into a huddle, speaking so quietly she couldn't hear a word they said.

Her skin already fair, paled further as she envisioned what was going to happen to her. She clasped her hands tightly to keep them still.

"So," his chiseled face hard as slate, like he had a bad taste in his mouth, Jancarlo said, "I was correct. She did try to kill you."

The professor smiled slightly and nodded. "*Ja.* Sometimes your sixth sense is even stronger than mine. I agreed she was suspicious and probably had an agenda but killing me wasn't one of my suspicions."

Taciturn Knox said through unmoving lips, "What did she say, why did she try to murder you, and how, I mean…" he shifted a glance at the petite girl across the room with the big frightened blue eyes then to the professor's massive arms.

Robinson chuckled wryly. "Well, she didn't try to break my neck with her bare hands. She used this," he pulled out the knife and showed them. The knife was small enough to hide under clothes but the four-inch blade would kill easily.

"Nice," Johnson said.

"A steak knife?" Knox scoffed at the implement. "What professional kills with a kitchen utensil?"

They all looked over at her, her eyes dropped to the floor, mortified red brightened her cheeks.

His dark skin shining in the overhead lights, turning back to his boss, Johnson Brown asked, "So, what did happen? You look still alive, as does she," he nodded towards Tirsa. "But you sick *vuilehond*- dog, what're you-showing off? You should have let her get fully dressed before bringing her up here."

The professor glared at Johnson. "I did not assault her." He looked slightly embarrassed as he explained, "Well, maybe I threatened her some to get her to talk, which she didn't. Anyway," he shook his head at the men's vapid interest. "She snuck in my room in the dark, even if I wasn't waiting for her I could hear the door open and her footsteps on the carpet, she's definitely an amateur.

"She held the knife over me for what seemed an eternity. I opened my eyes to bare slits, she was shaking like a leaf, the knife was going all over the place, she actually had her eyes closed and her head turned away. The direction the knife was heading when she finally got the nerve to stab it so unbelievably slowly, well, my mattress was in big trouble. Me, not so much, she was going to miss me by a mile."

The men listened intently, their eyes shifting back and forth from the professor to her, then Johnson said, "Obviously you turned the tables on her, but why was she trying to kill you?"

The professor shrugged. "Hell if I know. I'm pretty sure it wasn't her idea, yet under the threat of," he looked sheepish, "sexual assault, and uh, being gutted and tossed overboard for the sharks," he shrugged again, "she refused to tell me. Other than crying, she's hardly uttered a word."

Knox snorted, his lips twisted as he said with dour sarcasm, "Now I know there's something dead wrong about her, a woman that doesn't yak?" The others laughed at him.

Johnson said quietly, "Especially one that looks like she does." They all turned and looked at her again.

She sat with her hands under her thighs, legs tucked under the chair, head lowered and eyes closed. The blonde hair draped, covering the sides of her lovely face wet with tears. She occasionally dashed angrily at the tears with dainty hands.

"Okay, I'm going to lock her in my cabin, don't start," Robinson frowned at the seamen who were gleefully leering at him. "I have no intentions of taking advantage of…the situation. At least not tonight."

His face never cracking a smile, Jancarlo warned, "Watch your back, Colonel."

The professor winked at him as he turned and headed towards Tirsa. He could hear the men chuckling behind him.

Standing in front of her, he said coldly, "Get up." Without looking at him she stiffly slid to her feet.

Gripping her upper arm, he walked her across the room.

Head high, eyes lowered, she pretended she wasn't on a ship in the middle of the night in a foreign country alone with strange men, leaving with one of them that she had no less than twenty minutes ago tried to assassinate.

He took her back to his room. Opening the door, he turned on the light and gestured with his hand for her to go inside.

Tirsa's brain screamed, *Run!* But she knew there was nowhere to run to, nowhere to go. She glanced down the hall debating; maybe he wouldn't come after her if she fled.

"Don't even think about it. I want to go to sleep, not chase some homicidal woman down the hall. Besides, you won't get two feet before I catch you, then I'll be pissed for having to chase you. Now go in." He stared down at her, his patience thinning.

She entered the room, just a couple of anxious steps and stopped. Following her inside, he closed the door and locked it, then stood and stared at her, apparently trying to decide what to do with her. Her lips trembled, her skin had a faint green hue, she eyed the wastebasket like was going to throw up.

He went over to a set of trunks stacked against the wall. Opening the top one, he took something out, closed the lid then walked back over to where she stood quaking.

Her eyes dropped to what he held. The color drained from her face. She shook her head, not taking her eyes off the chain he held in his hands. "No…God no…please don't, please…"

Ignoring her pleas, he opened a wide circular clamp on the chain and snapped it around her neck. Her hands went right to it, she tried to pull it off. "Please professor, you can't do this!"

He held the other end of the chain and clamped it to a metal slate at the foot of his bed. Then he went and shut off the light He came back and stood in front of her.

Looking down at her terrified face, he said coldly, "You broke and entered, trespassed into my room, on my ship and tried to take my life. As I said before, I can do anything I want. Good night." He left her standing there in the dark and climbed back into the bed.

She said weakly, "I didn't break in, the…the door was unlocked." He made no response.

She stood like a statue for as long as she could, an hour passed, then she collapsed slowly, curling up in a ball on the floor at the foot of his bed. She was only slightly relieved, when she first saw the chain she thought for sure she was going overboard with a cement block or an anchor tied to the end.

Robinson lay on top of his bed trying to sleep, waiting for her to lie down. Now that she finally had, he listened to her trying to stifle her frightened weeping.

Chapter Four

*B*efore the dawn's light even started thinking about rising, Robinson woke. Remembering last night, he got up and went to the end of his bed.

She was still there, curled up on the floor like a child, her head on a bent arm, the long blonde hair splayed behind her. Resisting the urge to grab a pillow, and lay a blanket over her, he went into the head and took a shower.

After dressing in the head, he came out toweling his wet hair. He dropped the damp towel on the dresser, grabbed up a comb and strode to the door.

Tirsa was sitting up with her arms wrapped around her knees watching him. He was wearing jeans and a sweater; both outlined his strongly built body. His nerdish hair and beard looked so incongruent with the powerful muscular physique.

Last night, his professor's voice and demeanor had changed. He spoke with a subtler accent and his tone was hard and low. His goofy manner had transformed to confident and tough. It appeared she wasn't the only one in disguise. She climbed to her feet holding the chain and asked timidly, "Can, uh, you please take this off me?"

His hand on the doorknob, he looked at her with no emotion and said, "No." When he turned from her to open the door he heard her choke back a sob.

"Please Professor," she cried, tears rolling over rounded cheeks. "If the ship goes down, I'll...I can't get away...I'll drown..."

Opening the door, he said coldly, "You should have thought of that before attempting to plunge a knife into my heart." As he stepped through the door he turned back to look at her.

She had sunk to her knees, her head lowered. Clutching the links, her hands set on her thighs. Her face a veneer of abject distress, her shoulders shook with silent sobs.

Softly, but with conviction, he said, "It is not going to sink, Tirsa. If it does, I will come for you." He closed the door.

Up on the bridge, Jancarlo was at the helm also in jeans and a dark sweater.

The professor entered moving to stand beside him. He reviewed the hydrographical charts for navigation, and the position fixing instruments making sure they were up-to-date.

Everything on board including the electronic chart display and information system met the SOLAS requirements. Paper charts hung within easy reach. Three whistles blew and the ship started to move, slowly, ponderously. The two men looked out the window at the bay.

"Aren't you going to ask me what I did with her?" Robinson inquired of his friend.

Jancarlo shrugged. "You are alive, that is all I care about." He rubbed his face as if washing it then scrubbed his tanned hands over the closely trimmed beard.

The Professor smiled. "That's good to know." They watched the port pass by as they moved through the bay. Gulls squawked flying overhead, circling the boat. Robinson turned slightly to look at Jancarlo.

"Don't you want to know what happened, later? Aren't you the least bit curious to know if I…" he watched the chief mate skillfully direct the ship through the channel and out into the Coral Sea.

His dark eyes intent on driving, Jancarlo made no comment.

"Seriously, Jan," the professor said slightly curious, "you don't want to know if I did her?"

His face a mask, Jancarlo remained silent. The men stood side-by-side, feeling the restraints of land let go, the ship forged smoothly through the rocking water.

Once out in the open sea, Jancarlo glanced at the gyrocompass then put the ship on autopilot and faced the professor. Crossing his arms over a chest thick with cut muscles, he leaned a slim hip against the counter.

"She is going to be trouble. I can see it, I can feel it. She is going to be trouble for the mission and she is going to be trouble for you. If she were a man or an ugly female you would have locked her in the storage room and then dumped her on shore leaving her with the Australian police."

Jancarlo sat down on the leather swivel chair at the helm, crossed an ankle over a knee. "Which is what you should have done."

The messy hair hopped when the professor shook his head. "*Neen*. I kept her close because I want to get as much information as I can out of her, find out exactly what we're dealing with."

Jancarlo snorted a contradicting grumble, his narrowed eyes grated at his friend, he insisted, "*Neen,* you are intrigued by the woman, I saw the way you looked at her."

"Jan, we were all looking at her like that, she's young and beautiful with a rocking hot body."

Shaking his head, Jancarlo said, "We looked at her in lust, you looked at her with lust and interest."

"That's what I said, I am interested in who sent her and why someone wants me dead."

Jancarlo turned away from him. "Whatever, E. You have a lot of enemies, choose one. Get rid of her."

With long sleek strides across the deck, Knox entered the bridge wearing his ever-present scowl and knit hat. His body so lean, and with exceptionally long legs, his huge shoulders were always a shock. He was looking down at a log extract in his hand. He held it out to the professor.

"E, how would you like me to word last night's issue on the 'howgozit' sheet?" The sheet covers time at sea, time under pilotage, time in port, and types of incidences.

Knox and Jancarlo blankly watched the conflicting expressions cross the professor's face as he thought about how to report the intern's actions.

His brows drew down. "I know you guys want a reaction out of me. But you're not getting one. I'll let you know later what to record." He strode out of the bridge letting the wind slam the door behind him.

Jancarlo and Knox, generally stoic men shared a rare grin. Their normally tough, harsh friend was abnormally captivated by the young murderess.

"She's going to be trouble," Knox pronounced.

"*Ja,*" Jancarlo agreed.

"I think it's going to be interesting trouble."

"*Ja,*" Jancarlo agreed, the grin gone.

"We won't let the bitch hurt him, Jan."

Jancarlo's jaw grit, the corner of it worked.

Knox left the bridge and went outside to the top deck to give the new seamen instructions. He set the new ranks, Ordinary Seamen, (OS), Owen and Ji to mopping the deck, and Bruno and Lil Dam to polishing the rails.

Johnson stepped out onto the deck. "You," he pointed to the fifth new seaman, Stav standing idly, "follow me." He took him down to the engine room to work.

The interns stood in a clutch off to the side. "What are we supposed to do?" Max said to no one in particular. Raine watched Owen and Ji thinking they looked funny together.

Owen tall and thin with a bowl mop of stringy hair, and the severely neat Ji, half his size but he worked out. Ji's muscles flexed against the loose, off-white shirt all the new seamen wore with the baggy, slightly darker pants. The two went and got buckets, filled them with water and added detergent.

"I'm not swabbing no stinkin' deck, that's all I know," Lindsey announced, her nose puckered, the freckles merged together over her pale skin. The four interns stood aimlessly for a while talking.

Dia said casually, "I wouldn't mind checking out the engine room, I dig those big machines."

Raine looked her full figure up and down in her skin-tight t-shirt and jeans and said to her, "I bet you do." They all laughed.

"Where's that other girl, um, the one in the knit hat and glasses, what's her name, Terry or something?" Raine asked.

"Who knows, who cares. Maybe the homely chick already got herself a boyfriend on board," Lindsey replied with a snide scowl. "She was hardly friendly, didn't say a word to any of us."

"I think it was like Tersha or Tisha or something," Max offered. "You couldn't really see what she looked like anyway in those baggy clothes and dark glasses. Couldn't even tell what color her hair was, if she had any with that hat covering half her head. She also has a very faint accent like the senior seamen and the professor have, but hers is totally different, French I think."

"Who cares?" Lindsey repeated. "She was a stuck up bitch. Come on." She had tied her long red hair into braids, they striped down her back like strawberry suspenders. "Let's go to the day room and play cards. We're here to learn, not to clean." She strode haughtily to the stairs leading to below decks.

Dia moved past her, flitting fast down the stairs disappearing before the rest even set a foot on the first step.

When Max reached the last few steps he leaped in the air, his legs straight out in a split then landed lightly on his toes.

Lindsey watched him in awe. She checked out the young man, lithe but with a hard body, short smooth dark hair and a neatly pared goatee. "Hey," she said, admiring the athletic intern, "that was incredible, are you like a dancer or something? Like those people on TV that do the contests?"

"What are you," Raine said disparaging to Max, "a fairy or something?"

Max made a face at him, his nose in the air. "A man can be a dancer you red-haired prick, and not be gay." He turned and winked at Lindsey. "Not that there's anything wrong with that. My favorite uncle just married his sweetheart, Benjamin. But I'm straight as an arrow." They linked arms and walked down the hall together.

Raine called out, following them, "Yeah, well, you just stay on your own side of the fucking cabin. Hear me? And my hair is not red, dickface, it's auburn."

Dia branched off and went aft to find her way to the engine room on the bottom deck. Finding it, she opened the heavy steel door, the warmer air and noise rushed out.

She stepped inside and closed the door. It was hot and very loud, and dirty.

Once past the soundproofing insulation, metallic grating and clanging from the propulsion, auxiliary engines and generators, high pitched whirring from feed pumps and fuel pumps, even the cooling system flushing water added to the sound level.

Dia wandered only briefly before coming across one of the OS's.

New seaman, Stav, was in front of the water-cooling exhaust manifold. He had one hand on a riser connected to the exhaust discharge, and a screwdriver in the other when she approached him.

Thank goodness it was quieter where he was working. Tugging the neckline of her super tight shirt down to reveal more ample cleavage, she announced her presence saying, "Hi there."

The big blond seaman looked surprised to see a woman in the engine room. "Well, hey yourself, good lookin'." He set the screwdriver down on a pipe.

"Whatcha doin'?" she asked, shimmying close to him. Fluffing her shoulder length, curly dark brown hair, she pretended interest in what he was working on.

One husky shoulder rose slightly. "Nothing much, just supposed to be checking for rust on these elbows." He tapped the riser with his hand. "I don't know why, they're made with stainless steel, but I just do what I'm told. What are you doing, I mean down here? This isn't exactly a place for a lady." He wiped his hands on his off-white shirt then pushed the long sleeves up.

Her smile took in his square head with blond hair, the big broad shoulders and all the way down his thick legs; he looked like a yellow mountain. "Well," she simpered, "I never said I was a lady." She leaned against a gearbox.

The seaman looked like he didn't know how to take this, was she joking or should he make a move? "Uh…"

She moved right up to him and slid her hands up his thick chest. "Has anyone ever told you that you look like that Thor guy on the Avengers? Big and blond, and," standing on her tiptoes, she pushed her full breasts against his chest and kissed him.

He hesitated for only a second, then roped his thick arms around her, pulled her close and tightened the kiss. After a minute he pulled back. Sliding his hands down then over her large posterior, squeezing the globes, he said with a smile, "Nice. More cushion for the pushin' like they say. You wanna-"

"Right now," she affirmed bluntly, cocking her head and batting her lashes. He grabbed her hand and led her down the rubber-matted aisle. Over his shoulder he said, "There's not a lot of hidden space around here but I know of a perfect place."

The couple slipped into a supply room. As he closed the door, Dia asked, "What's your name again, honey?"

Chapter Five

$\mathcal{M}$ost everyone ate together at 1700 hours in the mess. Knox and Jancarlo stayed on the bridge and Johnson had gone down to the engine room.

The professor moved uneasily down the hall to his cabin. Unsure of the condition his prisoner would be in, especially her attitude, he unlocked the door, opened it and went in quickly, he didn't want anyone passing by in the hall to see the girl chained to his bed.

He stood just inside the doorway closing the door behind him. He was quite surprised to see her sitting on the floor leaning against his bed, her legs crossed, with a book in her hand. Dry-eyed she was calmly reading. She looked up at him, folded the book closed.

Glancing at the cover, he asked, "How did you get my book on New Guinea Rivers?" He had expected tears or screaming or something on that level, not her sitting peacefully reading.

She moved to kneel, sitting back on her heels. "I hope it's okay," her voice trembled, now she appeared fearful. "It was there on the dresser. I could just reach it. I...I didn't touch anything else, I swear." Her winsome heart-shaped face was strongly earnest, hoping he wasn't angry.

If he could read her mind, he'd see a picture pop in her head of him whipping her with his belt for daring to touch his property. Virtually at his mercy, she was in the most vulnerable position that she could be in. He could do anything he wanted to her and no one would know.

Robinson inclined his head to her not sure how to respond. He hadn't told her she couldn't move around, at least as far as the chain would let her, and that was only about four feet. The book was harmless.

Next time he would make sure there was nothing she could use as a weapon within her reach. Except for his seasoned team, not knowing the rest of the people on the vessel, he'd locked up anything valuable or dangerous.

He wasn't worried about Tirsa stealing anything. She might be a murderer, well, an inept attempted murderer but she didn't act like a thief. A thief would have tried to lie to him, make up the name of whoever sent her, or use her wiles on him, and she had a surplus of those, to divert him from her actions.

Yet, she'd kept her mouth shut, and didn't try to trick, lie to, or seduce him. Trying to recall her paperwork, he thought she was 21-22 maybe, she looked younger and she appeared incredibly innocent. It was hard for a person not to show their feelings or experience in their face, but those big blue eyes that regarded him fearfully shone straight out pure and guileless.

He scratched his chest over the sweater then set his big hands on narrow hips and answered her, "*Ja*, it's okay."

Still kneeling, she let out her held breath and very softly said, "Thank you." Holding the book closed on her knees her eyes dropped nervously to the floor.

Looking down at her kneeling so small and defenseless at his feet with her head lowered, an odd feeling struck him. His shoulders stiffened, he'd be dammed if he was going to feel guilty about keeping her locked in his room with a chain around her neck.

Relaxing his shoulders, he hadn't thought about her being bored sitting there all day chained up with nothing to do.

He'd had his first mate, Jancarlo, bring her a sandwich and briefly free her to use the head. Jancarlo reported that she never looked at him, and hadn't said a word the few minutes he was in there except a quiet thank you for the sandwich.

She hadn't even demurred when he'd locked the clamp back around her neck, just kept her eyes lowered, never once looking at him.

Of course Jancarlo was such a hard as nails man like the toughest of longshoremen, with a harsh inscrutable expression in his hooded dark eyes, even the fiercest men avoided pissing him off. Most just avoided him.

The boat suddenly rocked steeply, knocking her off her knees. Falling to the side, her elbow banged on the hardwood floor, the book dropped with a clunk.

Before he thought about it, Robinson crouched beside her, wrapped his large hands around her slim shoulders and helped her sit back up. At her frightened expression he said, "It's all right, it's just a big swell. They'll get bigger the further out to sea we go."

Alarmed, she stammered, "We're not sailing, not moving- are we?"

He nodded, not understanding her surprise. "*Ja*, of course. We're going to New Guinea, that was the plan."

33

She scrambled to her feet; her face lost color, the eyes grew even bigger if possible. Her hands pressed together as if in prayer she cried, "No! I can't go to New Guinea! I was supposed to get right off the ship, fly home from Australia, I can't…I don't have…they're going to hurt my-" Feeling the boat sway under her feet she realized it was too late. Not wanting him to see her cry again she covered her face with her hands.

Standing in front of her like a linebacker, sounding as if he wanted her to deny it, he said, "I see. So the plan was to kill me and sneak off the ship and get clean away."

She didn't respond, just kept her hands over her face, shoulders hunched, her head lowered, tears leaked through her fingers.

His stomach panged. There it was again, he thought, that guilty feeling. Hell, he wasn't the one that had done wrong, he was the victim, goddammit. He felt a little foolish thinking of himself as the victim. Here he was twice her size and she was chained by the neck.

The professor had known all along he was never in any danger of her. Even without Jancarlo's suspicions and their preparation to watch her, she was breathing so hard with nerves and fright, he had heard her coming last night a mile away.

With her clumsy attempt at stabbing him, even if she had kept her eyes open and brought the knife down straighter, harder, faster, there was no way she would have been able to do any great damage to him. She was too scared, and, he admitted to himself, her heart definitely was not in it.

She obviously had no desire to kill him. But someone did, and he needed to learn who that was before a second attempt was made.

The vessel rocked hard again, tilting then slammed back down hard. Tirsa fell sideways letting out a little yelp. He grabbed her arms to keep her from falling. The chain shook and jangled. She looked up at him, terror striking the lovely face. She cried, "Are we going down? Are we-"

He grasped her arms tightly, his sturdy legs shoulder-width on the floor to brace them both. "*Neen*, no, we're fine. It's just rough seas. You'll get your sea-legs soon."

The boat pitched hard again throwing her against him, he caught her and wrapped his strong arms around her to hold her steady, her forearms pressed up against his chest. His nose dipped into her hair, he inhaled deeply, then leaned back and gently pushed a few strands of hair off her face, letting them tumble with the rest down her back.

Feeling oddly reluctant, he released her and another sudden huge swell shook the ship and she pitched sideways, the chain snapped hard yanking her head back. Her hands went to the clamp; she gripped it with her fingers trying to protect her neck.

"Dammit," he cursed. Winding one hand around her arm again to hold her steady, he fished keys out of his pocket. He said harshly, "Tilt your head back."

His hard, commanding voice reignited fear in her eyes; she tried to pull away from him.

Keeping his grip on her arm tight, he said more gently, "I'm not going to hurt you, Tirsa, I am going to remove the chain, move your head."

Warily, she obliged.

Thinking he couldn't believe he'd put a steel chain around a girl's neck and chained her to his bed, made her sleep on the floor, Robinson shook his head, what a man. He unlocked the clamp, took it and the chain and threw them with disgust on the stacked trunks. She touched her neck feeling the freedom from the heavy clamp and chain.

"Let me see." He pushed her hands aside and examined her neck to see if she needed the medic. Red rings gouged parts of the fair skin of her thin neck. The flash of guilt stuck him again.

Annoyed, he shoved the feeling away. He said gruffly, "Everyone should be up in the mess having dinner about now. Let's go."

Balking, she asked fearfully, "Are you going to- to throw me overboard now?"

His mouth pulled down in dismay. "Of course not. We're are going to go eat dinner."

Saffron brows arching in surprise, Tirsa's voice held doubt, "I'm to eat with…everyone?" Obviously she believed he would keep her restrained where she couldn't hurt anyone.

Nodding, he muttered, "*Ja*, of course." He moved to the door, but she didn't take a step.

He waited, perplexed when she didn't look too happy, but she must be hungry. "What's wrong?" Maybe she was embarrassed for not being around the whole night and day, people certainly were wondering what was up.

She looked down at her shirt she'd had on for a couple of days and slept in. "I uh…"

He got it. She wanted to get cleaned up. Funny, he was thinking how nice her hair smelled when she'd been in his arms. "Oh. Okay. Why don't you take a shower, I'll wait."

"Um…"

"What?"

Her cheeks tinged pink. "I only have a couple of changes of clothes, I wasn't supposed to be-" she turned pinker, last thing she needed was to keep reminding him of her plan to leave the ship right away, and why. "Um, but, they're in my, um…"

It dawned on him. "*Ja*. I get it. You want your clothes. I'll get them. What's your bag look like?"

Blinking at him, surprised at his willing to fetch her bag, her words slightly stilted she replied, "It's, um, the little brown one. Can't miss it, the others brought, well, you'll see." She smiled at the comparison of her one small bag to their numerous huge suitcases.

Her sudden smile, brief though it was, gave Robinson an odd prickly feeling. It was the first time he'd seen her look other than scared to death. He smiled back. "They're going to be quite surprised when they find out they're going have to leave most of it on this ship."

A laugh bubbled out of her pretty lips, the blue eyes twinkled, she said, "There's going to be a mutiny when Lindsey doesn't have her Jimmy Choo's and Dia doesn't have her makeup."

"What's a Jimmy Choos?" he asked.

She grinned. It pricked him again, a weird feeling. He put it down to this being the first time he'd ever had a woman in his cabin, particularly a stranger, a beautiful mysterious stranger, he was just having an odd reaction to it.

"Never mind," she said, shaking her head, the fat yellow curls sailed around her shoulders.

"Okay." He told her, "Go ahead and shower, there are clean towels in the cabinet inside the head. I'll get your clothes."

Trusting her to not search his room for weapons, of which he had many, most were safely under lock and key anyway, he moved across the room. During the day he had a Glock holstered at his hip, as did the rest of his close team,

Jancarlo, Knox and Johnson. They'd had run-ins with pirates before.

He strode down the hall past the cabin the new seamen shared, and then past the male interns' cabin, all the way to the end where the females were appropriated. Although he knew everyone was probably up top, he knocked.

The only cabins that locked from the outside were his, the cook's and his teams'. He waited a sec then opened the door and went right in.

It looked like a bomb had gone off inside. Clothes and shoes were strewn everywhere, makeup and curling irons and perfume and other girlie stuff littered the tables and dresser.

Next to the wall lay two humongous suitcases, their lids up, matching smaller cases were piled next to them. It was easy to tell which bunk was Tirsa's. There was nothing on it except a small brown overnight bag. He picked it up and headed back to his cabin.

On the way, he searched the bag. He had the right, he told himself, she might have a gun or different ID, or something that could tell him why she had come to kill him. But the bag only contained clothes, a toiletry bag and a brush, not even a lipstick or a mirror.

Rummaging through the bag, he pulled out a silky lavender bra. Picturing her wearing it, his fingers involuntarily rubbed the soft material, he tossed it in the bag like it was on fire and quickly closed the case.

Inside his room, he set her bag on his bed, and went to find a clean shirt. He was rifling through a drawer with his head down when the bathroom door opened. The sound brought his head up. His throat tightened.

Tirsa was standing with a towel, a very small towel wrapped around her. It didn't do much to cover her plump breasts and trim shapely legs. The buttery hair hung wet down her back. Her hand went to her mouth. "Oh! I didn't hear you return. I'm so sorry," she streaked back into the head and quickly closed the door.

"Don't be sorry on my account," he muttered under his breath. Taking a long-sleeved shirt out of the drawer, he closed it, and pulled off the shirt he was wearing, tossing it on the floor near the small closet.

She opened the door slightly and stuck her head out. Her embarrassed eyes swept his bare chest then dropped. "If I could just, uh, get my clothes I can change in here…"

Holding the clean shirt in his hand, Robinson went to the bed and got her case and brought it to her. The blush spreading across her face only made the half-naked girl all that more enticing.

He handed the bag to her and turned away quickly, mumbled, "Take you time." Shrugging on the shirt and buttoning it, he pondered how very self-conscious she appeared, like she hadn't had many lovers, if any at all.

In five minutes she emerged, dressed, and her wet hair combed.

Robinson was sitting on the end of the bed staring at the outside door. He stood up when he heard her come out. "That was quick. No makeup or whatever else you girls do? I mean not that you need any." His hands in his pockets, he rolled one shoulder indicating her pure complexion.

"No. I don't have a lot of experience with it, and it makes me feel sticky."

"Okay then. Let's go." He opened the door, she walked out, he followed, closed the door and locked it.

The mess was on the same deck, it only took a few minutes to walk there. The room was filled with movement and chattering, everything came to a halt when they entered. All eyes were on Tirsa.

She hadn't slept in her bunk, had been missing all night and day, and here she was with the professor. He had been clearly visible on the bridge most of the day. Everyone was confused; Tirsa and Robinson didn't act like a couple that had had sex, yet where else could she have been?

The professor's team knew, but they were all close-mouthed pretty much all of the time, except with each other.

Astonished at her radically changed appearance, everyone in the room gawked at her.

"Wow," Raine exclaimed, "she's hot."

Lindsey sniffed then looked away, remarked, "She has no style."

"Hell, she doesn't need any," Raine snorted. Checking Tirsa out, his eyes roamed from the top of her blonde head down to her tiny shoes, then settled on her chest. Before, she'd been wearing an over-sized shirt over another shirt. Now, she was wearing a more form-fitting blouse, rudely, Raine openly ogled her.

Max's eyes popped. His elbows on the table, he flattened his forearms and leaned forward. He wore long shorts exposing rocky calves, he crossed his legs at the ankles and tucked them under his chair and rhapsodized in admiration, "She's like a chrysalis blossomed into a butterfly."

Giving him a dirty look, Lindsey said nastily, "Flowers blossom, butterflies emerge you dope." She barely glanced at Tirsa before sticking her nose in the air. "She's hardly a butterfly, more like a moth, I'd say." She leaned to the side and nudged Dia in the arm, "Right Dia? She's still plain as cold mud."

Dia smiled. Dia wasn't particular about who she had sex with, males or females, she liked them both, and anything in between. "Hmm, more like hot melted butter."

Lindsey rolled her eyes.

The professor led Tirsa to the food counter and grabbed a tray. He set two plates of meatloaf, mashed potatoes and corn on a tray on the tray. Next, he got himself a beer and a soda for her and then he took her to a table that Jancarlo, Johnson and Knox were sitting at.

At the table, Robinson pulled out a chair for her and she sat down keeping her eyes on the table. She was well aware of the hush when they had entered and the stares and whispers as the professor led her to his table.

"Who's at the helm?" Robinson asked Jancarlo.

The first mate was shoveling in meatloaf, he mumbled not looking up, "One of the new guys, Ji Wook. He has more time in under his belt than the others."

Everyone at the professor's table ate silently. Slowly, the chatter in the room picked back up.

The interns sat at one table. New seamen Owen and Stav hunched at another, and Bruno and Lil Dam were walking back and forth getting seconds.

While waiting for seconds, Lil Dam was rapping, dreads and gold chains swinging, and Bruno was singing with him but in Spanish. The cook, Seymour, heavyset with glasses and a swirly mess of straw colored hair, stood sweating behind the counter laughing at them.

"You guys are good," the cook said, "you should go on tour." His laughter rang out heartily like big men's do.

"Yeah." Lil Dam finished his rap and said, "It'd be the Lil Dam and Bruno tour." He pounded his new friend on the back.

Bruno shook his head emphatically. "Naw, bro, that's the Bruno and Lil Dam tour. Get it straight, yo." They started arguing, Cook laughed harder.

"I got to tell you girl, you clean up spectacularly." Husky with strong hefty muscles in cordons across his back and down his brown arms, Johnson stared unabashedly at Tirsa. "That wet hair baby, you look like a damned mermaid come climbed outta the sea."

The professor shot him a *have you lost your mind* glare.

Johnson didn't care; he just stared at Tirsa, looking her up and down and up and down. His black face shiny, he grinned a wide mouth of very big, very white teeth.

Tirsa ignored him. She could feel Knox's dark eyes on her. Like the rest of his team, he was expressionless but his eyes seethed angrily at her. She set her fork down and said softly, calmly to him, "Can we please go somewhere for just a moment and talk?" All four men gaped at her.

"What?" Knox barked, his long face dumfounded and angry. He shoved at his wool hat in irritation.

Tirsa pushed her chair back and stood up. Pulling her long hair over one shoulder, she caressed it while waiting patiently with a pleasant yet unsmiling expression.

Surprisingly, Knox reddened. He looked at the other three men; they were as baffled as him.

Urging him, "Go on, you lucky bastard," Johnson mocked.

The professor looked about to stand up too, but didn't. Yet. The men stared at Tirsa in confusion and curiosity.

There was no way Knox could refuse her, he would look ridiculous afraid of the petite young woman. Slowly, he got to his feet, took a big swig of beer and set the bottle down.

Tirsa started to walk away, she turned her head slightly back at him.

Knox wiped his mouth with the back of his hand and glanced at his fellow mates. The professor, looking pissed and possessive, frowned. Johnson was grinning, and Jancarlo as always was deadpan. Knox followed her out of the room.

Again, everyone in the room stopped what they were doing to watch.

Chapter Six

*T*hey knew no one was in the dayroom so they went there. Tirsa walked over and sat down on a small sofa. Smiling gently at Knox, she patted the cushion next to her. He hesitated, then guardedly sat next to her. She studied him for a moment with kind eyes.

Trying to hide his apprehension and his anger at what she tried to do to his friend, he clasped his long fingers like a piano player's together in his lap, and stared as if bored at the doorway, but on alert in case she planned on making him her next victim.

He wasn't the least bit afraid of her; it was a joke this slip of a girl had tried to take out the professor.

Crossing her slim yet curvaceous legs, Tirsa folded her hands in her lap and said quietly, "Knox, listen to what I say. Don't shut me down without hearing me out."

He didn't look at her, didn't respond, his cross, gaunt face stiffened trying to keep the pretty voice from penetrating his ears.

"Knox," Tirsa said, "Katrina."

He gasped and turned shocked eyes at her. Holding up a hand, she kept going, "Katrina says, she loves you, she wants you to know she is happy where she is. She is loved and cherished."

His face a mask of such rage, the beard shook with agonized fury, he barked, "What the fuck is this? What do you think you're-" he stopped at the look on her face. It was ethereally angelic; her gentle smile bathed him in trust and warmth.

"Katrina says, '*Bin.*'" Tirsa went on, " 'Remember the day at the lake? The yellow butterfly that landed on your shoulder? We named it Sunny. I let it fly onto my finger; it hovered for a moment then flew off. We swam, ate a picnic lunch, then made love'..." Tirsa set a hand on his knee; he was gaping at her in disbelief and astonished awe.

She let her words marinate for a moment, then she said kindly, "I told you that, Knox, so you could open your mind, let go, know that what I tell you is true. Katrina says only you and she know about that day and her pet name for you, *Bin*, she told me so you would know what I say is real."

He pulled off his knit hat, brown hair stuck up straight from the static. He held the hat in his hands; tears glistened in his dark eyes. "Tell me, tell me...more...how is, where is she?"

Tirsa patted his knee. "You could not understand where she is, you will one day, but not now. Trust me, I don't know where it is either. I only have a short message for you from her."

Knox's harsh lips parted in anguish, he struggled to keep his composure. He asked urgently, "What, tell me, please."

Tirsa turned more fully to face him, her gaze gentle, serious, leveled at him. "She is moving on with her...existence...and she wants you to also. She says she wants you to let her go, and find someone worthy of you, to love."

Frowning, he shook his head. Tirsa kept talking, "Yes, she says she will never be truly content until she knows you are loved, and love someone and are happy. You must, for her." She fell silent.

Knox just stared incomprehensively at her. Then he said like a drowning man, "Anything, did she say anything else?" He grabbed Tirsa's hand squeezing it, trying to squeeze out more words.

Tirsa shook her head. "I can't control it, I only hear brief whispers on the wind and then they are gone. They say what they have to say and then they…move on."

The pair sat quietly. Knox struggling to digest her words, believe and comprehend them, to understand…then accept. And finally, feel the peace slowly fill him, push out the mindless rage, the relentless resentment, and the all-consuming grief.

Tirsa stood up. "They will be looking for us, we need to go back."

Unmoving, he gazed up at her in fascination. "I don't understand, how did you…talk to her…?"

His hand still holding hers, Tirsa pulled him to his feet. He let her like he was a child. "You mustn't tell anyone," she admonished gently. "I told you, they are whispers on the wind. I have a…kind of gift…an intuition of sorts…I was brought up in seclusion to protect me from people who would use and exploit me.

"The thing is, I have no control over it. I can't seek things, they come to me, or not. Katrina came to me, for you. I could feel her the moment I met you. I could feel your tormented grief and seething anger at the world."

Knox stood holding her hand. Looking into the sincere blue eyes, he asked hopefully, "Can you talk to her again?"

She shook her head, said gently, "She won't again." Her hand touched his arm. "Cherish what she said, Knox. Let her words meditate in your heart, then do what she said. She is setting you both free to move on."

They stood for a few moments not moving. Tirsa was weary, and Knox was trying to take in what had just happened.

Together, still holding hands they went back to the mess. When they entered the room, all eyes were immediately on them.

The professor frowned at their clasped hands. He was startled to see Knox behave like that, he'd made it clear he hated the girl for trying to kill Robinson and he thoroughly distrusted her. And now…?

Knox clutched his knit hat in his hand; he never took that hat off. The strangest of all was the look of wonderment on his gaunt, scraggy face; he appeared to be on the edge of…*no way*…a smile. The beard couldn't hide the uplifting of his mouth.

The professor couldn't remember the last time he's seen the dour Knox smile. After his fiancée, Katrina, had died in a car crash, Knox had withdrawn into himself and had never come back out.

The couple walked to the table and sat down and started eating like they hadn't stopped and left the room at all. Johnson went to open his mouth but the professor threw him a short shake of his head. They'd talk about it later when the team was alone.

In bemusement, Knox put his wool hat back on and almost cheerfully, scooped up some mashed potatoes and enjoyed them. Before, everything tasted like paper to him, but suddenly, like a dark cloud had passed, everything changed from black and white and was now infusing with color, he felt human again. The flavors were sweet and savory like manna, he ate with happy gusto.

His friends goggled at him in bewilderment. Their eyes flit from him to Tirsa who sat calmly eating with her eyes on her plate, and back to their bizarrely transformed mate.

Tirsa said in a soft voice, "I…I'm going to the counter and get a cookie." She announced it in case the professor objected to her leaving the table. He said nothing, just stared at her with his inscrutable dark eyes. She asked if she could get anyone anything, they all declined.

At the counter, she introduced herself to the cook.

Seymour was instantly smitten with the quietly gorgeous girl. Being part of the professor's team, he knew what had happened. Taking note of the guileless face, he did not believe she was capable of such a dastardly act; she had obviously been forced to try to attack the professor. And she was innately incapable of completing the dastardly deed.

"Here ya go, honey," he said with a friendly smile and gave her a plate of cookies to take back to the table for the men. On the way back, she passed by the interns' table.

Raine stood up and approached her. As she kept walking past him he snagged her arm to stop her. Taken aback, she looked up at him in surprise. The intern was quite handsome with his height and auburn hair, brown eyes, and strong jaw.

Still holding her arm, the handsome face turned sinuous, he said with snark, "So, first you screw the professor and now Mr. Knox, you're quite the crafty shadow, eh? You've already been passed around the senior seamen, so I believe I'm next in line. What do you say we slip down to the-"

"Please let go of me," Tirsa said quietly, trying to tug her arm from his grasp.

But, he held her fast. His handsome face shuttered and his tone nasty, he said, "Come on honey, everyone knows you're a slut, I want my piece of the action. If I'd known what you were hiding under that…that disguise I'd have tapped you first. Come on." His grip tightened as she tugged away harder.

"Raine, let go of me right now." Realizing her voice was rising, she instantly lowered it, she didn't want to make a scene. If she had to go with him to keep things quiet she-

A hand circled Raine's arm like the steel clamp that had been around Tirsa's neck. "Release her. Now." Knox ordered, his voice deathly low. He may be long and lean but he had extraordinary strength.

When the other men had seen Raine accosting Tirsa, the professor had gotten to his feet but Knox was already striding across the room. Robinson watched him confounded. What the hell had happened to the reclusive, taciturn man that altered him in the few minutes he and Tirsa had been alone?

Knox and Raine stood eyeball to eyeball. Not used to rangy sailors with hats and beards hiding their faces, Raine struggled to not back off timidly, he didn't let go of Tirsa. He said almost friendly, "Listen mate, you've had your shot at her, let the rest of us play with her-"

Knox slammed his fist into Raine's gut. With a gagged grunt, the intern dropped to his knees like a sack of dirt. Without a beat, Knox took the plate of cookies from Tirsa then gently cupped her elbow, walked her back to the table and pulled out her chair.

After helping her sit, he set the plate down in the center of the table, returned to his seat and added more butter and salt and pepper to his potatoes before gleefully gobbling them down.

The room was so quiet a leaf could be heard leaving a tree. One by one, everyone slowly got up, deposited their trays. The other interns, Stav and Max picked Raine up off the floor. Raine groaned and gagged as they dragged him out. Then everyone else quietly left the room.

Through a mouthful of corn, thickset Johnson, his cinnamon colored skin gleaming in the dining room's bright light, said to the taller, narrower Knox, "You must be getting old, man, it used to be you hit 'em and they didn't get up for a week."

Knox kept eating like this was the first time he had ever tasted food. Said through the side of his mouth, "He's young, he just needed a gentle message."

When they finished eating, Knox and Jancarlo took off to check the bridge. Johnson found the new seaman Ji and they went to the engine room. Under Johnson's instructions, the Asian seaman picked up Johnson's instructions and lessons quickly, better than Stav had, and was fairly non-talkative which was fine because Johnson loved to talk.

The professor brought Tirsa back to his cabin. Once inside, she stood awkwardly as he gathered a few articles of clothing and his toothbrush. He set them on the dresser then opened a drawer and pulled out a shirt. Handing the shirt to her, he said benignly, "Here, I know you haven't brought anything to sleep in. You can use this."

She tentatively accepted the shirt, not knowing his meaning. He ran hot and cold, mean and kind; she didn't know what to think.

He picked up his clothes and went to the door. At the door he said, "I'm bunking with my team, you sleep in my bed." He didn't say it like he was giving her an option but like it was an order. Without another word, he opened the door, stepped through and closed it. She could hear the key in the lock, locking her in.

Standing mystified, unsure if he meant what he said, or if he was coming right back to catch her doing something wrong, she shook her head. It was still early, everyone else was probably playing cards or getting to know one another.

She stood in front of the dresser, her image reflected back wistfully at her. Feeling lonely, she wanted to be with the others, but then didn't think she could stand the stares, the judging her, looking down on her. Especially if they knew what she'd done, or tried to do.

Raine had called her a slut; they all thought she had slept with the professor and Knox. Her skin crawled, appalled at them thinking that about her. Redheaded Lindsey had looked down her freckled nose at her then away like she was unworthy trash.

On the other hand, Dia was watching her differently, with a sly smile and gleaming eyes, like she was dessert on a silver platter. At least Robinson hadn't chained her again. Not yet.

Settling on the bed with the river book, Tirsa thought her conversation with Knox would be disturbing her concentration, yet it was the professor's unfathomable, dark glowing eyes that kept wavering in front of the words on the page.

****

Around seven o'clock, leaving one of the new seaman, Lil Dam, manning the bridge, Robinson went to his team's cabin. He was going to use one of the extra bunks in the room. He opened the door.

They looked up. The three of them were all lounging on their bunks. Johnson was watching a movie on his hand-held, Knox was studying charts, Jancarlo had maps spread out on his bunk and was marking them with a yellow marker.

"Hey E, 'sup?" Johnson paused his movie.

The professor went to a vacant bunk and set his clothes down. "I'm crashing here tonight."

A big grin splitting his husky face, Johnson asked, "Who don't you trust, yourself or the girl?"

Chapter Seven

A few hours later, Tirsa was sitting in the middle of the bed, her legs curled to the side, immersed in the river book when there was a soft knock at the door. Not sure what to do, since she couldn't open the locked door, she waited.

The door opened. It was the professor. He had some books in his hands.

"Hey," he greeted her without a smile. "I thought you must be bored to tears so I brought these for you."

She quickly slid off the bed then stood next to it not sure what to do.

He couldn't help it; his eyes were drawn to the bare legs his shirt didn't cover. He'd never seen a woman in one of his own shirts before, normally it would have annoyed him, but right now he couldn't stop staring. For a small woman, she had damned long shapely legs.

He forced his eyes to move up to her face but on the way he realized he could see the dark shadows of her aureoles through the revealing white shirt. The more nervous she grew, the harder her nipples poked through the thin material. He awkwardly settled his gaze on the wall behind her. Beads of sweat splintered across his forehead. He needed to get out of the cabin quickly.

"Um…" Tirsa was obviously highly uncomfortable standing there in only a shirt, alone in a room with a strange man. A man she'd tried to kill. Her cheeks bloomed bright pink.

Holding the books against his chest, he blinked. "Oh." He held out the books. *"Zich excuseren,* I mean, ah, I'm sorry, we have some paperbacks that others have left behind, the river book is probably quite tedious, so I thought…here…" he moved to hand them to her then saw how the sleeves of the shirt were so long even after she'd rolled them up, they'd slipped covering her hands.

"I'll just set them here." He stepped past her over to the nightstand and put them down. Turning, he frowned seeing her flinch when he moved by her.

She took a few steps back, away from him. "Thank you," she said, her breathy voice tight with apprehension.

He swiped a hand over his messy black hair then tucked his hands in his jean's pockets to appear less threatening and studied her, trying to read her mind. He obviously made her very nervous. Normally women were avid around him, not terrified.

He found this young woman's fear of him an unpleasant feeling. It made him feel like a monster, and he didn't like that role. Not from a female.

Of course if he put himself in her shoes, or bare feet at the moment, a young woman being held prisoner by a man she doesn't know, that she tried to kill, who looks like a damned crazed, muscle-bound lumberjack, locked in his room aboard a ship on foreign waters not knowing her fate, he would be terrified too. In her mind, he thought, she must be thinking about sexual assault, and maybe being passed from man to man, possible arrest, or to be thrown over the side for the sharks. *Ja*, Robinson smiled, he would flinch from him too.

"Oh," he said again with a slight jerk, remembering he'd brought something else for her. He reached into his back pocket. She stepped back until she was flat against the wall.

Frustration at her fear of him furrowed his brow. He pulled a black object out of his pocket, held it out for her to see it wasn't a weapon.

Her confused eyes flicked from the device to him.

Keeping his voice soft, he said, "It's a walkie-talkie. It's for you to use if you need me, or need something. Here, let me show you how it works." He moved slowly towards her, she watched him warily.

"See, you just dial it to 2, that's our station. You hold this button down and talk, then let the button go. I'll hear it beep and respond. I can't hear you unless you hold the button down while talking, then let it go to hear me. Do you understand how to work it?" He held it out for her to take.

She nodded. Her arms were wrapped protectively around her body, her head was lowered, she peered up at him through long lashes obviously still uneasy with his close proximity.

When she made no move to take the walkie-talkie, he reached out and took her hand, opened her fingers and set the device on her palm then closed her fingers over it. Her hand so slight in his bigger calloused grasp, he nearly jerked his hand back when he touched her baby soft skin, feeling not an electric shock, but something, an unexpected tingle.

Regardless, she was still clearly fearful of him. It was starting to really bug him. He dragged his fingers through his beard then through the messy thick hair. It struck him that the beard and hair he used to appear the goofy nutty professor, had now possibly given him a more sinister, barbaric appearance.

Fluidly he swiveled and headed for the door. "All right, then. If you need anything, use the thing," he pointed at the walkie-talkie. "Don't worry, I promise, I won't come back tonight. I'll come get you in the morning for breakfast."

Her hands behind her back, her lips pulled in, she just nodded. He fidgeted with his beard, tried not to, but against his will, his glance stroked her head to toe in in his shirt again then quickly left.

She didn't move for a long time waiting to see if he was coming back. When it didn't appear he was returning, Tirsa checked out the books he brought, surprised at his kindness. Choosing one, she sat in a chair and read for an hour.

Her eyes grew heavy, closing the book in her lap she looked over at the bed. She hadn't slept well last night chained and lying on the floor, she might as well take the opportunity no matter how short to sleep in the bed.

Closing her eyes, she snuggled down and pulled the sheets over her. Aware she was still at his mercy and not knowing what he planned to do to her, with her, she drifted off inhaling his masculine scent on the pillow.

****

So intent on pushing the image of Tirsa in his shirt out of his mind, walking with his head down, the professor didn't see someone coming towards him.

Lindsey couldn't believe her luck. The professor and her, alone. At the last second she swerved so he ran into her.

"Oh!" She pretended he hit her hard enough to knock her back.

Instinctually, he reached out with one arm and caught her. Steadying her, he said with polite apology, "*Zich excuseren,* I am so sorry, miss…" he hesitated at her name, trying to recall it. He saw the irritation flash across her freckled face. She was a very pretty girl; men didn't usually forget her name.

"Lindsey," she mewed and clutched his arm when he went to draw it back. "It's so nice to finally be alone with you, Professor Robinson. Just you and me," she nuzzled her stylishly rail thin body against him, "and me. What should we do about it?"

"Oh, *ja*, Lindsey, yes. Sorry." He looked blankly at her. The picture of Tirsa half-naked in his shirt was still in front of his eyes. Recalling the feel of her soft curvy body under his on his bed the other night, hell, he didn't really even hear Lindsey's words.

Hiding her anger at his practically ignoring her, Lindsey tried harder. She ran her hands with long, blue nails up his arms. Feeling the bulging muscles under his t-shirt she simpered, "Wow, who knew you were so built?" She mewed again, wriggling closer to him, pawing his biceps.

"Professor, you've been hiding an insanely fantastic body under all those loose clothes," she declared, looked up at his face, "and hair."

He was no longer wearing the glasses he had been after the first introduction. "I would sure love to feel," she giggled, "I mean see what you can do with all those lovely muscles." She raked her splayed fingers over his chest drawing them down to his hard abdomen.

Now she got the professor's attention. He grabbed her wrists and pulled them away from his body. "Miss Lindsey,

I have things to do. Young ladies shouldn't throw themselves at a man. It's unbecoming." He dropped her hands and stalked off down the hall leaving her standing with her mouth hanging open, she couldn't believe he'd refused her advances.

Shaking his head as he headed back to his bunk, Robinson had to agree with Jancarlo that it was a bad move to bring women on board. But he had needed them to make his research team look credible, like a real research team.

He hadn't expected everyone on the ship to be so damned randy, especially the young women. Rumors of Dia sleeping her way through the crew were already getting back to him.

Now that the others have seen the way Tirsa really looks, he'd need to keep her under lock and key, or with the way the men were hopped up on this voyage, she'd be pregnant before they reached land.

He couldn't trust one of them to not snatch her out of a hallway and drag her off into the dark somewhere. That fucking intern, Raine, had already manhandled her. And in public. Who knows what he was capable of if no one was around. Shaking his head again, he went back to his friends' cabin.

Chapter Eight

*E*arly the next day, Tirsa made sure she was ready when the knock came at the door. It opened, Knox entered. She gave him a full wattage smile. "Good morning, Knox, how are you?" Dressed in jeans and a blouse, her hair in damp waves from the morning shower, she moved closer to him.

Amazingly, the stoic man's mouth turned up slightly at the corners. "Good morning Miss Tirsa. I've come to take you to breakfast."

Tirsa didn't ask why he and not the professor came, just followed him out the door. He locked it behind them. They trod down the hall in wordless companionship. In the mess they joined Johnson who was already tackling a stack of pancakes.

A glob of butter was melting on top of the stack, he poured a generous heap of syrup over the butter, it oozed down the sides and pooled around the stack. A huge ration of bacon was on the plate, a mug of coffee still steaming sat next to it, he tossed down a glass of orange juice as they joined him.

The room was mostly empty, just Cook and Seamen Lil Dam and Bruno were cleaning up with him.

"Everyone is up on the top deck. It's a beautiful day," Johnson uttered cheerfully through spongy forkfuls of pancake. Stabbing a pile he tried to get it into his mouth before the syrup dripped off onto the table. His mouth wide open like a hippopotamus, half the gooey mess hit the side of his mouth before he could shove it all in.

Tirsa laughed. Knox watched her, a tiny grin sprouted under the long beard.

They finished eating just as Lil Dam and Bruno had completed the cleaning up. They all went up top together. It was a nice day, blue skies with a few downy clouds, and just a shade coolish.

Tirsa walked to the side and peered over the railing at the rolling dark blue sea. The wind tossing the fat blonde curls around felt refreshing. She laid her forearms on the rail and looked off over the sea.

The professor was in the bridge; he saw Tirsa come up with Knox and Johnson. She'd made it clear she was petrified of him so he'd sent Knox to fetch her. At least that's what he told himself. Since he didn't really know what she was about, he kept her locked in his cabin.

He wasn't afraid of her hurting him or his team, or for that matter even any of the new seamen, after all, she was just a bit of a girl, but he had the others, the interns to think about.

The thought of the men fighting over her also crossed his mind, and maybe her even choosing to be with one of them. He rubbed his head, clueless as to why that bothered him. Anyway, there was already enough turmoil on the ship.

"E." Knox opened the door to the bridge and stuck his head in. "I think you need to see this." The professor set down the chart he had in his hand and followed his mate outside.

The air was perfect, low 70's; the puffy clouds blocked some of the sun making it bright but keeping the extreme heat and humidity away.

The two men traipsed to the bow and stopped at the railing. A pair of binoculars in one hand, Knox crossed his arms, gestured with his head, and said, "There."

A boat was coming towards them; it was smaller but designed for speed. "What's the flag?" the professor asked.

Knox lifted the binocs and peered through them. "I can see a diagonally divided triangle. The upper segment is scarlet with a yellow bird of paradise; the bottom is black with five white stars representing the Southern Cross. It's New Guinea."

Next to him, the professor agreed, nodding. He said, "Doesn't matter." He could see why Knox brought the vessel to his attention. It didn't look like a pleasure boat, or a fishing boat, it had a rag-tag appearance. As it got closer they could see paint peeling off the sides, rusty metal, barnacles clung to the hull.

The flag was New Guinean but it was ragged, torn. No good, proud, seaman would allow that. What really caused him concern were the guns, more like cannons sticking out of portals all around the sides. The vessel was coming on them fast.

The professor left the railing, abruptly jogging to amidship. "Jancarlo, Johnson," he called out to his team, Knox was right behind him. They waited, all eyes on the professor. His voice low, he said, "*Piraaten.*"

All four turned their heads to see the ship. "No guns, if possible," Robinson instructed quietly, "they might draw others."

The team nodded then without another word they separated.

Chapter Nine

*T*he professor yelled out to the interns, "Raine, Max, take the women and go down to the lowest deck and lock yourselves in."

The interns had been watching the team, the four men had turned deadly serious in a second then darted away and were now returning with extra holstered guns, machetes and knives attached to their bodies. The interns' dismayed eyes grew as big as satellite dishes.

Jancarlo came up beside the professor, and the new seamen all charged over as well, interested and concerned.

The professor said, "They want to rob us, they don't know about the women. Get them below, if they see them they'll be relentless, especially they get sight of that yellow hair." He glanced over at the interns; they had frozen in their spots.

Jancarlo said evenly, "I told you the bitch would be a danger to us."

Robinson said, "The other *junolinos* are a draw too, Jan."

Jancarlo narrowed his eyes across the deck at Tirsa. She looked back at him unwavering. "*Ja*, but, they might leave without the others but they will fight to take her."

"I know." The professor scanned the new seamen that were gathering around him. He had chosen them for the expedition because they all had a strong background in hand-to-hand combat. They had received knives and guns from Johnson and knew how to use them.

"Bruno," seeing Raine and Max hadn't moved, the professor said to the smaller but still hard-bodied seaman, "go take the interns below deck, lock them in then come back."

The Spaniard nodded sharply and took off towards the interns.

Robinson turned next to the mop-haired, tall, thin seaman with the round head and told him, "We want no guns if possible, Owen, but go man the weaponry just in case. All cannons out and ready." Nodding his obeisance to the order, the seaman turned on his heel and ran.

"They are here," Jancarlo announced in a calm voice.

The other ship was drawing up alongside starboard. A parade of sun-weathered dark men lined the rail. One of them was grinning like a hyena. Robinson moved a step forward.

"Sir!" the grinning man called out cheerfully. In pidgin he said, "We find we need help. We run out of food and our radios no work, perhaps you take your kind hearts to aid us." While he spoke, his men were judiciously climbing up on their railings like they planned to quickly board the Silenus.

The professor strode forward, his hand on a machete attached to his belt. He called out, "What is your name?"

Crooked teeth showed in the intruder's big smile, the smile a nicotine-stained crease in a face that looked like a squashed brown pumpkin. "I, sir, they call me El Muil. No need for those mean looking cannons, kind sir. Thank you for helping us-"

Next to Robinson, Jancarlo muttered, "An animal's snout? He calls himself a snout?"

The professor shook his head at the pirate. "What we will do is call the patrol to come and assist you. In the meantime, you will back away."

El Muil pulled off his hat and held it to his heart. "Oh, kind, sir, I know you no mean-"

Robinson took another step forward. "I do mean it. You have 5 seconds to reverse from us."

El Muil sneered, "Or what?" While they were talking the pirate had taken account of the Silenus. It didn't look like there was a large crew. The cannons though, worried him though; the Silenus had more firepower than he had. He also didn't want to have a gunfight as it might draw the attention of the authorities.

Then his eyes drifted to the interns cloistered near the stairs. Bruno was literally pushing them down the stairs, but they were resisting. They wanted to see what was going on.

El Muil's face lit up. "You have women," he said with a broad oily grin like he'd spotted a pot of gold.

Addressing the professor, he said, "Give them to us and we no slaughter all of you and take your ship. We let all men go." The squat dark face suddenly morphed from a friendly sailor with boat trouble into a savage beast.

His eyes hardening into black flint, a chilling edge in his voice, the professor said, "This is your last chance, El Muil, back off."

El Muil smiled again, regarding the bearded man. He taunted, "What will you do, bear-man, if we refuse?" Other than the cannons on the ship, the Silenus in no way intimidated him.

"You'll see. Last warning," Robinson said coolly, his hands on his hips.

The pirate grinned again, then the grin turned eerily icy. "No, sir, *you* have had *your* last warning. I take yellow hair for myself; the other two womens will go to my men. I do you a favor sir, women on boat- bad luck, redheads especially- they are witches." He sneered across the deck at the girls. "The rest of you die- *attawa!*" he screamed a battle cry to charge, raising his machete in the air.

The pirates scrambled over the side, hitting the deck shrieking curses and victory calls.

Robinson yelled, "Go!"

The seamen on the Silenus whooped and charged. The professor ran to the crow's nest, a rope hung down from the top. He grabbed the rope and scrambled up the wireless mast next to the nest.

Pushing off the mast with powerful legs, he swung out in the air flying over to the pirate's boat feet-first slamming right into three pirates – knocking them to the ground like bowling pins but they all jumped back up to their feet.

The three of them pulled out their machetes and started fighting, slashing, cutting, stabbing. El Muil ran back towards his own bridge.

With a machete in one hand and a dagger in the other, Jancarlo ran up to the closest pirate that boarded the Silenus, stuck the dagger in his neck, yanked it out, and like a shot he stabbed it in the next one, then pivoted on the balls of his feet spinning to slice the man that came up behind him with the machete, cutting his head almost clean off. Two of the pirates screamed before they all dropped to the ground.

Then Jancarlo bolted to help Knox who was surrounded by five pirates. At the bow, Johnson and Stav were back-to-back fighting off attacking pirates. Seaman Ji Wook sprinted then jumped in the air letting out a shriek, he kicked a pirate in the head, landed on his toes, twirled and kicked another.

Cook stormed out of a hatch with three guns strapped around his big stomach and a knife in each hand. He came out like a mad bull dressed in white kitchen garb and charged a trio of pirates.

While he fought them, another pirate came at him from the side- suddenly Lil Dam, dreads and gold chains flying dashed over, lifted his steel-toed boot and stomped sideways on the pirate's knee. The crack could be heard a mile away. The pirate screamed and buckled.

In one motion, Cook ducked a butcher knife swinging at his head, and stuck his knife in the pirate with the busted knee's belly, then sliced his throat with his machete and swung it right around to fight two more.

Blood splattered across Cook's glasses. He removed them while still swinging and stuffed them in his pocket.

"Bro," Lil Jam exclaimed, amazement ringing, "you the man." Grinning, several gold teeth glistening, he whirled and kneed a pirate in the groin then stabbed him in the chest.

Cook grunted, punching a man, replied, "You, my young friend are like a biting black Chihuahua."

"Humph," Lil Dam elbowed a pirate, put a foot to his chest and shoved him. "I prefer pit bull, Cook."

Cook's laugh, like a thunderclap, kept fighting beside him.

Bruno shoved the interns down the steps. The last thing they saw was the Professor swinging like Tarzan over to the pirate's ship taking on a group of pirates single-handedly slashing and punching, and Jancarlo stabbing with his dagger like a boxer jabbing, jabbing, jabbing, sticking pirate after pirate. The deck was swimming in blood.

Once he closed the hatch, Bruno didn't need to push the interns down the hall, they were running. They went all the way down to the boiler room.

Once inside, Bruno said, "There's an inside lock on this door, when I close it, lock it. Don't open it to anyone, hear me? No one except one of us? Clear?"

Five pairs of terrified eyes like frightened saucers stared at him, they all nodded. Raine's face was green, he looked about to puke.

"Lock the door behind me," Bruno said closing the door. He saw Tirsa, scared but determined come to the door.

Her face pale with terror, she stammered, "Is there anything w- we can do help? Load guns or something?"

Bruno flashed her a grin. "No, but thanks for the offer. You people would only get in our way and get hurt. Lock the door." Tirsa nodded then closed the door. He heard the lock click and he hurried to join his mates up top.

As Bruno threw the door open with a machete in his hand, a pirate was right in his path- Without hesitation, Bruno shoved the knife through the man's belly and yanked it right out. The man crumpled.

Bruno saw the professor was back on the Silenus, now he and Jancarlo were back-to-back, kicking, slashing with one hand, stabbing with the other. Bruno ran to them, making a fighting triangle.

Robinson, covered in blood and sweating like a pig, actually looked like he was enjoying the fight. "They okay?" he asked Bruno.

Bruno nodded, laughed short as he thrust his knife making contact with a pirate's chest. "The girls were calmer than the boys."

The three men grinned and continued to fight. Off starboard bow, a dagger in each hand, Knox vaulted in the air flinging himself at two pirates, took them both down, knelt quickly and stabbed them both at the same time. Behind him, Johnson hurled a knife in the back of a pirate about to chop Knox's head off with a hatchet.

El Muil yelled from his ship, hollering something in a foreign language. The few pirates still alive stopped fighting. They hauled off those that were critically injured but not dead and fled to their ship, quickly hopping over the side.

Before the last man got aboard, the pirate boat was already turning off.

Chapter Ten

A loud cheer burst up from the Silenus, the men trotted around bumping fists and congratulating each other. After throwing the dead overboard they came to circle around the professor.

Owen said, "Professor Robinson, sir, you are obviously more than just a meek mild professor. I've never seen anyone fight like you, not even in the movies, you're a damned ninja freakin' warrior!" The other new seamen babbled excitedly saying the same thing.

Bruno asked, "What gives?" We've heard your team call you colonel, and them majors. We have the right to know what's going on."

Ji said in awe and respect to Jancarlo, "Dude, you are a damned killing machine."

"Good job, men," Robinson praised them. "You all were great. None of us got seriously hurt. Before anyone does anything, I want everyone to line up so Knox our medic can give you the once over. Then let's get this mess cleaned up."

He said to Jancarlo, "Crank up the knots, we need to get to land." Jancarlo instantly strode towards the bridge.

The professor, or colonel, whatever, said to Bruno, "Release the interns, tell them to come up top but be careful of the slick deck. They can help clean up."

Bruno replied, "Yes Colonel. Are you getting in line to see Major Knox?"

The colonel's brows arched in question. Bruno motioned with his head. Robinson glanced down; his shirt was almost slashed to pieces, as were his jeans. Bruises, cuts and blood covered his face and arms. He rolled the long sleeves up over his rocky forearms. "Later."

Bruno grinned; his respect for the goofy professor had exploded into the highest esteem. He saluted the bearded man then hurried to do his bidding.

Knox was still bandaging those that needed it and everyone else was swabbing, cleaning up the blood and guts when the interns came out. They looked shaken and pale, their frantic eyes searching the boat for pirates.

His voice shaking, Max asked the bulky Johnson, "Did you get them? Are they gone?" His head slunk down his chest ready to duck and run at the first sight of a pirate.

Johnson's big chest filled with blocks of heavy muscle puffed, his grin bragged, he replied, "Oh *ja*, the *piraaten* turned tail and ran like little girls." The interns breathed sighs of relief when they saw the coast was clear.

Seeing some of the men limping and bandaged, Tirsa asked Johnson, "What about ours? Were any of our, um, I mean your men hurt…or…" her hair tied back in a ponytail flipped while the blue eyes scanned the area.

Everyone seemed to be all right, and downright happy, singing, humming, whistling. Lil Dam was trying to teach skinny Owen how to rap while they scrubbed down the railing.

Filled with pride, Johnson said, "*Neen,* everyone fought like skilled gladiators extraordinaire. Just minor injuries. Hey-"

Tirsa walked away while he was still talking. She spied the professor with a mop in his hands wiping the deck while talking with Cook. Her hand pressed against her mouth, she walked slowly to him, troubled eyes fastened on his bloody face.

As soon as he noticed her, Robinson was no longer listening to Cook. Cook hid a grin and waddled off to get some food started. When the adrenalin wore off there'd be a hungry ship.

"You're hurt," Tirsa whispered redundantly to Robinson.

Setting the mop against the rail, he swiped the back of his wrist across his forehead to keep the blood from seeping into his eyes. "I'm fine. What about you, I mean you, uh, interns, you all okay?" he asked, not taking his eyes off her to view the others. He was thinking she looked like a young teenager with that ponytail and bright eyes.

Tirsa reached up and pushed back a lock of wild hair that flopped over his brow. "We're good. You're hurt," she repeated, then took his hand tugging him to come with her.

The line between his brows deepening in puzzlement, he allowed her to pull him with her.

She brought him over to Knox. "Knox, he needs attending," she smiled up at the long-limbed, bearded medic. His knit hat splashed with blood was still on his head. Knox smiled at her.

The professor couldn't believe it. Stoic, brooding Knox, smiling at their attempted murderess? The world was awry.

"I know," Knox said. "I've tried to get to him but he scampers off."

A brow arched. "Scamper? I do not scamper."

Before the professor could say another word or take off, Knox poured a bottle of alcohol onto a swab and dabbed at his face. Laughing at his wince, Knox said, "E, you need to go wash up, I can't fix what I can't see. You're drenched in blood." He dropped his hands and insisted, "Seriously, mate."

The professor started to say something but with both Knox and Tirsa staring un-budging at him he muttered, "Fine," and stomped off to go shower.

Tirsa tilted her head up at Knox. Smiling, with light sarcasm she said, "It's a good thing we were told there was little fear of pirates attacking us in these waters, otherwise I'd be worried."

She had noticed what the seamen had. Her countenance turned serious, she said, "Tell me Knox, what's really going on here? You all call him the professor, but slip here and there and say colonel or just E. You refer to each other as mates then majors then, well," her forehead wrinkled, perplexed.

"I saw him in action. I saw him climb a steel mast without a ladder, and swing over on a rope into a ship full of fierce pirates and fight like a gladiator, and come back alive. He's obviously done this before, he's not the bumbling professor he pretends to be."

Stav came over holding his arm; he was covered in cuts and bruises too. "Knox," he said. Knox reached out and took the big blond's arm and felt it for a broken bone. Stav had washed his face and arms so Knox could see his wounds clearly. He poured alcohol on a new sponge and patted Stav's square face.

"The arm is not broken, just sprained," Knox pronounced. Taping a butterfly bandage on Stav's forehead, the medic said to Tirsa, "You're not the only one with secrets, eh?" He smiled to soften the barb. "You need to get your information from the colonel," he dabbed Stav's face, "uh, the professor, I can't speak out of school."

Tirsa was quiet for a minute watching Knox work. The long narrow fingers moved gently over Stav's face like he was a concert pianist. She asked, "Can I help, Knox?"

Knox glanced around, shrugged. "*Ja*, sure honey. Hand me that roll of gauze and that cloth, I need to make a sling for this big yellow block's arm."

"Hey," Stav pretended to be insulted.

Jancarlo had been the one training the seamen for battle. They were used to calling him Major. Now, bewildered, they all regarded the professor in a different light. His mates referred to him as Colonel. He appeared to be in charge not just of the expedition but militarily also. They were unsure how to address him, but they sure as hell had a lot more respect for him now.

His hair still damp, the colonel came out of a hubbed doorway to return to the deck. Strolling to the bridge, he noticed way off to the side Tirsa with Knox still treating injuries.

Knox said something, Tirsa laughed prettily, which made Knox smile. Knox seldom cracked even the tiniest upturn of lips and here he was gaily laughing away with the intern.

As the colonel kept making his way to the bridge, he saw Knox set an arm around Tirsa's shoulder and give her a hug, her head brushed against his chest briefly.

Robinson shoved the door to the bridge open so hard even Johnson at the helm jumped. Beside Johnson with his arms crossed, Jancarlo remained mute. He had observed the colonel's watchfulness as he'd made his way to the bridge, but he said nothing. After checking their course with Jancarlo, calming himself, Robinson went back out on the deck so Knox could tend to his relatively minor injuries.

The rest of the day was uneventful. The seamen had dumped the dead bodies overboard before the interns had come out and now everyone helped clean the blood-splattered deck.

Cook made a great lunch of tacos and salad. Lunch was boisterous as everyone expounded on their own fighting skills, and praising each other. The interns excitedly, now that the danger was gone, asked a hundred questions about who did what to whom. Even Johnson and Knox joined in the revelry. Having fans was a nice change.

The professor, whom everyone was now calling Colonel, was sitting with Tirsa and Jancarlo. Tirsa had no choice in the matter. No one explained why the colonel had pretended to be a bumbling professor. At this point he discarded the role because no one was fooled by it anymore.

Jancarlo ate stone-faced. The mixing in of their team with the other new seamen and interns was like a tack in his shoe for him. Someone was bound to let down their guard and spill private information about their mission. He didn't believe in all the mixing in of their team, the new seamen and the interns.

The three ate without conversing. Both Tirsa and the colonel were smiling watching the others engaging in storytelling and one-upping their embellished exploits. Even Cook was bombarded with praise.

Robinson leaned back with an ankle on a knee, his arm rested across the back of Tirsa's chair. He had showered and changed. Knox had neatly stitched up the side of his face between his beard and hairline.

Owen was babbling his prowess to Lindsey. When he took a quick gulp of soda, she stood up. "Where you going?" he called out to her. Lindsey kept her body almost too skinny. She believed the adage that you can't be too rich or too skinny.

She sashayed her bony butt across the room over to the colonel's table. A foot in front of him she bent her knee into her other leg and set a hand on her hip in a coy stance. Twirling a length of red hair around her finger, her voice all kittenish, she said, "You were so valorous today, Colonel. Everyone is talking about it."

Robinson glanced up at her thinking *who wears a dress on a research ship?* "Um, *ja,* everyone was courageous today, and I'm proud of you interns for taking the situation seriously and doing as instructed. It was excellent the way you all pitched in to clean up."

Aware Tirsa and Jancarlo were watching this discourse, he took his time deliberately skimming the intern from her six inch wedges, up the sheer, blue babydoll dress that had been gaily whipping around- and up, in the wind showing flashes of her thong when they were up top deck, his gaze moved to her hair. She'd styled her tresses in kinks that looked like long, red serrated knives.

Ignoring the others at the table, Lindsey leaned over putting a freckled manicured hand on his arm. "You are so daring, Prof- um, Colonel, I was wondering," she slid her hand up his arm moving closer, inches from his face, bending so he could get a real good look down the front of her dress. And he could. Her small breasts were encased in a tiny, red push-up bra.

She cooed, "Maybe you could give me some self-defense lessons. Just you," she tapped his arm with her finger flirtatiously, "and me. So petite, you see, I am such a defenseless woman, Colonel, I need your help to protect me from," she glanced around snootily at the other occupants in the mess hall, her nose wrinkled, "the, you know, riffraff." She tried to sit down on his lap but he kept his ankle on his knee so there was nowhere she could sit. Instead she leaned a hip against the table.

Tirsa and Jancarlo shared a rare look that turned to surprise when the colonel said, "Sure, Lindsey, I can make time to teach you some defensive moves so you can feel safer." His dark eyes trolled from her little breasts to her hazel eyes lined with kohl.

He smiled at her, his almost even white teeth just barely showed under the beard. "But, uh, now, if you'll excuse us," he nodded at the others at his table, "we have somewhere we need to be."

Lindsey clapped her hands and gushed gleefully, "Oh, I can't wait, Colonel, you just let me know when and where and I will be there, appropriately attired, with," her lids lowered seductively, "let's say, loose clothing?" Her brows quirked briefly with annoyance at Jancarlo's snort.

"Okay, well," Lindsey said in a sexy drawl while running her hand back down his arm. "I'll be seeing you, soon." She waggled her fingers over her shoulder and sashayed back to her seat with Owen.

Jancarlo growled, "E, what hell,"

The colonel interrupted him. He said to Tirsa, "Why don't you go grab a soda or water bottle and a snack to take back to the cabin. I'll be right with you in a minute to walk you."

Tirsa looked from the colonel to Jancarlo who was scowling at the colonel, and back to the colonel who had a smug look on his face. Looking like she wanted to slap it off him, she stood up without a word and traipsed over to the front counter.

Jancarlo waited for her to get out of earshot and said, "What the fuck were you thinking, E? The *blondine* is trouble enough but you will never get rid of the redhead, she will cling to you like a stripper on a pole."

A corner of the Robinson's lip turned up at the major's idiom, then he let out a long sigh. "I know. I suppose it wasn't the best move."

The major sat back in his chair with a knowing look. "You were trying to get a rise out of the *blondine*. You are letting a pretty face and a nice set of tits fuck with you."

He leaned forward, curling his hand on the table into a fist, his dark eyes warning. "E, I am telling you, get rid of the *blondine*, she is trouble. Or bang her and get it out of your system, then get rid of her. It is clear as glass that you want her."

The colonel jerked his head at his mate. "I do not want her, Jan. don't be ridiculous. Even if I was interested, she's way too young. I don't sleep with children. Maybe I want a little action too like the other guys, and Lindsey is willing," he scowled around the room.

"Humph." Jancarlo said, "The *blondine* is not a child, E, as you accidentally let us see the night she tried to kill you and you dragged her half undressed into the bridge. She has to be less than ten years younger than us. Besides, she is the same age as the redheaded coquette if maybe a year or two younger. I know you, E, you are not the least bit interested in the skinny redhead."

His brows rose as he considered it. "However, on second thought, maybe it is a good idea you fuck the redhead and then maybe you can get the *blondine* out of your pants, I mean off your mind."

Robinson leaned back again and crossed his legs. "Stop trying to read me, Jan. In experience years, Tirsa is years younger than Lindsey."

Jancarlo leaned back too, still angry. "But you know I can read you, *mijn broeder,* my brother. And it is clear what you want, at least to me. The *blondine-*"

The coronel pounded his fist on the table and uncrossed his legs, "Stop calling her 'the blonde' Jan, her name is Tirsa." He got to his feet.

"*Ja,* sure," Jancarlo muttered to him, "yesterday you called her the assassin." He finished his soda, crumpling the can in his hand. He peered staunchly at his friend seeing that his needle had hit.

The colonel's lips pulled in, he glared back at his friend and left to retrieve his prisoner. He picked Tirsa up where she was chatting with Knox and Johnson. "Let's go," he said so tersely Knox and Johnson frowned at him.

Tirsa brushed away her hurt feelings at his sharp tone and went with him. He escorted her to his cabin, opened the door and she went in. He said stiffly, "I'll send someone to get you in the morning." He closed the door.

Hearing the lock click, Tirsa stood for a while staring at the door choking back her misery.

Chapter Eleven

*H*alfway through the next day, the Silenus neared the side mouth to the Fly River. The boat slowed, everyone was on deck to get sight of the land they were going to explore when something clunked. It sounded like the boat ran over something.

Johnson and Jancarlo looked over the port side but couldn't see anything. Johnson said to the major, "That was pretty loud, I wonder if we got any damage."

Robinson approached the pair. "What do you think?" he asked them.

Johnson shrugged, "Dunno, might have hit something, might be damage."

Jancarlo replied, "There is only one way to tell. I will go down."

Looking over the side of the ship, the colonel nodded. "Okay."

The major kicked off his boots, pulled off his shirt and dropped it on the deck. He took out his cell phone and tossed it on his shirt.

The other seamen and interns started to wander over. Dia elbowed Lindsey and motioning her head towards Major Mercury, she said, "Now that's a bangin' body."

Lindsey admitted that the major had an amazingly shredded body. Then she countered with, "But what about that hunky Stav, you said he was the type you like, kind of a young Arnold Schwarzenegger, only blond."

Dia rolled a shoulder up and down in consideration of Lindsey's words. "Yeah, he's okay, but he's like too big, too thick. Now, Major Jancarlo Mercury there, like the colonel, is lean, look at those lean hips, they would fit nicely between my thighs, ya know?" Drooling, she cooed in a lusty haze, "And that six-pack, right up to a perfect, hard, chunkahunk broad V. I'd take either one, the major or the colonel."

Tirsa was trailing a few feet behind them and she could hear their conversation. Which they knew but didn't care.

The girls strolled closer to the men at the railing. Lindsey said, "Yeah, Major Jancarlo has a great bod, and he's handsome in a hard, scowling way, but what an ice-cold bastard. He looks at us like he would like to chuck us all over the railing. Never says a word to any of us."

Dia nodded. "I know." She chuckled then confessed, "But I don't care about talking, he's hot, and I like the rough-tough dangerous ones."

Lindsey confided, "I can't wait to see the colonel without that awful beard. I'm dying to see what he really looks like." Swooning, she fanned her hot face watching the colonel speaking to Jancarlo.

Jancarlo removed his gun and handed it to Knox who had just joined them, then, Jancarlo easily jumped up on the railing and did a perfect dive into the deep blue sea. Everyone ran over to the edge to watch.

In a few seconds his head popped up like a cork. He sent a short wave to the colonel then dove underwater. He went down and up several times but didn't call out anything.

Losing interest, people wandered around the deck and chatted. "I'm hungry," Stav said to no one in general.

"You're always hungry," beanpole Owen passing by told him.

The three girls leaning over the railing watching Jancarlo suddenly screamed in unison, so loud it sounded like a train whistle. Instantly everyone hurried to the side of the ship.

"What is it?" the colonel asked quickly.

Speechless with alarm, the girls pointed down to the water.

The colonel ran to the railing and looked over. His face tightened.

Beside him, Johnson looked over too, grimaced, and said ominously, *"Krokodil."*

Not one but two crocodiles were swimming right where Jancarlo was underwater, their scales rippling through the water. They weren't the small native New Guinea crocs but huge, twelve-feet-long saltwater killers.

The colonel knelt, quickly untied his boots, kicked them off and with one hand over his back grabbed his shirt, yanked it over his head and tossed it.

"We're coming too!" Johnson yelled, unbuttoning his own shirt; Knox was doing the same right behind him.

"Neen." Emptying his pockets, the colonel barked, "No. Everyone stays here. No one else leaves the boat, for any reason. That's an order." Setting his gun and the contents of his pockets down, he climbed up on the railing, in a flash he was gone.

Everyone hung over the railing to watch, trepidation swung widely in the air for the two men in the water.

Knox stood next to Tirsa. Seeing her eyes fill with droplets of fear, he slipped an arm around her shoulders and whispered, "He'll be okay, he's tough as iron. He's done this before." Sniffing back her tears, she nodded, biting her lip.

The entire group collectively held their breaths. The colonel came up for air once then they didn't see him or Jancarlo again.

The crocodiles started swimming in circles, jerking their long bodies and thrashing their tails. Like dragons they hissed and growled short grunts, opening their powerful jaws wide enough to show the pink inside with every huge, razor tooth ready to tear flesh then snapped them closed, then opened them, chomping closed again and again. The water around them frothed with their thrashing.

Tirsa clamped her hands over her mouth. Knox tightened his arm around her shoulder. He was tense even though he believed in his friends' abilities.

Owen and Lil Dam threw life preservers tied to ropes overboard. They floated down like giant white lifesavers barely making a splash when they landed. One of the crocs promptly swam over and took a bite out of one pulling it underwater. Only a piece of it popped back up.

Lindsey screamed nonstop until Johnson clamped a hand over her mouth. "I don't mean to hurt you honey, but you're not helping."

When she stopped screaming, he released his hand and quietly asked her, "Okay?"

Her head bobbed weakly. "Yes, sorry." She clung to Dia they both hung over the railing straining to see the two men in the dark rocking sea.

Ji Wook and Bruno started to climb over the railing but Johnson grabbed their shirttails and yanked them down.

"We need to help them-" Stav shouted, putting a foot on the railing too, his square face crunched in anguished fear for the two men in the water.

"*Neen*," Johnson said sternly, "his orders were for us all to stay here."

"But, sir," Bruno stammered. "What if they don't…" out of the corner of his eye he saw the women with eyes rounded in fright watching them.

Johnson shook his head adamantly. "*Neen*. Doesn't matter, we follow his orders no matter what, whether we agree or not, even if they're in dire danger. No one else goes overboard."

Antsy to do something constructive to help, Ji still had both hands on the rail holding so tightly his knuckles were white. His face grim, dark almond eyes darted all around the surface of the sea. Bending over further to look down, the wind smacked his straight black hair around; he spastically swatted it back.

Ready to stop any anxious seaman that decided to disobey orders, Johnson bookended them on one side, Cook braced on the other side.

"The crocs look like they're leaving!" Raine cried out. "Look!" So excited, his pointing arm bounced up and down.

It was true. The two behemoths were swimming away. Everyone held their breaths again, waiting to see the blood pool, or the bodies, or pieces. Then Jancarlo's head broke the surface. Treading water he watched the crocs leave.

There was dead silence on board. No one dared to speak or breathe, where was the colonel? Knox's arm tightened harder around Tirsa so hard it had to hurt but she didn't feel a thing, her heart was in her throat.

Then, a roaring cheer as deafening as when they ran off the pirates, even louder blew up around the deck. The colonel popped up next to Jancarlo. Tossing his head to clear his wet hair, he waved indicating they were all right.

They both swam to the uneaten life preserver and clung to it. Owen, Lil Dam, Bruno and Cook ran down below to help them get back on the ship.

Tirsa dropped her head into Knox's chest and wept. He put both arms around her, patted her back. "It's okay, he's okay, they're fine, honey," he soothed softly.

An hour passed by, people came and went. Knox and Tirsa hung by the railing. Lil Dam holding a soda wandered over to them. His face was lit up. "Hey, you guys haven't been below so you didn't hear their story."

Knox shook his head. "No, I'll get with them later. What's the word? By the way, you look different. But I can't put my finger on it…"

Lil Dam grinned, the gold teeth sparkled. "I cut my dreads, put away the gold chains," he pointed to his head now covered with short buzzed hair. "Colonel said they weren't acceptable on the ship or off if I was working with him. Said they could be dangerous for me, catch in trees, maybe a cannibal catching me," he laughed at Tirsa's gasp. "You haven't heard about the cannibals, girl? Where you been?"

She turned to Knox, he was giving the young rapper a *shut your mouth* look. "Knox? Cannibals?" Her voice squeaked, "Are- are they where we're going?"

Shooting a scowl at Lil Dam, Knox tried to sound reassuring but, "Well, honey, there haven't been a lot of reports about cannibalism in the past number of years, but truth be told, the stories get back about, um," he hesitated knowing the colonel would whip his butt for scaring the girl, but Lil Dam already spilled it.

"Uh, anyway, they say they do the, uh, head-hunting stuff really between clans fighting against other tribes, not visitors so much. We really have nothing to worry about." To distract from the grisly conversation, he switched to Lil Dam with a threatening frown. "You were telling us what happened down below?"

Lil Dam blinked dark round eyes, then talked fast, "Yeah, yeah, so they didn't want to talk about it but we dragged it out of them. Supposedly, the major kept looking but he didn't see what we hit, or what hit us and he couldn't find any damage. He would come up for air right next to the bow hull on starboard where we couldn't see him.

"So, then the colonel seen the crocs and he dove in. The major said the colonel basically got under the crocs and pushed them, poked 'em a little with his knife just to keep them from having the major for dinner. He kept 'em busy until the major was done clearing the props then he ran them off."

"Why didn't he just shoot them, or- or stab them?" Tirsa inquired. She and Lil Dam waited for Knox to answer.

Knox told them, "The colonel, you saw him in action with the pirates. He'll kill without hesitation if it's necessary, but he doesn't like to kill just to kill. Even deadly crocs. If he can get rid of them without hurting them too badly he'll go that course. Besides, they both left their guns up here. And, well, stabbing them," his mouth twitched at the corner with his shrug, "no one wants blood in the water."

Chapter Twelve

That evening after dinner, everyone gathered on the top deck to enjoy the balmy night air. The world seemed endless with the wide-open rolling ocean below and the vast, clear sky above. Stars twinkled like the black nightscape had been salted with silver. Knox was at the helm.

Amidship, the interns had set up a makeshift bar. Someone had hooked their phone to some speakers and set it up on the deck.

Music flowed through the yawning expanse of sea and the dark, celestial crown. A slight wind brought an intermittent chilliness occasionally pushing aside the tropical warmth, and just enough breeze to sweep hair and Lindsey's dress.

Closer to the bow, the colonel was off in a corner with Johnson and Jancarlo deep in private discussion periodically watching the interns goof around.

The OS'; Stav, Owen, Ji, Bruno and Lil Dam joined the interns who were now taking turns dancing. They all hoofed the fast tunes with Lil Dam in the center showing off his talents. Bruno and Max sang with the music, the slower songs found Lindsey and Dia with plenty of partners.

Off to the starboard, a soda in her hand, Tirsa rested her arms on the railing letting the wind whip her hair while she solemnly gazed off into the dark, trying to clear the turmoil in her mind of her failed mission, the consequences of the failure, and contemplating what would happen to her when they landed in New Guinea.

Naturally, as the alcohol flowed, the more boisterous and risqué people became. Raine was changing the music to a different playlist. Dia and Lindsey were refreshing their drinks. Both girls peeped over at the colonel and Jancarlo talking with Johnson. "Go ahead." Dia nudged the redhead with her elbow. "I dare ya, you're dying to ask him to dance."

Chewing on the edge of her straw, Lindsey tilted her head to study the colonel without blatantly staring at him. "Maybe. In a bit. You first." She smirked at the Latina who was fluffing the tight curls of her brunette hair.

"I'm not a scaredy-cat like you, Red," Dia said sarcastically, taking a big swallow of her tequila. Her brown eyes were steadied on Jancarlo.

"I bet Major Mercury runs you right off or tosses you over the side," Lindsey teased.

Dia set her glass down on a table. Wiping her mouth with her hand, she said, "We'll find out." Already a couple of buttons on her blouse undone, she opened a few more and tucked the hem tighter in her jeans. Clearly not wearing a bra, she bounced over to the three men who did not look up at her approach.

She sauntered straight to Jancarlo. Tunneling between him and the other two, she angled herself right next to the major. Her hair swooping sexy over one eye, voice low and husky, Dia interrupted the men mewing, "What's goin' on,

Major?" Pushing up against Jancarlo, she batted her dark brown eyes at him, beguiling him to pay attention to her.

Johnson and the colonel bit back mocking grins at the major.

The colonel let his gaze drift over to the blonde standing off starboard. Watching Tirsa looking so pensively out into the dark he wondered if she was contemplating jumping over the side, and if he could reach her before she did.

"How 'bout you coming over and dance a little with me?" Dia's voice a deep silky tassel, she nestled a big breast against Jancarlo's arm and flapped her lashes up at the hard-faced, impassive major.

Jancarlo barely glanced at her. With a total lack of feeling of any kind in his face or voice, he said shortly, "*Neen,*" and dismissively sipped his glass of whiskey.

Undeterred, Dia nuzzled more of her untethered bosom against his arm while trying to wriggle further under it and against his chest.

Johnson elbowed the colonel in the ribs, he thought it was hysterical watching Dia vamp all over the major not realizing the tough man liked to do his own choosing and he wouldn't touch anyone on the boat with a ten foot pole.

Dia's voice lowered to a guttural invitation, she crooned, "Come with me, my big tough major, I can show you a good time," and burrowed further into his embrace.

Trying to extricate himself from her blowsy clinging, Jancarlo's voice a rumble of detached coldness, he said bluntly, "I would rather mate with a rangy cur." He tried to disengage her grasping fingers but she held on.

Next to him, his hand covering his mouth, Johnson's snigger was still audible. Jancarlo shot him an acrid frown.

Robinson watched on with bemusement. For once the shoe was on the other foot and Jancarlo was the object of one of the interns' lust.

Thinking he was just playing hard to get, Dia didn't give up, really, how could any man resist her full figured lush body? Rubbing her body over his like a dog in heat, her voice drenched with lewd solicitation, she purred, "Oh, come on, you guys never relax, have fun, let loose, come on with me and-"

The planes of his face sharpened like the blade of his knife, scars glowed against his darkening tanned skin. Jancarlo's deep growl, a thrum of distinct warning, he snarled, "Get the fuck off of me."

Dia froze.

Jancarlo's muscled body was rigid with aggravation. Extricating herself from him with a sulky grumble, she said, "What are you, gay? It's okay, I do both, and, honey, I can turn you-" then she saw his dark eyes, the violent threat in them was unmistakable.

"Fine," she huffed and stalked away. She didn't see Johnson slapping the major on the back in glee or the piqued look Jancarlo shot at him.

The group minus the senior seamen huddled for a while, dancing and drinking.

The colonel strolled over to the makeshift bar and was pouring himself another scotch when suddenly Lindsey was at his side. "What about you, Colonel?" Chewing on the end of her straw, she tipped her head slightly giving him a thoroughly besotted smile, her hazel eyes flirty behind a sheet of kinky red hair.

He glanced briefly at her, put a stir stick in his drink and stirred the ice cubes around before taking a swallow. "What about me, Lindsey?" He poured two more drinks, one for Jancarlo and one for Johnson.

Lindsey slipped her hand into his. Holding his big hand, she squeezed it indicating it was fine with her if he wanted to take her away somewhere private. "You and me dancing, what do you say? I bet you're real good, I'm sure those big 'ol arms can hold a lady real tight, huh?"

Detaching his hand from hers, he picked up the three glasses, said as he walked away, "Some other time." Now he had to suffer the mirth of his mates as he rejoined them. He handed the majors their drinks, and leaned against the railing.

"They're getting drunker, rowdier, and bolder," Johnson commented. The phone had been turned up, the interns and junior seamen were gyrating all over the deck, laughing, singing, drinking more.

"*Ja*, I guess I should put a lid on it before things get out of control," Robinson said, taking a swig of his scotch.

Jancarlo nodded emphatically next to him. Poking his elbow in the colonel's side, he motioned to starboard. They watched Raine and Max strut drunkenly over to Tirsa.

Looking out to sea she didn't see them coming. They got on either side of her.

"Hey, Tirsa," Raine said looking around, making sure Knox had gone into the bridge. "It's your turn to dance, come with us."

"Yeah, let me show you my moves, baby, we can do a boy-girl-boy sandwich," Max added from her other side, twisting his wiry hips in a sexy undulation.

Tirsa swung around, found herself with her back to the railing and the two men boxing her in. Shaking her head she said nicely, "No thank you, I really never learned to dance. I would be all left feet I'm afraid." Smiling politely, she held her empty soda can in clenched hands in front of her chest like a shield.

"It's all right, I'll teach you, I'm a great teacher," Raine declared, grabbing her wrist he pulled at her.

Max said a bit miffed, "Actually, I am the professional dancer, Mr. Baseball," he mocked his friend. "I should be the one to teach her."

Rained tugged at her. "You get her next, me first."

"No, really," Tirsa objected still trying to be polite. "Please let go of me."

"Don't you two have other things to do? The music needs changing."

The three interns turned at the colonel's interruption.

"No, Colonel, we were just gonna have a dance with Tirsa," Raine argued, still tugging Tirsa's wrist.

Raine was a big man, but the colonel was bigger. Robinson didn't say anything, just wrapped his fingers around Raine's wrist of the hand that held Tirsa.

Feeling the superior strength, Raine released her in a heartbeat. "Go change the music, Raine, put on something slow," Robinson ordered, a mild command but still a command.

Barely covering his scowl, Raine said, "Come on, Max, help me choose."

Embarrassed again to be the center of an awkward situation, Tirsa didn't know what to say. Of course he would be angry with her, which wasn't fair. She was deliberately staying away from everyone to avoid trouble, and here it came to her.

His voice temperate, not displaying any anger, he asked her with interest, "Is it true you don't know how to dance, Tirsa?"

Mortified at everyone seeing how unworldly she really was, Tirsa didn't know what to say, so she stared at her feet.

The colonel gently cupped her chin to tip her head up to look at him. "Is that true?" He could see her embarrassment before she lowered her eyes.

She answered in a shallow breath, "The way I was brought up had little opportunity for things like dancing."

Letting go of her chin, he clasped his hands behind his back and stared enigmatically at her. He wanted to ask her what she meant by that statement, but judging by the way she continued to stare at the floor instead of him, he figured she wouldn't tell him. Instead, he said softly, "I see. I can fix that, let me show you-"

Blanching, her eyes darted up to his, she whispered swiftly, "No!"

He regarded her calmly. To appear as non-menacing as possible, he kept his hands clasped behind him. His voice quiet and low, he said kindly, "I won't force you, Tirsa, but I would like you to give me a chance to show you. I swear I won't embarrass you, we will hardly even move."

Watching the blush creep up her cheeks he felt bad for her, but he had this feeling, by her words and her quiet reserve, as well as her seeming unworldliness, that for some reason she had been kept maybe in some kind of isolation. Judging by the haunted glimmer in her eyes, she was missing out on a lot of good things in life.

He waited patiently, his dark gaze watchful but not saying another word. Intimidating her into doing it would take away the essence of dancing as being fun. He murmured softly, "What do you say, give it a little try? You don't like it we'll stop immediately."

She lowered her head again, then raised it slowly. "I, um…all right." She said it so quietly he almost didn't hear her. She was clearly surprised at his grin.

Raine had put on a slow tune and was dancing with Lindsey. Stav and Dia looked more like they were having sex than dancing, the others stood around drinking and talking.

The colonel took Tirsa's hand and moved her away from the railing but not over to where the others were dancing. Away from the ship's outside low lights, they were immersed in the cloak of the black velvet night with only the hue of her blonde hair reflecting a shimmer of the silver moon as they moved.

Holding her hand, "Okay," he said in a deep quiet voice. "The main thing, Tirsa, is to relax. Dancing is meant to be fun, not a job."

They were both wearing black jeans, she had on a short-sleeved sweater, and he wore a dark blue, button-down shirt, the sleeves rolled up his brawny forearms. Standing in front of her loosely holding her hands, he said, "Take a breath, honey, let it out slowly."

Feeling silly, she did what he said. He waited until he could see some of the tension leaving her shoulders then said, "Here, put this hand on my shoulder," he moved her hand to his shoulder and put his hand on her waist. "Then this hand here," he picked up her other hand, curled his big palm around it and held it lightly against his chest.

"For lesson number one, all we're going to do is sway really, just move slowly back and forth to the rhythm so you can get used to feeling the music with your body." He looked down at the top of her head, "But you have to look up at me."

It took her a moment to raise her head and shyly meet his low-lidded gaze. He asked her with a smile, "There, that's not so bad, is it?"

Her eyes still on his, she shook her head with a tiny smile.

His black hair was neatly combed back, even his beard was clipped taming his rugged face and showcasing his strong features. His reflection in her bright eyes glowed with vitality.

Aware of his strength, he held her dainty figure gently a few inches from his body, and they just rocked back and forth. As she relaxed more, he pulled her a little closer.

Across the deck, Jancarlo and Johnson watched them. Knox came out and joined the majors.

"Who's driving?" Johnson asked him with a mellow tranquility, shifting his thickset body to lean an arm on the railing. He was drinking and listening to music with his friends, watching people dancing, he was in a contented mood.

Knox's gaze travelled the deck, over the people drinking and dancing, and settled on the black-haired colonel with the blonde in his arms. His smile interested, he answered, "Ji relieved me. What's that all about?" He nodded to the colonel.

Johnson followed his gesture, seeing that now Robinson held Tirsa cuddled in a very close embrace, she was looking up at him with a slight smile, and he was smiling down at her. They were talking so softly to each other their voices didn't drift up the deck. He shrugged with a serene pull at his drink, replied, "Dance lessons."

His brows arched, Knox muttered, "Uh huh." He clinked glasses in a cheer with Johnson and said, "It's nice to see everyone relaxed and having fun for once."

"Ha," Johnson snickered, "let me tell you about Jan here and the spicy brunette hoochie-mama." He grinned at the scowl Jancarlo threw at him.

Across the deck, the colonel pulled Tirsa closer and nudged her head to rest against his chest. Subtly, he drew her hand down from his shoulder and brought it around his lean waist.

Still clasping her hand curled in his against his chest, he moved his other hand to spread across her lower back, fitting them together comfortably, more closely.

Lowering his head, he murmured in her ear, "You all right, Tirsa?" She sure felt okay to him all snuggled up in his arms.

She nodded, hummed a soft, "Hmmm." Her head rubbed up and down his chest.

Biting back a groan, he swallowed the feeling her movement elicited in his groin. He turned his hips away from her slightly so she wouldn't feel what she was doing to him by being in his arms and pressed against his body.

They were hardly moving, just swaying. His face against her hair, he inhaled her fresh scent, feeling like he was holding a soft, purring kitten, it was a struggle to not stroke her.

Her nerves and tension had finally dissolved, she unfurled completely relaxed against him. His arm tightened, closing her curves against his granite torso.

Ji came out of the bridge and hurried over to the colonel. "Sir, there's a call for you on the bridge," he said then jogged back to the helm.

Swallowing a curse, the colonel reluctantly wrapped his big hands around Tirsa's tiny waist setting her a few inches away.

She looked up at him with a dreamy smile.

A heavy sigh drawled reluctantly from him. "Ahh, I'm sorry, Tirsa, I have to go to the bridge." He rubbed his thumbs delicately over her blouse feeling the warmth of her skin through the light material.

"Okay." Soft and drowsy, she smiled again at him. "Thank you, Colonel. That was really…nice." Her hands had moved to splay her fingers on his chest.

"Hmmm." Nice wasn't the word to describe how he felt. His eyes on her lips, his voice a low rumble, he said gently, "I'll be right back for lesson two, all right?"

Her happy smile of acquiescence brought a reflexive smile to his own face. Taking each of her hands from his chest, her fingers curled delicately around his, he gently kissed her knuckles. Not wanting to leave her alone again at the railing he brought her to where his team was hanging.

They had found some chairs and now lounged comfortably, drinking. Jancarlo was smoking one of his skinny cigars.

Raine switched to a fast song, the interns and OS's all jumped up to dance.

Robinson got Tirsa a chair and settled her on it before heading to the bridge, he repeated, "I'll be right back." He strode quickly across the deck, the sooner he handled the call the sooner he could return for lesson number two.

Without his warm arms around her, Tirsa was feeling the wind's chill. She murmured to no one in particular, "I'm going to get my jacket." The men deep in conversation nodded absently at her as she got up and started for the stairs.

Winding down the steps to the hall, she passed the great room when suddenly Raine popped out in front of her. "Hey baby, where you going, the night's still young!" Not expecting to come across anyone, he startled her. Realizing people would probably be coming down to use the restrooms she relaxed thinking he wasn't stalking her.

She started to walk by him saying, "Oh, I'm just going for my jacket," when he suddenly reached out and grabbed her arm, pulled her over quickly and pressed her against the wall.

"Now that your babysitters aren't around, maybe we can get to know each other a little better. What do you think?" He staked her against the wall with his hand, and trailed a finger down the side of her face then her neck to her collarbone, pushing a lock of hair off her shoulder. He bent to kiss her.

Jerking her face away, she demanded fiercely, "Raine! Let go of me!" When he didn't, she flailed her arms at him trying to hit him to make him let her go.

"Give me a fucking minute, girl, I just want to see what you got-" with a coarse growl he suddenly yanked at her blouse, several buttons popped open. His eyes lit at her exposed bosom. "Oh yeah," he uttered with a carnal hiss. Dipping his head, his hot breath blew over the swell of her breasts.

Tirsa quickly put her hand on his chin to keep him from planting his mouth on her flesh. She tried to reason with him, "Raine, are you trying to cause trouble? Please go back to the top deck and let me be on my way." She pushed to move from him but he shoved her back so hard against the wall a grunt of pain burst from her.

He replied with a nasty mirthless grin, "No. You put it out for everyone else, I want my share." Pinning both her arms against the wall, he lowered his mouth nuzzling her cleavage.

Struggling against him, Tirsa cried angrily, "Stop it! Let go of me, you can't hold me against my will and molest me, let go of me right now!"

He threw his head back and laughed loudly. Still holding her arms secure on the wall, his lusty snarl steeped with eager promise, he said, "You are a little tigress, honey, you will make a spectacular notch on my bedpost."

Then his brows drew down, the shallow lines around his mouth deepened, he got close in her face. "Now, let's do this without any drama or attention, I don't need any of your watchdogs at my throat. Come on, we can go to my room, there's no one in there."

Panicking that he will force her to go, Tirsa shoved hard at him and opened her mouth to scream, he promptly slapped his hand over it stifling her cries.

Digging his fingers into her arm, Raine shoved her back against the wall again and pressed his hips against hers to hold her immobile then ground his arousal between her legs. With a greedy growl, he rasped, "You're so tender and juicy you make me burn, baby."

He held her arms pinned to the wall and shoved his face back into her cleavage. She kicked at him, hitting one of his shins.

Anger turning his face red, Raine leaned in, gripped a lapel of her opened blouse in his fist then moved his mouth close to her ear and threatened, "You fucking come peacefully with me, girl, I don't want to have to hurt you-"

Hands grabbed his collar, he was suddenly jerked from her and sent flying across the room. Skidding and bumping over the wood-planked floor, he landed on his butt with his auburn hair flopping over his face. Impatiently, he shoved it aside to see the colonel, his skin flushed dark, rage spitting from his black eyes, he was standing with his shoulders bunched and his fists clenched ready to come at him.

"Get up you little motherfucker," the colonel cursed. "I'll kill you, you fucking piece of shit," he took a step towards the intern.

"Uh..." Raine garbled in fright, scuttling backwards away from Robinson like a crab on his hands and feet. "Uh..." He got to the corner of the grand room, jumped up and ran down the hall as fast as he could.

Steam pouring out his ears, the colonel turned to Tirsa, his ire quickly melted at the ashamed look on her face. When he had completed his phone call he had rushed back to continue their lesson and saw right away she was gone. His men told him she said something about getting her jacket.

Glancing around, he had noticed Raine wasn't present. Knowing the licentious group that was onboard, he quickly left to find Tirsa.

Boy was he right. Barely down the hall and he saw that fool Raine practically raping her against the wall. The intern was lucky he only threw him and didn't go after him. As mad as he was he would have seriously hurt the boy.

Robinson wanted to touch Tirsa, comfort her, but after already getting manhandled, he knew it would freak her out more so he resisted the impulse. He shoved his agitated fingers through his hair then stuffed them in his pockets instead.

Her body stiffened, tears gathered in the eyes that just moments ago had gazed dreamily at him, and now regarded him with fear.

Calmly, he said, "Don't look at me like that, Tirsa, I am not mad at you. You did nothing wrong." Now he did touch her. He set his large hand on her slender shoulder then stroked it down her arm to her hand and clasped it.

He curled his fingers under her chin and raised it so she was looking at him. "Are you all right? Did he hurt you?" He pushed his fury at the asshole male intern down and kept his voice gentle. She was already scared; he didn't want to add to it with his fuming rage.

Blinking back her tears, Tirsa's gaze lowered to his full masculine mouth, then up to his enigmatic eyes that at the moment held a flicker of a flame. His big body cocooned around Tirsa as if he wanted to protect her, his solid warmth enveloped her.

She shook her head.

Reluctantly, Robinson released her, his eyes dropped to her open blouse. Following his gaze, her cheeks flared with mortification. Her face grew redder seeing his hard stare at her exposed breasts.

He cleared his throat, swallowed, turned his head to save her further embarrassment while she awkwardly buttoned her blouse with the remaining buttons.

His skin darkened realizing that the bastard had ripped her blouse open. His fists clenched, teeth grit, it was all he could do to stop himself from going after the rapacious prick.

When she was done, her head stayed bowed.

Robinson lifted locks of curls off her shoulder letting them shuffled down her back. He said softly, "Tell me, Tirsa, what you would like to do. Do you want to go back upstairs, or…"

Her breath labored out, Tirsa wearily stroked the back of her hand across her forehead. Her voice small, she said with a sad sigh, "I would like to go to my, I mean your, I mean the room you have me in, if that's okay."

His heart twisted at the dejected way she looked having to ask permission for every move she made. There was nothing he could do about it though, until he found out what was being held over her head and by whom and he could deal with it.

Swallowing his disappointment, Robinson said kindly, "All right." Lightly cupping her elbow he walked her to her room.

After he locked the cabin door, he glumly went back up top. He needed a stiff drink.

Chapter Thirteen

*T*he ship travelled slow and steady for another couple of hours. Half the group worked on the vessel's maintenance, the other half napped or played cards.

The colonel told Tirsa she could stay out of the cabin as long as she was with Knox. Knox was happy to take the young woman under his wing. She'd lifted the black cloud of grief that had completely encompassed him since his fiancée's death. He felt he could now, at long last breathe, finally let Katrina go and move on with his life.

His mates had asked him what had occurred that day between he and Tirsa, but he avoided answering, knowing they would not believe it. They would likely make fun of his being drawn into Tirsa's fabrication.

But, Knox knew the truth, and like the cliché, the truth had set him free. Set his damaged heart and his soul free. He would always love Katrina, however, he knew now that she was at peace, content, and wanted him to be that way as well.

Three whistles blew, they were approaching land. Everyone had already packed up their belongings and were waiting on the second deck for disembarkment.

Because most visitors weren't allowed to enter New Guinea through the straits, Robinson and Johnson left the Silenus by small motorboat to meet with the officials. They had everyone's paperwork, VISA's and passports.

The colonel had already paved the way with his government contacting the officials who contacted customs and immigration. After a couple of hours they returned to the Silenus. Johnson was in the small motorboat, Robinson was piloting a live-aboard right behind him.

The group gathered below deck waiting with anticipation. Thinking about and planning and traveling to the strange, wild land was not the same as actually setting foot on the soil. They were in a land heavily unexplored with unknown, undocumented natives, and new fauna and flora frequently being discovered. The newness and danger were exhilarating. To most.

The seamen got the motorboat back onboard then when the colonel got fairly close with the live-aboard, they put up a walking platform between that and the Silenus then commenced transporting the belongings. Once the gear was aboard, the interns crossed over.

Johnson was first off the boat to assist the others. The colonel and Jancarlo would be the last off, and Knox was in the middle to ensure all went smoothly. Once they were all on the live-aboard the seamen would transport the equipment to it.

Feeling Tirsa's body quaking beside him, Knox put an arm around her and asked, "What's the matter, honey?"

She took a deep breath; let it out slow trying to calm herself. It wasn't working. Her voice shaking, she stammered, "I- I uh, I'm trying to prepare myself for when the colonel turns me over to the police." Biting her nails, she was trembling all over.

The very man she was fearing came down the stairs from the bridge and was heading straight to them. He walked quickly but not hurried, his stride purposeful and confident in his powerful strength, combat experience and military skills. Pumped biceps and pecs like brick slabs strained at his black t-shirt.

As he passed Lindsey, she stuck out a hand and said something to him but his eyes on Tirsa, he strode right past the redhead without acknowledging her. Lindsey's face screwed up and turned ruddy, her freckles flecked across her skin like measles. Scorned at Robinson's indifference to her, she crossed her arms in a huff over her chest.

"Tirsa," the colonel said as he reached the pair at the back, "you'll be with me." He told Knox, "You can start getting things moving with Johnson."

"*Ja,* E, um, Colonel." Knox took Tirsa's hand and said gently, "It'll be all right, honey. No one is going to hurt you. Trust me, okay?"

Her head down, Tirsa's blue eyes rolled up to Knox then to Robinson. Knox smiled encouragingly. Patting her shoulder he said, "Trust him, Tirsa. Trust the colonel. I'll get with you in a while, we'll go right from this ship to the smaller live-aboard, the Zoeken." He squeezed her arm then left them.

The colonel said to Tirsa, "I'm going back up on the bridge, come with me." Watching Knox's tall head covered with the knit hat flow through the middle of the people exiting the boat, he commented, "Ji Wook and Lil Dam will stay aboard until we're all clear then they will take the boat where it'll dock down land."

One hand in his pocket, the other ran through his beard. He didn't know why he was telling her all that, it wasn't any concern or business of hers. But those blue eyes were shaking and she was gripping her hands together to stop biting her nails.

He frowned, apparently without Knox to cling to she was becoming unhinged. "What's the matter, Tirsa?"

Her head down she asked, "Then, um…will you take me…will I be arrested?"

Robinson's brows rose in understanding. She thought he was going to turn her in for attempting to kill him. No wonder she was beside herself with anxiety. She must have been having nightmares about being held in a New Guinea prison.

He could relieve that anxiety but he chose not to. She would be more malleable if she had the threat of prison held over her head, yet he didn't want her living in constant panic.

"*Neen*, Tirsa. Not…now."

Her doubting gaze skewed up sideways at him from under her lashes, then, her head lowered so he couldn't see her shame. She clutched her fingers so tightly together they were white, she pushed a knuckle into her mouth to keep her teeth from chattering.

His stomach twisted, he couldn't leave her hanging on the frightening precipice of impending arrest. "I promise, Tirsa, you will not be arrested."

She kept her head down, she had no reason to trust or believe him.

"Tirsa," when she didn't look up, he gently cupped her chin, lifting it, forcing her to meet his steady gaze. Her shaking blue orbs disturbed the hell out of his stomach, twisting it more.

Stroking her cheek with his thumb, he said, "I swear, I have no reason to lie to you. Please calm down." He kept stroking her face until the shakes left her and she let out a heavy sigh.

"Come on, let's go," he took her arm and led her down the hall, opposite from the others to go back to the bridge.

They walked side-by-side down the hallway. "So," he mused, "you and Knox seem to be getting along quite, uh, well."

She'd tied her hair back in a ponytail in preparation for being arrested. With her hair pulled back the colonel could see her entire heart shaped face that normally was partially covered by the loose tresses. She barely looked 16.

The ponytail bounced when she nodded. "Oh yes," she agreed, a tender smile lit her almost translucent skin. "What a sweet man he is." She trod more energetically alongside him since he said he wasn't going to have her arrested, for now.

Taken aback, the colonel croaked, "Sweet?" A picture of the tall man built like a lamppost, lanky and narrow but with huge shoulders, a long dark beard, a knit hat always on his head, and the perpetual dour expression came into his mind.

"Hmm, that's not how he's normally described. Seems like you two made a connection," he sounded pleased and disgruntled at the same time.

That tender smile curved her lips. "Yes," was all she offered.

They walked in thoughtful silence to the bridge.

Jancarlo was inside. He stared unsmiling at Tirsa, ascetic mouth taut, then turned back to the helm.

Robinson said to her, "You can sit over there." He gestured to a soft leather chair near the windows so she could watch the activity outside.

It took hours by the time everything had been transported. Ji and Lil Dam reported to take over the helm and move the Silenus for dockage.

By the time the colonel, Jancarlo, and Tirsa boarded the live-aboard, everyone was already settled in. The Zoeken was large enough to transport them all but small and thin hulled to manage the sometimes shallow Fly River.

The constitution of the tunnel-shaped river can change dramatically from a languorous, aggrading, rambler with a 50-mile wide mouth to that of a torrential, charging down mountain tsunami.

The boat contained four sleeping compartments. One miniscule cabin for the women, one tiny one for the colonel, one bigger for Jancarlo, Johnson, Cook and Knox to occupy, and the fourth, the largest was stacked berths for all the other males, the OS's and interns to share.

Also, there was a small galley with an eat-in area that Cook was already setting his things up in, and a small covered salon to hang out in. The widest open space was the deck, which was where most everyone had clustered.

As soon as Robinson boarded, Lindsey came up to him and complained, "Colonel, this boat is too tiny for all of us, you can't possibly think that we will-"

The colonel plugged right on past her with Jancarlo and Tirsa.

The ever-cheerful Johnson went over to Lindsey. "Miss Lindsey, this is an expedition, not a holiday vacation." His voice was upbeat, thick lips in a friendly grin. He was the heaviest out of the colonel's team, but as they all had, he was chock blocked with thick cordons of muscles too.

Setting a beefy hand gently on her arm he told her, "We're only going to be on this boat a short time. We're going to traverse a ways up the river then stop at a land structure for our base then we'll branch out from there on foot. The boat has to be small enough to navigate the sometimes shallow and narrow channels. Plus we-"

"Whatever," Lindsey snapped. She rudely spun away from the jovial mate and flounced over to where the other interns lounged on the open deck.

Leaving Stav and Owen at the helm, Robinson took Tirsa to where she was to sleep. His compartment consisted of two tiny spartan spaces with a wall and door between them. He opened the door to the cabin and brought her inside the first space. His belongings were inside the room.

He said, "This is where I'm sleeping. Normally Jancarlo would be in the other room, but you'll be staying there for now."

Reaching back, she tightened the band around the ponytail then pushed the hair off her shoulders where it coiled down her back. The colonel watched the unconscious way she fussed with her hair. Even with her hair back and dressed in khakis and a tee she was very beautiful.

Her lips pursed, eyes ashamed, she said quickly, "Really Colonel, I swear on my honor I won't hurt anyone, and...and I won't run, I mean, Major Jancarlo shouldn't have to suffer because of my disgraceful-"

He wound his fingers lightly around the top of her arm pulling her further into the room. Their boots scuffed across the planked floor. Robinson said blithely, "The major has suffered a lot worse, take my word for it. He seldom cares where he lays his head. He's as hard on the outside as he is on the inside."

Shaking her head vigorously, Tirsa protested, "Nevertheless, to displace him because you think I-"

Not liking the guilty feelings that suffused him, and angry at himself for the soft way he regarded her, especially when she would not open up to him and tell him who sent her to kill him, he angrily swung her around hard to face him.

Glowering darkly, he ground through gritted teeth, "It's too late to take back your reprehensible actions. Everyone must now suffer the consequences of what you did. I can't let you loose amongst the other vulnerable people, it would make for unsafe conditions."

Her face crushed by his cruel accusations, shameful tears springing, she put her hands over her heart and cried, "Colonel, I swear on my life I would never harm them, I swear to God."

Still holding her arm he shook her, the ponytail flew back and forth. "*Ja*? But what about me? Do you swear you would not try to hurt me again?" He was harder to understand as his accent thickened in agitation, his midnight eyes bored into hers willing her to answer him honestly.

Disconcerted blue eyes gawked at him; her mouth opened but no words escaped, her lips quivered then closed.

The colonel waited, hoping she would tell him she would never attempt to harm him again. Yet she said nothing, just stood there gaping at him. He could see her struggle to say something, reassure him, swear to him, lie to him, her skin reddened, eyes cast about, her lips parted again but she said nothing.

Disappointed and angry, he roughly let go of her arm as if she was covered with thorns. Her face whitened then flushed.

Closing his eyes, he scratched his eyelids with his fingernails, ground out, "That's great, Tirsa. Great." He opened eyes as black as night, shot with thunder. "You can swear not to harm another, but me, are you saying you would make another attempt to…to kill me?"

Looking at the angelic young woman standing so distressed in front of him he couldn't even believe the discussion they were having. There was something about her; she had charmed the hardened sullen Knox. Cranky and dour with everyone else he was downright gentle and caring of her.

The colonel realized that since the night she tried to kill him nothing had changed. So, if she'd had orders to kill him, those orders would still stand. Someone had something they were holding over her, he was sure of it. But what? He had no answers to these questions and Tirsa wasn't talking. Frequently he would try to question her about who had forced her to attempt to kill him, but she refused to discuss it. Jancarlo had people investigating her so they should have some kind of information soon.

The cornflower eyes dropped to the floor, the ponytail swung around landing to curl over one shoulder. She uttered not a word of denial to what he said.

He set his fingertips lightly under her chin and tilted her head up. Tears glimmered making her eyes look as blue and fluid as the turbulent sea they'd just crossed. Tenderly, he brushed back loose tendrils that clung to her face, sweeping the tips of his long fingers across her silky skin. How could he get her to open up to him?

They stared at each other like lovers at odds. He dropped his hand to hold her upper arm again and demanded, "Tell me, Tirsa. Tell me what's going on. Who sent you to kill me?" He waited, she said nothing, just looked back at him miserably, then lowered her head.

"Tirsa," he stroked her arm, "you can trust me. There's no way I believe you're here on your own with your own mission. Someone sent you to..." He set his fingers under her chin again and tilted it back up for her to look at him. "Trust me, Tirsa, I have capabilities you couldn't know or understand. I can take care of the situation, whatever it is that's got its clutches on you. Let me help you."

Her breath ragged, she said in a small voice, "You could only make it worse." Her forehead creased, lips parted again like she was going to say something else, she wanted to tell him, he could see it in her eyes. Then something distressful crossed her face striking anguish in her eyes. Her lips slammed closed and her lids shuttered.

He'd been holding his breath, he let it out. He let her go and turned his head so she couldn't see his own dispirited expression that she couldn't, wouldn't trust him. He crossed the room to the door of the adjoining rooms and opened it.

"Okay. Until you are able to trust me, tell me the truth, let me help you," sighing heavily his voice hardened, "you will not be out of my sight this entire expedition, unless you are with me or one of my team, Jancarlo, Johnson or Knox. This is an order. My orders, for the safety and wellbeing of everyone on this trip, cannot be disobeyed or questioned for any reason. Do I make myself clear?"

Tirsa just stared miserably at him. She was afraid to respond, to question him again about the police. When would he be turning her in? He just mentioned the entire trip, would it be when they got to a particular town in New Guinea? Or wait until they returned to Australia? Maybe she should trust him, maybe he can help…she gave an imperceptible shake of her head, no, she couldn't trust anyone. She pressed her hands against her stomach to still the quelling.

Seeing the frightening thoughts flit across her face, Robinson said sharply, "*Tirsa!*" to get her attention.

She blinked rapidly, trying to calm her insides. Twining her fingers together she tensely clenched and twisted them.

"Tirsa," he repeated, "if you don't answer me, say right now that you understand and will follow what I say to the letter, I will lock you in that tiny room," he pointed inside the other space, "and you will stay there until everything is…resolved. Days, weeks, months, however long it takes to do what we came to do."

If it was possible, she grew even more frightened of the bearded, angry, threatening man whose accent she couldn't place but it thickened when he was disturbed, like now. He said he had capabilities, what did he mean by that?

Her eyes narrowed in suspicion at him. Who was this man? He hadn't yet revealed who he really was. They were all calling him Colonel now. The interns and new seamen gossiped, saying the name Russell Robinson was a false name and that he wasn't really a professor. It was a pretense to get into New Guinea for…well, no one had come up with anything yet.

Of course she wasn't often alone with any of the others to hear their theories, and his close-knit team, Jancarlo, Johnson and Knox were tightlipped. It mortified her that she was in this disparaging untenable position. She hated that her stonewalling, not trusting him, upset him so much.

So quietly he had to strain to hear her, her head turned aside, without looking at him she said, "Yes."

Resigned, looking down at the top of her head Robinson exhaled. He walked towards the exit, "All right. Let's go up top."

Outside the room he stopped. Then he said gruffly, "*Dank u*, ah, thank you, at least, Tirsa, for not lying to me." His strides away from her were so long she was far behind him when they emerged on deck.

Chapter Fourteen

*T*he Zoeken live-aboard had pulled anchor and was cruising into the mouth of the Fly River. The river delta was studded with low swampy islands covered with mangroves and nipa palms.

Chugging along, the boat slowly made its way through the wide mouth and was moving towards narrower water where the banks crept closer. Scrubs and dense trees crouched right up to the riverbanks like a tropical dike.

Along the way they passed wooden shacks called *rumah thingi*, like tree houses up on poles that were dispersed beside the river bordered by open savanna. The sediment that washed down from the mining churned thickly under and behind the boat as it rolled through.

After a meal of hamburgers and potato salad, biting a spear of dill pickle, Johnson was telling the people about the Fly River and New Guinea. "*Ja*," he was saying, "the Fly wasn't named after a pesky ol' bug, it was named after a ship. In 1842 Captain F. P. Blackwood discovered the mouth of the river and named it for the ship he commanded, the HMS Fly."

The group took turns telling what they knew about the little explored mystical land they were travelling in. It was growing darker, they meandered out onto the open deck to watch the vast, remarkable blazing sunset unobstructed by buildings. The group waved at a half dozen canoes rowing by so quietly there was barely a splash from their oars and rumbled talking.

Chestnut brown grebes dove, and shearwaters soared about looking for places to roost as the sunlight dwindled. Cormorants hunched on tall dead trees preyed the river for dinner. Palm fronds fluttered in the evening breeze. Far off in the distance deep in the jade scrub, a tunnel of smoke flowed dissipating into the darkening sky.

After a long day, the group hit the sack soon after the sunset. They slept uneasily to the hum of the diesel engine and strange birdcalls and whistles, grunting frogs and the occasional splash from jumping fish.

An uneventful day and half of travelling up river, the bored occupants on the boat were starting to pick and snipe at each other. The seamen had very few duties and the interns were tiring of each other and the boat. The cabins were too small to do any more than sleep in so everyone was hanging around the salon with some up on deck.

The boat turned down an overgrown tributary, trees hung over the water shading the boat, their limbs catching and dragging, scraping across the roof like nails on a blackboard.

"Hey guys, check that out," Lil Dam called, gesturing over the side.

Several got up to see. Lindsey let out a squeal. "It's a snake!"

"Eew, gross," Dia said, watching the bright yellow snake with large eyes the vertical slit pupil easy to see, coiled languidly around a tree limb.

"It's freakin' enormous," Bruno's fear unmistakable in his voice.

"It's a juvenile, green tree python." Johnson said joining them. The numerous tats on his dusky arms shimmied when he adjusted his dark sunglasses; the single gold earring glinted every time he moved in and out of the sunlight.

"That's a juvenile?" Lil Dam sputtered. "It's gotta be at least five feet long!"

Johnson folded his hands together and rested mahogany forearms as thick as fence posts on the rail. He wore a baseball hat to keep the hot sun off his shaved head. "Yeah, practically a baby. He won't bother you if you don't bother him."

"Really?" Dia asked, leaning over to get a better look as they passed under the limb. The others cringed back in case it dropped from the tree.

Johnson smiled, "Sure. Unless he's hungry." He grinned slyly at Lil Dam. "I hear they like tender dark meat."

Lil Dam quailed, backed away from the edge of the boat and quickly disappeared off the deck. Johnson roared with laughter.

Tirsa sat by herself over in a corner. The colonel was with Jancarlo and Knox in the cockpit. Johnson was out on the deck, so going by what the colonel had said, it was all right for her to be out there. It was painful, to be treated like a prisoner, or a child. The others glared at her with disdain and abject curiosity.

They'd gotten the word, secret conversations overheard on the Silenus manufactured rumors and suspicions. The unconfirmed word was *killer*. The girls ignored her mostly, they didn't believe the shy, slight young woman capable of anything that heinous.

When the male interns tried to get close to talk to her, they were thwarted by the colonel keeping a cocoon of his team around her most of the time. He made it virtually impossible to have a long conversation with her. Since being punched by Knox, and thrown by the colonel on the ship, Raine had stayed clear of her.

However, Max was feeling his oats today on this still mildly cool, slightly overcast day. He thought Raine was a sissy and a coward after he'd told Max what happened when he tried to get Tirsa alone the other night. The way Max figured it; everyone on the ship was fair game. They had to know how it would be before they signed on.

Lindsey and Dia had no compunctions shagging it with the guys, but little Miss Killer thought she was too good for them, and the colonel let her be all uppity. Well, they haven't met the incredible, indelible, non-turn-downable Max Kovsky yet!

Far be it for the good-looking dancer to let a beautiful girl lie, or sit, untouched. He strolled over to where Tirsa was, grabbed a chair and scraping it across the wooden deck, pulled it over to her. "Hey, how ya doin'?" he said, his tone friendly in a machismo manner.

She smiled politely at him. He took that as a yes, please join her. He sat down and scooted the chair closer. "Would you like a fresh drink?" He pointed a strong arm covered with silky black hair at her soda.

"No thanks, I'm fine."

Max felt his heart flutter. Beautiful, with a soft, lightly accented, melodious voice, hardly killer material. "So, uh, let me know if I can get another for you, okay?"

"Um, sure, but I'm fine." Tirsa couldn't help her eyes from flicking to the bridge where the colonel was. Heaven forbid he would see her and storm out to rescue the innocent, endangered Max from the murderess' clutches the way he had with Raine. She folded her hands in her lap and stretched her legs out on the lawn chair.

Dressed in a dark green polo shirt and khaki shorts, Max crossed his legs. Olive toned legs covered in springy dark hair, swinging his foot, the sockless deck shoe he was wearing flipped back and forth of the end of his toes.

He cleared his throat then said, "So, um, we haven't seen a lot of you," he broke off thinking they all assumed she was sleeping with the colonel since she didn't stay with the other women. They decided she had also had sex with Knox, and probably Johnson and Jancarlo too. Maybe all at the same time.

When they were together, the interns let their imaginations and gossip run wild. The more salacious the better. Speaking of better, Max told himself that those guys were no better than him and Raine, so they need to bugger off and get out of Macho Max's way.

"Anyway," he said quickly, "where are you from?"

She thought about her answer. It was hard to explain. "I grew up mostly in a very rural, tiny town in France. I moved with my…um…family…to the states when I was 16."

Max settled back, put his hands behind his head, elbows stuck out like bat wings. Blatantly, his gaze poured over her figure, his attention lingered on her breasts. For the rest of the conversation it hardly moved, he was clearly picturing her naked.

He remembered she had bright blue eyes but he only looked at them once. "Where in the states do you live?" he asked.

Uncomfortable, Tirsa crossed her arms over her chest unaware this only caused her cleavage to deepen. As his pupils expanded, she wrapped her arms more tightly around her body. "I uh, lived in Washington State." Changing the subject off of her, she asked him, "So where are you from?"

Ah, his favorite subject, him. "I'm originally from Brazil. I've lived in New York since I was 6. There's no place like New York City, huh? The pace, the beat, the constant changing, nothing stays the same for long. I get a crazy thrilling mind race just walking down the street. I am a professional dancer and attend university."

Tirsa set her arms on the chair arms. "I've never been to New York."

He uncrossed his legs and leaned over closer to Tirsa, his forearms on his knees. He was devilishly handsome, suave with his neatly pared goatee, rich brown eyes, rippled dark hair.

"Actually," he leaned closer and spoke low so no one could hear him. "I'm getting excited, you know what I mean, just talking about the city."

He set his hand over hers on the chair arm. "I should take you there, you'd love it." He scooted his chair right against hers and stroked his hand up her bare arm. "You're like sugar on a stick, baby, you'd be like sweet taffy on my arm."

Nervously, Tirsa looked around the boat for Mr. Imperious, thank goodness the colonel was nowhere in sight. She went to pull her hand away but Max grasped it and held it tight on the chair arm.

Before she could move, he got up out of his chair and sat next to her on her lawn chair. His feet flat on the ground, he still held her hand down, and planted the other next to her shoulder against the chair then positioned his head inches from hers.

"What do you say we-"

Extremely uncomfortable, Tirsa cut him off, "Really, Max, you need to back away. I have no interest in doing anything with you. Can you please move back to your own chair?" Trying to tug her hand free, she tensed further when he didn't move back or let go of her hand. She tried to keep her voice level and unperturbed, but her words sounded strident in her own ears, "Please move back, Max."

Still holding her hand down, his face floated close, his gaze finally moved from her chest to her eyes. He tried to draw her in like a magnet with his rich, bedroom eyes. With his long curly lashes and sexy lips, women told him all the time he had bedroom eyes. And that's where he took them, and usually without any hesitation on their part. This one just needed a little more coaxing.

Tirsa put a hand to his chest and pushed at him. "I'm serious Max, go back to your own chair. I don't want a scene, *please*." Now she knew her voice was thinning. Why did this keep happening to her? Was there an aphrodisiac in the water for heaven's sake? Did she have a sign over her head that said 'hey everyone, feel free to molest me?'

He trilled a string of musical words in Spanish, then informed her, "That's a love song, baby, tell me that doesn't get your juices stirring." Serenading her, he moved closer, his lips almost touching hers. Her one hand trapped, her other was ineffectually pushing against his strong chest. "Come on, girl, give it up," his voice silky sultry, "give me some sugar, you sweet thing."

His breath moist on her face, his lips about to latch onto hers, Tirsa turned her head, but he followed her movements,

Jungle Treasure

mirroring them, trying to kiss her. "Max, *please*, leave me alone. I don't want to kiss you, get away from me,"

"Come on pretty baby," he sang, gripping her jaw to hold her head still. "I give you a taste of me and I promise, you will be begging me to bed you."

Tirsa was unable to speak because of his strong clutch on her jaw, and he still held her hand trapped. She pulled at his wrist with her free hand to release her face, and she tried to twist out of his grip but he was too strong. She tried to pull her knees up to put between them, but he leaned his body against her pinning her legs. Panicking, she jerked her body to get him off her, snapping her head to break loose of his grip.

Max's eyes were closed now as he zeroed his mouth in to hers, but then something drew them open. A shadow hovered over them. Pissed that someone would bother them at this moment he looked up, his mouth opened in a scorching retort, the words died in his throat.

Standing over them was the colonel. His expression was unreadable, but his jaw flexed.

Tirsa squirmed in the chair, Max still had her pinned. A vein at the colonel's temple pulsed and his eyes tapered to angry slits.

Tears of embarrassment and frustration gleamed in her big eyes. Tirsa feared the colonel would accuse her of acting like a slut in public. Her upbringing had been strictly sheltered; she had no training on how to handle these situations. It must be her fault for somehow sending out the wrong messages.

Max didn't move. This wasn't any of Robinson's business. His tone arrogantly insolent, Max asked with a hint of a sneer, "What can I do for you, Colonel?" Still holding

121

Tirsa's jaw, he twisted his neck to look up at the colonel, not hiding his annoyance in the least at the interruption.

Frustrated at being treated as a mindless toy, a mortified tear slipped from Tirsa's eye landing on Max's hand. Max didn't pay it any mind, but the colonel's gaze fell to it. The vein at his temple beat harder.

One eyebrow arched at the young man's audacity. Robinson wasn't all that much older than the intern, it was the wars etched in his face, and the things he'd seen and done, shadows plaguing his steely black eyes that gave Max pause.

The colonel's penetrating gaze moved to the hand that held Tirsa captive.

Max ignored the silent order to let her go. Not hiding the irritation in his voice, he said, "I asked you, Colonel, what can I do for you? You can see we're busy."

Dismissing the colonel, he turned back to Tirsa who sat rigid with trepidation. Smiling at her, Max let go of her jaw, and slid his hand over her shoulder and behind her head to pull her to him. Ignoring her struggles, her small hand pushing at his chest, he opened his mouth to latch onto hers.

"What you can do for me, young man," Robinson's deep voice glacial, rage burgeoned underneath, "is get your *bloedig* fucking hands off her, get your ass up off that chair and get the hell out of here before I see what *I* can do for *you*." The threat grated through the air.

For one second Max was thinking of staring down the colonel, really, what could the man do to him with witnesses around? Then he caught the hard warning in the colonel's dark eyes. He tried to get up nonchalantly; failing miserably, he shot out of there as fast as he could.

Robinson sat down where Max had just deserted, next to Tirsa on the lawn chair. Her face as pale as a daisy, plush lips pulled in with a tremor. Rubbing the hand Max had held down so tightly, she lowered her eyes and waited for the reproof. It came.

"Tirsa." He leaned arms as hard as granite on his thighs, clasped his hands together. Tone autocratic, he said sternly, "Look at me." Slowly, she raised anxious blue eyes blurry with tears of frustration at her involuntary helplessness.

"I told you that you weren't to be out of your room without being with me, Jancarlo, Knox or Johnson. These are exactly the situations I'm trying to avoid, first Raine, now Max. It's likely they will try again to force themselves on you."

Sniffing back her tears and fear, suddenly angry at his bossy attitude and her untenable situation, Tirsa said boldly, "Really?" An eyebrow cocked. "I recall you saying you feared for their lives that I needed to be locked up for their protection lest I go maniac on them and slaughter them. As you can see, Max was in terrible danger." She slapped furiously at the annoying tears.

"That's not what I said," he paused, a shadow of a smile started, "well, *ja*, it kinda was." He explained, "Tirsa, I have been on a lot of ships and expeditions. Whenever there are women, there's trouble. I'm trying to prevent that from happening here."

"Uh huh. I don't see you breathing down Dia and Lindsey's backs. Only me. Besides the homicidal stuff, why are you so high-handed when someone is..." she didn't know how to put it.

"Accosting you?" He almost smiled at her blush. He went to set a hand on her knee but held back. "Because, Tirsa, you're...different. Dia and Lindsey can take care of themselves. You don't know how to handle...men. And they can see that so they think they can just...take you."

Her brows, a shade darker than her hair drew down. "What do you mean, what do you know about me? You don't know anything about me, my experience with...men..." she kept her hands from covering her blooming cheeks.

The colonel set a palm behind him on the chair and leaned back, the other hand on his thigh. His glinting onyx gaze trailed down her body then back up to her guileless eyes. Raising his hand from his thigh, he combed his wild hair back with his fingers.

A slight smile softening his chiseled lips, he said, "Honey, your face is like an open book. There's virgin ingénue written all over it. Plus, you're a nice person, Tirsa. It pains you to hurt a person's feelings. You don't know how to assertively extricate yourself from...prowling wolves."

Another tear escaped, rolled down her rounded cheek. He touched it with his fingertip, then smoothed wisps of curly hair off her face. Running a knuckle lightly down the side of her face, he leaned over setting his forearms back down on his legs and twined his fingers together. "Back to my point. I told you what the consequences would be if you didn't obey my orders."

Her mouth dropped open. "But Colonel, I didn't, I mean, Johnson was, is here. He's right over-" anxiously she scanned the deck. Only Bruno, Ji and Lil Dam were there and they were far down the deck against the rail with fishing poles, the lines hanging over the side. "I swear, he- he was there, right over there with..." she sighed, what was the use; he would believe what he wanted.

Robinson stood up. "Maybe he was, however, he's not here now and he wasn't aware that you were here, and I think you knew that. If he had been, that punk cad wouldn't have been hassling you. This is the last time I'll tell you this, obey my orders or you will not like the consequences."

124

From behind him someone said, "Colonel."

He turned around. Knox was there. "We're here, E." He took in the colonel's stiff stance and Tirsa's indignant, frightened face. "I'll stay with her while you bring us into shore."

Robinson looked at Tirsa then Knox, sighed heavily. "All right. Don't let her out of your sight," he stalked off to see to the docking of the boat.

"No prob." Knox smiled at Tirsa.

Chapter Fifteen

A long, skinny weathered dock stretched like a centipede across the olive colored water. The colonel expertly maneuvered the boat against the grey wharf.

Bruno and Lil Dam hopped off the boat to the pier. They wrapped lengths of rope around the posts, adroitly tying nautical knots to hold her.

Once the Zoeken was secure, as before, the group walked single file carrying belongings and equipment down the lengthy pier, picking their way carefully over the uneven old planks.

The tropical sun pierced the low hanging clouds, pushing heat and humidity onto their backs. If it weren't for the coarse breeze it would be uncomfortably hot and sticky.

Tripping down staggered planks in high wedges, Lindsey's dress was doing a tribal dance in the wind. It was hard not to watch it flap and flutter against her legs and swoop up suddenly at a brisk gust. She seemed oblivious that the world could see everything she was wearing, or not wearing, under the dress.

Enjoying the view behind her, Owen, his arms stacked with boxes asked, "Girl, how do you walk in those high heels?"

Over her shoulder her smile brassy, she said, "Hon, I was born in heels. These are my flats." Dragging her suitcase on wheels clumpity clump over the wood, she swung her saucy thin hips harder.

Owen looked back at Stav, his eyes rolled. *Wait until they hit the jungle*. They shared a smirk.

Ji stopped and looked down into the water. "Hey, check out the ugly turtles." The three seamen peered into the mucky water, several rocks protruded in the shallow coast. A twelve-inch turtle, olive colored same as the water basked on a rock, another was in the water.

"That's a pig-nosed turtle," Owen told them.

"Ugly," Stav said. The turtle on the rock slid into the water with a tiny splash and both turtles disappeared.

At the end of the pier, they walked down steps and onto a dirt path. Spinifex grass with its spiny leaves stabbed at their legs, and thick overgrowth tugged at their shoes as they made their way.

All around them, flowing palm trees with flexible trunks swayed in the wind. Like long lissome fingers, the narrow leaves rippled and waved. Johnson led the way stomping quickly and heavily in thick boots to run off any wildlife that might be hanging around the path. His main concern was the variety of poisonous snakes that littered the land.

It was close to an eighth of a mile before they reached the structure. Lindsey was complaining up a storm by the time they reached it. Leaving her suitcase at the entrance, she clattered up the steps to the brown weathered porch made of montane oak and dropped her exhausted, sweaty body onto a rattan chair.

Johnson set the stack of boxes he was carrying on a wicker table, and wiped a beefy hand across his damp face. His hands on his hips he said cheerfully to Lindsey, "You know honey, we usually sweep and dust up a bit before we sit on anything around here, 'cause, well, we are in the wild."

Her head was hanging draped off the back of the chair, Lindsey's hazel eyes blew wide. Letting out a piercing shriek she leaped out of the chair, the braided pigtails hopped like red exclamation points she ran away a few steps before looking back. A black and yellow spider eloquently strolled up a web from the chair disappearing into a crack in the wall.

Johnson chuckled. "Aw honey, that's just a little 'ol St. Andrews Cross Spider. He ain't nuthin'. Wait'll you see the giant spiders, size of small dogs that-"

"Giant what?" Lindsey slapped her hands over her ears screaming, "Shut up! Shut up!"

The others caught up gathering on the porch. Robinson with Tirsa in front of him was the last to tread up the porch steps. "What's going on, why are you screaming?"

He took in the redhead hovering knock-kneed in the corner with her arms wrapped around her skinny body, her eyes flying all over the porch in search of other creepy crawlies. Then he saw the amusement on Johnson's dark face shiny with perspiration. Using his toe, Johnson nudged an orange-eyed tree frog off the porch.

Jancarlo moved past everyone to unlock the door. Balancing boxes on his hip, he pushed the door open with his foot. The others trooped in behind him gathering in a long entranceway used to hang outerwear and muddy boots.

Johnson led the way to the first room, he said, "This room is the great room. It's where we can hang out." A large open space containing mostly cushioned rattan chairs, a couple of sofas and tables scattered over area rugs spread on the hardwood flooring.

He continued describing the building, "The structure, is kind of like a lodge, named Copestone, it's a jumble of rooms patched together."

Mostly made out of merbau, a termite-resistant wood, the dark reddish-brown, coarse-textured wood was planed smooth and glossy with gold flecks in its wavy texture. Through a big window, a jeep was visible parked on the gravel and dirt drive extending a few dozen yards from the front of the building.

Johnson took them on a brief tour. "The building is in the shape of a bunchy capital I with rooms appearing to be added at different times. There're seven small bedrooms in a block in the center and to the back of the building. A wide hall runs from the great room with the bedrooms to the right and to the dining area with the kitchen at the end." He took them down to the other end; to the left of the great room was a library.

"Who lives here?" Raine asked checking out a row of books on the bookshelves. "Are you guys here all the time?"

Shaking his head, Johnson said, "Different people use Copestone for different things at different times. That's why the bookcases in the great room and the library are lined with an assortment of books."

He watched Lindsey and Dia whispering together. In the big center room, long windows with overhangs let in muted light. Several gold and green flowered cushiony chairs, sofas, and oak tables made it an airy and comfortable room.

Tirsa wandered over to look out one of the windows. With a sly eye, Raine saw the colonel and Knox weren't in the room. He sidled up to her. His arm raised and was just about to drape across her shoulder when he felt something next to him.

"There are more boxes to bring in. Get them," Jancarlo said in his cold voice, dark eyes sharp with threat pierced Raine. He moved between Raine and Tirsa.

Color flooded Raine's face before he turned and left the room to do as the major ordered.

Jancarlo stood silently beside Tirsa who was acutely uncomfortable with the tough hard man standing rigidly next to her. He had never said a word to her, clearly indicating he thought Robinson should have dumped her with the police back in Australia. When the colonel came in, Jancarlo headed out of the room.

In the back between the dining area and kitchen was a workroom where the group put the equipment. There were four bathrooms, one at each end of the building, the other two between the middle bedrooms.

A study where charts, maps and research books were set up was between the bedrooms and the kitchen. Behind the building was another structure like a bundled series of big barns for storage, tools, and equipment.

The colonel's room was at one end, then Jancarlo, Knox and Johnson shared, Cook had his own room. Lil Dam, Bruno and Ji bunked in the biggest room. Stav and Owen in the next, Max and Raine shared a space, and the last bedroom Dia and Lindsey would occupy. Johnson showed everyone where they were sleeping.

Back in the great room, Lindsey stood in the middle of the room, her head snapped around and around like the exorcist inspecting for bugs. Her fingers clutched the sides of her dress loath to sit down; she didn't trust that something wasn't lurking under a cushion.

Owen and Max came over to stand with her. Owen said, "It's okay, Linds, the colonel hired locals to clean this place for our arrival. It's safe." He saw her shoulders relax, her eyes stopped shopping, she let out a loud exhale.

Max said wryly, "I don't get it. You came here knowing what a rustic, wild, treacherous land this was. Yet here you are in dresses and heels and scared of bugs. What's the deal?"

She took one more scan of the room then perched on the edge of the nearest chair and looked up at Max the dancing intern, and Seaman Owen, the beanpole with the bowl-shaped mop of ochre colored hair. Sparse light whiskers stuck out around Owen's jaw like he was trying to grow a beard but it wasn't happening.

"Oh," she said, crossing her legs and laced her fingers placing them around one knee. "My folks made me go to college or they said they'd cut me off. I had been spoiled rotten they said, and now it was time to get my life in some direction. I'd taken every lousy elective I could take, I was running out of non-major classes to take."

Owen folded his long thin body to sit in a chair next to Lindsey. Max flopped on one in front of her. The rest of the people buzzed about putting things away and going back to the boat for more.

Lindsey cocked her head, said the seaman beside her, "So, I read about this class, studies of the BC and AD eras, the modern changes in thought about the time period and renaming it to be more politically correct, and blah, blah, blah. It sounded easy, and basically it wasn't too bad. Boring, but I didn't have to kill myself studying or anything." She shuffled her butt back into the chair and sat back. Hiking the short skirt up higher she uncrossed then re-crossed her legs.

131

"Uh huh." Listening with one ear, Max watched the others maneuvering back and forth putting stuff away and exploring the building. "So, this expedition, how did you get dragged into this?"

Lindsey groaned. "My parents again. Thought it would be good for me. Widen my horizons; take me out of my comfort box, blah, blah, blah. My mistake was I didn't read the flyers the folks had picked up at the school for recruiting. I mean, really, who has even heard of New Guinea? I thought we were going to a tropical island for crying out loud." Her arms draped dramatically over the chair arms. "I packed my tanning oil and my best bikinis."

"Hmm. Well, it is a tropical island," Owen said.

Lindsey snorted. "Ha. I mean tropical as in luxury resort with spas and 5 star restaurants, not tropical as in jungle."

"Actually it's a rainforest," Max informed her.

"Whatever. Who cares." She flit a freckled hand at him.

"I was lucky," Owen said, stretching his long arms over his head and yawning. He exhaled loudly and rough, shook his head. Combing his mop with his fingers, he scrunched down in the chair, crossed his legs.

Plopping his elbows on the chair arms, he set his hands loosely in his lap. "I had the type of folks that always went to bat for me. If a teacher gave me any flack my mother would fly down there and give them what all. No one was to ever speak harshly to her baby."

Smiling, his chin grew longer in his round face. He scratched at the few light spindles of whiskers. "I was totally spoiled too. It was great. And boring. I had to inject some excitement in my life. I was getting a bad juvy record and Daddy was getting tired of paying the cops off, so the folks thought it a good idea for me to go to sea, become a sailor and get away for a while."

After a glare from Robinson, the trio got themselves up and went to put their own gear away.

The unloading done, Cook grabbed Bruno and Lil Dam to help him set up the kitchen and start preparing for dinner. Jancarlo went to ensure the boat was secured and the covers pulled down to keep out rain and animals.

The colonel brought Tirsa down to the farthest room at the end of the hall. He said to her, "I chose this room because like on the live-aboard, the Zoeken, designed for families with young children, it also has two adjoining, windowless rooms." He nodded to the door standing open to the side.

Her lips pulled in with claustrophobic sadness, she didn't ask, she just stated, "You're going to keep me locked in there."

He turned his palms up. "Only at night. For your protection as well as the others. As I told you on the ship, when not sleeping you're to be with either me, or one of my team, Jancarlo, Johnson or Knox at all times. Or Cook, that is Seymour. If you are not with one of us, then yes, you will be locked in."

She looked so dejected he said flatly, "It's better than the police, jail." Tirsa agreed but didn't smile and made no comment.

"Come on," he said, "let's see how Cook is doing with dinner."

Once in the kitchen, feeling like a child for having to ask permission, Tirsa asked Robinson if she could stay and help Cook fix up the kitchen.

Bruno and Lil Dam had put up some boxed and canned food. Dishes, glasses, utensils, cookware were already there. Cook gave the two seamen directions to the nearest town that was 50 miles away, tiny and rural with only basic amenities, to get supplies.

The men took the jeep into town. There were some groceries they'd brought from the boat and stored in the fridge, Cook was taking them out and opening cans when Robinson and Tirsa came in.

"I'd like to help, sir, if I may," Tirsa asked shyly, barely looking at the big man. She felt embarrassed, figuring as one of the colonel's team he must know about her reprehensible actions on the Silenus.

"*Ja*, sure." He grinned, an apron tied around his portly belly. "I would appreciate the help." A twinkle in his eye he said, "Please call me Cook. Sir would be my commander, not me, honey."

He went to a drawer and took out an apron and handed it to her smiling to take the bite out of his words. "I hear you don't have a huge wardrobe so we don't want to sully the clothes you do have, right?"

Tying the apron around her waist Tirsa didn't see the look the two men shared. The colonel had told his team that Tirsa was never to be left alone. "All right," Robinson said, "I have things to see to."

The group enjoyed a supper of spaghetti and meatballs, garlic bread and salad, with chocolate cake for dessert. Afterwards, Tirsa and Ji Wook helped Cook clean up then everyone met in the great room.

The colonel stood in the center of the room. He had long given up the laborious way of speaking he'd done on the Silenus that first night. His tight jeans and black tee stretching over the strongly muscled chest revealed he was a lot younger than he had seemed as the bumbling professor.

He did still have a thick beard, long curly messy hair, and the accent that Jancarlo, Knox and Johnson, and even

Cook shared but weren't forthcoming about where they were from.

"This is how we'll proceed at first," while the colonel spoke, he browsed the room. His team, the new seamen, and Tirsa, Max and Dia gave him their earnest attention.

Cozy on the couch, Lindsey and Raine were having their own whispered conversation. Frequently giggles slipped out from the pair. They petted and stroked each other.

The colonel said, "For the first few days we're going to branch off in groups, going in different directions. There are some landmarks we need to locate from this map." He had an ancient yellowed, cracked paper folded up in his hand. "Once we've located those landmarks we will head out on foot through the forests towards the mountains."

"Why not use ATV's?" Owen asked.

"Good question." Robinson nodded. "The forests can be too dense to drive through, there can be flash floods and mudslides, swamps and invisible sink holes. The ATV's can't climb up tree-heavy steep mountains. On foot we can see the pitfalls before they get us, plus we have things we need to look for and speeding past on vehicles we might miss them."

"Horses?" Owen suggested.

"Transporting them back and forth would be a hassle, and again, we've found where we're going that the travel is easier by foot. Plus, we'd need so many for all of us there's not suitable barns or food for them here. We will bring a pair of burros though, we're picking them up in a few days to carry our supplies."

Robinson waited for more questions. When no one else asked anything, he said, "Well then, let's get a good night's rest, we leave at dawn. There are alarm clocks in each room, set them for 5." Ignoring the groans he said, "See you all in the morning."

He figured half of the group would probably hang around for an hour or so before going to bed. It looked like Raine and Lindsey would be searching for a clandestine place to…get together. He went to have a quick private word with his team. In a low voice, he said, "I'll see Tirsa to her room then meet you guys in the small study behind the workroom." He left them to go get Tirsa.

The occupants still in the room watched the colonel take her out of the great room. Gossip sprung up like mushrooms. They couldn't figure the pair out. The colonel kept her with him but they didn't look like a couple that was having sex together.

She shied away from him when he was near her, he frowned a lot when watching her, and except when he was escorting her, they never touched. Her eyes would flash to him and then quickly away before he caught her looking at him. Maybe she wasn't willing to have sex and he was forcing her.

They concluded it was a mystery.

Chapter Sixteen

*T*he next day they broke into four groups. Cook stayed back at the lodge.

Robinson, Tirsa, Ji and Owen were group 1, they went south. Jancarlo, Bruno and Dia group 2 took off towards the north. Knox, Max, Stav, group 3 headed east. Johnson, Lil Dam, Lindsey and Raine group 4 headed west by the river channel.

The colonel told them they were looking for a trail of lava tears, black volcanic glass. They would be searching for a glimpse of black crystals laid out by nature in a loose, crooked row, hidden in the tall savanna grasses. It would be the first arrow Robinson was searching for.

Two fruitless days of searching passed, they were going to spend the next day regrouping, resting, getting supplies and reviewing the maps and charts. At the lodge, everyone had a task. Tirsa was with Knox, Raine, and Lindsey doing laundry in a shed out back.

Lil Dam and Owen were mowing the grass near the shed. Cook, Max and Dia bustled about in the kitchen.

Johnson, Bruno and Ji had gone to the small town for supplies.

The colonel and Jancarlo had also left the lodge; they said something about a special meeting with some officials.

The laundry mostly done, Lindsey accidentally cut her arm on a sharp shelf and cried like a baby. Raine finished the laundry while Knox took Lindsey to go back to the first bathroom to treat her cut.

"Come on, honey," Knox said to Tirsa, "stay with me."

Lindsey peeped over her shoulder at Tirsa following behind them and smirked at her. Lil Dam had put up his mower and trailed them.

They shuffled through the long grass, grasshoppers jumped out of their path. The sky a pure blue dome overhead reflected the gentle sun not as overwhelmingly hot, as it was not yet into the drier season. A bristling breeze kept the humidity and mosquitoes away.

Knox took Lindsey to the kitchen to wash her wound and sent Lil Dam to Knox's room to retrieve the first aid kit. Everyone busy doing something, no one noticed Tirsa wander off.

She made her way to the library. It was cool in the paneled room lined with bookcases. A stone fireplace took up the far wall. She saw a comfy looking chair beside a French glass door that was partially open to let in the breeze, where after she found a good book she would settle on to read.

Her back to the rest of the room, Tirsa carefully read the titles of books, occasionally pulling one out to read the back. So focused on what she was doing, she didn't hear the glass door open further or the soft steps on the floor behind her until it was too late.

A hand slammed over her mouth and another wrapped around her waist, she was swung around and jerked against a hard male body. One man held her, another man stood near the open door.

The man by the window said, "Hello there, Tirsa Auret."

He grinned at her and bowed. He was swarthy and dressed in dirty rumpled ranch wear. His fortyish face was heavily tanned and leathery from years outside in the elements. A soiled bandana hung in a loose knot around his neck, his boots were scuffed and worn and he had black oily hair.

From what Tirsa could tell, the man holding her looked more or less the same. Both men, big and undeniably strong, looked to Tirsa like renegades, brigands, stone cold killers.

Tirsa's eyes widened over the hard calloused hand covering her mouth. How did this man know who she was?

He smiled but the smile didn't reach the dark brown eyes. He said calmly, "Do not scream, girl, or Paara there," Tirsa felt the man let go of her waist and then she felt cold steel at her neck, "will cut your throat. You get me?" He had a thick, unrecognizable accent. Pitiless cruel eyes under thick dark eyebrows cut like a terrifying sword across the room at her.

The man, Paara, holding Tirsa, slid his hand off her mouth and put it around her waist to hold her still, keeping the knife at her throat.

"Now," the man at the window instructed her, "you will be coming with us. One word, one scream, or refusal to move and you will never be able to speak again. Your vocal cords will be gone." He made a cutting motion across his neck with his hand. "You get me, girl?" He waited.

The knife pressed against her neck forced her head back. She was too terrified to utter a word.

The man shouted impatiently, "Answer me!"

Trying to catch her breath, she gulped wordlessly like a fish. The man holding her was well over a head taller than her.

The oily smile left the other male's leathery face, his amiable voice dropped to violent menace, he warned her, "No fighting, no screaming girl, don't make me have to make Paara hurt you." He repeated in a harsh hiss, "*Do you understand me?*"

Unable to speak, Tirsa nodded.

"Thank you," he said with insincere politeness. The smile returned and he sounded pleasant again. "Paara, bring her here, we need to go before-"

"Adullam, let her go."

All eyes turned to the doorway.

Almost unrecognizable to Tirsa, the colonel stood over the threshold. He was dressed in a long-sleeved black tunic, black pants, boots. The beard was gone and the black hair was cut and combed straight back.

He looked years younger. The glittering black eyes were the same. His arms at his sides, legs akimbo, he wasn't looking at Tirsa, he was staring at the man by the window.

"Ah, van Eleman," said the man the colonel had called Adullam. He said ruefully, "My Intel told me you were not on the property."

"Your Intel was wrong."

Adullam shrugged indifferently. "Oh well, good help and all that. Anyway, I don't expect you to interfere; all will go smoothly if you just look the other way while we take Miss Auret with us. We will pay you well for her."

The colonel's brow arched at the man's use of Tirsa's name. His voice cool, deep, he said, "She is not for sale. What do you want with her?" His eyes flicked to the man holding the knife at Tirsa's throat, then to her. Harrowing terror convulsed in Tirsa's unblinking eyes fixed on him.

Adullam studied the colonel for a moment. "Ah, it seems you really don't know. Other than the obvious attributes she has," he let his creepy gaze slide down Tirsa's body. "I have other needs for her. You'll find out anyway so I'll tell you. She is an Intinitt. Her ancestors were Intints."

"So?"

Wiping a dusty hand across his mouth, Adullam explained, "The Intints travelled here thousands of years ago from a distant country that was sinking into the sea. They are one of the undocumented, unseen, virtually unknown tribes that lives hidden deep within the rain forest."

"Again, so what?"

"You've heard of the rare red diamonds?" Adullam asked.

The colonel raised one shoulder casually up and down. "*Ja.*"

"Well," Adullam said, licking his lips. "There are stories about these newly discovered gemstones that have a similar structure to regular diamonds but are made up of different atoms. Two kinds, wurtzite boron nitride, and a hexagonal diamond called lonsdaleite. The significance of these is that they are up to 58% harder than diamonds. The wurtzite is more stable in oxygen at higher temperatures and can be used for instance, as a corrosion resistant film on the surface of space vehicles. I have diligently studied research on these new gems."

The colonel said with cool impatience, "Good for you. Speed it up, Adullam."

"Huh." Adullam spat on the floor. "It is I that hold you captive." But he liked to show off his acumen, so warming up to his subject he continued, "They are so rare because one is formed from meteorites and the other during volcanic eruptions. The word is, the Intints have both crystals and are sort of guards or guardians or some such of the mines where they were found."

His eyes sparkling greedily, he went on, "There's a rumor the red diamonds can be found there. The problem is, no one has seen these people. Except the one guy, an Intinitt, that found them and brought back some of the diamonds, and he is dead. No one else knows where his people are. But, the Intints are, somewhat empathic. They can find each other by…not thoughts exactly, but an aura, a feeling. She," he nodded at Tirsa, "can find them."

Adullam, shrugging as if it was nothing, continued, "Unfortunately, the Intinitt that had the diamonds was tortured too far when questioned about the location of the mines, and he died. But," his grin gleaming white against his swarthy skin, he said, "He was able to spill info about her before perishing."

"Who arranged to get her on my ship?" Robinson snapped his question without moving a hair from where his boots were planted.

A corner of his mouth pulled up, Adullam shook his head. "Now, you know I can't tell you that, Eleman. Come on then, we will share the riches with you. That's why we want her, so if you will just look the other way and go on about your-"

"Adullam," the colonel said, his voice so deep and deadly low and accented it sent chills through Tirsa. "That man has three seconds to let her go, or I'll kill him."

Adullam's head flopped from his man to the colonel. "Aw, come on now, Eleman, we're not going to hurt her, we just need her for a bit then I'll return her. We will make you a very wealthy man. Don't worry, it will only be me and Paara that bang her, I will bring her back practically untouched."

"Two seconds."

Adullam frowned. "You're making this harder than it-"

Bang!

A gunshot rang out in the room- Paara turned rigid then dropped to the ground in a heap.

Tirsa saw the colonel with one arm stretched out like a rod, a small gun in his hand. There was a rustle, they looked to the glass door and Adullam was gone. In seconds, hoofbeats pounded outside, disappearing quickly.

"Tirsa, don't look at-" Robinson called out but it was too late. Tirsa had turned and looked down at the man behind her on the ground.

He lay with one leg crooked, the knife had clattered to the floor next to his open hand, and there was a bullet hole in his forehead like a third eye, a line of blood poured out of it and down the side of his head.

Tirsa gasped, her legs buckled, she started to crumple into a faint. With long fast steps the colonel ran to her, catching her before she hit the ground.

Footsteps banged into the room. Jancarlo and Knox came running in.

Robinson swooped Tirsa up in his arms, her head draped back, the blonde curls swept back and forth. He motioned to the glass door, "It was Zadock Adullam, he left through that door."

"I will go." Jancarlo started for the door.

"He's on horseback, you won't catch him," Robinson told him, looking down at the girl he held in his arms.

"I will try anyway," Jancarlo replied and sprinted out of the room.

Knox asked with concern, "What happened to Tirsa?"

The colonel said wryly, "Our little murderess fainted when she saw the guy with a bullet hole in his head."

Smiling at the irony, Knox walked over to the colonel with his arms held out. "I'll take her, you'll want to go with Jan?"

The colonel never took his eyes off the unconscious woman he held, her spine arching over his arm, her head hanging, the t-shirt tightened across her breasts, and then he looked at Knox. The major was staring at Tirsa.

Robinson pushed his arms up so her body curled inward and her head rested against his shoulder. "I've got her. You go after Jan. We'll talk later about why she was alone."

Knox faltered, stricken, he hadn't remembered that he was supposed to have eyes on her. He'd gotten complacent out here in the woodland, and involved with Lindsey and her cut, no excuse, he gulped down his guilt and hustled out the door after Jancarlo.

Johnson came running in, stopping in his tracks when he saw Paara on the floor. "You've been busy," he observed. He nodded at Tirsa. "She okay?"

"*Ja.* Get someone you trust, Lil Dam or Bruno or both and have them help you get rid of the body."

A quick snap of his head in acknowledgment, Johnson quickly strode out of the room.

Robinson carried Tirsa across the room to the door, she stirred. Blinking confused, she jerked when she realized she was in his arms. "Colonel what-"

"You're all right," he stated, and walked out of the room with her and into the hall without explanation.

Her face flushed, she squirmed to be set down on her feet. "If I'm okay then please put me down."

He kept walking down the hall and into the great room where he went to the sofa and set her gently on it. Her face a muddle of disorientation, she shifted to perch on the edge of the cushion staring with tense confusion at him.

Sitting down next to her, he turned his body to face her. "Do you remember what happened?"

She was staring oddly at him. Then her hand went to his face stroking it with one soft motion. "Your beard."

He didn't move. Her touch had startled him. Normally she cringed whenever he was near her. He could still feel the feathery fingertips warm and creamy against his face, his skin tingled, the tingle coursed down his body.

Her eyes went to the shorn black hair combed straight back. A smile tugged at a corner of her mouth. "You needed a trim. You look-"

But then the picture of the dead man flashed in her head. Her mouth dropped, a green tinge colored her face. Her eyes rolled in the back of her head.

The colonel quickly put his hand at the back of her neck and eased her against the cushion.

Tirsa looked queasily at him, her hand covered her mouth, she said through trembling lips, "You...shot...him. Is he...dead?"

His hand still under her neck he nodded. "*Ja.*" He dropped his hand, sliding it from her neck over her shoulder, down her arm, then onto the cushion.

With a shrug, he said matter-of-factly, "I warned him." He got up and told her, "Don't move, I'll be right back."

No worries there, Tirsa thought. Her stomach was churning and her knees were shaking.

He came right back with a bottle of scotch and two rock glasses. Leaning over, he took her hand and pulled her gently to her feet. "Come on. You need something to settle your nerves."

He led her outside off the front of the structure, to a swinging bench in an alcove. "Here, have a seat." He helped her to sit on the bench then set the bottle and glasses on a wrought iron table in front of them.

Sitting down next to her, he poured a few fingers of scotch in one glass and a quarter as much in another and handed that one to her.

Uneasily, Tirsa took the amber liquid, staring down at it. "Um, I don't really drink, I mean, I had a glass of champagne once."

"Go ahead, take a tiny sip. It'll calm your stomach. I won't let anything happen to you, I promise. Go on." He gestured with his hand for her to drink.

He took a healthy sip of his own glass, then said gently mocking, "You had a helluva reaction, you know, being an assassin yourself and all. I would think that kind of…violence, you'd take easily in stride." He watched a pink hue spread up her neck and across her cheeks. She dropped her humiliated eyes to the scotch in her hand.

Very unsure, Tirsa raised the glass and took a tiny sip, and made a face. In seconds she could feel the liquor ease down her throat, heat sliding lower to her stomach where it spread warmth, easing her belly and her head. She relaxed back against the bench and took another sip, made a face again, stuck out her tongue.

He chuckled at her puckered nose. "You'll get used to it."

They sat for a few moments, his long legs on the ground pushing the bench, swinging them gently, slightly.

To distract her from her thoughts of the ghastly sight of the man with a bleeding hole in his head, and her near kidnapping, he said, "Tirsa, I distinctly remember telling you that you were to always be in the presence of one of my team." He waited for her response, his gaze level on her.

She drank the rest of her scotch and set the glass on the table. He picked up the bottle and poured her a little more, handed the glass back to her, and refilled his own.

Tirsa took a sip. Slipping her fingers under the back of her head she drew them through her hair, then passed the glass to her other hand and did the same to the other side of her head. Stretching her neck, she shook her mane, it shimmered in the waning sunlight. She curled one leg up on the bench and turned sideways to face him. A trace of rose shined on her cheeks and the tip of her nose.

The big blue eyes glowed at him; the liquor softened the rigid tension from her jaw, her shoulders settled. She told him, "I was with Knox, Colonel. He had to help Lindsey with a cut on her arm. I didn't want to be in the way. I didn't think it would be a problem if I went and got a book and hung out in the library. It's cooler and blocks the glare of the setting sun.

She glanced at him, seeing the glower she turned away. "I don't see why it's such a big deal, Colonel, I swore to you I'm not going to hurt anyone, why don't you believe me?" Her eyes turned dewy with shame, she lowered her head so he couldn't see her struggle to hold back the tears of frustration.

"You never swore you wouldn't try to hurt *me* again, Tirsa." His voice husky, there was a hint of a question in it.

She kept her head down, her hair covering her face. He waited for her to object to his comment, in vain.

He took a deep breath, exhaled. "Anyway, as I've said before, it's not all about you harming…others, as today showed."

Her head stayed bowed hiding her shame.

"Tirsa, look at me."

Composing herself, she raised her head and took a big swallow of scotch then immediately coughed and spluttered, her face burnt red, the tears leapt from her eyes, her tongue blew out. He took the glass from her, set it on the table, then patted her back gently until she stopped coughing.

It took a minute before she was able to breathe normally. Smiling gently when she caught her breath, he said, "You're not used to it, you need to take it slow." He stroked light circles on her back until she leaned against the bench wiping at her eyes with the heels of her hands.

He settled back beside her. "As I was saying," he continued, "after what happened today you must be able to see that you yourself are in peril." He handed her glass back to her and resumed pushing the swing.

After a few moments of silence, he asked, "Tirsa, do you know why that man, Adullam, came for you? Do you have any idea what he was talking about? You, the diamonds? Those natives?" His back against the wooden swing, he watched her under lowered lids.

She turned her bewildered face towards him. "I- I, I thought he was making up what he said. I assumed he was there thinking no one was around and he could rob the lodge. It was all so…surreal…" she sipped her drink and rested her head against the swing's back.

"Hmmm," he murmured in agreement. "*Ja*, that it was." It would take a lot of scotch to wipe out the picture of that

148

fuck holding Tirsa with a knife at her throat. If he'd been a few moments later coming back from town- he shook his head and smoothed his hair back off his forehead with his palm.

They watched the sunset searing orange behind the dark poles of palm trees, fringe-topped like long tapered fingers. Pretty as a postcard, the sky slowly darkened, stars flickered on one by one.

Frogs croaked somewhere near the river. Every so often a gust of wind blew over the savanna tickling it like grassy hair. As they sat, the wind picked up a little more, the palms shimmied in the moonlight.

"Oh!" Tirsa exclaimed. An enormous, iridescent bluish-green butterfly with a yellow belly and gold spots on the hind wings, fluttered up and down and around them, sweeping its vast wings like bird wings only more gently and gracefully. It hovered under the outside lamppost.

They watched it flit away to the closest tree then from branch to branch then it was gone.

He explained, "That was a Queen Alexandra's Birdwing. A male. The biggest butterfly in the world pretty much and quite rare, on their way to going extinct. The females are larger than the males. We are very fortunate to have seen it." Robinson watched Tirsa watch the butterfly.

"It's breathtaking," Tirsa marveled, her voice and face filled with reverence.

His eyes still on her, he murmured, "*Ja.*" Then he said quietly, "Tirsa," he waited until she drew her gaze from the butterfly to him. "Back to the subject. From the moment I met you, I felt...something...I felt you would be in..." he trailed off.

Starting again, he said, "I don't know if the danger brought you, or you brought the danger." He could see her pale face in the dusk. "Until I know what's going on, I have to ensure the safety of everyone on this expedition, including you. So I will do what I feel is necessary." His gaze drifted down to the drink in his hand.

"But," she began.

His head was lowered but his eyes rolled up to her.

"If you let me be by myself, or...or somehow let me go...home... don't you see, your own team, you, can be putting yourselves in jeopardy by enforcing one of you to be with me at all times. That person, that brigand knew my name, if it's true that he- he really did come for me..." she trailed off in confused wonder. Then she looked up at him. "Don't you see? Everyone here can be in danger because of me! You must let me go!"

He listened to her, his expression growing darkly serious, angles on his face sharpened. He retorted angrily, "You don't know my team, Tirsa. They can take care of themselves, they'll take care of you too but only if you damned let them."

Heat rose in his voice, he took a breath to calm himself. "You committed a crime, Tirsa. Several crimes. I'm not sending you home. And," he gripped her arm spilling her drink, "this is the last time I'm warning you to obey my orders. If you flaunt them the others will too, then we're all at risk. I mean what I say. Recall the dead man on the library floor-" he broke off at her swift intake of breath.

"Are you...threatening to kill me?" her voice cracked, a small delicate hand fluttered at her throat.

"*Neen*, no, God no, Tirsa," he said swiftly. "I didn't mean that at all." His hand still on her arm he brushed his thumb gently over her skin. "I meant that I will follow through with consequences when my orders aren't obeyed. For everyone."

Recalling how quickly and easily he had killed that man; fearful of him again, she tugged her arm from his grasp and shifted her body further from his. This annoyed him, although he had said it on purpose to make his point.

Still, he said crossly, "Stop looking at me like I'm a deranged psychopath. It was necessary to shoot him; they were going to take you. They would have executed you after they used you, in more ways than one." He deliberately ran his gaze down her body then levered back up at her comprehending, frightened expression. She looked green again, he changed the subject back.

Deep voice exacting, he said unequivocally, "Anyway, I can't run this thing effectively if I don't have everyone's obedience. That's not said out of pomposity, I have been put, ah, I am in command and my orders have to be followed without fail. I've given you leeway because you're a civilian, unused to…" he shook his head.

"Regardless. This will be the last time you don't obey my orders, the consequences will be severe." He let out his breath and sat back. His arm stretched across the back of the seat, his hand almost touching her shoulder, he took a long drink.

She said nothing. He craved to know what she was thinking. She just sipped quietly, the swing see-sawing gently again, her hair swirling in the wind. He said, "Tirsa-"

"I hear you," came the reply.

"Colonel." Jancarlo appeared out of the dark. He took in the scotch and the glasses, and the couple that sat with a big space between them. The scene looked romantic but they didn't. She was glaring at her drink and he was glaring at her.

The major advised, "We did not get him, Adullam got away. He took the horse through the trees, the jeep could not follow. Cook sent me to find out where you guys were, you are holding up dinner." His eyes flicked to Tirsa. She was now gazing up at the moon.

The colonel reluctantly stood up. "*Ja*. All right." He held a hand out for Tirsa to take. She ignored it sliding to the end of the bench then off to her feet where she stumbled.

Robinson grabbed her arm. "Here, the scotch will make you unsteady."

She giggled engagingly, the alcohol making her lightheaded, then she tripped. Steadying her, he pulled her against his chest, his arm belting her to him. She giggled again, the yellow hair spread across his black tunic like a star against the night sky.

Jancarlo looked over her head at the colonel. His expression impassive, the colonel still got his point.

Chapter Seventeen

*O*n the way in to join the others at the dining table, Robinson said to Jancarlo, "I want you to set up perimeter guards, 24/7. Two walking, one clockwise and the other counter-clockwise with a changing pattern and speed."

Jancarlo nodded. "I will make a schedule. Knox and I will check outside after dinner and then start them."

Cook had made pans of thick, cheesy lasagna. Most of the group was seated at the long, plain wooden dining table. The furniture in the lodge was stark but functional. Simple cushioned chairs and two sofas, the dining area contained the table and an extensive longboy for buffets.

Stav dug into a pan with a spatula, scooping up a hunk he plopped it on his plate. Bruno tore off a hunk of toasty Italian bread and passed the basket to Owen.

The colonel motioned to Johnson to step away from the table. They moved to the hallway out of hearing from the others.

Robinson said, "Listen Johnson, I need you to go into the town tomorrow morning. I need you to…um…well, I need you to get Tirsa some clothes. She hadn't planned on staying in New Guinea, you know, the old kill and run," he smiled drolly, "so she didn't bring much."

At Johnson's confused look, the colonel pulled money out of his pocket, peeled off some bills and handed them to Johnson. "You need to get her another couple of pairs of pants, shirts," his face reddened slightly, "uh, and under things,"

Johnson sputtered, "What? You want me to buy ladies underwear? Are you joking?"

Shoving the bills at Johnson, Robinson said, "Come on, Major, you told me you used to go shopping with Jayda all the time and helped her choose…stuff."

His brows arched high with rebuttal, Johnson retorted, "Jayda's my wife, E, for Pete's sake. Why don't you do it? Or Jancarlo, or-"

"Because I'm asking you to do it. You have more experience in this kind of thing, besides Jayda, you have five sisters. Think of Tirsa as a little sister. Her clothes are lying on the bed, go write down her size. I also need you to get her like an outfit. A dress. Nothing splashy, just something she can wear to that little dive there in town. I'm not taking her shopping because I don't want her seen yet, I have a meet and I need a cover and she'll do."

Rolling his eyes, Johnson, sighed, "*Ja*, sure." He took the money, folded it and put it in his pocket. "Is that the only reason you're taking her with you?"

The colonel stuffed his hands in his pockets and ruffled his shoulders. His face grim he replied, "*Neen*. I'm taking her to keep an eye on her since none of you are capable of doing it."

Johnson was hurt. "That's not cool, E."

Robinson looked apologetic. "You're right. *Zich excuseren,* sorry. It's just, after today, those men trying to take her. What if I hadn't come looking for her at that moment? What if-"

"You were in time, E, that's all that counts. We'll all be more diligent, we didn't mean to be lax. She's a girl, a gentle young woman, who would think, well, whatever the hell is going on?"

Nodding, Robinson mumbled in agreement, "I know. I know. We need to research that shit Adullam said about her, and the red diamonds." He snapped his fingers. "Oh, and get her some shoes for the outfit, sandal things with heels or something."

Johnson rolled his eyes again. "What do I know about women's shoes?"

Robinson said, "Her boots won't look right with a dress. Ask one of those girls in the store to help you. You need to get girl things, a brush, shampoo, female stuff, the girls at the shop will tell you what she needs. It'll give you a chance to flirt." One side of the colonel's mouth turned up in, ribbing the major.

Johnson crossed his arms. "I'm getting plenty of flirting with those other two here. They act like female Tomcats for crying out loud. By the way, women working in the stores don't like to be called 'girls.' This is the 21st Century, E, calling them girls is disparaging, it's putting them down. Sometimes you sound as backwards and chauvinistic as Jan."

Robinson responded innocently, "They are not men are they, they are girls aren't they?" He walked back to the dining area leaving Johnson shaking his head at his back.

After dinner, everyone left the table except Knox and Tirsa. The colonel went into the kitchen where he found Cook putting away left overs. "Seymour," he said.

Cook closed the refrigerator door. Friendliness beaming from his chubby face, he asked, "Hey, what can I do for you, E? You look good by the way, finally getting rid of that crazy disguise. I noticed you had tossed the glasses right away."

Robinson set his palms on the table behind him and leaned back against it, crossed his ankles. He rubbed his jaw then put his hand back on the table. "Feels good to have that shit off my face. I was afraid birds were going to start nesting in my hair."

The men shared a chuckle. Then the colonel said, "Those damned interns are of very little use. They're not taking the search seriously; they spend all their time sniffing after each other. I feel like I'm running a bordello for cripe's sake."

Cook reminded him, "They were necessary for cover."

"*Ja.* Tomorrow I'm going to that meet in town. I want you to take them out to the buildings out back and get them to cleaning and organizing all three rooms. I've been thinking about that kid's suggestion with the horses. There'd be too many for this expedition, but if we need to come back we can use the buildings as stables and supply storage."

"*Ja, goed* idea. What about Tirsa, her too?" Cook asked.

"She's coming with me to the meet," Robinson said nonchalantly.

Cook's forehead furrowed. "Uh huh. Okay, I'll get them started later in the afternoon. I wish we could find the black glass and get on with the search."

"I know. We'll find it." The colonel pushed off the table to return back to the dining room.

The next day was another disappointing search. In the later afternoon, Robinson and Jancarlo were in the study.

Johnson came in with bags in his hands. "I got the stuff. The salesgirl- person, was a big help. I gave her the list, told her to include female stuff, and she chose everything and bagged it up." He grinned large showing rows of big white teeth.

"I didn't have to participate, just sat and read the newspaper while she did it. So, what do you want to see first, the underthings?" he asked the colonel with a leer. Reaching in a bag he rummaged around. "What first? Sheer panties? Silk bra?"

The colonel frowned at him and crossed his arms. Even Jancarlo looked on with some interest.

Glaring at the major, Robinson said, "*Neen*. Just go take them to her, tell her to get dressed and ready to go out. Explain to her where we're going then tell her to come in here when she's dressed. She's in the library with Knox."

"Oh?" Johnson remarked with a sly raised brow. "They're getting quite um, cozy, aren't they?" He and Jancarlo watched the colonel for his reaction.

But his face remained expressionless, he said, "Whatever. Go give her the clothes. I'll change and meet you all back here."

Sharing a jeering smirk with Jancarlo, Johnson left to get Tirsa.

Not long after, Robinson came out of the shower freshly shaven, his hair still damp and went back into the study. He was wearing pressed, dark brown Dockers and a white, button-down long sleeved shirt. The brown boots he wore were dress boots, not his normal scruffy, steel-toed black boots.

Johnson, Knox and Jancarlo were already there waiting. Johnson whistled, "Don't you look purty, E, for your date," he grinned.

"Whatever Johnson, knock it off. It's not a date and you know it," Robinson gruffed, buttoning the cuffs on the sleeves.

"Oo," Johnson teased, "aren't we surly today?" Clicking his tongue against the roof of his mouth, he shook his head, "Your date isn't going to like her man cranky…"

Not biting Johnson's attempt to rile him, the colonel asked, "Did you tell her to come straight here when she's ready?"

"Of course. She was definitely confused, and I'd say she had a bit of fear. I promised her she wasn't being taken to town to be arrested. That you have a meet and prefer not to leave her alone with us untrustworthy knaves." He and Knox and Jancarlo crossed their arms and pretended they were offended and hurt.

"Come on you guys, don't be stu-" Robinson broke off, Tirsa was in the doorway. His eyes widened like black moons, mouth slacked. The four men stood with their eyes popping.

Her hand on the doorframe, Tirsa said shyly, embarrassed, "I, uh, need some help…"

"Come in," Robinson told her while shooting Johnson a rebuking look, but the hefty black man was too busy gawking at Tirsa to see it.

"I…uh…" She hesitated.

"Are you deaf girl, I said come in," he snapped at her, shocked at his own physical reaction.

She stepped gingerly into the room in her bare feet. She was wearing a thigh-skimming short skirt that showcased long, slender legs and she was holding part of the top.

It was a long, one-piece fabric. It was designed to wrap around the waist then go into a halter-top tied behind her neck. Not familiar with the style, she was struggling to hold the thing against her bare breasts, wherever she held it trying to tie it, it would slip somewhere else.

"I need one of the girls to help me but I can't find them, I thought they might be in here." She was mortified, standing there half-dressed again in a room with these same men. Déjà vu all over again.

The colonel tried to speak but the words strangled in his throat. Half-dressed and with her hair in disarray floating around her shoulders and down her back, cheeks rosy in embarrassment, licking her lips dewy, she looked like she had been in the process of either starting or ending having sex. His men were getting an eyeful and enjoying every minute of it. He moved quickly to block her from their view.

"Here, ahh...let me...try." He grasped one end of the fabric from her then the other trying to figure out how to tie it together. His hands brushed her waist, her back, he dropped the end he was pulling behind her neck and swept his hand up her breast trying to catch it before it fell completely. He could feel his neck burning; he knew his ears were turning red before he heard the men behind him snickering.

"Here," he said huskily, handing the ends of the fabric back to her. "Cover up, I'll take you back to your room and find one of the girls to help you." He put his hand at her back ushering her out the door, the snickers growing louder as they left.

He found Lindsey and told her to go help Tirsa. Taking no notice of the redhead's resentful expression at being ordered to assist Tirsa, he strode back to the study. Outside the door he took several deep breaths to still his racing heart and calm his betraying body, then smoothed his hair back with his palms before going in.

"Great," he groused, when he saw all three of his team; normally severely stoic men all grinning at him like loons.

"What the hell were you thinking, Johnson? I'm going to have to keep a hand on her all night. You know what kinds of dogs frequent that dive. I'll be lucky if I don't get out without having to give some asshole a black eye." Scowling at Johnson, he said, "For God's sake, she can't even wear a fucking bra under that thing."

Knox tittered, "Good thing you're not going horseback riding then, huh?" All three men guffawed ignoring the black glare from the colonel.

"I can't believe you're even complaining. I'll go if you don't want-" Johnson cut off at the colonel's narrowed eyes. He raised his shoulders, turned his palms out. "Hey, I didn't ask to do the shopping. Besides, I told you, I didn't even see the clothes, the clerk did the choosing. But I will say," he said slipping a leer at the others, "she looks damned amazing. I know I wouldn't be able to spend the evening with her and keep my hands to myself, and I'm a happily married man."

"*Ja*," Knox snickered, "good luck, E."

Jancarlo slapped Knox on the back, they all laughed, except the colonel.

Knox said, "If you don't trust yourself alone with her why don't you just take one of the other girls? We swear if you leave her here we'll all keep an eye on her."

Johnson said, "*Ja*, E, and it will be hard... wait, I mean it won't be a *difficult* job-" they roared with laughter.

"I'll be back when you girls are done giggling." Robinson went to splash cold water on his face.

When he came out of the bathroom, Tirsa was with Knox alone in the library. Her hair was brushed and the outfit was put together. Lindsey did a great job, except Tirsa looked even sexier than when it was falling off her because the top fit almost snug, but not snug enough to keep her held firmly. He barked a terse, "Let's go."

Knox bent over and gave Tirsa a kiss on the forehead. "Pay no mind to his bark, honey. Have a good time."

A little too roughly, Robinson hooked her arm and quickly pulled her to the door, slowing down when he realized she was tripping along in heels.

Wordlessly, he helped her into the 5-speed jeep then climbed in behind the wheel. The Copestone Lodge was over 50 miles across the savanna from the town. The road was only where the jeep had recently worn down the grass going back and forth to town. It was bumpy travelling over grass and rocks and holes.

He kept his eyes glued to the ground in front of them; he didn't dare look at her, dressed in what that idiot Johnson had gotten her. Her legs were crossed, the short skirt rode way up her thighs. She didn't have a purse, her hands were folded demurely in her lap, the halter thing did nothing to hold her- steady.

Every bump and jostle his throat got drier. His neck felt tight, he stuck a finger inside his collar dragging it around to loosen it, wishing it was cool enough for her to need a jacket, a long thick jacket. He kept his eyes fixed on the road, the pulse at his temple beating like a drum.

The sun had set. The black sky with no lights around blazed with stars. The air was balmy, if not for the circumstances and the rough road it would have been a nice trip. It took well over an hour to get to where the colonel needed to go.

The town was basically four corners of a grungy two-lane street consisting of a tiny pharmacy, ratty food market, several derelict bars, a tawdry four-room inn, several shops, and a cruddy diner. Robinson pulled in front of one of the better looking bars.

He shut off the engine then set his elbow on the steering wheel and turned to her. "Tirsa, I brought you here because I have a meeting and it would look better, um, for me if I had a girlfr- uh, lady on my arm. I need you to stay with me at all times. This is like the Wild West out here, there's no law nearby, don't put us both in a bad situation by…um…"

"Throwing myself at some cowboy?" she snipped sarcastically. He looked guilty. "Colonel, why didn't you just bring Dia or Lindsey?"

He turned to look out the front window. Then he faced her again. "Listen, I know you're not the flirtatious type, but men are still going to come on to you. As far as the other girls, they both would definitely flirt with anything in pants. Dia would probably be drunk before I could even get her here, and Lindsey is too fastidious to come to this place."

Her brow arched in offense.

"I'm not saying you're any less a lady, actually you're ten times the lady either of them are, and I needed a lady for this mission…I mean meeting. Anyway, I doubt you even know how to flirt."

He continued quickly at her frown, "Lindsey has her nose so high in the air she would offend everyone in the place. And, both women are so brazen I'd have to peel them off the cowboys here. Besides, with you here with me I don't have to worry what trouble you're getting into back at the ranch." He had the grace to look contrite at the hurt look that came over her face.

"Come on," he climbed out of the jeep and came around to open her door. She gracefully swung her legs out before he could look away. He sighed, and thought not for the first time, *it's going to be a long night*. The jeep had a very high step.

Taking her hand, he said, "Put your other hand on my shoulder to brace yourself, it's a big step down and you have heels on." He set his other hand on her waist in case she tripped. She had to come close to him for him to help her down.

With her feet firmly on the ground, she was closeted between the truck and him, and he didn't back up. Their bodies pressing together, he released her hand and curled both of his around her waist. His eyes boring into hers, he pulled her closer.

Uncertain of his intent, to hurt her or kiss her, or what, she stepped back.

Seeing her trepidation, he wordlessly closed then locked the door and pocketed the keys.

Chapter Eighteen

*T*hey walked up to the saloon, he pushed the door open but instead of letting her go first. Robinson stepped in. He wanted to check out the scene before he brought her inside. Although tamer than the other bars in the rural town, it did have the nebulous notoriety as being a rough place. Glancing around, he decided it was docile enough tonight and ushered her in.

The saloon was mostly timber, walls, floor, ceiling. The bar counter was a varnished circle taking up the left side of the rustic room and was knee-deep with customers. Like a neighborhood bar, people were mostly in groups drinking and laughing. Almost all of the plain wooden chairs and tables were occupied.

A cluster of people holding beers gathered around a jukebox arguing about what to play next. Some were in grubby jeans and t-shirts; most had dressed up a bit more in khakis and polo's, although it was a casual place it was a step up from the other ramshackle dives on the street. Two barmaids serviced the floor wearing bland black pants and blue striped tops, the two bartenders were up to their elbows making drinks.

Finding an empty table through the sea of heads, Robinson held Tirsa's hand as he threaded his way to it. He pulled out a chair for her, helped her sit then he sat facing the door. The room was hazy with smoke, all kinds, tobacco, cigar as well as the sickly sweet.

His gaze kept drawing to her like she was a magnet and his eyeballs were metal. He'd sweep her body then he'd look away, and then back at her again like he couldn't stop looking at her no matter how hard he tried. Clearing his throat, he asked her, "What would you like, maybe a glass of wine?"

"Um, I guess." Tirsa felt so out of place, and bewildered as to why he had brought her here.

The barmaid came over, the colonel ordered for them, "A glass of wine and a draft."

Laconically the barmaid scratched her head with her pencil and asked with the tone of *she shouldn't have to ask*, "Red or white?"

The colonel looked at Tirsa. "Um, I guess white," she said in more of a question than a statement.

"You got ID?" Chomping on a wad of gum, the barmaid scratched the fuzzy mound of bleached, platinum blonde hair again with the pencil.

Pink filling her cheeks, Tirsa mumbled, "I don't have-"

"She left her purse with our babysitter. I'll vouch for her." Dropping his arm over the back of Tirsa's chair, Robinson leaned back in his chair, crossed his legs, confident, a little cocky. Tirsa's cheeks grew brighter at his insinuation that they were married.

The barmaid's eyes swept his strong legs, lean hips, even in the dress shirt his huge biceps bulged whenever he moved his arms, he had serious, but nice looking lips. With the thick black hair and lacquer eyes, he appeared relaxed, but there was an edge, like a panther leashing its energy until it was needed. She glanced at his and her fingers, no rings. She shrugged. Under-aged loggers and miners came in all the time. "Okay handsome, I'll be right back."

Not talking, the couple each surveyed the room, she to see what it was like, he searching for the person he was meeting. The barmaid brought their drinks.

Robinson drank through the foam until half the beer was gone before he set the mug down. Tirsa took a small sip of her wine. Trying to make conversation he said, "So, um, you and Knox seem to be, uh, hitting it off."

She took another sip, her smile sweet. "Yes. As I said before he's a nice man. He was devastated over the death of his fiancée; he seems to finally be working through it. The," she searched for the words, "somber sullenness is being replaced by a thoughtful, charming, kindness."

He grunted. "Humph. Charming…" His arm still around the back of her chair, he threw down the rest of his beer then set the mug down a little hard. "It appears that you are…helping him through his pain." He looked off to the side like he wasn't interested in the conversation waving at the barmaid for another beer.

"Sure. Of course. It helps to have someone to talk to." She smiled into her wine glass.

He leaned forward and set his forearms on the table. Uncrossing his legs, the dark brows drew down over surly eyes. He grumbled crossly, "Is that all you do, talk? You seem pretty cozy every time I see you two together." He'd wanted to ask Knox what was up, they're close friends, but he didn't want the teasing about jealousy that would go with his questions.

Not getting what he was hinting at, the guileless blue eyes searched his in question. "Of course, what else would we-" her eyes dropped, she blushed. Then, frowning, she looked at him, ire shooting out of the formerly sweet eyes. "How dare you speak to me like that. Knox is like a...a brother to me. And it's none of your business anyway even if-"

Holding the mug's handle the colonel tipped it peering in to see if a drop of beer was left then slammed it down on the table. Leaning towards her he said fiercely, "You can't tell me-"

"Eleman." A man was standing at their table.

The colonel hadn't seen him come in. Irritated at himself for being distracted, he shoved his chair back and stood up. He held out his hand and greeted him, "Manasseh." They shook. The colonel didn't introduce Tirsa. The less known about her the better. He leaned over with his palm on the table close to her so no one else could hear.

"I'm stepping outside for one second. Do not move. Do not talk to anyone. Okay?"

Furious at the way he spoke to her, she crossed her arms and dipped her head in a brief nod.

Not caring if she was annoyed, he took stock of the stunning eyes fringed with long lashes, perfect bow lips, creamy complexion and cloud of blonde curls, not trusting himself to look at the rest of her, he shut his eyes for a second, kicking himself. He was probably going to have to knock out some asshole when he comes back that would no doubt swoop in the second he leaves the table. He should have brought Jancarlo with them, or not brought her at all. Too late now.

"I'll be right back." One more swift glance at her then he left with the man.

Tirsa sat patiently sipping her wine when she realized she really needed to go to the ladies room. The barmaid came with the colonel's beer. Tirsa asked, "Where's the restroom?" The barmaid pointed. Tirsa said, "I'll be right back. Is that all right?"

The barmaid assured her she wouldn't clear the table. Tirsa stood up quickly glancing at the door; surely she could get to the bathroom and back before he returned. She hurried across the room. Many pairs of eyes followed her.

She was washing her hands watching a woman who looked Middle Eastern, finishing diapering a baby. Cooing at the infant, the woman picked the baby up and left. Tirsa felt tingly.

Leaving the restroom the thought of the colonel's orders to stay put went right out of her mind. The woman was crossing the room heading towards a back entrance. Tirsa hurried after her.

Outside was a patio with only a few patrons scattered around it in the low lighting. Tirsa saw the woman and the baby alone, off to the side sitting on a low brick wall. The woman's head was down, the baby was crying. The woman seemed unable to console the baby. Tirsa went over and sat on the wall near them.

"Hi," she said softly.

The woman held the baby on her lap trying to still its wails. She barely glanced at Tirsa.

"Here," Tirsa said, holding her arms out, "let me."

Startled at first, the woman held the baby to her chest eyeing Tirsa suspiciously until she looked deep into the blue eyes. With only slight uncertainty, she handed the squalling baby to Tirsa who took it and held it against her breast, patting its back.

"Her name is Lucia," The woman murmured in wonder as the baby quickly stopped crying and fell asleep with her head on Tirsa's chest.

"Yes, Lucia," Tirsa whispered. She looked directly into the woman's dark brown eyes. "And you are Asha."

The woman was shocked, her mouth dropped. "How did you-"

"It's okay, don't be alarmed. I've come to talk with you, to tell you about, Lia." Tirsa watched the shock, sorrow, then anger spread across the woman's dark-skinned face.

"What do you, who the-"

Tirsa spoke softly, "Lia says to tell you it wasn't your fault. You couldn't have done anything." She let the words sink in.

The woman Asha, stared at Tirsa, eyes so filled with pain they looked about to bleed. She murmured in a broken whisper, "My sister."

Tirsa waited, patting the sleeping baby. Lucia smelled like baby powder and shampoo. Tirsa ran her fingers over the soft as cotton skin, tugged gently at the tiny toes, listening to the soft spurting breaths the baby expelled.

Her hand on her heart, the woman's voice shook, "What...did...Lia-" she choked her name, "say?" She moved her hand to Tirsa's arm, begged, "Tell me,"

Tirsa shifted the sleeping baby slightly, smiled warmly at Asha. "She said you couldn't have talked her out of driving that night. Even if you were together and not on the phone. She was so mad at Mohammed she couldn't think, couldn't stay there, she had to go. She was speeding, around a sharp curve on the mountain," she paused and waited.

Asha was nodding, staring so intently at Tirsa, her face a sketch of anguish, tears filled then flooded out of her dark eyes. "She...she went over, the cliff," she sucked in a cry of pain.

Holding the baby with one hand Tirsa patted the woman's hand, "Yes. Lia says, you couldn't have done anything, even if you'd gone looking for her, it was immediate, she died instantly, without pain."

Asha bent her head to her hands and wept into them. Tirsa patted her back then put her hand back under the baby's legs.

Asha gazed up with wretched eyes, her voice wounded, "I...was so...scared that she laid in agony waiting for help, waiting for me... these past three years I..." she broke down weeping.

Tirsa cradled the baby's silky head, fine tendrils curled under her hand. "The last thing I have for you," she waited until the woman's weeping lessened then said, "she said to tell you, she is in tremendous peace and gloriously happy where she is, where you'll see her one day. There's nothing else, that is all I can tell you."

Asha put her hands together as a steeple in prayer, "Thank you, Miss, thank you for giving me my life back...thank you..." Tirsa handed her the baby who didn't waken when her mother took her into her arms. Asha clutched the baby to her chest and wept over her.

Tirsa stood up watching mother and child, then turned to go to the door- she gasped.

The colonel was standing near the door in the shadows, his arms crossed over his chest, his shoulder against the wall, watching her. Her heart beating like a hummingbird's wings she made herself walk to him. *What was he going to do to her?*

Without a word, he took her arm firmly and led her around the outside of the bar back to the jeep. Opening the door, he held her elbow helping her into the truck, then went around and got in.

He still said nothing as he drove out of the lot and down the street. He drove until the dirt road ran out and he had to find the trail in the dark that led across the high grass back to the structure.

When they were near enough to see them, the lights on the lodge helped guide them in the twilight. Copestone loomed like a hulking set of trains that had gotten derailed and crunched together in a crooked line, surrounded by tall waving grass, and palm trees like dark skinny ghosts. Robinson drove up to the lodge, parked and turned off the engine.

They both sat mute. Tirsa was weary, drained, and very afraid of him.

He was trying to absorb what he'd seen, heard. A couple of lights went out in the lodge, others came on. Moths danced around the light over the front door.

Sitting in the quiet darkness, Robinson bent his head over the back of the seat and stared at the roof. He rubbed his face, scratched his jaw suddenly missing the beard.

Finally, he leaned his back against the corner of the jeep and set an arm on the steering wheel and one across the back of the seat. She turned slightly in her seat to face towards him.

He opened his mouth, said, "I…" then he saw her eyes. Luminous as blue gossamer, her face pale and ethereal, his gaze dropped to her lush lips slightly parted in nervous anticipation of whatever punishment he planned to do to her. Feeling himself drawing towards her like a bear to sweet honey, he closed then covered his own eyes with his fingers.

Rubbing his lids, mystified and incredulous he said, "It was true what Knox said. You have something…he couldn't quite explain it…a phenomenon."

This was what her guardians had kept her from, people thinking she was a freak, a ghoul.

Sifting a strong hand through his thick inky hair, he turned more towards her. "Explain it to me, Tirsa. Help me to understand, this…gift."

"Huh," she grunted, "or curse."

He shook his head faintly from side to side, said softly, "*Neen*, what you do with it, the relief you give people, the peace, that is a gift. Tell me about it."

Tirsa cocked her head to the side as if trying to determine how sincere he was. He'd started off the Mediatrix Expedition with a pretense, a façade, but other than that he'd been true to his word, candid, without affect, direct.

Taking a deep breath and letting it out slowly, she said, "There really isn't much to tell. I grew up in a place in rural, remote France, with guardians. They said my parents sent me when I was too young to remember, for my protection. That if people knew what I…it's hard to explain. They thought I would be sought after, taken away, locked up, maybe studied, maybe exploited. What people didn't understand was that I have no control over it."

When she didn't continue he prompted, "It?"

Her lids fluttered tiredly. "Things come to me in a sort of dream-state. Like tonight with Asha. When I was near her in the restroom, something like a veil enveloped my…head, words, voices come to me. Her sister said to me, well you heard what I told Asha. And that's all. I can't control it, it just happens. I become, compelled, to tell the person. Like with Knox and Asha I was guided, kind of forcefully to tell them, it's very hard to fight it. I felt it the minute I met Knox, but I fought it desperately knowing he would push me away before I could get the words out. But then," she smiled lightly, "I gave in, as did he."

She grew quiet waiting for him to say something. He just sat there, dark brooding eyes under hooded lids watching her.

"I, uh, I guess that must be why those men came after me."

"You said you didn't know them."

She shook her head, pushed the long curls off her shoulders. Her shoulders shivered, recalling the colonel that she was sitting alone in the dark car with, shooting the man who had held a knife to her throat. "No." Her expression revealing her thoughts, now he would really be afraid of her, think she was crazy, and lock her away, or hand her over to the police. She anxiously watched his face as he took in her words. Yet, as usual like the rest of his team, his face was unreadable, the black pupils glittering under the partially lowered lids made her stomach tighten with nerves.

He rested his head against the corner of the jeep. He found *her* compelling, the luminous eyes, the lovely way her full lips move when she speaks in that hushed, sweet way. He felt he could sit there forever and listen to her. He shook his head to clear it.

Tirsa rested her head against the back of the seat and closed her eyes.

He tried to understand what she was saying, how she was psychically compelled to do things and it was hard to fight it, whether or not he believed in this type of thing was not something he wanted to dissect at this moment. Remembering the anger he'd felt when he'd come back inside and saw the table they'd been sitting at was empty, came flooding back. Feeling the blood rush to his head he had sought out the waitress to ask if she knew where Tirsa had gone. The waitress informed him that *his wife*, as he had implied, had asked for the ladies room.

Throwing money on the table he had gone straight to the restrooms, his head thumping harder as the anger grew, then fear gnawed at his gut, pushing aside the anger. What if she was gone, had run from him? Was abducted? Hurt? Without hesitation, he pushed the door open to the restroom, fortunately it was empty or there'd have been complaints.

Letting the door close, he noticed there was a short hall going in the opposite direction. He had followed it to the outside exit and saw her in the dimly lit patio speaking with an unfamiliar woman. The anger overrode the relief when he digested the fact that she'd disobeyed him again. However, he admitted that he would have been angrier if he had found her with a man.

Staying in the shadows eavesdropping, he waited to see everything play out before he made any moves. Maybe this woman was Tirsa's contact, the one who had given her the order to kill him. Pissed at the whole thing, Robinson's curiosity raised ten-fold when he saw Tirsa was holding a baby. Listening to the women's conversation, it was bizarre, mystical; he battled his own pragmatic realism to comprehend what the hell was going on.

He couldn't pull his eyes away from Tirsa holding the baby so gently, naturally, like she was born to do it. When Tirsa finally finished, got up and then saw him, the surprise, guilt, then fear scrolled all over her face as she walked uneasily to him, feminine curves undulating in that indecent, but damned hot outfit Johnson bought.

He decided he would swallow his ire and bide his time before unleashing his *displeasure* on her. It was one thing for him to feel fury at her for once again not listening to his orders; it was another for the profound fear that warred with that anger when he'd first seen that she was gone.

Now, sitting in the car, the dark night peaceful around them, he said, "Tirsa, look at me." Stamping down the anger, he kept his voice calm, reasonable. He could see that part of her was still with the woman on the patio. She rolled her head to him, opened tired eyes.

He said, "Again, I'm tiring of saying this to you repeatedly. When you disobey my orders you put yourself and everyone else in danger. You wandered out of a place you've never been before, in a foreign land to go out into the dark with a woman you didn't know. Surely you can see how foolhardy that was?"

She brought a hand up to delicately cover a small yawn and rub an eye. "I didn't think about it at the time." Her brows drew down in consternation. "Colonel, I don't see the world as you do. You see a dangerous, wicked place where everyone is out to hurt everyone else. That's not how I view things. Your existence has been at the opposite end of the spectrum of mine."

Exasperated, he rubbed his face with his hand then grasped her arm lightly. "You keep claiming you're an adult, Tirsa, but you think like a child. The world *is* a treacherous place. Just ask any victim of robbery, murder, assault, war." He leaned in to her, the cinder eyes snapping with anger, "You, my God, Tirsa," his voice shook, "you were almost taken by fucking knifepoint, for the love of-"

"Colonel, you-"

"Enough. I don't want to talk about it anymore, I'll just get mad again and we're both too tired for that. Come on, let's go."

He got out and went around for her. Seeing how truly drained she was he just reached in, slid an arm under her knees and around her waist, lifted her out, set her on her feet careful to keep space between their bodies, he needed to get some sleep tonight, and recalling how he felt earlier when they were pressed against each other he didn't need that acute arousal to happen again. He brushed a tress of hair out of her eyes, she looked so weary. Apparently whatever happens to her during the…episodes, sucks energy from her. He wondered if it was harmful to her.

They went inside, he took her to her room. Inside, he said, "Tirsa, I ken what you're saying, sort of. Also that it compels you and you can't fight it." His hands on his hips he said darkly, "But you must fight it while you are here. If you are compelled to…" he searched for words, "help someone, I need for you to tell me first, or if I'm not here one of my team." At her rueful look the corner of his mouth turned up. "Even Jancarlo. I cannot have you running off unprotected."

He set his hand on her shoulder, felt her stiffen. "I mean it, Tirsa. I mean it." He gave her an uncompromising look then locked her in and went to meet with his team.

Inside the study, he told them what happened. Knox was nodding, Johnson appeared totally accepting. Jancarlo scowled darkly and said, "I got the background on her. Basically same as what she said, she was brought up in seclusion, in hiding, until about three or so years ago she moved to the states. She is younger than we thought, barley legal depending on what country you are in. Even then there is little on her. She has not been married, never been arrested, did not go to school in the states."

"Really?" Robinson was surprised.

Jancarlo nodded, "*Ja*, the paperwork that got her on this expedition was obviously falsified. She is not in college, not an intern. Do you see you cannot trust her?" he demanded quietly.

The colonel ran his hands across the top of his head. "Okay, let's turn in, we need to go early tomorrow, maybe the morning sun will shine on the black glass and we'll be able to see it."

Chapter Nineteen

*T*he next day, they all headed out just before dawn. Less than an hour later someone yelled out a whoop, "I found it! I found it! Colonel! I found it come look!"

They all went running to see.

Practically jumping up and down, the normally reticent Ji was pointing at the ground.

It looked like a six-inch high jagged glass wall. A crooked line of black volcanic glass lanced through, partially hidden in the high grass, they couldn't see how far it went.

"Wow," Max exclaimed with wide eyes.

"I'm picturing a fab necklace," Lindsey purred.

"Wonder what we can get for it, how much it's worth," Dia pondered.

The colonel patted Ji on the shoulder. "Good job, Ji. We've searched before but were never able to find it." He said brusquely to Dia, "It's not for sale. It's an arrow for us, it stays where it is." The interns' faces fell.

"Just a useless treasure?" Owen whined. Disappointed, the gangly beanpole scratched his mop of hair making the squiggles flop over his small, light brown eyes. His nose a tad pointy, with a round face and long thin body he resembled a stop sign, except instead of red and white it'd be white and ochre.

"*Neen*, like I said, it's an arrow. It's what we've been looking for. It's pointing us in a direction, to the next clue so to speak, another plot on the map to follow," Robinson explained to him.

Even though they weren't going to make any money off their find, the group went back to Copestone elated. They gathered in the great room. Cook came in at their excited voices and they told him that they found the first directional clue. He grinned and went over to congratulate the colonel.

"Ah, finally, E, you found it."

Robinson grinned back, then turned serious. "*Ja*, but it's only the beginning. It will lead us to the next one. We'll get ready tomorrow, get supplies, then the day after we will pack the mules and head out."

The next day everyone had a task to do, they were all bustling around in the house.

Tirsa went outside with Johnson to get supplies out of the jeep. Snapping his fingers, Johnson said to her, "I forgot the keys, I'll be right back." He jogged back to the house.

Tirsa plucked a flower out of the grass and twirling it leaned against the jeep enjoying the quiet, away from the other people's constant chattering.

Deep in her ponderings, the sound she heard at first she thought was Johnson returning. Then she heard a bunch of clumping, a snort, she looked up and screamed. Three men on horses, the same man as before, Adullam, and two others. One of them galloped straight at her, she screamed again and cried out, "Colonel! Colonel!"

She started to run but one of the men barreled right at her, barely slowing down- with one smooth move he bent and grabbed her under her arms, picked her up and threw her in front of him on the horse, swung the horse around and galloped off. He slapped the reins with one hand and clamped her back against his chest with the other.

Adullam and the other man were pulling their horses' reigns trying to turn them around in the gravel drive when the colonel hearing her screams, came charging out in time to see the man heading into the brush disappearing with her.

Adullam took a moment to laugh triumphantly at him then pulled his horse up and galloped off. The third man was just getting his horse turned around to take off for the scrub when Robinson raced over to him, reached up, grabbed his leg and jerked him right off the horse. The man crashed to the ground, the colonel leapt onto his horse and tore after the other two.

Digging his heels into the horse's side, Robinson bent over as far as he could on the horse's neck for speed and to keep from getting knocked off by low branches.

The horses he chased, hooves thundering, flying through the grass were almost to the beginning of a dense forest. Keeping sight of Tirsa's bright blonde hair whipping like a yellow flag around the man that held her, the colonel rode at breakneck speed.

He caught up with the thug who'd captured her, rode right up next to him, the hooves deafening pounding hell for leather. Robinson pulled the reins hard to the left forcing his horse to come so close to the other that the huge galloping beasts knocked against each other.

The man holding Tirsa slashed his reins hard back and forth, whipping the steed to go faster, clods of dirt kicked up behind them. He held Tirsa so tightly she couldn't breathe. His filthy face a picture of wrath and madness, he glanced over at the colonel and whipped the horse harder.

At that second, Robinson leaned over and jabbed a knife into the side of the man's neck.

The man clutched the knife and then fell right off the horse banging and bouncing against the hard ground- At the same time, the colonel reached out, grabbed Tirsa and pulled her onto his horse facing him, straddling him. He slammed an arm around her, strapping her to his torso.

Before they could catch their breaths gunshots exploded in front of them, Adullam was coming at them shooting.

The colonel jerked the horse to swing it around, the steed stepped back on its hind legs, raised his front hooves up scraping at the air then he leaped and took off. Robinson held Tirsa's head against his chest covering it with his big hand, keeping his own head low, he slapped the reins and kicked the horse to go faster. Tirsa wrapped her arms around him and hung on for dear life while bullets rang out and whizzed past their heads.

Suddenly, the jeep came flying through the grass, roared past them and went straight after Adullam. The jeep hurtled by at full speed, jumping and banging over the rocky land with Jancarlo at the wheel, Johnson shotgun and Knox in the rear. As soon as Adullam saw them he jerked his horse around and ran for the woods with them at his heels.

Seeing they were safe, holding the reins loosely in one hand, the colonel slowed the horse to a bare trot to let them catch their breath. Tirsa was hugging him so tightly they could feel each other's hearts banging against their chests. Terror still constricting her throat, Tirsa couldn't catch her panicked breath.

They slowed further, Robinson whispered in her ear, "You're okay, you're safe, *mijn luttel zeldzaam men*." He soothingly stroked her back feeling her soft curves jostling, rubbing against the hard slated surface of his powerful chest.

Now his worry was that she'd feel something else straining at his pants and it would ignite her usual fear of him. The steed slowed to a stop. The colonel cupped Tirsa's chin, lifted her head.

Her eyes were wild with fright, lips parted; the pupils huge in the blue irises searched his face for security. She could see her reflection in his black orbs bathing her in a safe warmth, his rock solid arms bound her to him like a vice. Still holding onto him, gasping her terror, she started to relax in his embrace, her chest still heaving with crazed panic.

Feeling her settle against him, molding to his hard body, still holding the reins he put a hand behind her neck, cupping her head, and he lowered his lips to hers, kissing her so lightly it was as gentle as a butterfly flutter. When she didn't push him away, he leaned back slightly to look at her.

Tirsa's eyes were closed, lips slightly parted. As light as the kiss had been it was enough to enflame him. He brought his mouth back to join hers, the gentleness hardened, quickening in a flash to raw, inebriating passion. He brought this other hand up to grasp her head, his fingers tightened as his arousal spiraled.

Surprising them both, Tirsa wound her hands around his neck pulling him closer. The reins dropped unnoticed down his wrist and the kiss deepened. Cradling her head in both hands he slid his mouth away to kiss her jaw then her neck, down to where her pulse beat, her head fell back, she moaned, it about undid him.

He returned to her mouth, his tongue parting her lips, rolled across the soft petals then pushed inside tasting her. Rough sounds of male desire rumbled in his chest, he licked her lips and bit at the soft skin on her neck.

Tirsa laced her fingers in his hair, arching her spine her head fell back again, her hair dusting the horse's back.

Robinson's hands stroked to her waist, his palms hot against her shirt he roamed them up her back then moved to her head, molding it, pulling her back to him.

Fusing his lips to hers, the kiss deepened so intensely, his hands so forceful, so fervent, physical feelings Tirsa had never experienced before confused and frightened her, he frightened her, she suddenly put her hands against his chest and tried to push him away.

Consumed with having her, at first he didn't realize she was pushing at him.

Turning her head from his devouring lips, "Colonel, stop, please," her whispered cry sifted into his fevered brain.

Hearing her plea, he dropped his hands to grip her upper arms. Breathing hard, the pulse at his temple throbbed, the glazed lacquer eyes poured bemused into her blue seas of apprehension. Struck dazed with mindless passion, his hands tightened around her arms squeezing hard until she cried out in pain.

Coming to his senses, Robinson loosened his grip, cognizant that they were out in the open without protection, and he had been just about to drag her off the horse and lay her in the grass, and…

He shook his head. What the hell was he thinking? What had gotten into him? One look at those sultry eyes, and lips plumped and red, he didn't have to ask himself that question. At first she had surrendered, it seemed she wanted him as much as he wanted her, yet now, her gaze dropped as if in shame and uncertain fear.

He'd forgotten her inexperience with men. He could feel it through her kiss, but it was so sweet and fresh he wanted more, a craving like one taste of ice cream. Through a throaty hoarseness, his accent thick, he said, "Tirsa, it's okay, I…I'm, it wasn't right for me to…*zich excuseren,* I'm sorry.

We'll go back." His strong fingers splayed across her spine, he gently pulled her back to rest against him, giving her the protection and comfort of his body.

She nodded against his chest. He settled an arm around her and softly kicked the horse.

After a minute he looked down at her, thinking maybe in this vulnerable position, Adullam taking her and him coming at the last second to go after them, she would be so afraid that she would open up to him. He asked, "Tell me Tirsa, can you tell me now who sent you, why?"

She just shook her head, eyes so sad they wilted looked at him then away.

Pressing, he said it again, "Tell me Tirsa, *vertrouwen mij,* trust me. Who sent you?" Her head drooped further, tears slipped out.

His voice stronger, he asked, "Have you been told to try to kill me again?" Her eyes darted to his, frightened, desperate, silent. He repeated, pressuring her, "Tell me, Tirsa, are you going to try to kill me again?" The tears flowed; she covered her face with her hands, weeping, but didn't respond.

He put his fingertips under her chin lifting it to look at her sodden eyes. "You must trust me, Tirsa, I can help, I promise I can, you don't know what I am capable of. I can take care of whoever has a hold over you. Just trust me." The tears fell, she remained mute.

Frustrated, he let her go, grabbed her around the waist picked her up and twirled her around to sit in front of him facing out. His arm loose around her so she wouldn't fall, he made a tsk sound and the horse moved a little faster.

As they neared the ranch area, Tirsa said so softly he almost couldn't hear her, "You ask me to trust you, *Colonel.*

But I don't even know your name. I don't know who you are. You pretended to be a professor, Russell Robinson, to lure us out here for a false mission. They say that's not your real name and that you're not really a professor, and your men call you Colonel or E. Since we've been on this- this expedition, I have seen you...kill, two men, skillfully and without hesitation, with only one movement, I..."

She shuddered, closed her eyes trying to clear the pictures of the man he shot in the library in the head from at least 20 feet away, and now, stabbed another without a qualm or hesitation while riding a galloping beast. Not to mention fighting with the pirates, and not one but two crocodiles...who was this man?

It was like being in a movie. So bizarre. She breathed deeply, twisting to look up at him, he looked so different without the wild hair and beard. Yet the man himself was wild, dark, and mysterious. Although he had scars on his face he was extremely attractive, the scars only gave him an edginess, a violent aggressive edginess that made her feel very unsettled. Especially since he didn't hesitate at any menace and attacked like a seasoned warrior. "And you ask *me* to trust *you*?" She fell silent.

The jeep was back before they got there. Jancarlo went to them, Johnson and Knox hurried right behind him. Breathless, Johnson huffed, "E! Are you okay?"

The colonel stopped the horse and slid off. He held the reins out to Johnson who took them then reached up, put his hands around Tirsa's waist and lifted her off the horse setting her on her feet. His face a stony mask he said, "*Ja*, we're fine. I want whoever was on watch, in the study in 5."

"Got it," Johnson said, and started for the lodge.

Jancarlo held his hand out. "Here is your knife, E. Adullam escaped into the forest, we could not follow in the jeep. The other man that you pulled off the horse here disappeared while we went after Adullam."

Wordlessly, the colonel took his knife and slid it into a sheath on his belt. He turned from Jancarlo and looked down solemnly at Tirsa.

His hands clasped behind his back, legs braced, he said quietly, "My true name is Etam. Etam van Eleman. I am Dutch and a Kolonel in the Royal Netherlands Marechausse, the Koninklijke Marechausse, military police. And, the mission is very real."

He nodded to Knox and ordered, "Lock her in her room." Ignoring Tirsa's confused, flabbergasted face, he stalked off.

After Johnson told the two that were on patrol duty to go to the study, he took the horse to the back of the building. Knox walked with Tirsa to the lodge, and Jancarlo went after the colonel.

Chapter Twenty

Johnson went to get some OS's to help him get the dead man out of the jeep and onto some ice.

Jancarlo followed the colonel into the equipment room where Robinson AKA Etam van Eleman took a key out of his pocket and went over to a cabinet on the wall. He stuck the key in and opened the steel door.

"E, what are you doing?" Jancarlo asked calmly, watching the colonel take out a Glock and buckle it on. Then he removed a diemaco C7A1 assault rifle, set it on the floor against the wall and added an M590A1 shotgun to it.

He took out a holster with a pistol in it and buckled it over the Glock, swiveling it over to the opposite side like a cowboy. He removed a long wicked knife and attached it under his clothes then stuck a small knife in his boot.

"What's it look like?" van Eleman said, reaching for a box of ammo. "He's not going to stop, he'll come back for her again. I'm going after him, I'll stop him." He poured bullets into a case and shoved it in his pocket.

"Etam, think about this. What about the mission? The two on patrol are waiting for you in the study, we have things to-"

187

"Screw the mission, Jan, it'll still be here. The idiots that failed on their patrol can wait." He slammed the door shut and locked it. "You guys track the black glass. See where it leads. When I return I'll-"

"Do not be an ass, E, I am coming with you."

Before Etam could say anything, Johnson and Knox came in, they both said, "Don't count us out."

The colonel studied their unmoving expressions, shrugged, went back to the steel cabinet and opened it and the men came over to take out arms. Etam said to Johnson, "You stay here, I don't trust all of the OS's, I need you to-"

"I know," Johnson said banally, "don't let her out of my sight. Got it."

"All right," Etam said, moving to the door, "let's pack up."

Johnson brought the horse back out and they stuck the shotguns in the saddle and tied a roll of blankets on the back of the saddle. Etam mounted the horse, Jancarlo and Knox followed in the jeep.

Out in the tall grass they found the dead man's stallion. Jancarlo exited the jeep and hopped on the horse. Knox stayed in the jeep following the two men on the horses. They tracked Adullam past the savanna, through a dense grove of trees and into a freshwater swamp.

Knox had to leave the jeep; he mounted the steed to sit behind Jancarlo. Sometimes they had to get off the horses and walk. The oozing scummy water tugged at their boots, the horse's tails swatted constantly at the bugs.

It was easy to follow Adullam's trail in the swamp because nothing moved for days, the scum layering the water was motionless except for mosquitoes dive bombing it. The trail Adullam left was a slightly clearer trace in the scum like a green road in a white pond. The humidity lay on the swamp like a heavy haze.

Knox rubbed his nose with a knuckle. "The swamp doesn't smell that bad. Kind of musky."

"*Ja.*" Jancarlo said over his shoulder, "If you like the cloying tropical smell of humid rotting vegetation and mud."

"*Broeds,*" Etam whispered a short nip to be quiet.

The trail led from the freshwater swamp to a lowland, broadleaf evergreen forest. Adullam's horse left clear hoof-prints in the mud. He was moving fast, he had a big head start, the colonel and his team moved more cautiously, on the alert for an ambush.

It grew dark, when they couldn't see a hand in front of them they stopped for the night. They laid out the blankets and set the shotguns near them.

After chowing on powerbars for dinner, they went to sleep in their clothes with their weapons strapped on, while listening to the forest sounds of chirping tree frogs, crickets and things scurrying through the bush.

Before the sun even thought about rising, they packed up without a sound, and headed back out eating more power bars.

It wasn't long before they came across the flattened grass where extra hoof prints showed Adullam had met up with another person and they had spent the night. They had also been forced to bunk down; everyone knew the forest was too dangerous at night to travel with the zero visibility, peat bogs, sinkholes and hungry critters.

They caught up with them as they crested a clearing of grass going over a small hill. Knox slid off the horse so Jancarlo could go faster.

Adullam saw them coming, he yelled to the man with him to go- Kicking their horses brutally, and whipping the reins against their backs with all their might, they flew over the hill and down the other side with Etam and Jancarlo hot on their heels.

Charging down the hill, Adullam and the man twisted in their saddles to shoot behind them. Firing wildly, Adullam screamed as the team closed the gap, "You won't take me in! I won't go, it's you or me, Eleman!"

"Fine," Etam said grimly, "have it your way." He and Jancarlo opened fire.

Adullam and the man with him screamed as they were hit. The other man tumbled right off his horse, ricocheting off the hard ground, he rolled and bumped for a dozen feet before he stopped moving.

Jancarlo raced over to the body and hopped off to check the man's status. He bent over, checked for a pulse then stood up and made a slashing motion across his neck indicating the man was dead.

Etam went after Adullam. The horse was still going, but Adullam slouched over further and further until he slid down the side then fell. His foot was caught in the stirrup. The roan dragged him; his head banged against the ground until Etam caught up and captured the reins to stop the steed.

The team tied the two dead men lying on their stomachs over one horse, then each climbed on a horse and they went back the way they came. They picked up Knox and when they got to the jeep, they put the dead men inside, tied the extra horses to the jeep and Knox drove it back.

Arriving at the ranch, the colonel called the police. Fortunately, Copestone Lodge was near enough to the tiny town to get cell service. He was told it would be a while before anyone came out for the bodies.

Etam called his commander and gave the report. His commander would smooth the way for him with the local police. He went in and took a shower.

At dinner everyone talked over each other asking the team what had happened. The team just ate their dinners with gusto not replying. The five interns stared unblinking at them. They couldn't believe they were on a university expedition and men had attacked them, tried to kidnap one of them and had a shootout with the team that ultimately killed them.

After Etam had told Tirsa who he really was, Johnson had explained to the rest of them that they were all members of the Koninklijke Marechausse, the Dutch, actually the Netherlands military police, which explained their accents and their battling prowess.

Very importantly, his chest rose with pride, Johnson said, "Besides ships and jets, Kolonel van Eleman can operate a Chinook helicopter."

That peaked the already impressed people. Because Etam ignored their inquiries about himself, they pummeled Johnson with questions. He was unable to reveal much because most of what they did was clandestine. They tried to wheedle info out of him anyway.

He eventually regaled them with some of their more lethal missions. Explaining how Etam was a colonel at such a young age, the successful, dangerous, covert missions he commanded had moved him up the ranks quickly, as had the majors themselves.

The OS's had been prepared before they started the expedition, the mission. They knew they had been chosen for their armed and hand-to-hand fighting abilities, so they weren't shocked that something violent had happened, but they were resentful they had missed the action.

They asked the officers what the Dutch Military Police was doing in New Guineas, was it to find the book of Jesus or papers, or did they have another agenda? Not giving them any other information, the team remained mum on their true mission, neither confirming nor denying they were there to find the book.

Two days were wasted while they waited for the nearest police to get there. They had kept the bodies under ice in a bathtub, that the girls all swore they would never use again.

A four-wheel drive could be heard crunching over the gravel driveway. Etam went out to meet the two officers. He spoke with them for a few minutes before bringing them into the house. They wanted to take everyone's statement.

Everyone gathered in the great room. First, the team was taken one at a time into the study and interviewed, and then each of the others was questioned about what they'd seen and heard.

Tirsa was hiding behind Knox sure this was it for her, believing once they interrogated her she would be arrested. Especially after she pushed the colonel away on the horse and refused to answer his questions. He looked so…well, she wasn't sure how he looked. But he was undoubtedly not pleased with her.

She had stayed in her room since the colonel had rescued her. Knox had come and retrieved her as the police made it clear they would be speaking with her. She had hoped if the police didn't see her they would forget about her.

Then, one of the officers stated in a loud voice, "The woman next, the one taken, please."

Seeing her pale face behind Knox, Etam went to Tirsa. He said quietly, "It'll be okay, honey. Just tell them what happened, no more, no less."

"Will they be taking me with them?" The big eyes trained on him revealed her fear but her voice was flatly calm. Tirsa tried not to sound panicked, she would face her punishment as bravely as possible.

Etam set a strong hand on her delicate shoulder, then turned it slightly so his fingers stroked her nape. "*Neen*. They are unaware of what you tried to do to me. I'll be with you, Tirsa," his voice dropped, "you will be fine, I won't let anything happen to you. Just tell the story as Knox explained to you." He moved his palm to the small of her back and brought her to the officer.

Prowling her figure with a heated gaze, the policeman said to Etam, but gaped at Tirsa, "I will speak alone with her."

Raising his arm to curl around her shoulders, with authority Etam started in Dutch, "*Neen, sprach-*" he switched to English, "no, she is young and fearful, it was a traumatic experience for her. I am her guardian, I will stay."

The officer studied Etam. The colonel's stance was strong and braced, he was wearing a buttoned-down shirt and black slacks, his black hair slicked back in thick waves. His sober expression was resolute.

His superiors had briefed the officer before he had come to the lodge about who Etam van Eleman and his team were. He could argue that Tirsa was an adult and didn't require a guardian, but one look in Etam's chilled eyes, formidably dark under hooded lids, he shrugged, then began his questions.

The questions were brief, to the point. Knox had told Tirsa to tell the complete truth except leave out the part of what Adullam had said about who she was and about the diamonds. Adullam's story was so outrageous that Etam was worried the police may think Tirsa was somehow complicit with the thugs and would require her to go with them to the station for more in-depth interrogation.

Etam wanted there to be zero connections between the deceased Adullam and Tirsa. Things could easily get wrongly concocted and spiral out of suspicious control, she could be held in account of their deaths.

Knox had told Tirsa to just tell the basics about the two attempts of Adullam's abducting her. She was beautiful; let the officers draw their own conclusions as to why the brigands would want to kidnap her.

Concluding his inquiry, the policeman stalled, clearly coming up with repetitive questions because he wanted more time with Tirsa, Etam politely, yet sternly called a halt and escorted the officer to the door of the study.

When he was gone, exhaling her held breath, Tirsa said, gratefully, "Thank you…Colonel, for not having them take me."

He said firmly, "I told you that you were safe. I did not come after you and then go back out and…eliminate the threat against you, to turn you over to the police." His arm still around her shoulders, he drew her around to face him.

Her curves weren't pressed against him, yet his body reacted as if they were. His voice softened, he said, "You need to learn to trust me, Tirsa. Right?"

She didn't answer him. Their eyes linked, a warm light shone in the ebony orbs that streamed back at her.

With faux sternness, he said, "Say 'Yes, Etam.'" Then watched her mouth as she spoke.

The smile crossing her face made his mouth twitch in a slight smile as he waited for her to respond. She said shyly, "Yes…Etam."

His lips stayed together but his smile broadened. He felt a peculiar shiver at the way she pronounced his name with her strange little accent. It sounded slightly like French. Soon, he would ask her personal questions again. But for now, they all needed to let things calm down from the excitement.

Their gazes still connected, he drew his fingertips softly down her round cheek then down her neck to her collarbone. His body tensed as if he wanted to say more, do more, instead, he sighed, then he took her hand and brought her back out to the great room where the others waited.

The police completed their interviews then loaded up the bodies and the horses and were gone.

Everyone blew a sigh of relief. They hadn't done anything wrong, but being in a foreign country, involved in a kidnapping and a deadly shootout, one never knew what could happen.

When the police left, Jancarlo told Bruno and Lil Dam to take their turns guarding the perimeter. He warned them they weren't to stay together, to follow the circle plan, change patterns often, and no earphones, no talking, he looked right at Lil Dam when he instructed no singing, dancing etc. they were to stay alert.

He gave them walkie-talkies and they left.

The others went back to playing cards, reading and napping.

Chapter Twenty-One

*E*tam joined Knox, Johnson and Jancarlo in the study. He pulled out a chair, turned it around and straddled it. "Knox," he nodded to the long-bearded man.

Knox was bareheaded for a change. Short, wavy brown hair flopped in disarray. "E?" he answered, clipping the chart he was looking at to a board and then laid it on his bed.

"We never discussed in detail what happened that day with Tirsa, when she…helped you with Katrina, you only gave us a brief answer," the colonel said with a questioning tone. The others turned with interest to their mate.

Knox smiled. The smile gave them pause; it was so contrary to his normal dour, brooding demeanor. He scratched his head with both hands then said, "I'll tell you, but you're not going to believe it." This comment drew enhanced attention from the men.

Etam prompted, "So, tell us." He patiently laid his brawny forearms over the back of the chair and rested his chin on his arm.

Knox told them what Tirsa had said about he and his fiancée's time in the park, and what Katrina wanted her to tell him.

"Bullshit," Jancarlo spat. "That is bullshit. She is a con artist, she is scamming you." An unlit skinny cigar stuck out of the corner of his mouth, it flopped up and down when he spoke. The brown eyes totally shut down Knox's words. He palmed his short trim of beard, took out the European cigar and set it on an ashtray.

Johnson watched Knox carefully. Knox's face was shining like he'd won a lottery or something. The black man's eyes flitted from Knox to Etam, his boss and friend. The colonel said nothing, his expression revealed no reaction to Knox's revelation.

Knox replied calmly, "I said you wouldn't believe me. Doesn't matter. She said things no one on earth could have known. Positively. She even told me my own thoughts that I've never spoken." He sat back comfortably, crossed his legs, rested his hands on his stomach.

Johnson scootched his burly body to the edge of his bed, closer to Knox. "*Broed*, Brother, I can see it. There's a..." he thought a moment, "a...like an aura around Tirsa, but not really an aura, but there's something about her."

Knox nodded. "*Ja*. I can't explain it, but there's...something. She has a kind soul."

"Bullshit," Jancarlo swore again. "She is a hired killer, a fucking assassin. Beautiful and deadly. Have you blockheads forgotten she tried to do E in?" He shook his head, nettled at the obvious taking in of his mates by the female grifter.

"True that, Jan, but she didn't," Johnson said quietly. "You heard the colonel tell it, she wasn't carrying through with it. Whoever sent her did so because they must have thought the young woman was a benign ruse we wouldn't expect. We would have taken no notice of the nondescript girl who blended into the woodwork in her disguise."

197

"Exactly," Jancarlo retorted. "She was in a disguise. She knew if we saw her as she was we would have noticed her, paid attention to her. She could not slink around without us seeing."

Etam finally spoke. He said flatly, "She doesn't slink. I don't think she's even aware of her beauty."

Jancarlo grimaced at him. "Oh come on, E, the way she looks? Give me a break, there are mirrors all around you know." He didn't hide his disgust at his mate's being pulled in by the con-woman.

Knox shrugged. "I agree with E. She was brought up differently than most, she mentioned something about seclusion."

Johnson nodded his agreement garnered from some of their talks.

"Probably reform school." Jancarlo said harshly to the colonel, "E, the girl is just a scamming *hoer*. You need to just take her, bang her, get her out of your system, force her if she is not willing, who cares? We are in a jungle, who is she going to complain to?"

Etam responded angrily, "She's not a whore, Jan. I've seen her use her gift on a total stranger, like Knox says, it's for real. She was brought up in remote isolation, they tried to hide her...talent. She's had little experience with the outside world, especially with men."

Jancarlo bit back, "So what? She is just a woman, she needs to learn her position, she will get used to it." He went on, "You gave up your room to her the day after her attempt on your life, obviously because you could not trust yourself alone with her. At this point you need to relieve yourself, E, you cannot think properly when you are stressed like this, the girl already has your balls twisting in this short time. Just do it and end this. Fuck her once or twice, get her out of your system, then you can give her to the others or the police and you can move on."

Etam said, "I didn't know you were such a hard man, Jan."

"I did not know you were so weak." Jan scowled at his friend.

The colonel's brow rose thoughtfully. He said with a ponderous tone, "Who's more a man, one that throws a woman to the ground, spreads her legs, and fucks her against her will, or one who resists the intense temptation?"

Silence. Then Jancarlo said impassively, "Whatever. You know I do not think rape is right. But, in self-preservation you need to do something, either do her, or brand her as yours to keep the others off her. Right now she is free game and you are going to spend all your energy fighting the other men off all the time."

Etam glowered at his friend. "Come on, Jan, she's practically a child."

Jancarlo snorted his response, "She is a grown woman, E. She is a killer and she has your balls all tied up in her tiny delicate hand." In mime, he held his hand up, closed it into a tight fist, and twisted it.

Shaking his head Etam said quietly, "You're nuts, Jan. I have absolutely no interest or desire for that girl whatsoever. She's just some fiend's innocent pawn, and I will discover who and end it."

"*Ja*, right." Jancarlo grunted his disbelief. "Whatever." Scowling, Jancarlo picked up his charts again, dismissing Etam. But, he muttered, "I have D'Jon Samuels working on digging up more on her background." He bent his pissed off head to his charts.

Chapter Twenty-Two

*I*t rained a third day in a row further stalling the search.

Etam had taken to not lingering in any of the rooms. A few times he'd been in the kitchen and Dia strolled in after him. She was bold, came right up to him, stroked her hands up his chest over his shoulders and whispered how much she wanted him. He caught her wrists, held them away from him, and told her he wasn't interested.

Yet, the next day he was in the study, she came up behind him, pressed her breasts against his back and let her hands roam at free will. He'd seized them again, in his most commanding voice he told her to keep her hands to herself and don't touch him again, then banished her from the study.

Still, when she was nearby wherever he was, she sidled next to him, rubbing any part of her hourglass body she could against his. He regretted having the interns on the expedition, but he'd needed the cover. He couldn't wait until he saw the last of them, most of them. They were all running around blatantly having sex with each other and the OS's.

The fourth day cabin fever hit. Late into the evening they had grown tired of playing cards and reading. Most of them started drinking right after dinner.

Etam and his team were in the study, drinking and talking. The rest were out in the great room, they wandered in and out, to the kitchen, the library. The only ones not drinking were Ji, Lil Dam, Cook and Tirsa.

Owen threw down his cards with a curse, "I'm fucking out."

"Cool it, Owen," Ji remonstrated him, "there're ladies present." He made a bid and tossed a chip into the middle of the table.

"Yeah, yeah, sorry, sorry," The beanpole seaman mumbled his apology. He got up and paced. "I'm just going stir crazy. At least the guys got to go out on a chase-down and shoot out, while we sit here bored, or worse outside in the rain patrolling until our legs give out."

He took a big swig of his drink, wiped his hand across his mouth. "I coulda done it, you know, gone with them on their manhunt, I've been hunting since I was a toddler practically. What a bunch of shit."

"So what. You didn't get enough with those damned pirates? Chill out, Owen, and sit back down. You playing the next hand?" Ji asked him.

Owen shoved his hands through his moppy hair and plopped back down in his chair. "Yeah. What else is there to do?"

The group drank until half passed out.

Stav left the card game and went over to Tirsa who was sitting near the window in an easy chair reading a book. Dressed in jeans and a blouse, she'd kicked off her shoes and curled her legs on the chair.

Occasionally, she'd look outside at the raindrops as big as fists battering the window. It came in sheets and the sun had long set hiding behind black clouds making it futile to see more than a few feet. Due to the severe weather, even the toughest thug wouldn't be able to get through so there was no patrol.

"Hey, Tirsa," Stav said softly. She looked up at the man who was a few inches above average height and as big and muscled as a blond mountain. She closed her book and smiled up at him.

"Um…" Stav hesitated appearing slightly embarrassed.

Tirsa slid to her feet. She smiled sympathetically, said softly, "You want to talk about your father."

His eyebrows hiked over brown eyes, then leveled, he grinned crookedly. Nodded unsure, "Uh…"

"Come over here." Tirsa took his big paw and they went across the room to a corner away from the others for privacy. When they got there, Stav stuffed his hands in his pockets; he was hunched over, uneasy. The brown eyes skipped around the room to see if anyone was making fun of him, or watching them.

Relieved that the others were all into what they were doing, he was drawn to the blue eyes waiting patiently, compassionately for him to relax. Her face had that ethereal veil, to Stav she was so angelic at that moment he believed in her. Dia had been eavesdropping outside the study door the day Knox told his friends about what had occurred with him and Tirsa. Of course Dia told everyone else. Naturally none of them really believed it. Still…

"Yeah," he said faintly, "can you tell me anything about…my father?"

Tirsa's smile turned tender, she nodded. "Yes. I can tell you what he wants you to know. That he didn't leave the family because of you. That his sickness and debilitating pain is gone and he is new and fresh like a baby where he is."

Stav nodded eagerly at her words, he leaned closer to her.

Tirsa said, "I will tell you what he said, for you, to you."

At the card table, Owen was still grumbling. Ji had a big pile of chips in front of him. Raine and Max were both staring miserably at their paltry chips. Lindsey was in her room napping and Dia was watching a movie on a hand held.

In the study, the team was drinking heavily knowing nothing was going to happen until the monsoon rain ended. Every time a glass was half empty, Johnson would refill it to the point where none of them knew how much he'd had to drink.

Etam stood up and swayed slightly. "I think I've had enough, I'm hammered," he announced, then stumbled turning to go to the door. The men all laughed, including Etam. He slurred, "I'm going to the library, grab a book, then to bed."

Etam made his way unsteadily down the hall with his team straggling behind, chuckling and talking.

When he got to the great room he saw a blur of people. Then, he caught a glimpse of two people in a corner hugging. His lips pulled in, "Lovers..." then his eyes narrowed. He saw Tirsa with her arms around Stav. Stav's head was down, near her face, *was he kissing her?*

Feeling the heat rise up his neck, rage beat at his heart, his hands clenched into fists, arms bowed. Without a thought, he strode over to the pair and grabbed Tirsa's arm jerking her away. He snarled in a jealous hoarse whisper only she and Stav could hear, his voice thick with drink and accent, "You won't give to me but you'll play the whore with him?"

Shocked, Stav stuttered, "No, sir, no it's not what you-"

"*Shut up*," Etam spat the harsh words. Tightly gripping her arm, he half dragged Tirsa out of the room past his surprised team without a word to them. Blinded with fury, he saw nothing but the picture of Tirsa and that fool with their arms around each other, kissing, about to go into the fool's room and screw, Etam was sure of it.

"Etam, what are you doing? I haven't-" Trying to stop him, Tirsa tried to pull his hand off her arm and dig her socked feet into the floor, to no avail. He roughly pulled her down the hall, past the dining area and through the kitchen, Cook tried to stop him.

"Don't," Etam barked, moving briskly out of the kitchen into the hall and down to his room. He threw open the door, it banged against the wall and bounced back, he blocked it with his arm and yanked her inside. Slamming the door, he locked it then turned to her in the duskily lit room.

Tirsa was struggling to stand straight, not cower, find out why he was so mad. "Colonel-"

He grabbed her, picked her up, carried her to his bed and threw her on it. His feverish eyes like burning coals in the dark room bored drunkenly into hers. Unbuttoning his shirt, he jerked it off, tossed it on the floor then unbuckled his belt, never looking away from her.

Rage and lust radiated in hot waves off the shredded strapping body. Low light from a small lamp cast gold and shadows over every hard sinew and cut hollow of his powerful bare torso that seemed to pump bigger with his wrath.

His intent becoming clear, Tirsa sat up and backed away. She held up trembling hands, murmured, "Wait, stop," but he came closer.

She rolled off the other side of the bed and ran for the door. Quickly unlocking it, she turned the knob, he slammed his hand on the door over her head keeping it closed then reached down in front of her and relocked it. His voice harsh, low, a grizzly growl, he snarled, "You are staying right here."

She turned in a panic to run again, only getting a step away when he caught her. Grabbing her around the waist, he picked her up and took her back to his bed, set her down and quickly knelt on the mattress, pushed her on her back and climbed on top, straddling her.

"Colonel! Stop! Please!" she cried, struggling, her flailing hands as useless as fluttering bird wings against his brawn.

He took her hands and pinned them over her head. Furious and drunk, his vision blurred, voice slurred and heavy, so deeply accented he was barely understandable. Leaning over her, gravel coating his throat, he growled fiercely, "I should have done what Jancarlo said, taken you that very first night, gotten you out of my system then turned you over to the authorities. But, *neen*. I wanted to trust you, respect you, *help* you."

"Please, Colonel, Etam, you-"

He bellowed, "*Shut up!*" He bent over, putting his face inches from hers. "I've had enough of your lies and deceit. I will take what I want now, I don't want to hear any more of your lies." He lowered his head and crashed his lips against hers.

It was not a gentle kiss, he sealed her words inside, binding their mouths together with such punishing force she would have cried out in pain if she'd been able to.

Under him, she thrashed, trying to wriggle away, struggling to turn her head from his. He held her wrists staking her arms to the bed with one hand and gripped her jaw with the other. Forcing her mouth open, against her lips, he groaned, "I have been so fucking hungry for you," he shoved his tongue in, devouring her as if he was a wild vicious animal and she was trapped prey to be plundered.

In the great room, Knox said, "I've never seen him look so mad, or trashed. The expression on his face- even I'm afraid of him. What if he's hurting her, maybe we should-"

"He is not hurting her," Jancarlo reproached, "mind your own business."

His hands on his hips, Johnson said with concern, "I don't know, he might not be hitting her, that's not him, although he sure looked pissed, in a helluva rage, his face was as black as mine. I'm afraid he might be doing, you know, what you keep telling him to do, Jan." Johnson tilted his head in accusing disapproval at the major.

Jancarlo crossed his arms, said in an acerbic monotone, "He thinks she is a virgin, he would not destroy her that way."

Knox pulled his knit hat down with both hands then pushed it back up, said anxiously, "I don't know, he looked out of his mind, he might not know what he's doing. We have to go get her." He turned on his heel and started for the hall. Johnson hurried right behind him.

Shaking his head, Jancarlo followed them. They argued all the way down the hall about what Etam was capable of doing to a helpless woman that he was enraged at and clearly lusted after.

"I've never seen him this way, he's acting like a jealous lover," Johnson remarked.

Agreeing, Knox said, "Because he is, he just won't admit it, especially to himself."

When they reached Etam's room they stood outside debating what to do. "She's not screaming," Johnson noted.

"I hear her crying and he's yelling, I'm going in." Knox started for the door but Jancarlo stood in front of it blocking him. "*Neen.*" His expression as caustic as always, he said, "He is not hurting her, we wait."

Inside, Etam tore his lips from Tirsa's, in his intoxicated vision she was a wobbly haze, a fuzzy Jezebel, her tears blurred into the haze. He leaned over her still holding her arms against the bed.

She cried, "Etam- Colonel, please listen to me, you don't know what you're-"

Still holding her wrists together with one hand, he bent down close to her face and clamped his other hand over her mouth.

"I told you," his voice coarse, craggy from the liquor and fury, the onyx eyes glittered under half closed lids. "I don't want to hear anything you have to say. We're done talking." He let go of her, grabbed the front of her blouse with both hands and ripped it apart.

She opened her mouth to scream-

He lay down on top of her, pushed himself between her legs, spreading them apart, and brought his mouth back down on hers to still her cries.

Bracing himself on a forearm, he shoved the parts of her blouse aside and paused to drink in the sight as she frantically, futilely punched at him and tried to push him away. Lowering his bare chest onto hers, he clasped her hands again holding them above her head.

Her lips parted as she started to plead with him, "Please, I-"

Silencing her with his mouth again, he slid one leg outside of hers, the length of his rigid erection raging against

207

her leg, he reached between them with his free hand to unbuckle her belt.

Outside the room, his brows like daggers, Knox said, "Step aside, Jan, I'm going in, he can't-"

Jancarlo held his hands up to stop him, "*Neen*. He will not hurt her."

Inside, Tirsa's screams and pleas were muffled by Etam's mouth.

Fumbling with the button on her jeans, his mouth ravishing hers, he was just about to give up and tear the jeans apart too, when he tasted the salt from her tears. It brought him back to his senses. Lifting his head, he put his hand on her neck. Her liquid eyes screamed her fright that he was going to strangle her.

He bent, as gentle as a puff of air, kissed her swollen lips then released her wrists, took his hand from her neck. Still on top of Tirsa, he propped himself on his forearms on either side of her.

The lovely lips were bruised, tears streamed down her face, her heart pounded against her heaving chest as she choked on deep sobs. The only sound she made was her struggled gasping breaths.

His big body hovered over her delicate frame, barely touching her but he could feel her panic in her soft breasts undulating against his granite chest with her gulping sobs.

Etam stared down at Tirsa, his eyelids flickering, bringing her into focus. Blinking rapidly to clear his alcohol addled brain, he tried to break the insane fury that still raged.

With his fingertips, he traced the side of her face, touching the swollen lips and wiping the tears with the pads of his fingers. It pained him, a knife right in his heart to see the way she looked at him, in terror. Finally realizing what he had been about to do, he clenched his fists, his head dropped, his hair brushing her face.

He rolled to the side of the bed, sat there unable to take his eyes off her, yet it was unbearable to see what was in her eyes. He'd done to her what he had almost beaten others for doing. It was his duty to protect her from assault, *fuck*, and he was the one who hurt her, assaulted her.

He had worked to get her to trust him, and screwed it all up in one uncontrolled, insanely jealous moment. He dug his fingers into his face and scrubbed them down, wiped the back of his hand over his mouth. He knew he had to leave her, but he couldn't tear himself away, but, with her palpable fear of him, he had to get away from her.

Tirsa lay on her back unmoving, tears streaming down her face, her arms still up where he had pinned them, leaving her vulnerable. Even when she saw his tormented gaze move from her face to her half exposed breasts, she didn't move. Her chest still heaved from trying to stifle her sobs.

He moved slowly to not startle her, took the lapels of her shirt and pulled them together. *God*, he'd been so crazed with rage when Raine had done the same exact thing to her.

His voice shaky and hoarse with remorse and shame, Etam wiped his eyes and said, "Tirsa, I'm so…sorry. I-" his mouth shut. What else could he say that could undo his abominable behavior?

Then their gazes locked for what seemed a lifetime, the pain in her trembling wet eyes was unbearable, he looked away. He got up, picked up his shirt and put it on without buttoning it, buckled his belt and without another word walked out the door.

Outside, his team, Jancarlo, Johnson and Knox were standing in front of his door, they all jumped guiltily when it opened, he almost ran into Jancarlo. Giving them a cursory, beaten down, haggard look, Etam muttered, "Lock my door," then strode off with his head down.

They could hear her crying inside. Knox said, "Now I'm going in, get the fuck out of my way." He scowled at Jancarlo until the major moved aside.

Knox went inside the room. He saw Tirsa curled in a ball on the bed. He went to her, gathered her in his arms and let her cry against his chest.

Chapter Twenty-Three

*E*tam took the jeep and disappeared from the house for two days.

When he returned, dark stubble covered his face and an aching burden clouded his shadowed eyes.

Knox took him aside and told him what Stav and Tirsa had been doing. Stav's father had left the family when he was very young, and as children do, Stav thought his father left because of him. Before he got to high school his father died of an illness. Tirsa was telling him what his father was saying to him.

Stav had become so emotional he was filled with tears and relief, and weakness. He was weeping, she was holding him, comforting him. That was all. Etam avoided looking at the condemning accusation in Knox's eyes and left him without comment.

Knox followed him to the study. Etam went inside and sat behind his desk.

Knox closed the door. "What the hell is going on with you, E? I've never seen you in a jealous rage before. You are a fucking cop for God's sake. You are the guard and protector, especially of women and children. She's young, and the way she was brought up she still has a child-like innocence." His fists clenched, he said, "You would kill anyone who brutalized her the way you did."

Etam set his elbows on his desk and put his head in his hands. "I know, Knox."

Knox wasn't done. "You're treating her despicably. You would beat anyone to a pulp that dared treat her or any woman the way you yourself abused her."

His head down, Etam scraped his fingers through his hair, said in a tortured voice, "I know, Knox, I know." He looked up at his friend with agonized eyes. "I don't know what to say, I lost my head, my control, it's sick, it's wrong." His eyes dropped to his desk. "I can't explain, she's like an intoxicant, I…"

"I know, E. She has like a vulnerable sexuality, you want to protect her and fuck her at the same time. Kind of a young Marilyn Monroe thing that she is totally unaware of. It's worse for you because you've got your head wrapped in there too, you have feelings for her even though you deny it. We can blame your unconscionable actions on Johnson for keeping our glasses full until we were obliterated. When you took off from here you were so wasted you couldn't say your name."

Etam put a hand over his face. "It's no excuse, Knox, no excuse at all. If it were, every Tom, Dick and scumbag would be running all over town raping and pillaging and getting away with it because they were drunk. It was my fault, I'm to blame for my lack of control."

"Send her back to Australia. For both of your well-being."

Etam slouched back in his chair, his palms flat on the desk. "I can't."

Knox pulled at his beard then leaned over, put his hands on the desk, long fingers spread like drum sticks. "You mean you won't. E, listen, you-"

Etam banged his fist on the desk, shouted, "Enough!" Rubbing his eyes, he pulled at his chin, dropped his hand back to the desk. "I need to be alone." He stared blankly at the desktop.

Knox watched him for a moment. It was excruciating to see his friend suffering and unable to do anything to help him. He and Etam had been friends and part of this team for a long time, but he himself had feelings for the girl that grew stronger every day. Not romantic feelings, just, caring about her as a person, a little sister.

Knox liked her, she was a good person. If she hadn't tried to kill E it all would be a different story. The colonel had to keep her under lock and key, and couldn't let himself fall for her until everything was resolved. Knox knew she wasn't really capable of committing the act, but not everyone believed that, the law was the law.

The next day the weather had cleared, the land was drying.

Etam gave the order to head out. He didn't bother with the walkie-talkies, they had no way to recharge them out in the field. They packed the burros with supplies, a cooler, tents, weapons, and started early.

Etam went over to Tirsa and asked her to wait.

When everyone was out and heading across the savanna, not meeting her eyes, his hands slung loosely on his hips, with a formal tone he said quietly, "Tirsa, I need you to promise me that while we're out on this expedition that you won't run. We'll be deep in the rain forest; swamps, maybe mountains and you won't survive if you take off alone. I don't want to have to tie you to me to keep you from escaping." He should have said he'd tie her to any one of his team but he wouldn't do that. Couldn't do that.

Avoiding eye contact with him, she looked at his shoulder, her voice very hushed, she said, "I promise, Etam…Colonel."

Etam winced at his name on her lips. The lips he'd hurt. She said his name differently than the others with that hint of French accent, it made his heart flip-flop. He did to her what he'd break another man's neck for doing. His gut twisted, her demeanor towards him had gone from friendly back to fearful, and distant. They caught up with the others.

Returning to where they found the black volcanic glass, the group followed it for several miles. Etam couldn't believe they'd never found it before then he saw it disappear into the earth constantly reappearing in a different direction like a corkscrew maze. They found it and lost it all day. When they passed a bronze quoll that resembled a chinchilla they'd seen twice already, and it was growing dark, they set up tents, Johnson and Raine made a fire and cooked hamburgers. The fire kept the bugs away. Two coolers were strapped to the burros.

Tirsa volunteered to do the cleaning up with Cook. When she finished, she joined the gang sitting around the fire eating and talking, sharing stories and jokes. She sat between Knox and Johnson. Jancarlo was with Stav and Ji doing an initial patrol of the area. Lil Dam and Bruno would have first guard of the night.

Etam sat watching the fire, voices bounced around the camp, he heard nothing. Through the dancing flames he saw Tirsa sitting peacefully between Knox and Johnson like they were her pillars of protection. What he should have been. Now they felt she needed to be protected from him. Wait until they saw the sleeping arrangements.

Cook added a few more big logs on the fire and everyone said goodnight and started for their tents. Johnson and Knox still beside her, Tirsa sat on the log wondering if that was where she was to spend the night. Then, she saw Etam's gaze cutting through the smoke at her.

He got up and walked around the campfire to stand in front of her. He said to her without inflection, "You're coming with me." He ignored Knox and Johnson's watchful eyes.

She blinked back her thoughts and stood up. Her face calm and collected, she followed him to a tent. He lifted the flap for her to enter. Her stomach churning, she bent slightly and went in. There were two sleeping bags inside. A lantern burned between them. Clutching her hands to her stomach she looked wide-eyed at him.

The dark eyes bleak, he said wryly, "It's just as hard for me. Lay down. You will not leave this tent. If you need to, you know, go out, then wake me, I'll take you."

Her brows flew up, pink stained her face. *That's not going to happen*, she'd burst before suffering that indignity. The bag was unzipped. She knelt down, squirmed into it. Seeing earlier that everyone else had a flashlight she asked politely, "If there's an extra one, could I have a flashlight?" It was scary being in the jungle in the pitch black.

"*Neen*." He climbed in his bag, then turned the lantern off. He didn't tell her he wouldn't give her a flashlight because there would be no way she could escape into the woods at night without a light.

The pair lay on their backs listening to the sounds of the forest. Beating wings, strange cries, hoots and howls, rustling all around the tents. Acutely aware of each other, it was a long time before either of them fell asleep.

215

When Tirsa woke the next day Etam was already gone. Rubbing the sleep from her eyes, she saw his sleeping bag was rolled up and tied, so she did the same to hers, then went out. The sun was rising, the air losing its nighttime coolness was turning warm.

Almost everyone was up. Lindsey hadn't stopped whining and complaining. Johnson had to take her into the town before they left to get proper clothes and boots. She wailed all the way back at having to wear flat footwear.

Etam was chewing Owen out. Owen admitted he'd had wandered off to explore. He'd tripped and almost broke his neck falling down a ravine. They found him by his yells. Bruno and Stav had to go down the ravine to help him up and back to camp. He was sitting on a log while Knox bandaged his leg.

"You had orders," Etam barked. He looked at all of them gathered around, his voice cold and harsh, he said, "All of you had, *have* orders to not leave the group. You were told to stay here. There are illegal loggers, miners, trappers, natives we know nothing about who still headhunt, at least each other when fighting. We don't know how they will act if they come upon one of you alone." He examined each face thoroughly, watching that they heard him, took him seriously.

"You will, you *all* will follow orders or face the repercussions. If it happens again, you will be immediately discharged. Returned to the house to wait for travel back to Australia." His hands on his hips, Etam gave Owen the full force of his wrath.

Owen had the feeling the colonel wanted to rip his head off and the only reason why he didn't was because everyone was watching.

The colonel's voice was so chilling, and commanding, everyone took him seriously. No one wanted to be Owen sitting there getting seared a new butt.

The rest of the day everyone went about their business quietly on eggshells, with hushed voices, afraid of Etam. Since tossing his goofy disguise as Russell Robinson, he had always looked stern, but the lashing he gave Owen and the scowl on his rigid face since they had left the lodge was intimidating.

After another two days, they lost the trail of the black ice completely. Disappointed, the gang cheered up when near to their camp they came across a fresh water pool fed by a small waterfall.

The OS's and some of the interns giddily removed their filthy clothes and jumped in buck-naked. Laughing and splashing and playing touchy feely they swam for an hour until they grew exhausted. Then they dressed and returned to the campsite.

Tirsa has spent the time helping Cook make lunch and clean up. Wasn't a lot to do since most of the food was either freeze-dried or dehydrated. She watched the others in envy coming back clean and relaxed.

"Go on now," Cook told her, "you've worked harder than any of them, you deserve a dip."

She looked at him skeptically. "I can't swim."

"It's not very deep. Go on now," he said, making shooing motions with his pudgy hands. "Be gone with you girl, it's a pleasant day. I think I saw Knox and Johnson go down to the pool, you'll be safe with them."

Convinced, Tirsa grabbed a bar of soap then found the trail and took off for the pond. When she got there she was enthralled with the beauty. A lightly cascading waterfall bubbled into a clear blue pool. No one was there but her.

Leafy bushes and colorful flowers made it look like the Garden of Eden.

Peeling off her clothes, she slipped into the cool water, it felt like satin on her skin. She scrubbed herself and her hair with the bar of soap.

She dove under to rinse off, when she broke the surface and wiped her eyes, her heart stopped beating. A crocodile was loping down the slight bank straight towards her, long scaly tail swishing the ground behind it. She opened her mouth to scream when a voice stopped her.

"Don't move, Tirsa," Etam said quietly. He was to the side of the crocodile. He had a gun holstered to his hip but he picked up a rock and hurled it like a baseball clocking the reptile in the head.

The animal stopped and swung around to charge him, Etam threw several more rocks. The one that hit him on the end of the nose did it. The croc grunted then lumbered off into the brush, twigs snapping and leaves crunching and rustling as he disappeared.

After making sure it was gone, Etam walked down the bank until he was near the water.

Tirsa stayed neck deep, covering her breasts with shaking hands. "Th- thank you, colonel. I was so scared."

When he didn't respond, just stared at her, her voice trembling, she asked, "How…how long have you been here?" She hated how her voice shook. She'd been terrified when she saw the croc and instantly froze. But it happened so fast. The colonel chased the reptile away in seconds. Tirsa sucked in relieved quick breaths of broken gasps.

He crossed his arms over his chest. The water lapped lightly at the toes of his boots. "When you started shampooing. I followed you, because, yet again, you disobeyed my order. And, Cook tells me you don't even know how to swim."

Not knowing what to say, Tirsa remained mute. She was getting cold, her teeth started chattering. She waited but he said nothing else, just stood there watching her. She didn't dare get out of the water; she was nude, which he was well aware of.

"Last warning, Tirsa," he finally said. "Now, get out of there before you turn blue."

"Uh," she saw her clothes in a heap behind him. She realized she had forgotten to bring a towel. "My, um, clothes, can you leave for a second so I can-"

"Nope."

"Really, Colonel,"

"*Neen*. I'm not leaving you alone. Remember that croc?"

Voices and rustling came from the forest. Max, Bruno and Johnson came into the clearing.

"Hey, E," Johnson said, "what's up?" He looked from Etam to Tirsa and back.

Etam smiled for the first time in days, "Nothing. Tirsa's taking a bath."

"Uh, she's turning blue," Johnson pointed out. Her chattering teeth could be heard a mile away. "We wanted a dip before it's dark, which will be in about 5 minutes." The sun was waning, the trees drew long shadows across the forest and the water. Birds swooped from tree to tree squawking seeking a place to roost.

Etam swung back to the freezing girl with her arms wrapped around herself. "Yes she is blue-ish," he said. Then he unbuttoned his shirt, peeled it off and tossed it to her. He walked back up to the grass where the men stood and said, "You guys can turn around for a second."

"Hey, why don't we all just swim together?" Trying to see her naked body through the water all Max could see was wiggly flesh. He started walking towards the pool when Etam's hand snaked out and grabbed his arm, "Do what I tell you, boy."

Max glanced down at the steel hand wrapped around his arm then up at the black eyes. "Sure," he mumbled meekly and turned his back to the water. The others including Etam did the same.

Catching the shirt, Tirsa stood up and pulled it on. When Etam heard her coming out of the water he turned around, then said suddenly, "None of you guys move."

Soaking wet, his white shirt turned so sheer it was see-through over her sodden body. He turned back around quickly. "Hurry up, Tirsa, get your clothes and let's go," he barked over his shoulder.

She ran leaving wet prints in the dirt, gathered up her clothes in her arms and said, "I'm ready."

Etam swung around, his gaze scorched down her body. "We're outta here," he said to the men, "don't stay too long, the animals will be coming by as it's dusk." Blocking the men's view of her with his body, he put a hand to Tirsa's back pushing her gently to the trail.

Walking behind her, he struggled to keep his eyes up on her wet hair because they kept dropping down to his sodden shirt that clung to her soaking body, revealing her little round bottom, as if she wasn't even wearing it.

It seems lately she was wearing more of his shirts than he was. If they were alone that would be okay with him, but they're not. *Shit, he'd never look at that shirt the same way again. He should go back and jump into the pool; he definitely needed a cool dunk.*

When they got back to the camp, Lindsey was leaving Owen and Raine's tent and slipping into hers and Dia's, while Owen was slipping out of the girls' tent into his, clearly having just left Dia. Etam rolled his eyes. He was running a rabbit palace for Pete's sake. Of course, he chastised himself, who the hell was he to pass judgment after his own reprehensible behavior?

At the end of the next day, Etam met with Jancarlo, Johnson and Knox. They came to the conclusion they were going in circles and leading right back to the ranch.

Etam said, "We need to go back, get more supplies, I need to study the book and maps again." During the day, although he kept her glued to his side, he and Tirsa did not speak, at night he waited until she was asleep before coming into the tent and was gone before she woke.

They broke camp the next day, packed up and headed back to the ranch. It took two days to get back. "We'll get supplies tomorrow," Etam told them, "then start out again the following day."

The group happy to be back on beds instead of hard ground, with electricity and running water were in no hurry to go back to the forest.

Later in the afternoon, Etam got a phone call. He found his team in the library hanging out. He saw Stav pass by the window outside on guard patrol. He told his men, "I got annoying news, guys. The police want us to come to their station, it's a good hundred miles out. They want to question us again."

"What about the *blondine*?" Jancarlo asked.

"They wanted her too but I managed to talk them out of it. I said she was so traumatized that she didn't remember anything that happened, it was all a blank and whenever we'd bring it up she'd start screaming for hours. They said it was all right to leave her here."

Johnson grinned. "Really? They didn't want a deranged female in their station screaming all day?"

Knox laughed, Etam smiled.

"*Ja*. Except I should bring her, I don't know about leaving her out here," Etam murmured thoughtfully. A few things bothered him about bringing her with them though; at this point he didn't want her around other unknown people, with her...gift. She could wander off again, and he didn't like the way that last officer looked at her when he wanted to interrogate her alone.

The person who sent her to kill him was also a concern. Etam didn't know, the guy could be in the remote town where the police station was, waiting for a chance to get to her. Etam wasn't worried about himself. If the guy wanted to kill him himself he wouldn't have gone to the trouble of sending Tirsa to do it. Plus, Etam was trained for that kind of situation. But he didn't want Tirsa out in the open vulnerable to attack.

Knox said baldly, "We took care of the men who came after her, there is plenty of security here. If she goes with us there is a chance for her to run, escape in the town, small as it is, it is bigger than the one we get our supplies from. She could hide out; we might not be able to find her. Not that I think she would even think of running."

Etam ruminated on the major's words. "*Ja*, we have security here," he scowled sarcastically, "but who's to keep her out of their clutches?"

Johnson agreed, nodding ruefully, "True that. Bunch of rutting animals you hired on."

Etam smirked at him. "I did the best with the information I was given." It had been Knox and Johnson's job to recruit both the interns and the OS's. They both looked aggrieved about their choices.

"They're all going to be like that," Johnson retorted, "It's their ages, they are in their twenties."

Jancarlo snorted. "Huh, so are we. We can control ourselves." He shot a side look at Etam, "At least some of us can."

The dig struck. The lightheartedness fell from Etam's manner. "Yeah, whatever. Let's go give instructions, pack a bag. We'll be there at least one night."

He found Cook as usual in the kitchen. He told him what was going on.

"Seymour, we need to keep everyone busy. You'll be in charge. Keep the OS's on guard patrol 24/7. Have the others work on the building in the back. There's three rooms the size of a barns. Have them inventory, box up stuff we don't need, clean the place up and then start painting it inside."

Cook pulled his white pants up, wiped his hands on his stained white apron. Pushing his glasses up his budgie nose, he rested his hands on his big belly. "*Ja*, of course, E. No worries."

"Seymour, you need to keep the girl, Tirsa, in your sight at all times. Don't leave her alone. You're in the barns; she's in the barns. Got it?"

Seymour nodded staunchly, pushing his glasses back up again, "Of course. No problem."

Feeling edgy about leaving the house without the protection of his team except for Seymour, Etam patted Cook on the back and left to pack a bag.

Chapter Twenty-Four

*A*s it turned out they were gone almost four days. The four men wearily entered the house, it was quiet. Ji was in the great room reading. He got up when they came in.

Etam greeted him, "Hey Ji, how's it going? Where is everyone?" He set his bag on the floor.

Ji raised his arms in the air while yawning. "Uh," he palmed his eyes then said through another yawn, "they're all out at the barns except Lil Dam and Bruno are patrolling." As he said that, Bruno walked past the front window.

"It's been quiet. Real quiet. Boring quiet." He yawned again. At that moment the side door opened and Stav, Owen, and the five interns came in, they were dusty, some had paint splotches on them.

White paint on her freckled face, Lindsey said, "Dibs on the first bathroom," she scurried down the hall without a howdy-do to the men who had been away for four days.

"I got number two-" Raine yelled and took off.

"Three!" Max was gone.

Dia went right over to Etam the second she saw him. "How about you and me takin' number four together, we can

224

conserve water?" She touched his arm, slid her hand down to hold his then squeezed it. "I'm feeling really dirty,"

Seeing Tirsa come in, Etam shook Dia off, this time he didn't bother to reprimand her. His eyes narrowed at Tirsa's appearance. She looked very tired, her spark was dimmed, her eyes trained on the floor. She went right to her room without a word.

"Where's Cook?" Etam asked Ji.

"Just saw him through the window, Colonel, he was behind them, he went in through the kitchen entrance. He'll know you're back seeing the jeep." Ji yawned again, wide opened mouth like a tiger then sat back down with his book.

Early the next morning, Etam got dressed, grabbed a muffin and went into the study. He decided he needed to start at the beginning of the book, read, study every word, every nuance. He was deep in thought when Cook barged in.

Etam looked up from his book. Smiled, said wryly, "Come on in, Seymour." He put a slip of paper in the book, closed it, and turned to the heavy man. "You look angry, what's up?"

Cook plopped his fat hands on his thick hips. "E, you made that girl fair game to all those jackals, branding her a criminal, and a *hoer*, then you banished her to the barns. The other interns are abusive to her. They make her do all of the hard work, they make her scrub the floor on her hands and knees with a steel wool pad instead of a mop."

Etam said with mild sarcasm, "I take it you're talking about Tirsa. I didn't brand her a criminal or a…whore, our team conversations have apparently been overheard. Anyway, why doesn't she refuse?"

Cook spat. "Really? You treat her like shit, keep her prisoner in your room, where would she get the idea she has any choice in how she's treated, or what work she is forced to do? The others think they can get away with doing what they want to her because she's going to jail eventually, who's going to care what's happened to her here?"

"Why don't you intervene?"

Pinching the end of his round nose, Cook complained, "I have, but I can't be there every second, there're three separate rooms to supervise and they ignore most of what I say. The tough girl, Dia, apparently she's bi."

"Bi?"

"*Ja*, she's slept with half the men here, she hits on you relentlessly but she also goes after the girl, Tirsa. Constantly she is groping her. Tirsa tries to fight her off but Dia is much taller and quite strong, muscular. *You* need to do something." He turned and stalked back out of the office. Etam heard the kitchen door bang shut.

Etam left the study, locking the door, he walked through the lodge and out the back door. His boots shuffled through the tall grass as he made his way to the barn. He stood silently looking in an open window.

Dim inside the cavernous room, the high round roof and a tiny triangle window at the top along with several along the lower walls helped make it a little lighter. In the back was a loft with a ladder leading up to it. Boxes stuffed with useless crap was piled against one wall; most of the rest of the wooden structure was empty.

All the way across the other side of the huge room, Tirsa was on her knees scrubbing the floor. Dia was standing next to her mocking her and making scuff marks on the wooden planks and then telling Tirsa to clean them.

While Tirsa was kneeling and bending over, Dia crouched beside her and ran her hands over Tirsa's back, over her black sweater then around the front trying to fondle her breasts. Tirsa pushed her hands away and told her to stop but Dia just laughed and put her forearm under Tirsa's neck to force her head back and shoved her other hand up her sweater.

"Come on, girl, you tasty bit," Dia said against Tirsa's ear, "dip a toe in the lady pool, you'll love it. I can teach you things!"

"Leave me alone," Tirsa demanded, twisting, trying to push Dia away.

Dia slapped her, her voice dark and ugly, she sneered, "You don't push me away, felon."

Tirsa tried to get away from her, Dia knocked her onto her back and jumped on her and began beating her with her fists. Then springing to her feet, shrieking curses, Dia started kicking her, then she knelt and yanked Tirsa half up off the floor by her sweater, raised her hand to punch her-

With one hand Etam caught her fist, with the other he grabbed Dia's hair and wrenched her to her feet.

Screeching like a howling monkey, she swatting savagely at him, "Let go of me you shit!"

Suddenly released, Tirsa fell back on her palms.

Still clutching Dia, holding her arm's length away so she couldn't reach him with her fists, Etam leaned over with his hand out, pulled Tirsa to her feet, and commanded, "Go to you room."

With her palm to her side where Dia had rained blows, following his order, hobbling slightly, bent over and painstakingly slowly, Tirsa left the barn.

Dia's hair still wrapped around his fist, Etam jerked her head around to face him, he said fiercely, "You *godverdomme* piece of *schijt*, you fucking lay a hand on her again and I'll take you out like I would a man."

Instead of cowering, Dia tilted her head and batted her lashes at him. "Uh huh, that's fine with me, honey, I like it rough, why don't *you* be a man and do me? What's the problem, honey, you don't like spicy Latin meat?" She cuddled against him, running her hand down the front of his jeans.

He grabbed her wrist and bent it back until she shrieked then he dropped her wrist giving her a shove. "Next time I'll break it. You need to learn to keep your hands to yourself." He stalked to the door, turned once and repeated, "You touch her again and I'll lay you out," then went out the door.

He caught up with Tirsa just as she was entering the house. "Tirsa," he called out, jogged to her, "wait."

She had a hand pressed to her side, and the side of her face was scarlet where Dia had slapped her. Turning slowly, she gave him a defeated, pained look of *what's next?*

"I want Knox to look at you," Etam said quietly.

Pale as snow, she rubbed her brow, dropped her hand to cover her eyes, still bent over slightly with her hand near her stomach, she didn't say anything, her head was spinning.

Seeing she was about to pass out, Etam slipped one arm under her back, the other under her legs and lifted her up in his arms.

Holding her high and tight against his chest, he carried her down the hall to a small room Knox kept as a makeshift infirmary. The door was locked. He set her down gently on her feet she wobbled against him; he kept an arm around her while getting his phone out of his pocket. He pushed a button, Knox answered right away.

"Yeah, E?"

"I need you to come to the infirmary."

"Check," Knox replied curtly.

Tirsa appeared to be about to fall over so Etam scooped her back up laying her head against his shoulder.

Knox was there in less than two minutes. He saw them as he came down the hall. Already puzzled, when he got close enough to see the mark on Tirsa's face and a bruise on her neck, he looked at Etam in outrage, like there was going to be a fight.

"Not me, Knox. Just open the door," Etam said, his voice dark with ire that his friend would think he would beat a woman. Especially this woman.

Knox opened the door and turned the lights on. Off center of the room was a small hospital bed, Etam went to it and carefully laid Tirsa down.

Knox rolled his sleeves up and leaned over Tirsa. Her eyes were closed; he tenderly touched the angry red palm print on her face. His head snapped up at Etam, he barked, "What the hell is going on here, E?"

His hands stuffed in his pockets Etam was upset too but he had been able to vent his anger somewhat. "It was the girl, Dia."

"What are you going to do about it-"

"I already did. Just see if she's okay," Etam indicated Tirsa laying so still, her face screwed up in pain.

Knox bent over her, muttered, "I mean, what are you going to do about this continual abuse of this girl? Whatever she was sent here to do, she was obviously forced to do so but she didn't, she needs to stop getting punished for it." He gently pushed open first one then the other of Tirsa's eyes, studied them briefly. "Tirsa, honey, tell me where it hurts the most right now," he said softly, his other hand light on her arm.

Wincing, Tirsa moved her hand slowly and touched her side where Dia had pummeled then kicked her.

Knox went to lift up her sweater, he said to Etam, "You can go wait outside."

Etam crossed his arms, planted his boots shoulder width apart. "*Neen*."

Knox glared at him for second, which did no good. He turned his attention back to his patient. He pushed her shirt up, and gasped. Her entire side was black and blue. Shaking his head in repulsion, he carefully set his palm on her side then patted lightly up and down the length from the bottom of her ribcage to her hip, she cried out at his touch.

Etam, his heart clenching at each whimper, covered his mouth with his knuckles and moved to the other side of the bed to watch.

Another bruise was spreading purple just under her ribs. Trying to keep his anger under wraps, Knox grated tightly, "E, help me lift her up, I need to take her sweater off."

Etam hesitated, frowning, "Knox…"

"You wanted to stay. I'm a licensed medic, I can look at her without getting my boxers in a tent," he quirked a derisive brow at Etam, "can you?"

Clearing his furrowed forehead, Etam stepped closer and slid an arm under Tirsa's back. "Ready when you are, Doc," he said blithely.

"Humph." To Tirsa, Knox said softly, "All right, honey, we're going to lift you up and take your sweater off, *neen*, don't struggle." With her eyes still closed she shook her head, and feebly tried to push him away.

"Shh, no, don't fight us, Tirsa, it's okay," Knox soothed, tenderly brushing her hair off her face. He took her wrists and carefully laid her arms by her head. He looked at Etam and nodded.

His heart bleeding, Etam's dark eyes radiated aching despair at the small, defenseless woman so injured she could hardly lift her hands to try to protect herself. Dia had kicked her with steel-toed boots.

Together, the men lifted her to sit up. Etam held her while Knox delicately pulled her sweater off and set it on the bottom of the bed. They laid her back down carefully. Etam made a strangled sound, he stepped back and walked over to the door, put his hand on it and leaned over.

Dia had done a job on Tirsa. As soon as Etam had seen her groping Tirsa he raced around and into the building. As he entered, he saw Dia slap her and was already pounding on the girl by the time he'd gotten to them. His stomach roiled right up his clenching throat.

When they'd taken her sweater off, they saw almost her entire torso, arms and neck included were covered in bruises. Even her breasts mounding over the lacey bra were black and blue. Etam thought he was going to be sick.

He could hear Knox talking in a low-pitched, friendly, doctor voice to Tirsa telling her exactly what he was doing so she wouldn't be nervous and hurt herself more by trying to fight him off. Knox decided he needed to x-ray her ribs. "Buck up, E, I need you to help me, it'll go faster."

Etam rubbed his face then went over to Knox keeping his eyes on the major. "Okay, here, help me put this on." Knox went to a cupboard, took out a lead blanket and they laid it over her hips and legs. Knox went to set up the machine. Etam watched the pain pass over her face. Her skin whitened, then darkened, her eyelids fluttered, lips parted with a moan.

There had been various injuries the last time they'd come out looking for the volcanic ice so they had the medical equipment brought in. It was easier than dealing with the rural clinics.

Etam set his hand on the uninjured side of her face and held it there, murmuring, "It's okay, Tirsa, *mijn luttel zeldzaam men*, I won't let anyone else hurt you. *God, I promise.*" He choked out the last words. She looked so beautifully delicate but battered and broken, and it was his damned fault.

Knox set up the machine; they stepped out of the room while he pushed the button. Then they went back in and put the machine away, lifted off the cover, put it away, and pulled the sheet over her. Knox went to a locked cabinet and took out some pills, he shook out one.

"Hold her up, E," he said.

Like before, Etam slid an arm under her back as carefully as he could and lifted her to sit, her whimpered moans killing him.

Knox got a cup of water and gave her the pill, helped her drink the water. Etam held her while Knox put her sweater back on, keeping his eyes askance so he didn't see either the ugly bruises, or what the lacey bra barely covered, he didn't need to be more of an ass and get a hard-on for the half-conscious battered woman.

They laid her back down. Knox motioned for Etam to follow him outside.

He closed the door. Speaking quietly he said, "E, there's nothing I can really do. I don't think there are any broken bones; the x-ray will take a minute to complete. She's just covered with bruises. That bitch beat her damned good."

Knox's face darkened with fury. He took a deep breath before continuing. "I gave Tirsa a pill for pain, but she'll be just fine in a couple of days. If you'll excuse me, I need to go see someone." He started to go down the hall but Etam snapped out his hand and grabbed his arm.

"*Neen*, Knox. You can't go beat the woman, it's enough the women are beating the women. I'll take care of it. She's done here."

A hand to his head, Knox shook it back and forth, then pierced Etam with a denouncing look. "Listen, E, you have to let her go, Tirsa I mean. Before she really gets hurt. I mean, even you, you're sworn to protect her, and even you have-"

"I know." Shameful pain flitted across Etam's face. Crossing his arms, his head down, he stared at the floor. Then he raised weary, lamented eyes to his colleague and friend.

"I can't let her go, Knox. If I send her back with her mission not completed, I don't know whom she's dealing with, I don't know what they'll do to her. Someone went to a great deal of time and money to get her on my ship; they falsified school records and background paperwork. Someone goes to that much trouble, they're likely to take her out whether or not she completes what they sent her to do."

"E, *mijn broeder*, my brother, we'll go after this guy, it's what we do."

Etam shook his head in frustration. "She won't tell me who he is. I've threatened, cajoled, begged, she refuses. This guy has something so heavy hanging over her that even upon the threat of death, rape or imprisonment, she's not talking. And, I think she has to still stick to the plan, to kill me. She vehemently denies she would ever harm anyone else, but when I ask her if she is to still try to kill me she clams up.

"Doesn't lie either and say no, just says nothing. Jancarlo has people trying to find out who sent her. He hasn't been able to get in contact with her guardians; we don't know where they are. I do believe her about not harming anyone else." He said dryly, "I saw firsthand today what a lousy fighter she is. And we all know how incompetent she is with a knife."

233

Knox cocked a brow at him. "I could have told you that. If you'd keep your brain out of your pants and stop lusting after her like a possessive dog in heat and talk to her, get to know her, you'd see what she's really about. She's compassionate and gentle, and unremittingly kind."

A tone of irritation rang as Etam scowled at his friend and said, "You don't have to tell me, I know what she's like. You sound like you're in love with her yourself."

Knox rolled his head back looked up at the ceiling, smiled and shook his head. "See, E, you think of her as yours and want to fight anyone else that looks in her direction. *Neen*," he held up a hand as Etam started to disagree. "Stop kidding yourself. For the record, I think of her as a little sister, truly. You and I go back a long ways, *broed*; there's never been deceit or competition between us. She has a beautiful soul, she's helped me get my life back and she's helped others."

"I know, Knox. However, at this point she is still a criminal, and I'm a cop. She's an innocent and I'm a...soldier. I can't have a relationship with-"

Knox cut him off, "I'm not saying for you to. But you are emotionally involved with her whether you admit it or not. I'm saying stop seeing her as a sexual object and find the person that she is. Don't forget to show her who you truly are too, right now she thinks you're a cruel barbarian. Or did she say caveman? I forget. Means the same."

Scowling, Etam growled, "Knox-"

Knox chuckled then said seriously, "However, I think you said the words, though, that you *can't* let her go, I think you mean you *won't* let her go, even if her safety wasn't at issue. Anyway," he said quickly as he saw Etam's pique building up, "let's go back inside and tuck her in. she should be asleep by now. I'll get one of the boys to guard-"

"*Neen.*" Etam pushed past him. "I'm taking her."

"E, that's what I mean, you're so overbearing and possessive when it concerns her. You are not her husband, or her father," Knox argued, following him inside. His words were to no avail.

"Help me wrap her." Etam picked a blanket up off a chair and held it out. The two men carefully wrapped Tirsa loosely in it, then Etam gently lifted her up but she still moaned even in her sleep.

"Really E, she should stay here where I can keep an eye on her," Knox objected.

"Get the door," Etam ordered.

Knox sighed and opened the door.

Carrying Tirsa, Etam turned sideways to get them through the doorway. As they left he said, "You can check on her in her room." He strode off down the hall.

Awkwardly holding her with one arm, Etam opened his door and went inside and deposited her gently on his bed. Then he passed through the room to the adjoining room where he pulled back the sheet and blanket.

Going back into his room, he picked her up, took her into her space and set her on the bed. He wasn't about to undress her, been there, hadn't gone so well before, so he put her in the bed fully clothed. He would retrieve her shoes still in the barn later.

Pulling the covers to her chin, he sat down next to her, his weight sinking the side of the mattress. He leaned over and set his hand on the other side of her on the bed so he could see her face. He stayed like that for a long time, just watching the way her lashes curled on her cheeks, lips closed, breathing softly, the nasty handprint still red on her face.

He got up, walked out of her room, passed through his then out. Locking the door behind him he stalked down the hall. It took him a while to find her.

Dia was up in the loft in the barn with Owen. Their heads popped up when he threw the door open so hard it banged the wall.

Seeing their bare shoulders he snapped, "Get dressed Dia and come down. Now." He stood a few feet inside the door, arms crossed, legs akimbo. He saw Dia roll her eyes just before she ducked back down. It was several minutes before they were climbing down the ladder.

"Okay," she sighed, impatient and annoyed, "what do you-"

Etam snatched her upper arm right under her shoulder, and practically lifting her off her feet, walked her to the door.

"Hey, you need to-" she protested. Owen followed meekly behind them not knowing what was going on.

Still holding her, Etam jerked her arm and snarled, "You need to keep your mouth shut. The sound of your voice makes me sick." He yanked her to the door and out, across the yard and into the house.

She was a tall muscular woman but he hauled her like she was a puppet. Inside, he swiveled her around to face him, let her go and said, "You're out of here. We'll take you to the town, a helio will pick you up and take you back to Australia then you're on your own."

At first her olive-skin darkened in surprise and anger, she snapped, "What the hell are you talking about? I'm not going any-"

"I told you to shut your mouth," Etam snarled, the rage at what she'd done to Tirsa climbing up his throat. He closed his eyes and could still see that creamy beautiful body covered in angry purple and black bruises. He knew if he looked at Dia he'd want to punch her in the face, even though he always told himself he'd never hit a woman. But she wasn't a woman, she was a savage animal.

He said grimly, "You are to go to your room, pack your things, and stay there until I send for you. I can't stand to look at you."

"Colonel, you can't mean this, please, I-" Her dark eyes suddenly distressed realizing he was serious. At his implacable expression, her face hardened. "Is this about that stupid girl? The bitch can't take a little discipline for Pete-" her words cut off as Etam suddenly cinched both of his hands around her neck and started squeezing. Her eyes bulged; she gagged, scratching at his hands.

"Colonel! Colonel! Stop, stop it!" Owen squealed, jumping up and down. "Help! Someone help!"

Jancarlo and Johnson came running with others behind them. They both grabbed Etam pulling him away from the woman.

"Take it easy, E, get a grip," Johnson spoke under his breath in Etam's ear, grappling with his brawny arm.

Her hand at her throat, Dia staggered backwards, brown eyes huge with fright. Coughing and choking, she turned and ran out of the room and down the hall to her room.

"I'm all right." Etam shook his men off. "I saw red, that bitch-"

"We know, we saw Knox. That's why we were here so fast. The sooner she's out of here the better," Johnson commiserated angrily. "Let's go to the study."

The rest of the gang crowded in the doorway. White as a sheet, Owen ran to join them. He was gabbling at them, telling what happened. They stared wide-eyed at Etam as he shouldered past them with his men. Even the OS's stepped back.

After he left, they all agreed he was a scary guy with one hell of a violent temper and they planned to stay out of his way.

It took three days before the helicopter Etam called his commander for arrived in the outskirts of the town. Johnson drove Dia in to board it.

It had been pretty quiet in the house for those few days. Etam had kept Dia locked in her room. He'd given her the walkie-talkie and told her to call Johnson if she needed to use the bathroom, and Johnson or Jancarlo would bring her food.

Neither Etam nor Knox trusted themselves to do it, and they didn't trust any of the others either. The intern was smooth and salacious. She could talk any of the OS's or other interns into opening her door and who knew what she would do in retaliation. She looked like a knife wielding kind of a girl and knew how to use one, unlike Tirsa.

The entire group actually breathed a sigh of relief when she was gone. She was a bully and no one was immune to her wrath.

Johnson said his little sister was gay and Dia gave lesbians a bad name. Rather bisexuals. His sister, Jessica, was as sweet and gentle a woman that you'd ever meet, except Tirsa of course. Good riddance to bad rubbish, he'd said, as he watched the helicopter take the sullen intern away.

Chapter Twenty-Five

*I*t rained again for two days after. They would have gone out on their expedition if it was just rain, but this was as before, a monsoon with gusts of winds so strong the palm trees bent over like they were hiding their heads. Limbs and other small trees ripped out of the ground sailed by in the gale.

The ground flooded so fast the tall grass was barely visible. The lodge was built up on high ground with a cement foundation so it stayed dry. It would be impossible for an animal much less a human to be able to move around in the vicious storm.

They were all eating breakfast together. As they were finishing, Tirsa, who was feeling better although still in pain, got up to carry her plate to the kitchen. When she didn't come back, Etam got up and went in. Cook was putting leftovers in plastic containers and Tirsa was filling the sink with water. She always stayed to help Cook clean up.

"Seymour," Etam said from the door. "Ask one, or better two of those lazy bored people out there to help you clean up." Ji's head passed by the window under the overhang as he walked patrol. His voice softened, Etam said, "Tirsa, come with me."

She eyeballed him warily, as did Cook. Knowing she didn't have a say in the matter anyway, she turned off the water and walked over to him.

"E," Cook murmured, with a quiet warning in his voice.

Etam smiled sadly at his old friend, sad that Cook was worried for Tirsa to be with him. "It's all right, Seymour." He said to Tirsa, "Come on." His fingertips brushed her back leading her out of the room. He brought her down to his study where he unlocked the door and brought her in.

This was the first time she'd been inside this room. It was actually quite nice. When it wasn't dark outside with rain pattering against the glass, a big window let in light. There was a desk piled with notes and books, charts, papers, maps. A sofa was against one wall with several old but comfortable looking easy chairs facing it. A liquor cabinet with glasses and a compact, generator-run fridge under it was next to the sofa.

A low table in front of the sofa had two glasses wetting spots on it; apparently some of his team had been in with him earlier. One was probably Major Jancarlo judging by the ashtray. It was empty but had ash residue on the bottom. The only one who smoked on the whole expedition was Jancarlo. He smoked the real thin European cigars.

"Here," Etam said, gesturing to the sofa, "please sit down."

Tirsa still eyed him warily, he was usually telling her to do something, not asking her. She moved to the couch and gracefully sat down wondering what he was up to. *A little rape on the couch perhaps?*

He looked particularly sinister to her this morning. He hadn't shaved so dark stubble covered his jaw, and he'd been outside, the wind had mussed his hair and he hadn't re-combed it other than dragging his fingers through the thick locks. He wore black jeans, boots, several buttons on his shirt were undone, black hair on his tanned chest was visible. He looked like a caged, menacing outlaw just waiting to break out.

Her fear of him was palpable, it was all over her face, and in the rigid way she held herself perched on the very edge of the couch ready for a sudden attack. A pulse at Etam's temple beat, he felt awful inside the way she avoided him like he was a rapacious creep.

She kept a big space between them as she passed by him, sliding nervous, sideways glances at him now like he was a serial killer about to pounce on her.

"So," he said amiably, going to the desk he picked up a book. "I thought you might like to see what started and is running this expedition."

Her eyes slanted to the book he held. "Really?" Rounded eyes showed her interest.

He let out a held breath the way she lit up. He went over, and making sure there was a space between them so she would relax, he sat down slowly and leaned back against the cushions trying to appear as nonthreatening as possible.

Sitting on the edge of the sofa, her ankles crossed and tucked off to the side, Tirsa folded her hands primly in her lap. She was wearing jeans and the black sweater she'd been wearing the day Dia attacked her. Etam wanted to burn the sweater but considering she only had a few things to wear it wasn't feasible. When he opened the book she kicked off her shoes, squirmed back against the cushions, pulled up her legs and crossed them tailor style.

"So, let me tell you in a nutshell the gist of the history of this book, actually it's more like a diary and what it says about the writings Jesus and others made after the resurrection." He peered at her to see her reaction.

Her eyes were glued with excited interest at the book. "Oh, I hadn't thought about how you came to know about it." She looked at him with curiosity and new esteem. Pulling her knees up she wrapped her arms around them and hugged them. "This is, I can't describe it. I feel like I'm *in* history in the making."

The side of his mouth curved up. It was always heartwarming when he came across someone as interested in all this as he was. Also, he was proud that he had the book and how it had come into his hands.

Her knees flopped back down and she crossed them again. "I'm sorry, I'm blabbing away, please tell me your story."

He smiled gently. "It's okay, Tirsa, it's great to hear you speak, uh, I mean about the book." The back of his neck heated because he did like to hear her speak, her voice was soft and lilting.

"Anyway, this book, diary, tells of writings of the apostles Andrew and Bartholomew, of the considerable time they spent with Jesus after he rose. With those writings are words Jesus Himself wrote about what He knew, felt, saw, heard, the day He was crucified, what He was thinking and experiencing nailed to the cross." Etam's voice lowered, "What His father, God, was saying to Him at the time."

Tirsa didn't move, couldn't move, it was too…fantastical, too amazing to hear. He could almost see her mind clamoring, *let's go now, I want to read it now!*

She curbed her impatience. "Whose diary is it? How did you get it?" she asked eagerly, thirsty for as much as he could tell her.

He couldn't help but grin at her enthusiasm. "Okay, okay, I'm going to tell you."

Settling her body into the cushions, she whispered, "Sorry, I'll be quiet."

His expression solemn with a shade of a smile, he told her, "Please ask all the questions you want, seriously. It's exciting for me whenever I share this with anyone else."

Her mouth straightened. A fleeting picture of him sitting here in his half unbuttoned shirt and tight jeans with another woman sharing this with her and- she pulled her knees up again and rested her chin on them. "Go ahead, I'm dying to hear the story."

"All right. So, by the way, there are also writings from Pontius Pilate, the Prefect of Judaea, who of course ordered the crucifixion, about conversations he had with Jesus months after he rose. Apparently, Pilate had told Him he deeply regretted his action and asked for His forgiveness. He said his wife had been against it and he should have listened to her."

"They said that in the Bible," she added, "about Pilate's wife being against harming Jesus."

"*Ja.* So, there's this thing called the Pilate Stone that was discovered in 1961. It had Pilate's name etched in it, it was found in an ancient theatre built in 30 AD. Hidden into part of a set of stone stairs was a tablet in a crumbled part of the stairs that hadn't been examined as carefully.

"A papyrus written in Aramaic by Pilate describes other works along with the writings of Jesus, Andrew and Bartholomew. Oh, and Barabbas. There's a brief mention of this in the modern record books made at the time of the discovery. Yet, in 1961 the actual works were missing."

Etam set the book down on the couch for a second, got up and went to the miniature fridge. Turning his head to look at her, he asked, "Would you like a soda?"

"Sure, that'd be nice, thanks Colonel."

He opened the fridge, took out two sodas, asked, "Do you like a glass?"

She shook her head. "No, the can is fine."

He popped the tab on the cans and handed one to her then sat down with his and took a long swallow.

"That was nice you pulled the tab for me," she said shyly, appreciating his thoughtfulness.

"*Ja*, well, women and their nails, you know." He drank some more then set the soda on the table in front of the couch.

Again the unbidden picture of him sitting here with another woman sifted into her thoughts.

"So then," he continued, "the diary along with other ancient artifacts were stolen, I'm ashamed to say by one of my ancestors. I have an ancestor whose history goes way back to the Frumentarii. The Frumentarii were officials of the Roman Empire who acted as the secret service in the 2nd and 3rd centuries. As a unit of military intelligence they spent a lot of time traveling as curriers and spies."

He picked up his soda, took a sip. "This gets kind of complicated. Supposedly there was a band of secret Frumentarii as early as the 1st Century. My ancestor was in that band. He found the book in the ruins and took it and the artifacts and hid them. At the time, there was this emperor Hadian, his whole name was Publius Aelius Hadrianus. He was born in 76 AD and was Roman Emperor from 117 to

138. He was credited with constructing the Temple of Venus and rebuilding the Pantheon.

"Apparently he came across information about the book. He went to question my ancestor but he was deceased. However, Hadrian got an idea. He dug up my ancestor's grave and lo and behold, they had buried the book with him. Because supposedly he always had it on him in a pocket or a tie-bag."

Etam glanced at her. Her eyes were wide in rapt attention to his every word. He had expected a yawn of boredom by now, but no, she kept looking from him to the book to him.

"Now," he continued, his eyes on her, "Hadrian travelled to nearly every province of Europe. The other thing he was famous for was for building Hadrian's Wall. This wall is in Great Britain. It marks the northern limit of Roman Britain at that time. I won't go into all that detail now. At the time they were building the western third of the wall due to lack of suitable building stone, they had to use turf to construct part of it."

He paused, studying her expression. He said, "Listen I'll completely understand if you want to beg off from the rest of the story. It's all kind of dry."

She reached out and touched his arm in enthusiasm. "Oh heavens no, Colonel, this is so fascinating, please go on." At his skeptical look she said with earnest keenness, "Really, I want to hear it."

Feeling her hand on his arm not only set his skin tingling but he lost his train of thought. His mind cleared when she removed her hand to hug her knees.

Etam cleared his throat. "*Ja*, um, so anyway, Hadrian supposedly brought this book with him and for some reason, hid it in that part of the wall. He had enemies, I guess like they all did then. So then, for some reason Hadrian told someone, who told someone else who recorded it. In the 1500's there was a lot of trading going on in the world, including the spice trade. One of the sailors of the West Indies learned of the book and signed on to travel with the spice trading. He jumped ship in Great Britain and went in search of the book."

Tirsa interrupted with giggle. "Naturally he found it or we wouldn't be sitting here."

"*Ja*. You are correct. He brought it back to the Netherlands and passed it down a few generations. There was always some mention of it in the family Bibles. Now, this part is where I come in. Until after the Second World War the western part of the island of New Guinea was part of the Dutch colony of the Netherlands Indies.

"The sailor that found the book brought it to New Guinea. This was recorded in my family Bible. The Bible had been in the attic for generations. We didn't come across it until a few years back. In the Bible, the sailor wrote how he'd gotten in trouble with his command for taking, maybe stealing, items from rural homes while in New Guinea, so now afraid to get caught with the book he hid it under a grave stone in New Guinea." He took a breath.

"And? So? How do you find the grave stone?"

"Every time someone found the book they made a note. The notes followed the book. This last time the sailor wrote in his diary how and where he hid the book. Since he was in a strange land he wasn't familiar with, he wrote down the landmarks, clues to where he hid the book. We've come out here a couple of times. The furthest we've gotten was finding this base, the start off location near the river. The next step was the black ice. When we find the end of the black ice it will point to the next clue."

He handed her the book and sat back, crossed an ankle over his knee and watched her eagerly open the book and pour over the pages.

Her head bent over, the blonde curls tumbled around her face and shoulders. The conversation he'd had with Knox came to his mind. Knox had said she had a crazy sort of vulnerable sexuality. No denying that.

"Colonel." She lifted her head, an odd, nebulous like mantilla shrouded the blue eyes. It was too bizarre to describe, a dusty mist. It was so mesmerizing he couldn't tear his own eyes away.

"I...there's a feeling I'm getting from this book..." Realizing how she sounded, her guardians had warned her to keep quiet about these things. She partially closed the book.

Adjusting his body so he was curved towards her, Etam set an arm on the back of the couch behind her and put his hand over her hand that held the book in her lap. Clearing his throat, his deep voice grave, with abashed hesitance, he said, "Listen, Tirsa, I need to...say something,"

The haze evanesced slowly until it disappeared and the bright blue eyes shone as intensely as before. She smiled, curious, he sounded unusually awkward and somber. "Yes?" she asked when he didn't continue.

He coughed, fidgeted with a button on the cushion, then wiped the corners of his mouth with his fingers, afraid what he was going to say would dim the happy, peaceful expression on her face that at the moment, was showing keen and sensitive interest in what he had to say. "I...um, I don't ask you to accept it just hear it. Okay?"

Now she looked perplexed. "Of course, Colonel."

He nodded. His hair had grown since he'd cut the bulk of it and now it flopped over his eyes like a sable brush. His bicep flexed against his shirt when he absently pushed his hair back with strong square fingers, he scratched the stubble on his face.

Taking a deep breath, exhaling slowly, he said, "I wanted to apologize for what I did the other night, to you. It was despicable. I behaved no better than a rabid dog. I was just as bad as those other two pigs that hassled you."

The coal eyes shifted over her, shame flickered through them. "I don't know what came over me, it was abusive, something I'd brutalize another for doing to you...uh, to any woman. It's even a thousand times worse to do it to an innocent, inexperienced...woman. And someone I genuinely care for."

Sounding softly forgiving, keeping her tone light, she replied, "Really? It was a kiss. You stopped before..." Her mouth pursed irately, she said, "Why do you keep talking about my...lack of experience? I've said before, you don't know me, you know nothing about me. I could have slept with a hundred men for all you know." She turned away; the blush tinting her cheeks negated what she said.

He twined his fingers together, bent and rested his elbows on his thighs, his shoulders hunched; he bowed his head, then raised it. "It was a kiss, and," he coughed then swallowed, recalling her ripped blouse and what he was thinking and feeling when he had started coming to his senses with his hands about to shred her jeans.

Looking at her under him with her wrists pinned helplessly over her head, looking so damned hot, and feeling her curvy body against his masculine planes, and what he had been about to do. Even as appalled as he was over his behavior, it still took everything he had to get off her and move away.

He said, "It was, uh a bit more," he could feel his neck burn again, "and it was against your will. That's never all right. Uh, and I treated you with anger, Tirsa," his expression sad and regretful. "I hate myself for speaking and acting so brutally to you like I did. I was, well, seeing Stav and you," he cleared his throat, "Knox told me it was all harmless, but that doesn't matter. I have no right to tell you who you can be with."

She sat silently, her face growing pinker as she stared at the floor. She had never even been alone in a room with a man before coming on this voyage, that was unsettling at best, and after what he did to her, and now he was *talking* about it- her skin heated in embarrassment.

Then he said matter-of-factly, "Regarding your...experience..." he settled back against the cushions with his feet flat on the floor, his knees spread like men sit, and set his hands on his thighs. "After we figured out you'd, well, duped us, came here under false pretenses and forged paperwork, Jancarlo had people investigate you more thoroughly. We know you were brought up in tight seclusion. Even when you came to the states you were home schooled, never let out alone."

The corner of her mouth pulled in ruefully, she said, "Yeah. Just like here."

He looked at her silently for a moment. Feeling guilty he said, "I want to say I'm sorry about that, Tirsa, but I can't. You brought it on yourself by your actions that first night. I have the duty to protect others from you." She looked so ashamed and sad he conceded, "Listen, Tirsa, I know it's not in your heart to kill, me or anyone else."

He chuckled, a dimple pulled in one rugged cheek. "I've seen you catch a lizard in a cup and set it free outside while Lindsey was screaming for someone to smash it." The dimple vanished, voice sobering, he said, "Nevertheless, I have to go by what is fact until I know differently, until I'm told differently." He waited for her to respond but she didn't.

Sighing his frustration, he said, "I've also had to keep you under lock and key to protect you. Someone is after you, besides the rest of us damned horndogs," he weakly half-grinned embarrassed at his own assault on her.

He turned serious again, "Until I get to the bottom of all this, murder stuff, I need to protect you from whoever sent you. They're going to come after you, believe me, whether or not you complete what they sent you here to do. We took out Adullam, so he is no longer a threat. You see, I swear on my honor, on my life, I can help you."

He bent closer towards her, displaying his steadfast sincerity, pleading with her to believe him, trust him, tell him.

The look on her face told him she fully realized that it was probable that whoever had coerced her into attempting to murder him would kill her either way. She knew who sent her and they would eliminate their witness and their tool.

Still, what they held over her head, her chest rose with a deep breath then lowered as it shuddered out. She said nothing.

"Tirsa," he murmured, setting his hand on her leg, they both looked down at it. "Going after these kinds of criminals, it's what I do. I'm a cop. I can help you. Please let me."

She stared at the large calloused hand on her leg. The warmth of it spread over her entire leg. "Help me or arrest me?" She angled her head towards him; the light from the window lit the soft features of the heart shaped face.

"Tirsa," he muttered, his voice rough, a wince creased his hard face.

She started, "The other night," pique blistered when she remembered what he'd said to her. With bitterness spiking through her hurt, she said, "When you were throwing me about and forcing yourself on me, you said you regretted wanting to help me."

"God, Tirsa," his voice coarse with guilt, he looked down at his calloused hand on her leg then up to the accusing blue eyes doused in pain. "I- I can't take back what I said and did. It's absolutely no excuse, but I was trashed, uh, drunk, I...I guess it just made me act more, ah, I was hurt," his lips pulled in, he sighed them out.

"I had thought you had played me for a fool, that you weren't really the sweet person I'd taken you for," he shook his head glumly. "Never mind. It was wrong of me to treat you, or anyone, that way regardless of whether it was true or not."

His gaze pierced hers, holding it, his tone somber, he said, "I regret that I behaved like an abusive monster." Etam picked up her hand, held it lightly, "I'm sorry, Tirsa, I'm so sorry for how I acted and what I said."

Lifting her hand to his mouth, he kissed it. "I am not asking for you to forgive me. I just wanted to say I was truly sorry. Not that it negates what I said that night, when I sobered up I realized I would still want to help you, even if you," he looked away then back at her, "weren't the person you portrayed yourself as. I would want to help anyone in your situation."

He lightly touched her chin with a knuckle, a serious glint pricked his dark orbs. "Tirsa, I meant what I said about helping you. I want to help you, I want it almost," his attention wandered down her body then back up to her baby blues, "more than anything."

Her thoughts were easily read on her pure expressive face as she listened to him. She was hurt. But then she looked down so he couldn't see what she was thinking and feeling now. Her head still down, she asked, "Tell me, Colonel, why did you stop the other night when you were…what made you stop?"

Taken aback at having to picture his humiliating behavior; lying on top of her, forcing her hands over her head as he tore at her clothes, violently kissing her when he didn't have his hand over her mouth smothering her screams.

Ahh, he sat back, interlocked his fingers and set them in his lap. Instead of answering her question, his brows drew down, he said, "Before…before, you were calling me by my given name, now you have reverted back to Colonel."

She glanced at him flustered, she wouldn't have thought he'd noticed, or cared if he had. "I um, that's what the others call you."

"Hmmm." He put his hands behind his head, his face inscrutable, he regarded her thoughtfully. Dropping his hands, he clasped them in his lap, shoulders slightly hunched. His head lowered, he peered up at her through a lock of black hair that had flopped over, and said in a low voice, "I'd like you to call me Etam. Okay?"

Thrown off by his request, she studied him. His expression was unreadable as usual, it seemed to be a training of some sort because Jancarlo and Knox also were hard to read, they were profoundly stoic. Johnson too, but he let his true cheerfulness and sense of humor show through often, and Knox was softening.

Yet they would all win at poker, and in the type of business, the life they led, the coldness gave them a lethal edginess. Etam seemed even more dangerous today, muscles tight with dynamism, dark stubble covering his hard jaw, hair tousled from the wind, and those unfathomable black eyes trained on her.

He waited, watching the thoughts flit over her face. When she didn't respond, he prompted quietly, "Tirsa?"

"Of...course, Etam," she uttered, confused.

"*Dank u.*" With a short smile, he nodded once.

Remembering her question he hadn't answered, she asked again, "Col...um...Etam," now she was ruffled, it was easier to keep him at arm's length in her mind by calling him Colonel. Saying his first name made it feel more...intimate.

Her eyes lowered to his partially unbuttoned shirt, to the tanned skin and masculine dark hair matting the powerful chest, she forced them back up to his face. "So...I asked you what stopped you...you know...the other night?"

His answer was quick, "I could taste your tears." His body moved of its own volition closer to her, curving towards her again. Laying his right arm behind her across the back of the couch, he leaned in, the long fingers of his left hand slid around her jaw then to the back of her neck. Lowering his head to hers, his gaze dropped to her mouth, his voice husky, he said, "I could taste your tears when I was...kissing you."

Unaware she was mirroring him, her head raised, she saw him staring at her lips, he was moving closer to them, then their eyes locked. Cradling the back of her head, Etam pulled her closer, she didn't resist, her lips parted, their eyes closed...

The door opened. They both froze. Keeping his arm around Tirsa's back, Etam dropped the hand that was holding her head. They both sat back against the couch.

Jancarlo stood in the doorway.

Frowning, his voice gruff not hiding his irritation, Etam asked impatiently, "What is it, Jan?"

Although he had to have seen them so close, taking in the colonel's messed hair, and her pink cheeks, as impassive as ever, the major said, "We need to get moving. I am getting the group ready to go." He stood there motionless, his face a harsh rock. He wasn't leaving until either Etam or Tirsa did.

Tirsa stood up. Knox came in at that moment.

"Knox." Tirsa smiled genially at him and asked, "Could you take me to my room?" She swiveled to see if that met with Etam's approval. He didn't look happy. "Is that all right, Colonel?"

He scowled. "*Ja*, sure, remember, Etam."

She left with Knox. Etam glared at Jancarlo. "You have great timing, *mijn broeder*."

"My brother," Jancarlo repeated Etam's words in English, "you are playing with fire." He said dryly sarcastic, "Giving up on the rape and going for the smoother seduction this time?" He kept talking when Etam opened his mouth, "I guarantee, E, I have this feeling in the pit of my stomach that you are going to get hurt because of her. You need to leave her here. She can stay with Seymour."

"You have ice water in your veins, Jan."

Jancarlo set his hands on his hips. "Maybe. However, surely you forget some of our, experiences together." The corner of his mouth twitched, "If you recall, we almost came to blows over that Peruvian *hoer-*"

Etam grinned, his head bobbing. "*Ja*, the one with the unreal huge *boezem*, uh, we'd been on a bender that whole weekend celebrating the arrest of that cartel, not only making and selling drugs they were terrorizing that poor little town. We ended up sharing her after all, and a couple of others." He narrowed his eyes at his friend. "It's a good thing you don't see Tirsa's attraction."

"I am not immune to her, E. I am very aware of how hot she is; no doubt she is easy on the eyes. You know damned well that I am as red-blooded as you, but, she is, different.

There is trouble attached to her, besides the insane draw she has for you, which I have never seen you like this before, there is that supernatural crap." He shivered. "It is freaky. To be able to change Knox like she has, he has changed like day and night. She is a witch casting spells on all of you males."

"Huh. This coming from someone who just said he had a feeling in the pit of his stomach, a premonition of sorts." Etam smirked. "Besides, Knox has changed for the better, more like night to day."

Etam got to his feet. He plucked his wallet and phone off the desk and slipped them in his pocket. "Jan, she's not trouble, she's in trouble and I will find out how and who and end it."

"*Ja*, let us hope she is not the end to you."

Chapter Twenty-Six

*E*tam told Raine, Max and Ji to stay at Copestone with Cook. The rest of them got their gear together, packed the burros and headed back out to find the black glass. Although the leersia grasses of the savanna were tall and wading through wasn't all that easy, when they tromped through swamps they wished for the open grass again.

"Everyone, stay in formation, follow the person's footprints in front of you," Etam instructed.

Jancarlo led the way, sometimes he struck with a machete to clear a path, fortunately most of the swamp was cleared, just mucky mud. There was a persistent sound of squish-squish and pluck-pluck as their boots sunk in then plucked back out.

They had all sprayed down heavily with bug spray to keep the mosquitoes at bay, and wore hats to ward off the sun. There wasn't a heavy canopy of trees in the swamp; the bright sun seared through sago palms and carallia trees like a carving knife.

Shortly after they entered the swamp, Lindsey jumped at a rustling in the bushes, then screeched when a bird ran out in front of her- it disappeared in the brush bordering the swamp.

"Just a red-billed brush-turkey," Johnson informed her. "If you'd been quicker we could have had a Thanksgiving dinner."

Lindsey shot him the bird.

He laughed, tilting his head the gold earring glinted in the sunlight, he scratched the top of his shaved noggin and said with a grin, "Well *that* bird we can't eat."

It took almost two days before they found the furthest they had traced the black ice the first time they searched. This time Etam had Stav record everything, the sun, the trees, stumps, rocks, the trail, the direction, to ensure they didn't circle back again.

They followed the black ice for another day. It grew dark, they made camp. As before, Etam had Tirsa stay in his tent with him, but he made sure she was sound asleep before he ventured in. All of the men rotated guard duty.

The next morning the dawn broke so red the sky was bleeding. "Crap," Johnson muttered. "Red in the morning, sailor take warning. It's going to be a rough one."

"What do you mean?" Lil Dam came up beside him, watching the sky brighten as the sun rose. Through a patch of trees they could see a black wall of tumbling clouds moving at a steady speed right towards them.

"Rain, hard rain coming," Johnson answered and jogged off to find Etam.

The colonel was sitting on a stump drinking a cup of coffee with Jancarlo.

"E," Johnson said, puffing, "big rain coming. Big."

Etam took one look at Johnson's face then up to the sky and stood up. Pouring his coffee out on the ground he said, "Let's go."

Jancarlo got up and cupped his hands around his mouth and shouted, "Pack up everyone, right now. You have five minutes or we leave without you." He took off to help Knox with the tents and supplies. Without Cook they had eaten dried food. Johnson walked over and kicked dirt on the small fire that had remained, putting it out.

Jancarlo went up to Etam who was tying stuff on the burros. "I saw a cave while on guard last night. I think we should make for it."

"*Ja,* okay," Etam agreed. "You lead the way, quickly." He glanced up at the darkening sky, it was coming black and furious, he could see streaks of lightening flash, white forks slashing against the dark storm clouds.

They made it to the cave as the first golf ball sized raindrops hit.

Johnson hurried in first to make sure they weren't looking to share space with an animal or two. The group was getting pelted with rain when he made the all-clear call. They rushed in, even bringing the burros in last. It was going to be a wicked storm, no place for man or beast to be.

The cave entrance was high enough that the women, and Bruno and Lil Dam could walk in without bending over, the other men had to watch their heads. They cautiously walked around checking out their temporary hotel.

Large boulders left by ancient landslides scattered on the dirt floor. Johnson and Knox surreptitiously scouted the area, brushing their boots across the ground to run off any scorpions, millipedes or snakes that might have also taken haven from the storm.

It was cold, damp and dark inside the natural fortress. Jancarlo worked to make a fire near the entrance. He searched around for something to block the fierce wind and rain that tunneled in.

"I'm freezing," Lindsey whined.

"Here." Owen untied his jacket off one of the burros and covered her with it.

Johnson informed them, "The burros will help keep us warm. That and the fire. If and when it gets going." He waited for Jancarlo to react to his taunt.

Jancarlo used some stones and sticks he found inside to hold up a blanket to block the wind. The dark, stoic man retorted to Johnson, "You could help, *eikel*, gather some twigs or branches that might be in here instead of standing there mocking the hard working." He turned back to tend to his fire.

"Language, guys," Etam murmured.

Grinning, Johnson said, "They don't know he called me a dickhead," he traipsed around with some of the others to scout around looking for any kind of wood to help keep the fire going.

"What did he say?" Bruno asked.

Etam playfully punched him in the arm. "Nothing. You've already picked up enough Dutch bad words from us."

Jancarlo got a good fire going and set it up so the smoke went out of the cave instead of in to suffocate them. Most of the group sat on blankets and rocks huddled close to the fire. The rain was so loud and dense it was like a door closed over the mouth of the cave. There was nothing to do but sit around talking and playing cards that Owen had thoughtfully brought along.

Tirsa wandered as far back in the cave as she could go which was about fifty feet. She came out holding the bottom of her shirt up carrying something. "Hey," she said to no one in particular, "look what I found." She knelt and carefully shook out the items onto the ground.

Bruno came over to look. "Shells," he noted in disinterest.

"Yes," Tirsa said, "but we're a distance from the ocean, how did they get here?"

Johnson came over to inspect them. He knelt beside her and picked up one, studied it, then smiled. "These are kina shells. The natives used to use these for barter. Now they make necklaces and stuff out of them. See this one," he held his hand out to show her, "this is a golden pearl lip shell, and this one," he set the white one down and picked up a reddish one.

"This one was rubbed with red ochre to color it. They all have holes in them. People probably came in here like we did to get out of the rain or sleep for the night and left them."

Lindsey strolled over and looked down at the small pile of shells. She snarked, "Really? Shells?" She sniffed and walked away, "Call me when you find something important like gold or diamonds."

Tirsa held several shells in her palm. She closed her hand, wordlessly watching Lindsey under a fringe of lowered lashes.

"Don't you pay any attention to her, honey, you are blessed that you can see and enjoy beauty in nature's simplest things." Johnson dropped an arm around her shoulders giving them a squeeze. Out of the corner of his eye he saw Etam who was standing by the opening with Jancarlo frown at him. Johnson stuck his tongue out at his colonel and hugged Tirsa harder.

The group grew bored quickly with little to do. Eating dried food that they couldn't rehydrate due to lack of extra water for lunch and dinner, they stretched out on blankets on the cold, hard ground, going to sleep early out of sheer boredom, listening to the rain pummel the cave sounding like machine gun rapid firing on the rocks.

Lying on his blanket with Tirsa between him and Jancarlo, Etam stared at the ceiling. He could see black things flying around in the darkness, some individually, some in clusters. He hoped everyone would stay asleep; he didn't need hysterical people screaming and running from the sight of bats sharing the limestone cave. He wasn't too concerned about the New Guinea giant rats coming inside; the fire should keep them away.

The rain stopped in the middle of the night. By morning, the sun rose like a burgeoning bonfire.

"It's beautiful," Tirsa remarked in awe after Jancarlo took down the blanket. A shaft of sunlight streamed down lighting raindrops that still clung to leaves. Glimmering in each drop were shades of brilliant greens, reflections of the lush forest.

As she stepped outside, a streak of light shone on her hair making it look like a golden halo circled her head. Eager to see their surroundings, she skipped around the clearing in front of the cave. The group packed up the few things they'd used and emerged like bears after a long winter's eve.

"Tirsa," Etam called as he came out. She pirouetted to face him looking like a child allowed out to play.

He forced himself to sound stern, "Please wait for us. Come back over here." It was hard to disregard her crestfallen face, or the way she reluctantly retraced her steps back to the cave. He explained, "Early in the morning is when a lot of the animals come out to feed, and reptiles, mambas, vipers, cobras will like this strong sunlight to bask in."

"All right." Tirsa suddenly pointed, pretending to duck, "Look out for that killer parrot! A flying mamba will be right behind it!" A parrot painted like pageantry flew across the clearing and into the trees.

The side of Etam's mouth curled up. "Funny, you're too funny. Actually we were lucky to have seen that, they're quite rare." They stood for a moment to see if it would return. It didn't, so they joined the others to head back to the last sighting of the black glass before the rain had struck.

As they walked, Bruno rapped, "The moist land from the rain's hard splash, smells clean like freshly mown grass, all pretty and green like newly minted cash." Playing air drums, he said to Lil Dam, "Bro, I think I'm poetic. We can make a song about it." The two had their heads together making up tunes and words to his rain poem.

The troop quickly found the length of black ice they had trailed yesterday. Etam said, "Okay, let's-"

Jancarlo cut Etam off, "E, look," he gestured to a clutch of boulders tucked between a stock of trees next to the cave and high scrub. So high it about hid the boulders.

"Oh, how exciting, rocks," Lindsey's sarcastic mutter was heavy with boredom.

Etam and Jancarlo long-legged it to the formation.

"What is it?" Tirsa asked Knox as they followed the men. Knox's answer held a hint of excitement, "They're what we've been looking for, they're the next on the map as a clue, a landmark."

Johnson caught up with them. He added to Knox's information, "They're megaliths. Stone tables. Large flat stones placed on top of smaller ones. It looks like there are stone rings, tsigoro, standing stones too."

Everyone gathered near the boulders. Etam and his team walked around the stone tables, examining them. Johnson took pictures of them. Johnson said to Tirsa who came up and joined them in their study of the stones, "It's possible that these monuments were created around 1000 AD. They are our next arrow."

She covered her mouth with a hand in amazement. "Are you kidding?"

Shaking his head, Johnson took more pictures. He took one with her standing in front of a table. "*Neen*. Serious as a heart attack. They were described in the colonel's book. We were going to start searching for them when eagle-eye Jan spotted them." He knew Jancarlo could hear him but the stoic man would ignore his compliment.

Lindsey took the opportunity to walk off to find a place to relieve herself. Normally, Etam's rule was that the girls went together with a male standing guard nearby, but she went off by herself.

Carrying her own package of biodegradable, coreless roll of toilet paper, she climbed through a web of vines and clomped through scratchy brush heading for a covey of wide trees to squat behind. When she was done, she climbed out of the mass of thatched bushes and grass and headed back to the stones. She was about twenty feet away when she heard a ghastly sound.

A grunt, then a blowing noise that turned into a roar. Her body rigid with dreaded fear, Lindsey turned and screamed. She'd startled a wild boar with husks a foot long and sharp as sabers. He went on the attack instantly charging at her-

Etam and Jancarlo raced over with knives drawn, both vaulted in the air and torpedoed the animal with their bodies knocking it on its side then they stabbed and stabbed the creature. It squealed and roared, kicked and tried to bite them and gore them with its tusks.

Stav, Bruno and Lil Dam were right behind Knox and Johnson; they all jumped on the beast like tackling a running

back on a football field stabbing it until it stopped howling and squealing.

Lindsey ran screeching to Owen and flung herself into his arms.

Once the creature ceased moving, Etam got up and brushed the dirt off his khakis. He stomped over to Lindsey who was still in Owen's embrace.

"Lindsey," he snapped, waiting until she wiped her eyes on Owen's shirt and turned around.

Her chin in the air, she said a haughty, "What?" Her face was like bubblegum, pink and swollen, the freckles spread fatter, hazel eyes globbed with tears.

Etam glared hard at her until she lowered her eyes in fright. "Don't stray alone from the group again," he commanded, barely suppressing his fury. He turned on his heel and went back to the dead boar.

Owen mumbled low enough so the colonel couldn't hear, "At least we'll have meat for dinner. Thanks to you, Linds."

The men butchered the boar, took what they could cook and eat and buried the rest to have the other animals take some time before they came after it. Enough time for the group to be on their way.

After they were getting ready to move again, Tirsa went over to Etam and asked, "Colonel, what's the significance of the stones to our expedition?"

Sitting on a boulder, he had his book in his hand and was looking from the book to the stones to the book. He was taken aback somewhat; she seldom came to him of her own volition.

Using his finger as a bookmark he said, "There's a design to the formation of the tables. It points in a direction. We need to follow it exactly forty miles due west. There it will point out the next landmark." Remembering the interest she exhibited when they were in his study and she had been reviewing the book, he said, "Tirsa, you were telling me before that when you were looking at the book you had a...feeling?"

"Yes." She sat down beside him. It was a few degrees cooler since the hard rain, and the wind had picked up. She fought at the locks the wind pushed in her face. "I can't explain it." She shook her head, mumbled, "Never mind."

Etam drew his feet up on the rock, crossed them and perused her. Still fighting her flying hair, her face was lightly radiating that ethereal glow he'd seen before.

He reached to her and brushed the tendrils back. She didn't shy away from his touch. He slid his hand around the side of her face, his thumb along her cheek. Cradling her head, he bent over and gently kissed her.

For a second she resisted, then her lips pulsed against his before she pulled back. He lowered his hands setting them on his legs and cocked his head slightly to look at her. Her face a blank, her attention seemed to be on his boots.

His deep voice low, he said quietly, "We decided that you would call me Etam, do you remember that?"

She didn't look at him but she could hear the slight smile in his voice. "Yes."

"E, daylight's burning," Knox called over.

Etam slid off the boulder, took Tirsa's hand helping her down and they strode back over to join the group.

Loading the burros and using a compass heading due west, they marched close to ten miles a day for more than four days. After a few hours, exhausted, Lindsey cried that she needed to rest. A long rest.

She plopped down on her rolled sleeping bag and took off her boots. "Gawd, look at my poor feet, my blisters have blisters. I need a pedi so bad."

Owen sat next to her. He said, "It's because you didn't have a chance to break in those boots."

Knox went over to them and knelt down, sitting back on his heels. He set his medic case on the ground and opened the lid. He told her, "Take off your socks, honey."

She slowly, painfully pulled her socks off. Her feet were red and blistered. Knox dabbed alcohol on the blisters, she shrieked, he dabbed more she shrieked more. He gingerly rubbed on an antibiotic ointment then bandaged the blisters.

When he was done he trod over to where Etam, Johnson and Jancarlo were talking. Jancarlo was smoking one of his skinny cigars.

Knox said when he reached them, "We need to take a day or so to rest. The redhead's feet are chock full of blisters. Tirsa's struggling to hold up, but she looks done in too, and even the guys look tired."

Etam nodded. "All right. We've been going for over four days." He pulled a map out of his back pocket and unfolded part of it. "Let's set up camp here. It's a nice clearing and there's a small stream to the north where we can get some water."

They set up their tents, took the burros to the stream to drink and refilled their supplies. They stayed the entire next day.

The following day Knox showed Etam Lindsey's sore feet.

Lindsey pouted in what she thought was a pretty way and whined, "Colonel, look at my poor feet. I think if we keep going, *someone* is going to have to carry me."

Standing beside Knox, his hands in his pockets, Etam shrugged without empathy. The two men stood dispassionately looking down at her.

One of her shoulders turned in, she inclined her head like a coy pixie. "Although you're all close, you look the strongest, Colonel, of all the men, so I think you-"

"Well," Etam interrupted her, "as it turns out, we've scouted around and found the next landmark. There's only one more and it should be right were the book is hidden. So I think after another night of rest you'll be ready to get up and at 'em. What do you think?"

Knox could hear the scorn in Etam's voice but judging by the way she stared at Etam with such lasciviousness he was sure Lindsey was deaf to it.

Her red brows rippled in annoyance. "Don't you see, Colonel that you should carry-"

He turned his back to her and said, "All right then, let's get some dinner going and then bright and early we're on the trail. You coming, Major? "

His face a perfect mask to keep from grinning, Knox was right with him as they stalked away from the fuming young woman whose face was turning as red as her hair.

When they got out of her sight they broke out laughing. "What a ridiculous female. I've never seen the like before," Etam said with light rancor.

Knox agreed, "And hope never to again when this thing is over. At least we're making headway and not just getting started."

Heading back towards the camp, Etam muttered, "Thank the stars."

Just as dawn was breaking, a noisy rustling in the bushes woke the group. Sleepy-eyed they all got up curious to see what was causing the commotion.

"Oh dear!" Tirsa cried out in pained compassion. Not too far away, just across the clearing inside a clump of trees, a rabbit looked like it was caught on something. It was frantically kicking and jerking to break free. Tirsa broke into a sprint running to the rabbit.

"No! Tirsa, stop!" Etam shouted.

She kept going, he ran after her yelling, "Stop Tirsa, stop! It could be a-" but she kept going, now almost to the rabbit.

Just as she reached it, Etam saw the string her knee hit, "Fuck-" he leaped in the air to tackle her, using his body to block her from the arrow that shot out of the tree, and went right into his back. He knocked her down landing on top of her. As soon as he landed he collapsed, unconscious.

She tried to squirm out from under him realizing right away something was wrong. "Etam? Etam, are you okay?" Wriggling out, she rolled to her knees and put her hand on his shoulder to push him so she could see his face. His eyes were closed. "Etam," her voice tight, her heart leaped in her throat.

"*Neen*, do not touch him you bitch," Jancarlo snarled. Dropping to his knees, he shoved her away. He cradled Etam's head, and yelled over his shoulder, "Knox, quick!"

Knox was already on his way with Johnson at his heels.

Tirsa climbed up on her shaking legs not understanding what had happened.

Jancarlo jumped up, face a mask of harsh wrath he raged at her, "If he dies you *moordenares* I will fucking kill you, do you hear me, I will kill you!" He went to grab her, Knox and Johnson each tackled an arm to hold him back.

Jancarlo's face was red and twisted in a hateful grimace, he clawed at her trying to reach her, it was all the majors could do to hold him away from her.

Gripping one of his arms, Knox said quietly, "You're not letting me help him, Jan, get it under control."

Still glaring hatred at Tirsa, Jancarlo shook the two men off. "I am *goed,* okay. Go, Knox." He knelt back down on the ground next to Etam and rolled him over gently. An arrow protruded from his upper back. Tirsa gasped.

Knox said to Jancarlo and Johnson, "Help me get him back to the tent."

Stav and Lil Dam came running over. All together, the men picked Etam up and carried him to his tent and laid him on his sleeping bag. Stav and Lil Dam came right out; it was too small for everyone to fit inside the tent.

Bruno, Lindsey and Owen hurried over. Lindsey shouted, "What happened?" No one answered her.

Knox shooed everyone out so he could see better.

Tirsa stood a few feet near the open flap of the tent wringing her hands. Jancarlo bent to come out of the tent, saw her and stalked straight to her. Though he looked like a building about to explode she didn't back away.

Jancarlo jabbed a finger at her and accused harshly, "This is your fault, *blondine,* you are nothing but a *bloedig* piece of *schijt hoer,* scum, you-"

Understanding the word whore, her ire and tension expanding in her chest, Tirsa hauled her hand back and slapped him across the face.

A pin dropped could be heard from the group that circled the pair. Tirsa figured she was dead meat now, even with Johnson hovering he wouldn't be enough to stop Jancarlo from beating her to death, but she stood her ground.

Surprisingly, Jancarlo didn't move, his hands stayed at his side, his face an unreadable stone. Then he said very quietly, "*Blondine,* this is your chance. To get away. It is what you have wanted. Stav and Johnson will take you back to Copestone; we will call for a chopper to take you back to Australia. The best thing you can do for the colonel now is go, go now. You do not give a *bloedig schijt* about him, you *moordenares*- murderess-"

Tirsa's hand flew at him, to slap him again- his hand shot out like a bolt of lightning snaring her wrist. He held it taut, eyes like iced obsidian marbles, he ground out, "I gave you the first one, *blondine*, because I deserved it. It is all you will get. Now go pack your *schijt* -"

She yanked her hand from his grasp and walked swiftly away.

"*Goed.*" Jancarlo muttered, then his brows rose in question as she ran into Knox's tent. "What the fu-"

She came back out carrying Knox's medical bag and hurried back to Etam's tent. Jancarlo stepped in front of the opening blocking her. "You are not going in there, *blondine*, you will never go near him again,"

Standing firm, ice clinging to her words, Tirsa said, "Get out of my way, *mijn luttel hart*,"

Jancarlo looked like he'd been struck with a two-by-four. He froze, his face turned to sheet metal. His skin whitened, eyes a tumult of disbelief, his mouth dropped open dumbfounded. He stood staring at her in a stupefied daze.

Tirsa looked him in the eye then pushed past him. Inside the tent she went over to Knox and set his medic bag down then knelt on the other side of Etam. "Knox," her voice trembling, her hands on her thighs, "how is…"

"Help me remove his shirt," Knox muttered, his arm under Etam's shoulder he lifted his back off the ground. Tirsa scurried over to help him take off Etam's shirt. There was a little blood on it but not a ton. Tirsa's stomach quelled when she saw the arrow in the top right of his back, just below his shoulder. She wanted to ask, but didn't want to distract Knox from his examination.

"Open my box, and give me the pliers and the swabs and the alcohol."

She obeyed quickly.

"Hold him for me," Knox instructed. Holding the pliers, he grasped the arrow with them. Tirsa let Etam's chest lay across her, she struggled to hold him up.

Sounding fearful, and like the professional medic he was, Knox told her, "I'm going to lay him on his stomach." Together they laid Etam down.

"Now, I know this is hard, honey," Knox said gently, "I'm going to pour alcohol on a swab and give it to you. As soon as I pull the arrow out I need you to cover the wound with the swab." He didn't ask her if she could do it, just knew she would.

Tirsa took the swab, trying to hold her hands steady. Using the pliers, Knox pulled the arrow out smoothly and set it on a towel and Tirsa immediately set the swab on the wound. Etam moaned. Tirsa's throat caught, she choked back tears.

Knox picked up the alcohol and another towel. "I want you to let go and I'm going to pour the alcohol all over it. Okay now." Tirsa pulled her hand away and Knox poured the alcohol over the wound. Etam moaned again.

"Don't worry, honey," Knox said reassuring her, "he really isn't feeling all of it, he's pretty much unconscious." After cleaning the wound, Knox added an antibiotic and put gauze over it taping it down.

Sitting on the ground, he crossed his legs and picked up the arrow. He studied it then sniffed it. Concern pushed aside the reassurance, worry furrowed his brow.

"What is it, Knox?" Tirsa couldn't keep her own concern out of her voice. She watched his eyes flit back and forth as he was thinking, researching in his mind.

He got to his feet and went to his bag and rustled around in it. Staying out of his way, Tirsa pulled a blanket over Etam, covering to his neck. Then she set a hand on his arm over the blanket to give him comfort, and she wanted to feel his warmth to ease her fears that he was dying.

Knox pulled out a vial and a syringe. He stuck the syringe in the vial letting it suck up the liquid, then spritzed it. He dropped to his knees then crawled over to Etam. Lifting up a corner of the blanket, he swabbed a spot with alcohol then plunged the syringe in Etam's arm. He put the syringe in a case to dispose of later and the vial back in his bag then sat back on the ground crossing his legs.

He looked at Etam but said to Tirsa, "The arrow wouldn't have killed him," he took a deep breath, let it out, "but there was poison on the tip."

Tirsa's hands flew to her mouth. Covering her face, she peered at Knox through her fingers. Fearfully she stuttered, "What...what...will he..." She couldn't form the words.

Knox looked as worried as she'd ever seen him. He shook his head slowly. "I don't know. I have no way of knowing what kind of poison was used."

"Knox." Jancarlo stuck his head in. His glance rolled over Tirsa then to Knox. "How is he?" He stooped then stepped inside. From the look on Knox's face, distress rocked Jancarlo's impassive mien. "What is it?" he asked, his voice strong but coarse with heavy dread.

Knox stood up, his expression bleak. "I...it's poison, Jan. I don't know what kind." He hesitated as he saw the major's alarmed reaction.

Jungle Treasure

Knox's head moved painstakingly slowly side to side. "I don't know, Jan, I don't know if he'll pull out of this one."

Chapter Twenty-Seven

*N*ever seeing his compatriot this bleakly disturbed, lacking of hope, shook the rock solid Jancarlo. He put his hands on his hips and said resolutely, "So, what do we do?" He was a man of action. His motto was; if you keep going, work at it, put one foot in front of the other, you will prevail.

Knox watched Tirsa. She laid her hand on the side of Etam's face, brushed back his hair and then left her hand there. She looked up at Knox waiting for his answer.

"I honestly don't know, Jan. I don't think we should try to get him back home. It'll move the poison more quickly through his body. We can only wait, time will tell. Let's try to flush him with water."

Jancarlo didn't say anything, just ran out. He returned in moments with a canteen. He dropped down beside his prone friend. He said to Knox, "The boys are getting more water, they will add the iodine tablets immediately. We will use the stored water the iodine has been sitting in. There will not be time to let the tablets act for 30 minutes but it will be better than nothing. Do it."

To Tirsa, Knox said gently, "You'll only be in the way, you can't help right now." She understood and quietly left the tent.

As soon as she went outside Lindsey and Owen asked her, "What's going on? What happened? How is he?" They questioned her, their words tumbling over each other. She told them about the poisoned arrow and what Knox said. The three stood in shocked silence.

Stav was the first to run up with a full bucket of water, he went straight to the tent and took it inside. Lil Dam was next, he handed his bucket to Stav, then as Lil Dam took off for more, Johnson and Bruno hurried up with buckets. Like a revolving belt they kept going.

Since there were no more containers to utilize, the girls and Owen went over and sat on some rocks to wait. The girls were told they would only get in the way if they tried to help, apparently Owen considered himself one of the girls.

An hour later, after they moved Etam and the tent from the wet ground, Jancarlo emerged from the tent, his face drained of color, eyes and mouth drawn. He walked over to Tirsa. On alert for an attack or worse, bad news about Etam, Tirsa straightened her spine.

He stopped a foot in front of her. In a voice as stony and cold as usual, he said, "Knox says to come." As soon as he spoke he turned on his heel and strode away presumably to have a smoke.

Jancarlo and Knox had argued about her. Jancarlo didn't want her within a mile of Etam. He wanted to pitch her over a cliff. Knox said he knew without a shadow of a doubt that Tirsa would not harm Etam, regardless of her initial actions and secret mission. He convinced Jancarlo that she would be the best person to help, besides there wasn't room in the tent for three big men counting Etam.

275

Realizing he was fighting a losing battle, Jancarlo had said, "Fine. But she is not to be alone with him. Ever." And he stalked off.

Johnson found him over by the stream smoking one of his European cigars staring off over the shimmering water. "Hey," Johnson said wearily as he approached. Jancarlo gave him a bare, narrow-eyed glance then stared back at the water.

Coming to stand beside the major, his normal cheerful manner flattened, Johnson said hopefully, "I think he'll be okay. He's strong as a bull, Jan, you know that."

Jancarlo jerked a shoulder up and down.

"We care as much as you do, Jan. You've been with him longer, a lot of time it's been just you and him on missions, but we're all *broeders*, brothers."

Silently, Jancarlo gave a short nod.

His hands in his pockets, looking out over the water too, Johnson waited a few moments before he asked, "What did she say to you?" He didn't have to explain what he meant. He knew even at this moment Jancarlo was pondering the Dutch words Tirsa had said to him that had Jancarlo looking like he was struck dumb with shock. An entirely alien expression for the harsh major.

Even now, his face had returned to its normal stoniness, but his reeling eyes were confounded, spooked. Still watching the water, Jancarlo said unemotionally yet with an uneven tone, "She said, *mijn luttel hart.*"

Johnson interpreted, "My little heart." He caught the swift reaction Jancarlo quickly hid. "What does that mean to you?"

Jancarlo hunched his shoulders, shoved his hands in his pockets. The breeze ruffled the top layer of the stream, and a few of the very short hairs on his head. "It is what my *Oma* used to call me."

"Your grandmother?"

"*Ja.* She died when I was 15." His face a steely blank, the timbre of his tone aggrieved, he said, "She always whispered it to me with a kiss on my head as I went to sleep."

Johnson didn't make any comment. He knew what Jancarlo was experiencing. There was no way on the earth Tirsa could have possibly known that.

Tirsa stayed with the unconscious Etam all day and slept beside him at night, as he fitfully shook, sweated, moaned. She wiped his brow with dry towels that the others laid out in the sun and brought to the tent. She only left to bath and relieve herself. Knox said at this point there was nothing they could do but wait and see.

For three days Johnson, Knox and Jancarlo took turns staying with her. She helped Knox clean and change Etam's wound. Knox and Johnson spoke quietly with her while they kept watch; Jancarlo said not a word to her. Just sat stoically staring at his friend as Etam writhed and tossed in his coma.

The fourth day, Johnson had just stepped outside the tent. Tirsa was still asleep lying on her side facing Etam, her hand on his arm, when something woke her. She slowly opened her eyes. Etam was looking at her, his dark eyes clear and glowing. A tender smile curved his lips, he murmured, "Tirsa, *liefje.*"

Tirsa propped herself up on one elbow, smiled tiredly, happy to see him alert, she said with joy, "Oh Etam, you're awake! How do you feel?"

Rolling over on his back, he winced, dropped an arm over his eyes and muttered, "Like I've been run over with a bulldozer."

Tirsa wriggled closer to him, pushed up on both elbows to see him better. At that point he slung a brawny arm under her shoulder and pulled her up and over to lie on his bare chest, pinning her there when she struggled to move away. "Don't fight me, *liefje*, I am too weary." He held her, hugging her body to his, his other arm still covered his eyes.

She relaxed against him, feeling the rise and fall of his chest as he breathed, saying a prayer of thanks that his heart was beating strong and sure. His chest hair soft matting for her face, she slid her fingers through it, amazed at how it felt. "I need to tell everyone the good news. Everyone has been so worried about you."

"Hmm, in a minute," he murmured.

They didn't lie there like that but for 2 or 3 minutes, when Knox slid under the flap of the tent looking surprised seeing Etam's arm around her holding her to him, his big palm stroking her slender back, her fingers sifting through his chest hair.

"I see my patient has gained his wits, so to speak," Knox noted dryly. His lean face was quickly wreathed in relief.

His eyes closed, Etam sighed. "Your powers of observation, Major, are keen as always." He moved his hand to Tirsa's head. Stroking her hair, he lifted tresses, letting one curl around his hand before filtering it through his fingers, letting it flutter back down on his chest.

"I hate to break this up, E, but I need to check you out. Blood pressure and all." Knox said to Tirsa, "If you will excuse us?"

She lifted her head and went to move but Etam strengthened his hold, curling his arm around her waist he pulled her closer.

"Okay," Knox chuckled. "You showed us you're feeling better, but really, help me out here, E."

His eyes still closed, Etam gave her another hug then reluctantly released her. She climbed to her feet, gave Knox a grin and a thumb's up and left the tent to share the good news.

Knox crouched at his medic box and pulled out his blood pressure monitor and stethoscope. Stepping around to the other side of Etam he glanced down. The blanket had gotten shoved down past his thighs. The bulge in his jeans strained against the denims.

Knox grinned at his friend. "*Ja*, I see you are feeling better. Hold out your arm." He wrapped the monitor's cuff around Etam's arm, put the ear-tips in his own ears, placed the diaphragm of the stethoscope on the inside crook of Etam's elbow and started pumping the machine.

Reading the numbers, Knox laughed, "Geez, E, she sure pushes your blood pressure up."

Chapter Twenty-Eight

*W*hen Knox was done with his examination and explained to the colonel what had happened to him, Etam sat up and asked, "Where's my shirt?"

"*Neen*, E. I think you need to take some time to recuperate." Sitting back on his heels Knox was putting away his equipment.

"I've rested enough. I'm hungry and I need a bath. Where's my shirt?" he repeated. The jeans they had put on him after soaking him to flush the toxin out were dirty, although the men had bathed him daily.

"Your shirt has a hole in it and blood stains. Johnson scrubbed it." Knox gestured to his shirt folded with clean underwear and a pair of jeans on top of it. He stood up, leaned over and offered his hand to his friend. Etam took it and Knox helped him get up.

Etam swayed, Knox held his arm to steady him. "E, you need to-" but Knox was speaking to empty air. Etam bent and picked up his shirt and jeans. Throwing the shirt on without buttoning it he went out leaving Knox shaking his head.

A few minutes later Knox found him bathing down at where the stream flowed into a little pool. His clothes were in a heap on the shore. "I brought you a towel."

Etam was scrubbing his hair; his head and hands were covered in white lather. He ducked under the water to rinse, stood up and tossed his head sweeping the wet hair back. "Ahh, that feels better," he exclaimed. Wiping the water from his eyes he said, "Although it would have been better with a certain curvy blonde mermaid scrubbing my back but you ran her off."

"*Ja*, sure. You need to gain back your strength. Of course you don't care that you're ruining my perfect bandaging," Knox chided him, holding the towel out for Etam to take as he strode naked as a jaybird out of the water.

Etam grabbed the towel, rubbed it over his head and face then body. Dropping the towel on the ground he climbed into the clean underwear, shirt and jeans then combed his hair back with his fingers.

"We've wasted enough time, let's go. We all need to talk. That trap was set deliberately for us. I'm thinking Tirsa was the one targeted because she would be the one compassionate enough to go to the rabbit and naive enough not to see the trap." He strode along the path, Knox beside him.

"Or," Knox offered, "it was set knowing she'd go for the rabbit and *you'd* go for her..."

After Etam met with his team, they packed up the burros and headed due west. Everyone wore hats and sunscreen to keep away the UV damage. Fortunately most of the way the hiking was relatively easy; they trod over volcanic rock, hard clay or ankle-high grass.

Times they were forced to make their way through the brambling thick forest, the men all took turns slashing at the heavy growth with machetes, chopping the broad leaves and prickly bushes, cutting a path through the almost impenetrable jungle.

Bruno yelped when startled by a tree kangaroo snoozing on a low limb.

The spooked chocolate brown and golden striped marsupial woke up, its eyes flashed back and forth getting its bearings then the agile fur-ball using its curved tail and spongy paws, hopped to another branch quickly bouncing from branch to branch until he disappeared into the cover of forest flora.

"Yo, that was way cool!" Lil Dam exclaimed. "I hope we get to see another one."

"*Ja.*" Jancarlo spoke for once. "Too bad it is yet another endangered species from logging and habitat destruction. Land cleared for production of coffee, rice and wheat, leaves them less shelter and protection from predators like dogs and vehicles. He was perched unusually low. They usually hang around the tree tops."

Lindsey quipped, "I guess the fur jacket I was thinking about is out of the question."

The look Jancarlo shot her withered her on the spot. Red blotches covered her face and neck the freckles all but disappeared. She discreetly dropped back to where Stav was, to hide behind the blond mountain.

The big seaman patted her on the back. His hand so large he accidentally knocked her forward, she stumbled over a root and crashed to her hands and knees.

"Gee, Linds, I'm sorry. Sometimes I don't know my own strength. Here, let me help you." He held a hand down to her.

She pushed his hand aside. Owen helped her up. Wiping her scraped hands on her khakis she snarled, "Ugh, you big clumsy brute," she sniped at Stav, "stay away from me." The haughty redhead tossed her braid behind her back, stuck her nose in the air and marched with Owen past the blond seaman.

Lil Dam strode up next to Stav. Dancing on dark sinewy legs, he poked him with his elbow. The two shared a grin.

The hikers grew quiet thinking about Jancarlo's depressing words. The mood lightened when they entered an open field bordered by the forest. Vividly colored butterflies disturbed by their presence swept out of the bushes that were abundant with bright flowers, and they flew off like a handful of tossed confetti.

At the head of the line, Etam put a hand out to touch Tirsa's arm to stop her. "Hold up," he called back to those behind them. Jancarlo jogged up to see why they stopped.

Strung across 30 feet or so of a crevasse was a footbridge made of uneven, discolored, heavily weathered wooden planks and the railing was made of twisted and tied vines.

"We need to cross it?" Jancarlo asked.

Etam was watching Tirsa; she'd already had a foot on the first plank and a hand on the railing. He took a long hard look at the swaying bridge that was tied to several trees on this side of the bank then it dipped over a steep ravine then was tied on the other side.

Carefully bending over he could see at the bottom of the ravine were rocks and boulders molding jagged out of a rushing stream. A person would definitely die if they fell from this height.

He tugged on the vine railing, it was flexible but felt secure. The vines were tied to trees but also vines had grown out of the bank of the ravine and someone had tied those to the railing for extra security. His gaze moved back to Tirsa who had set another foot on the plank and was looking down at the view below.

"*Ja,*" Etam answered Jancarlo, "we need to cross it."

They stood side-by-side as the rest of the group caught up. Lindsey's eyeballs about fell out of her head when she saw the bridge. Her skin turned ashen, mouth dropped, she shook her head. "No way, there's no way I'm walking on that thing, no way." Owen came to stand next to her. His mouth fell open in fright.

Lil Dam and Stav approached and peered down the crevasse, both exclaimed, "Wow." At the sight of the bridge, Lil Dam asked nervously but eagerly too, "We goin' on that? It'd be kind of like bungee jumping."

"Except we won't be tied to anything, bro," Stav said with an anxious undertone.

Johnson and Knox joined them. Johnson just barely tipped his head to look down the ravine. He stepped back scratching his cheek with a couple of fingers then over his lip then the sides of his face. "Whoa, E, really?"

Knox stood like Jancarlo, silently with his hands in his pockets.

"*Ja.*" The corner of Etam's mouth twitched back into a grin. "Piece of cake." He glanced at Tirsa who was waiting on the bridge. "I'll go over first," he said gruffly to her, grasping her elbow and pulling her back off the bridge. He turned to Jancarlo. "When I give the all clear, start them across."

Etam stared hard at Lindsey who had her knuckles over her mouth, hazel eyes shouting *no way was she stepping on the bridge.* Loudly Etam said, "Whoever doesn't want to come over the bridge is welcome to stay here, alone. With no supplies, water, or protection, in the pitch-black night. Is that clear?"

Owen dropped an arm over Lindsey's shoulders but he looked just about as scared as the redhead.

Etam said to Tirsa, "No one crosses until I say so." He trailed a finger gently down the side of her face to soften his order then stepped on the bridge and gamely strode not slowly but not too quickly across the bridge. Holding the railing loosely, he studied it and the planks as he walked searching for holes or wear and tear, anything that could cause disaster.

The bridge, he determined was in excellent shape. It wasn't that far, 30 feet give or take. When he reached the other side he waved the all clear.

Tirsa went to get on the bridge but Jancarlo pulled her back. "*Neen*. One of us needs to be there first with the colonel for safety sake. You wait."

Tirsa gave him the glower he had expected but of course it didn't faze him. He nodded to Knox who quickly stepped up on the bridge and trod across. Then Jancarlo gestured to Lil Dam, Stav and Bruno. "You and you and you go next. One at a time, slowly. No one goes until the person ahead is on the land on the other side. Clear?"

The three men nodded. "I'll go next," Lil Dam respected Etam and his team to such a high degree he wanted to look and be as courageous as them. He hopped on and started moving quickly.

"*Neen, luttel broeder*," Jancarlo called out to Lil Dam, a faint smile crossing his stern face, "slow, take it slow, *broed*." His grin broadened a fraction when the young OS waved back at him and slowed his pace.

"Little brother, is that what you called him?" Stav asked the major. "*Broed*, is that like bro?"

"*Ja*." Jancarlo nodded sharply.

Stav grinned. "I like that, *broed*."

"Uh huh. You are next, go." Jancarlo gave him a friendly shove towards the bridge. Stav made his was across with no hesitation. He trusted the colonel and the majors with his life. When they reached the other side, Etam gripped each man's arm and helped them off the bridge.

After Stav, Bruno went then Jancarlo gave Tirsa the go ahead. She strode lightly across to the other side into Etam's arms. Embarrassed in front of the others she stepped quickly out of his embrace. Smiling at her shyness, Etam watched for the next person to cross.

Owen went next. He gripped both sides of the railing so tightly his shoulders were up to his ears and rigid as poles. His steps were slow and plodding, but he was moving. Jancarlo smoked a cigar in the time it took the beanpole OS to get across.

"*Goed.* I will take the girl, then you go last, Johnson with the burros," Jancarlo instructed the huge, well-muscled black man.

Johnson nodded. Lindsey's eyes sunk in terror, as much at the bridge as at the coarse Jancarlo who everyone on the expedition except his teammates feared, but were also in awe of the hard-assed major.

Lindsey stood like a frozen sculpture. Jancarlo reached for her hand, she wrapped her arms around herself and shook her head the braid slapped back and forth like a whip. "I'll-I'll stay here. Right here." She plopped down, sitting on the ground with her legs and arms crossed.

Jancarlo looked over her head at Johnson. Johnson knew what the man was thinking, he was thinking he should knock her out; one light punch would do it, and then carry her across. Johnson shook his head ever so slightly stuffing his grin.

Jancarlo shrugged at him. He stood in front of Lindsey. She stared at his boots. He said, "I will not let you fall, *sproeten*. I swear on my honor." He held a hand down to her.

Her head down, she didn't move.

"There are wild animals, poisonous snakes, you do not want to stay here alone, *sproeten*, in the dark of night," the tough major spoke softly and patiently.

Her shoulders hunched, the hazel eyes darted around searching for hidden reptiles coiling towards her hidden in the grass. She reached up for his hand. Jancarlo pulled her to her feet and walked to the bridge with his arm around her shoulders.

Johnson stood by the bridge. He whispered at Jancarlo, "*Sproeten*, you called her freckles? Better not tell her that." Seeing Jancarlo's trace of a smile he chuckled under his breath.

Jancarlo brought her onto the bridge. "Do not look down. Look straight ahead at the colonel. We will go slowly but not too slow. The sooner we get there the sooner it will be done."

She nodded weakly. White as a sheet, Lindsey she gripped both sides of the railing while Jancarlo kept his hands on her waist from behind. It took a very long time but they made it. Everyone except Etam was sitting on the grass waiting.

When they finally reached the end of the bridge, Etam took her arm helping her onto the land, then she ran to Owen who stood up and said, "What a brave girl you are!"

Johnson joined them with the animals and they all got up and started hiking again. Lindsey mumbled to Owen, "I hope we're going back a different way."

Chapter Twenty-Nine

*T*he group plunged along with Etam and Tirsa in the lead.

Brooding about the trouble she had caused Etam and the time it took from everyone while he healed, Tirsa plucked a beautiful orchid and was twirling it, watching the purple, yellow and white colors meld like a pinwheel. It reminded her of when she had been captured and taken away on horseback.

Her mind swirled back, like then; she had once again not listened to Etam by being alone if only for a minute. He had yelled for her stop from going after the rabbit and he'd been the one to suffer. They'd almost lost him.

Just like he kept telling her, her actions did cause harm to another. Jancarlo told her he knew she was nothing but trouble and a danger to Etam. It was true.

Her voice drenched in remorse and guilt, staring at the ground ahead of them, she said, "Colonel." She stopped when peripherally she saw him turn his head to her with a frown.

"Etam," he reminded her.

She said, "Yes, Etam."

He waited she didn't continue. His brows perked curiously. "Well? What were you going to say?"

They were several feet in front of Stav, and Lil Dam who was rapping to himself. Tirsa stammered, "I…I am so sorry. It was my fault you were hurt, you almost died," she gulped sharply to stop the tears that threatened when she pictured him lying still as death. "You- you told me to listen, you warned me, you-"

He caught her arm and pulled her aside. When Johnson came up, Etam said to him, "Let's break over by those boulders." Johnson shot Tirsa a queried look to see if she was okay. She smiled morosely at him, shrugged. He hesitated, unsure.

Etam scrunched his eyes in irritation at the major. "For God's sake, Johnson, I'm not going to molest or beat her. Go on."

Johnson smirked at Etam, then winked at Tirsa. "Honey, if you need me, give a holler."

Etam waited for the others to troop past. When they were alone, he brought Tirsa to a large fallen tree and helped her to sit down on it then he sat down straddling the tree to face her. Woeful chariness prickled all over her face waiting for his furious reprimand for her ignoring his order to not go after the rabbit.

He felt a sting in his chest at the way she always regarded him fearfully, as if waiting for him to hurl her to the ground and commence beating her, or fucking her, or both. She was all rigidly defensive and wary, shoulders tense, fingers laced tightly.

Clearing his throat, he said, "Tirsa," keeping his voice mellow, "I'm not mad at you, I promise I'm not." He watched her shoulders lower imperceptibly. "I know you well enough by now that if you hadn't gone after the rabbit, or you had stopped when I said to, well," he smiled, "then the world would have probably fallen right off its axis."

Her surprised eyes swung up to his, she blinked with confusion, *huh*?

"What I'm saying is, is that it's engrained in your nature that when you see an animal or a person in distress you go deaf and blind to everything else in your orbit in an attempt to help it. I just," he slid closer to her and reached over and took one of her hands, held it lightly on his leg.

"I am so afraid that you are going to put yourself in such a deleterious position that could harm you terribly, or be...fatal. We are in a savage land, there are mercenary thugs after you, a single misstep, such as the rabbit can...well, you know what I'm saying. I've said it before."

"Colo...um, Etam, I understand and I've seen firsthand how my actions can endanger another person, you." Without thinking, she put her hand against the side of his face and held it there. Recalling the anguish of seeing him unconscious from the poisonous arrow, the bronze color of his skin waning, the lively fathomless eyes clouded with pain, the life fading from them. A shudder rippled across her shoulders.

He tilted his head slightly against her warm, gentle palm. When she dropped her hand his skin tingled instantly turning cold. Etam chuckled to relieve the tension. "I heard about you and Jancarlo."

His face darkened for a second when he thought about Jancarlo yelling at and cursing her, Johnson and Knox having to hold him back from hurting her. Not that Jan would ever strike a woman, Etam knows better, but Tirsa wouldn't have, she would have been terrified. He shook his head, set his hand over hers and said with admiration, "Anyway, you had brass balls- uh, buttons, to slap him. I have never seen someone your size ever attempt that. I wish I'd seen it."

Tirsa pulled her hand from his. "He was right though, it was my fault that caused you suffering and illness like he'd always prophesized. I deserved at the very least a tongue-lashing. If he'd struck me I wouldn't have complained." Her head lowered, she picked at her nails.

His breath sucked in his throat, he shook his head vehemently. "*Neen* Tirsa, a man should never hit a woman, it's never right." He thought back to Dia, he'd come close with her. Jancarlo had been beside himself with grief and fear that his best friend Etam was going to die and he said things he shouldn't have. He had admitted it. To Etam but not to Tirsa.

"*Liefje*, believe me, in the places we've been and the things we've done, he's had me in pretty precarious positions himself. However, he's…we're soldiers, cops, we're trained to take care of ourselves. It was wrong of him to treat you the way he did, say the things he said to you, and he knows it."

They'd had a long angry talk when Etam had recovered and heard about Jancarlo and Tirsa's altercation. He recalled Johnson relaying the words Tirsa had said to Jancarlo in Dutch, about his grandmother, it had shocked Jancarlo speechless, not that he ever was very talkative.

Tirsa raised her head to gaze off over the field. The sun was slipping down in a slow burn melting into the horizon. Yellow streaks and long shadows crossed the open grass making some of the blades blindingly bright while others merged into a dark mass.

Birds that were moments ago invisible were suddenly flying like boomerangs everywhere searching for places to roost. Dwindling rays of sun lit her pale, glum face.

Drawing her attention back to him, Etam said, "You know, your eyes are the same iridescent blue of the Queen butterfly we saw."

She looked up at him through half-closed lids. "I thought the butterfly was bluish-green."

"The point is," he said leaning into her, his eyes on her lips, "you are as beautiful, more so, than the butterfly."

Her gaze dipped to his mouth, she swallowed, then said earnestly, "Etam, I just want you to know that I'm sorry for what I caused to happen to you. I am so sorry."

He nodded, bracing his hands on the tree between them he leaned in further, muscles in his huge biceps flexing with the movement. Her lips were drawing him like a hummingbird to nectar.

His heated gaze tracing all over her beautiful face, landing back on her lips, he murmured absently, "Uh, huh, just, uh, in the future...try to listen, uh, when I...so...you know... Tirsa, the way you say my name with that hint of accent...it gets me..."

He gingerly grasped her legs and swiveled her to face him, then he lifted them up over his legs to straddle him. Tugging her as close as he could get her, he slid his hands around her back and drew her into the embrace of his thick arms.

She didn't resist him. With sincere assurance she vowed, "I will try, Etam, I promise I'll try with all my might to do as you ask."

"Hmm," he murmured, slipping a hand behind her head to bring her mouth to his. "Then *liefje,* I ask that you kiss me..." He edged his legs up as close to hers as he could get until she was mostly on his lap, and cradling her head with both hands, his mouth descended on hers.

Suddenly anxious, she said, "Wait, Etam," and put her hands against his chest starting to push him away. Then she stopped balking, and conquered her apprehension. Opening her mouth to his, she let him taste her and teach her what glorious intimacy a kiss could be.

She slowly stroked her palms over his chest feeling the strapping muscles, gripping them with unfurling virginal, exploring fingers, then she slid her hands up to his wide shoulders letting him deepen the kiss.

Groans rumbled up his throat to mingle with her soft moans. Etam ate at her mouth, bit her lips, sucked down her jaw to her neck, Tirsa pulled from his hungry mouth to catch her breath.

She leaned back slightly, her limpid eyes on his lips, she whispered shyly, "I hope, are we…friends now?"

Under heavy lids his dark eyes smoldering with heated passion, he drank her in. Her lips parted, licking them, she stared at his mouth. His body hardened to the explosion point watching the trail of her tongue over those plush lips.

"*Neen, liefje*, it is not friendly that I feel towards you." Bringing her head to his, he whispered against her mouth, "I want way more than friendship with you, *liefje*, way more." He moved his mouth to just barely touching hers, then brushed her lips lightly, tentatively. His tongue pressed, asking for entry. Yielding to Etam, Tirsa parted her lips and melted against him.

When he felt her respond, he pulled her hard into his arms and crushed her mouth with his. He wrapped his arms like steel bonds around her, holding her tight, she was a precious bundle of gorgeous femininity to cherish and desire.

Succumbing in his embrace, Tirsa's hands slid over those powerful shoulders then up around his neck, twining her fingers in his hair, now it was she who pulled him, pressing her body tightly against his.

Deep in his chest groans of arousal roiled. Slanting his head to bring their mouths closer, Etam's fingers clutched her hair, his hand moved to her back to hold her tight against him. The kiss burned through them both, again Tirsa breathlessly broke away.

Big chest heaving with heavy pants, Etam dropped his head back to look at her while his needful hands caressed her back, her arms, up over her shoulders, to tenderly touch her face, relishing the feel of her satiny skin. When he brushed his fingertips over her lips, it was electrifying for both of them.

He replaced his fingers with his mouth, devouring her fresh sweetness that had drawn him like it had that first time he had lain atop her the night she attempted to kill him. When she had looked up at him with such terror, the luminous blue eyes radiated pureness, innocence, he had wanted even at that moment to kiss away her fright.

Now, those eyes so transparent her beautiful soul shone through, he felt intense desire to be one with her, the pulse at his temple palpitated like a blinking sign announcing his deep need for the woman in his arms.

Their passion crackled, building like boiling lava in a New Guinea volcano. They were in their own world, unaware of the warm sun lowering on their backs, or the sand colored rusa deer crossing the trail, its large ears twitching, looking to munch on the purple orchids hiding behind tapering ferns.

Feeling an urgent flush building in him, another second and he would not be able to stop, Etam put both of his large hands around her waist, lifted her up and set her from him.

She looked so bereft he smiled weakly. He scrubbed his palms over his face then pushed his fingers through his hair. He couldn't believe how on fire he felt, so intense it felt like his skin was vibrating. He'd never felt this *moved* before.

"Etam?" She reached out to cleave to him.

Her eyes misted with passion, lips cherry red and breathless, he had to hold himself back from licking them. "*Liefje,*" he groaned, fighting the urge to gather her back in his arms. "You don't know the ways of men. I have to stop now, or-"

"Or what?" she asked naively, staring at his mouth beseeching him to return to her.

So beguiled by Tirsa he could feel himself sliding down like a fly into a pitcher plant. Wanting her so badly he moved away so he couldn't inhale her fresh scent. "Tirsa, if I continue, I won't stop at a kiss. I want what you're not ready to give. Do you understand?"

Comprehension pushed the haze from her eyes; she dropped her hands to the few inches of tree between them, blushing. "I…I…don't…"

"It's okay, *liefje.* I will wait until you are ready." His expression turned serious. "If you want me to."

Her gaze flipped dubiously to him. "What do you mean?" She laced her fingers laying them flatly on the tree bark.

He crept an inch closer to her. "It means, I want you. Obviously sexually." The edge of his lip pulled in as the blush deepened covering her creamy skin. He said, "I mean there's no doubt I want to make love to you," he watched her eyes dart away shyly, embarrassed, but then she looked at him, he could see passion burning in her shining pupils. He knew though that at the moment she was barraged with confusing feelings, physical feelings that were new to her.

"Tirsa, I have no intentions of turning you over to the police regardless of what happens…between us. I never did. When this expedition is completed I will take you back to Australia and you can go home, if that's what you want." He regarded her expression intensely to see her reaction to his words.

His stomach tightened when he saw relief curve her lips. Then her brows drew down while she contemplated his words. She finally looked at him, now he couldn't read her expression at all.

"I see." Very politely she said, "Thank you, Etam." When he looked so glum she asked, "What do *you* want, Etam?" A new allure lit her eyes, he had peeled away part of her that was still a child and now she was becoming aware of her femininity, and the effect it had on her, and him.

Now an unfamiliar shyness struck him. Yet he needed to speak now, or it might be too late later. He reached over and took her hand, held it. His loving gaze burned at her. "Tirsa, I want you. I want you sexually, mentally; I want every fiber of you to merge with every fiber of me. I want to wake up every morning for the rest of our lives with you next to me in my bed. Our bed. I love you." Rubbing his thumb over her hand, he gripped it and said soberly, "I want you to be my wife. I don't want you to leave me. Ever."

Pulling her hand away, she drew her legs up, setting her feet on the tree and wrapped her arms around her knees. Her chin resting on her knees, Etam couldn't see her mouth. He couldn't tell if she was happy, or considering what she was feeling, or, judging by the way she was sitting all closed up, it appeared she wasn't of the same mind as he.

A lovely thatch of orange Bird of Paradise grew at the stump end of the tree. Etam stared in unease at the flowers, his stomach dropping, he said, "You need to say something,

Tirsa. I've spilled my heart; I'm bleeding all over the ground. It's okay if you don't want to…be with me. You're young and pure, and I'm a hardened tough soldier, I understand. But I need you to say something. Be candid, don't be afraid. I won't take back what I said. You will be set free regardless." Taking a deep breath, he waited.

Her legs slipped down on either side of the tree. "Etam," her voice was so low he leaned forward to hear her. "You know, because you keep repeating it, that I have little…no…experience with men. I've found this whole expedition to be," she searched for a word, "um, an opening of my eyes. I didn't know how to handle, things, situations. I've never felt so vulnerable, people pawing me, and…"

His head dropped in shame.

"Etam," her voice tender, she said with a new maturity, "if anything on this trip, I've learned who you are. The man that you are. As worldly and, as unsettling as it is, you and your team make your own laws sometimes when you need to, do what needs to be done, take what you want by any means."

He couldn't see her smiling tenderly at the top of his head. "Yet I know in all my heart that if I hadn't responded, given you some look or touch, or words, that you picked up on that I was…attracted to you too…there would be no way on earth that you would have forced yourself on me. Even a simple kiss."

He raised his head; her direct gaze was disconcerting as hell. "*Liefje,* you always seemed to be terrified of me, yet whenever you were in real danger or distress it was me you called out for. After the pirates attacked us, you made me, not anyone else, see Knox to get medical attention. And the crocodiles, Knox said you cried in relief when you saw I was all right. Your initial ardent response to my kisses when we were on the horse. I tucked these things away in my hopeful heart."

She was looking at him but he couldn't tell what she was thinking, she didn't say anything about what he'd just said. So he plunged on, "Jancarlo told me while I was injured you never left my side except to bathe. *Ja*, you felt guilty, but if that was all you felt then you would have stayed away. I think you remained because you cared…about….me. When I woke and saw you lying beside me, asleep, so sweet, caring, innocent…your hand on my arm, my heart filled so much I could hardly breathe."

He looked down, feeling insecure for the first time in his life when she still didn't say anything. Then he raised his gaze to her lips, back up to those soulful eyes filled with warmth and purity. He smiled crookedly. "Did I hear you say that you are attracted to me?"

She turned her eyes heavenward at his obtuseness. "Really, Etam. We practically made love on this darn fallen tree here. You keep pointing out how green I am, do you think I'd do this with someone I just felt only an acquaintance to?"

His smile broadened so wide it hurt. He took her hand again, the smile dimmed. "You haven't said anything about what I…said about you staying…with me."

Tirsa swung her leg over the tree, sliding to her feet, she took a few steps to stand in front of him. "Etam, yes, I was, have been afraid of you, but I've always had feelings for you too, and after that first day when you were so upset when that chain around my neck injured me, I have always known deep down that you would never hurt me."

His face paled bleakly recalling that day he'd chained her to his bed, made her sleep on the floor without a pillow or blanket. He shook his head; he still kicked himself for treating her, or any woman that way. Just, at the time, she'd just attempted to take his life, but he was so drawn to her, he wanted her close by but didn't know what else to do to secure her.

His voice dismal, with deep remorse he started to apologize, "Tirsa, I so regret the way I've treated you. I-"

She put her fingers over his mouth. "Etam, I have been more afraid of the day when you would send me away. It didn't matter if it was to prison or Australia, I wanted to be with you, I didn't want to leave you. Don't want to leave you. I've been fearing the day you would send me away, away from you," the last words fainted into despair.

Her words chased away his dejection and a surging glow of happiness filled him. Etam put his arms out wrapping them around her and pulled her to him to stand between his open legs.

Cupping her chin with his fingers he brought her mouth to his, they came together in a sublime kiss. It was a short kiss. It was all he could handle. Letting her go he stood up.

"*Liefje*, I had never planned on letting you go, not since the night you held that knife over my head and I swung you onto my bed and rolled on top of you. When I looked at your beautiful frightened face, between being impressed with your guts, that soft body under me, and those winsome eyes, I was a goner at that split second. From that moment I never stopped plotting how to keep you with me."

"*Etam*," his name poured out as an elated cry of relief and joy.

With a quiet ecstatic moan hearing his name on her lips, saying she wanted him as much as he wanted her, he caught her up in his arms again. Holding her head to his chest they stayed contented that way.

Then, he tipped her head to look up at him and swore, "Baby, I won't let anyone ever hurt you again. When I call you my own the wolves will back away, or I'll make them wish they had." He set his hands on her shoulders, his dark eyes glowing he said, "Have I told you how much I love it when you say my name? The way you pronounce it gives me tingles. It is unique, makes me feel special."

She giggled. They embraced then he said, "We need to go before they come looking for us, catch us in an embarrassing position." Holding hands, they started walking to join the others.

Tirsa asked, "How much further, longer do you think before we find the, where the book is hidden?"

"What do you think?" he asked mysteriously.

"Me? How would I know?"

He stopped and turned her to face him, set his hands on her shoulders again. "Tirsa, you do know. You've been leading us since we left the stone tables."

Bewildered she said, "What? Etam, what are you talking about?"

Smiling down at her, he told her, "Even if we went due west like I had directed, there would be such an infinitely wide area to go in, seek in. Haven't you noticed the whole way from the tables that you and I have been at the front of the line? Except for the few times we had to forage through the dense jungle, you have been leading."

Her head swung side to side. "You're insane, I don't know where we're going. I've never even been here before, how could I-" something pricked at her mind, but she couldn't grasp it. She cried, "How?"

"Remember Adullam? Remember what he said that day in the library?"

She rubbed her eyes. "How could I forget? You killed that man."

Exasperated he said, "It was necessary, they would have taken you. Anyway, not that part, Tirsa. What Adullam said about you."

It had been so traumatic that day, she hadn't thought about what was said. Until now. "He said I am a...something...and my ancestors are here, and I can...um...he said I can find them by...intuition or something." Her face a mask of perplexity, and fear, she looked at him, big, strong Etam, for him to help her understand, and cope with what it was.

"We'll research it later," he gently reassured her. "It hit me when you said you felt something from the diary. I've been letting you walk a step ahead of me, to see, where you would go." He took her hand, held it tight. "I have the maps, notes, diary, I know the way. But it was you who led us, to here," he gestured to the distant sparse trail. "What will we find over there? Because I know."

Tirsa was quiet for a few moments, then her eyes widened, a transcendental acuity glimmering in them. Her gaze floated to where he pointed then to him. "A temple. Ruins. The broken tower will show the way."

He smiled at her and squeezed her hand. "*Ja*. See? Do you actually see, it?"

The blonde hair ruffled as she shook her head in wonderment. "No. I can *feel* it."

"We will learn to understand it, understand you."

"Thank you, Etam."

A brow arched curiously, "For what?"

"For saying 'we.' "

Chapter Thirty

*W*hen they reached the group, they could feel the excited energy. Bruno was hopping up and down. "Hey, Colonel, Tirsa, come see what we found!"

"Could it be a temple?" Etam teased, laughing when he saw the astonished expression on the young Hispanic's face.

"How did-" Bruno stammered as Etam and Tirsa walked past him.

They found the rest of the group crawling around an enormous pile of rocks. The crumbled temple looked like it was disintegrating back into the earth from where it had been originally formed from.

When it was built, the rocks had been plastered together with a mixture of mud, clay and grass. After a few thousand years, the structure had avalanched into broken piles of splintered rocks, some fragments ground to dust. Sections of the walls were still intact, along with some steps, altars, and places that appeared to be ceremonial stone groupings.

Mounds of ashes were strewn all over the inside of the demolished building. Johnson and Knox studied a dune of ashes surrounded by an uneven circle of rocks. "Could be for sacrifices," Johnson said.

Joining them Jancarlo muttered, "Or cooking."

Stav came over to look. "Do you think this building was destroyed by weather or humans?"

"Hmm." Johnson considered his question. "Little of both probably. There's also earthquakes in this Ring of Fire."

"Ring of Fire?"

"*Ja.*" Johnson nodded. "More of a horseshoe than a ring, it's where the folding and thrust of faulting of plates, where the collision of plate tectonics meet up with volcanoes and ocean trenches that are fathoms deep."

Jancarlo flexed a sarcastic eyebrow at his friend. "Damn, Johnson, could you have made that a simpler description of some extraordinary phenomenal acts of nature?"

Miffed, Johnson grunted, "Whatever. E's the professor you know."

"He was a fake professor," Knox said.

"Hey dudes, check this out!" Bruno called from deeper in the temple.

They all rushed to see. "Isn't that beautiful?" He pointed to a pile of black stones. Johnson bent and picked up one and held it up to the light.

"Wow, it's dazzling, like it has an inner fire," Lil Dam said, picking up a stone to study more closely. "Look," he said, "it glows inside when I hold it up to the light."

"Let me see." Lindsey pushed Tirsa aside so she could get one.

Lil Dam gushed, "It's like a mixture of layers of black and clear with a lace-like pattern flowing through it." He stooped and grabbed up a handful of the rocks. "They all look different, unique."

Lindsey plopped down on the ground and started piling stones in the hem of her shirt she held like a basket. "We couldn't take any of the black ice but I'm taking these."

Owen leaned over slightly and said in a low voice to Stav, "I cut out some of the black ice, had to use the pick, didn't everybody?"

Stav shook his head; he hadn't even considered it since the colonel had given orders they weren't to take any.

"Looks like midnight lace obsidian," Johnson stated, studying the stones.

"What's that?" Bruno asked the senior seaman.

"It's a gemstone, you know, made out of minerals. I didn't know there were any here in New Guinea," Johnson explained. "Some kinds have like a mahogany mixed with the black. It's said they have healing powers." In his teacher's voice he stated, "Volcanoes can produce or host deposits of aluminum, diamonds, gold, nickel, lead, zinc, and copper, among others."

"*Ja*," Jancarlo said acidly. "New Guinea has been mined to death."

"Ever the cheerful one, Major Jancarlo," Owen criticized sarcastically. "What are you, the Green Man of the team? You know, green earth and carbon footprints, crap like that."

His face as stoic as always, dark eyebrows lowered over simmering rancorous eyes, in a detached, empty voice, Jancarlo uttered, "That's Major *Mercury*." He took a step towards Owen- the beanpole quailed recalling the pirates, crocodiles, the hog attack, the major could snap him like a twig if he chose to. Jancarlo stabbed him only with a bone-cold stare then stalked off.

Owen let the breath he held drain.

The group stood stock still watching the pair's interaction. A few with fear, some with amusement, at least one had hoped the major would give Owen a good thump in the nose.

"So, uh, what's next?" Lil Dam grinned broadly trying for some levity.

"I'm hungry," Stav announced, rubbing his flat belly.

"Yeah? Tell us something new," Lil Dam joked.

"*Goed* idea," Johnson said, "let's chow." Instead of freeze dried tonight, they collected cans of food and started preparing dinner.

Etam followed Jancarlo. The major tromped around the back of the temple and lit a skinny cigar. He leaned his back against the building with one leg bent and his foot braced against the wall. Dragging on the cigar, he blew out smoke circles.

The air smelled of musky wine from the cigar. Etam joined him resting against the wall. He held out his hand. Jancarlo took his pack out of his pocket and tapped out a cigar. When Etam took one, Jancarlo pulled out his lighter.

Etam stuck the cigar in his mouth and bent his head. Jancarlo flicked the lighter and Etam cupped the flame until it lit. They smoked in companionable silence for a moment.

"The *blondine* finally got you," Jancarlo declared coolly, inhaling long on the cigar, blew out a tunnel of grey smoke. "You are keeping her."

Etam chuckled. He held the cigar up looking at the ember burning at the end. He could see the crescent moon above and beyond, a silver sliver with a sprinkling of stars around it against the black velvet sky. "First, *I* finally got *her*. I'm the one that got lucky. Second, she's not a possession for me to *keep*."

Puffing silently for a few moments, Jancarlo questioned his friend, "What about her murder attempt on you?"

Tapping the cigar, Etam followed the grey shower of ash journey to the ground. "Jan, you know she wouldn't have done it. There's not an evil bone her body. We will find out who sent her and take care of them. They're holding something over her head. Something worth more than her own life. That can only be a person she cares deeply for."

"Hmm. Where will you be keeping her?"

Chuckling while shaking his head, Etam said, "Again, I am not keeping her. She will however, go where I tell her to for her own safety."

Jancarlo spat out a mouthful of smoke. "*Ja*? Just like all the other times you told her what to do and… how has that worked out so far?"

Etam frowned at his colleague. He spurted angrily, "She will do as I-" he broke off thinking about what Jan said. A smile tugged at his mouth. "*Ja, broeder*, I get your point. She's a cookie with a mind of her own, that's for sure."

Turning his head, Jancarlo studied his friend's shining black eyes and happy grin. For once his own mouth relaxed into a slight, one-sided curve. Holding his cigar between a finger and thumb, he poked Etam in the arm and said glibly, "Cookie? I get scolded for calling her 'the blonde' and you call her a cookie?"

Looking a tad abashed, Etam countered, "*Ja*, well, you know, she's soft and sweet."

"I will remember, E, when you are evil to me, I will tell her what you said, and then what do you think your sweet cookie will do to you?"

"Come on, Jan, I'm never evil to you…much." He swung his head at the major in a mock plea. "Please don't tell her, she won't think it's funny, like we do." They laughed together like brothers.

"E," Jancarlo dropped his cigar, crushed it out with his boot. "You are practically glowing. If you were a girl I would swear you were pregnant."

"Huh? What the hell are you talking about?" Etam tossed his cigar, stepped on it and frowned baffled at his friend.

Jancarlo pushed off from the wall, clapping his hands together to shake off the dust from the ancient stones then wiped his hands on his pants. He bent and picked up the cigar butts to put with the container they kept their trash in. "It means, my comrade, that I have never seen you happier. If you want her, then I am happy for you. If she does not want you I will assist you in keeping her secured."

Etam slapped his forehead. "Jan, you don't get it. I care enough for her, I love her…if she is happier not being with me, God forbid, then, I would not hold her against her will. This isn't the dark ages you know." He rolled his eyes. "And she calls *me* the caveman."

Jancarlo shrugged. "Women seldom know what they really want. You keep her locked away somewhere with you long enough, give it to her good and hard and often, she will capitulate, eventually she will want to stay with you. You need to learn to control your woman."

"Jan," Etam laughed, "you are a helluva chauvinist. Women are human beings, not caged pets that are taught to love and obey their masters."

A rare smirk touching his hard mouth, in a salty tone Jancarlo quipped, "Really? You think that? Then you are as naive as your *blondine*." He strolled away before Etam could make a come-back.

Louise Furley

The center of the temple was mostly clear of fallen stones so they bunked down there. It had been a long hiking day, everyone was wiped out so they crashed early. Etam and Jancarlo stood night watch until Johnson and Knox relieved them. Seasoned military police, they were used to going days without sleep when on a heavy mission.

Without a canopy of trees to block it, the sun woke everyone as soon as it began to rise. Sitting on a large stone, Bruno held a spoon in his hand, he was about to scoop into the tin can he was holding then set his hand on his knee. He looked woefully at the can. "I don't know how much more of this freeze dried and canned food I can take. Don't they have like a McDonald's or a Subway or something out here?"

"You're missing the ambience of the jungle by thinking about fast food." Lil Dam dropped down on a rock next to him and dove into his can with relish. Shoveling the beans in his mouth the young rapper chewed vigorously. "Hmm, scrumptious!" he proclaimed, and stuck the spoon in for more.

Craning his neck, Bruno peered into Lil Dam's can. Baffled, he watched the junior seaman gobble up his food like he was enjoying it. "Watsup with that, dude? You act like you like that junk."

Lil Dam grinned while chewing, his coffee colored cheeks plumped out with food, he nodded, swallowed and licked his lips. "You bet."

"How the hell do you-"

Scraping the bottom of the can and eating the last spoonful, Lil Dam advised, "It's all in your mind, bro, you picture you're eating pizza and voila- it tastes like pizza!"

308

Bruno looked down gloomily at his beans, poked them a little with his spoon. "You're nuts." He set the can and spoon on the ground.

"Hey! Look what I found! Everybody!" Stav called out from the other side of a wall.

Everyone except Knox and Johnson who were on guard duty hurried to see what he found. When they got to him, Stav was bent over with his hands on his knees looking at the wall.

"What is it?" Etam asked, coming to stand beside the big, blond buffed seaman.

"Check it out," Stav pointed to the wall. The others joined them gathering in a semi-circle around the wall. "It's like hieroglyphics."

"Hey, cool," Lil Dam grinned with interest.

Studying them, Bruno asked, "Yeah, but what's it say?"

Stav mumbled as he looked at them, "There's a picture, a drawing of a figure and it looks like an animal, and, gee, I'm not sure."

Tirsa knelt on the ground, put her hand on the drawings and closed her eyes.

At first everyone was babbling about the drawings and what they thought they meant, until one by one they grew silent watching Tirsa.

She opened her eyes and said, "Yes, it is a figure and an animal, the figure has something behind its back." She leaned in closer to discern what it was.

"Looks like a pineapple," Bruno suggested.

Owen squinted at the drawing, "The animal looks like it's hungry, I think…"

"At least they had something other than beans and tuna to eat. I'd die for that pineapple right now!" Stav declared, they all laughed. "We had those wild fruits for a while on this journey, but we haven't come across any lately," he lamented, mourning the lack of variety in their menu.

"I agree, the animal is hungry and looking to the figure to feed it," Tirsa smiled at Stav then looked closer at the pictures. "So, um, in the next part the figure is still standing but the animal is lying down, looks dead. The next scene the figure is dead beside the animal."

"So, what does it mean?" Lindsey asked, managing to sound bored and interested at the same time. The group looked to Tirsa for an explanation.

She set her hand on the drawings again and said, "I think it's kind of like a parable. The being starves the creature, the being dies."

Her hands stamped on skinny hips, Lindsey asked, "What does that mean?" Impatience lined her smooth brow.

Bruno proposed, "It could mean that he died because he killed his food source?"

Lowering her head, Tirsa's hair fell over her shoulders, covering her face. Her fingers daintily traced over more scratches. "Yes, and no. He's dead because he killed himself. This says, 'What I do to you, I do to me.' "

His knees giving into the crouch, Stav stood up. "Huh? What does that mean?"

Tirsa brushed over the scratches wiping the old dust off them. "The person starved the animal because he was angry with it, therefore he ended up starving himself. These words say, "Our essence is each other. We are each other, linked by...our mutual...energy. We are not separate beings, we are all one. If I don't love you, I can't love me."

They all stood staring at the pictures contemplating their own thoughts on the words.

Lindsey sighed loud and long. "Ugh, what a bunch of crap. Who cares. Come on, Owen, let's go finish our grand beans." Her single braid whipped around as she turned and traipsed out of the temple.

Tirsa moved from her knees to sit on the ground, fascinated by the drawings and the thought provoking words.

Etam sat down next to her. "How are you able to read those etches?" He watched her studying the wall.

She shrugged. Then tilted her head slightly towards him with a small smile. "I don't know. But," her face stiffened. "I meant to tell you. I...that man, Adullam, he mentioned the red diamonds, when I was looking at your diary...well, I could picture the diamonds with the book. Totally bizarre, but..." she shrugged again, slightly embarrassed.

Etam's brows jumped then settled right back. Nothing was surprising him anymore about the woman he'd given his heart to. He bent slightly and without touching her with his hands, kissed her soft, long, then when it turned urgent, he moved back from her.

He was now eager to get the expedition he'd spent a good part of his life researching, studying, thinking, planning and working on, over, so he could take Tirsa to his home where they would have the time and privacy to get to really know each other.

It was a stab in his heart that Tirsa still sometimes watched him pensively, with a subtle but palpable apprehension of him. He wanted to free her of her fear of him, fear of everything. Agitation burned in his gut that he was impotent to eliminate the danger that was out there waiting on her. That she was too terrified to tell him who had their hold over her.

He rose to stand. "Come," he said, holding his hand down to her, "I want to show you something." She put her hand in his and he helped her to her feet. They traipsed to the front of the building a few yards out.

"There. Does that mean anything to you?" Etam motioned to a decaying tower. Tirsa walked close to it then touched it. Unaware how sorrowful she sounded and looked, her words foreboding, "A broken tower points to death in your circle, or friends."

Not expecting her ominous words, it was difficult for Etam to remain placid. Concern in his voice, he asked carefully, "What...um...how, who?"

Her shoulders bumped, mouth pursed in mystification. "I don't know, Etam, I just sort of feel these things, I can't explain it. Is that what you wanted to show me?"

He rubbed the top of his head with one hand then smoothed the hair back. "Uh, actually no. Not at all. That came totally out of left field." Staring up at the broken tower, he said, "In Dutch a tower is a *toren*. In the diary it said, follow the direction of the *toren*."

Nodding as she listened, Tirsa murmured, "Hmmm." Following the direction of the tower would be difficult due to its condition. She said redundantly, "It's broken."

"*Ja.* It fell towards the west."

They stood looking at the crumbling mess. She noted, "We don't know if it fell before or after the diary was written."

"I know. Going by the map it's west. I think that you will be able to define the more specific way. In a short while, we are supposed to come upon a trail of apparently very well hidden caves. At that point we should be about to our destination. What are your thoughts, *liefje*?"

Turning a blissful smile towards him, she said, "My thoughts are, what does *liefje* mean?" Her eyes dropped to his mouth to watch as he answered.

Etam cupped her chin and bent to kiss her, a slow, tender strum before lifting his head back. "You are too irresistible, it sounds different with your shade of accent. Much sexier."

Her eyes closed briefly expecting more. The blue eyes opened dreamy, lips turned up in a sultry bow.

He leaned over again, told her, "It means sweetheart," and kissed her more fervently, his arms wrapping around her, pulling her tightly against him. She hesitated, then sank into his strong embrace, like a statue coming to life, cool marble warming quickly into supple serum, Tirsa's desire blossomed for the colonel.

Her fingers splayed on his stomach, she couldn't believe how rock hard he was. Stroking her palms up his broad chest, she blushed picturing the times she'd seen him shirtless. In her realm growing up, other than infrequently on TV when she could watch it, she couldn't recall seeing a bare chested man before, it was frightening and erotic at the same time. She unbuttoned several buttons on his shirt and pushed the lapels aside. He had beautiful black hair on his chest and she wanted to stroke it.

His lips left hers as he dipped his head to watch her exploring his body. It only made him more aroused, he was tingling all over and wasn't going to be able to just stand there much longer. *"Liefje..."* his sigh too deep for words, his hands tightened on her waist.

Running her delicate hands over the stacked masculine muscles, she smiled, "I know, we have to go." Sifting her fingers through the hair she whispered, "It's like silk, rough silk." At his groan, before he could blink, Tirsa stepped out of his embrace.

Etam reached out to grasp her hand to pull her back, but then thought better of it. "There will be time, later, when this is done, Tirsa, for us to...learn about each other, *Ja?*"

313

Her smile softly reluctant, Tirsa combed her fingers through her tangled curls and agreed shyly, "Yes."

He did take her hand then and walked her back inside the temple to where the etchings were.

Knox, Johnson and Jancarlo were sitting there on low broken walls. Their eyes went right to Etam's open shirt. Their minds had been on each other, he had forgotten about it.

All three men were grinning like leering jackals, including this time, Jancarlo. Tirsa kept going, returning to the drawings, and sat down in front of them.

Etam buttoned his shirt and joined his team. Sitting with them, he forked thick fingers through his dark hair, and chastised his friends with a glower, "What are you, a bunch of teenagers?" The men laughed at him.

Johnson boldly asked, "So, what were you two doing out there? Have you-"

The colonel frowned at him. "Not that it's any of your business, because it's not, however, we are slowly getting to know one another."

"*Ja*, it sure looks like it! This time it's you that comes back half-dressed," Johnson snickered, the others joined in. "If we have a choice in the matter, E, we much prefer her to be the one lacking clothes." They roared with laughter at Etam's scowl.

Chapter Thirty-One

Stav and Lil Dam had relieved Owen and Johnson on patrol. Everyone finished breakfast and were gathering their things to prepare to venture on, when Lil Dam hastened into the temple making his way right over to Etam. He announced, "Colonel, we've got a problem."

Etam took one look at the young man's gravely urgent face and got right up. Knox, Johnson and Jancarlo followed, striding quickly out of the temple.

As soon as they stepped a few feet from the temple, Lil Dam wiped his face with his hands, stuck a finger in the corner of his eye anxiously, fidgeting, then wiped his sweating hands on his pants.

"Lil Dam?" Etam prompted the obviously agitated man.

"Dude, sir," Lil Dam scraped his fingers through his hair. "The burros are gone."

"What? Are you sure?" Etam bent emphatically towards the smaller man, his hands on his hips.

The seaman squeaked out, "Ye- yes sir. Stav and I looked and looked. They're gone sir."

His hand over his brow, Etam said, "All right, let's fan out. You go back on patrol with Stav."

Lil Dam saluted Etam and ran off. Knox, Johnson and Jancarlo took off in separate directions.

Etam rushed back inside the temple bee-lining for Tirsa. When he found her, he called out, "Owen, Bruno, Lindsey, come here, now!"

As soon as they reached Etam they gathered around him, flinching when they caught his disturbed expression. Bruno asked, "Colonel?"

"The burros are gone. They were tied up securely, someone may have taken them. The other officers and I are going out to search for them. Stav and Lil Dam are on patrol. I am ordering you four to stay here. Do not move until we come back. Is that understood?"

The four people nodded, puzzled and worried. Etam took Tirsa's hand pulling her to her feet. Cradling the side of her face gently, he said quietly, "Stay with the others. Please. I have to have your promise you won't go off alone."

Seeing how concerned he was, Tirsa quickly reassured him, "I won't. I promise. I won't go anywhere alone." She set a hand on his shoulder. "Please go do what you have to, don't worry about me. I'll be right here." She had been stringing the shells she found in the cave on a string of leaf stems tied together, she shoved them in a pocket in her khakis.

Cupping her face with both hands, he kissed her thoroughly. Drawing apart with a sigh, Etam kissed the tip of her nose, "Okay." He turned to the others, his face serious, brows low, mouth firm, he instructed, "If you have to go to the bathroom you all go together, got that? Otherwise, do not leave this temple." He gave Tirsa another quick kiss then left the ruins.

"Nice, Tirsa, you and the colonel, who would have guessed?" Bruno laughed, teasing. "Like we are all surprised- not!" He patted her arm when she blushed.

"It's nothing, Bruno, he's just concerned, that's all." Tirsa tried to make the sight of her and Etam kissing less significant, but her cheeks blushed pink.

"Yeah, right. Everyone can see how he looks at you, right guys?" Bruno laughed. "Right from the start, he scarcely takes his eyes off you."

Owen grunted. "Whatever. Let's play cards."

Using a towel, Lindsey brushed off a rock then laid the towel on it and lowered her behind gingerly to sit down. Her head up, she sniffed imperiously, like she was the queen holding court. "Who cares anyway." She looked at Owen. "Who's got the cards?"

Owen said to Bruno, "I think they're in Stav's or Lil Dam's backpack."

"I'll go get them," Bruno offered and left to search for the cards.

Lindsey stood up and said, "I'll help you," and she followed him.

As soon as they left, his hands in his pockets, Owen said to Tirsa, "Um, so I've heard about your...gift...power...what do you call it?"

Looking around for a place to sit, not wanting to talk about it, Tirsa murmured indifferently, "It's nothing, really."

Slightly embarrassed, Owen pushed his mop of hair out of his eyes, and said nervously, "Uh, well, there's been like something really bothering me, hurting me, I...I can't take it anymore, the pain..."

Her face instantly softened with compassion, she asked him, "What is it, Owen?"

His shoulders slumped, Owen glanced around like he didn't want anyone to hear and make fun of him. He said in a low whisper, "I...listen," he touched Tirsa's arm. "Can...can we just go a few feet away from here and talk privately? Please?"

She hated to turn down anyone in pain, but, she objected, "Oh, Owen, you know the colonel said for us not to move from here. I don't think-"

"It'll be okay. He said not to go off alone. We'll be together." He gripped her elbow, his face wreathed in discomfort he cried, "I can't take this...torment much longer. Please?"

She smiled kindly. "Of course. But just for a moment."

He breathed a sigh of relief. "Thank you, Tirsa. I can't tell you how much I appreciate this. Come on, let's go by that leafy tree with the under ripe wild tomato fruit in it." He took her hand and ushered her hastily out of the temple.

When they were outside, he kept going, pulling her along. They were several yards away when Tirsa said, "Owen, I don't think we should go any further, we should stay near the-"

His fingers tightened on her hand he kept moving bringing her with him. They went a little further then tugging her hand, Tirsa said sternly, "Really Owen, we need to-"

"Just to the bridge, okay?" He slowed his pace a bit, said with an abashed grin, "I mean the guys are out here searching for the burros and I'd die if they heard me." Walking faster he dragged her to the bridge.

Once there he suggested, "How about we just walk out a little ways, see the view. We came over so quickly I didn't get to see what the ravine looked like, Did you?" While talking, he kept pulling, nudging her to the bridge.

Her skin paling, Tirsa shook her head, dug her heels in and grabbed the first pole made of tree limbs and vines that held the railing. "No. Stop Owen. We need to go back right now." Suspicion of his intentions started niggling at her. She reminded him, "If the colonel finds us out here he'll be furious."

"Aw, come on, please Tirsa, just a-"

"No!" Holding the railing so he couldn't pull her, indignation with some trepidation creeping in she declared, "I'm going back right now. Let go of me."

Instead of releasing her, he roughly pried her fingers off the railing, quickly bent over, picked her up and tossed her over his shoulder then strode rapidly across the bridge. One arm holding a kicking, flailing Tirsa, Owen skimmed the railing with his other hand to keep his balance on the rocking footbridge as he hurried.

He moved so quickly, Tirsa was bouncing up and down on his back, her yells and screams muffled against his back. With his quick pounding steps, she was jarred about, her chin rammed banging off his back.

In only moments, he reached the other side and dropped her to her feet but stuck his hand in her hair, gripping a handful he held her tight, painfully so she couldn't flee.

"Owen!" she cried. "What are you-"

His fingers gripping her hair he shook her head and growled, "Shut up." He glanced all around like he was looking for someone, that's when Tirsa started screaming her head off.

"Etam! Etam! Help!" she peeled at the top of her lungs. Owen slapped his hand over her mouth but it was too late.

Having a bad feeling, the colonel had already returned to the temple and came across Bruno and Lindsey engaged in peeling their clothes off in the far back of the temple. He searched for Tirsa and Owen but they were nowhere to be found. He looked outside thinking maybe they went to the bathroom which displeased him thinking she shouldn't be with Owen doing that.

His blood froze when he heard her scream. Racing around the other side of the temple, he spotted her.

Owen's fist was twisted in her hair and he had his hand over her mouth.

Etam raced to the bridge. Just as he reached it, no less than six men came out of the bushes like rats on a ship and charged him.

As soon as he saw the first guy, he slammed his fist in the man's face and kicked another smack in the groin. Swinging around, Etam punched a third in the stomach. He twirled- shooting an upper cut to the fourth man, a left hook to the fifth, suddenly his body jolted. From several feet away the sixth man had shot him with a stun gun.

Etam dropped to his knees fighting the electric shock when the men all ran at him at once, pummeling, kicking, pounding him to the ground.

On the other side of the bridge, struggling with Owen, Tirsa screamed and screamed for the men to stop beating Etam, "Stop! Stop hitting him! Please stop!"

Behind her and Owen, a big man on a horse appeared out of the veil of trees. "Good job, Owen," the man praised the seaman, his wicked smile at Tirsa sent shivers through her. "Hello Miss Auret. You will be coming with us. You will be guiding us to your people."

At the shaking of her head, his face hardened, lines crimped around cruel eyes, he said, "If you don't come now without a fight and don't help us, I will give the order to kill him." He nodded over the bridge to where his men were beating Etam.

Tirsa cried, "No!" her eyes wild with horror at what the mercenaries were doing to Etam. "Stop them, please! I'll do whatever you say, please, God, please make them stop!"

The herculean man smile unpleasantly at her, he said to Owen, "Give her to me."

Owen put his hands around her waist and handed her up to the man who swung her in front of him on the horse. He whistled. His men on the other side of the bridge looked up, the man waved at them.

The thugs continued fighting Etam when four more men emerged from the bushes to join the melee. Another one ran to the bridge with a machete and started chopping at the vines holding it to the bank.

The horse danced around with its hooves in the air as the man jerked the reins to turn around.

"Wait!" Tirsa screamed. "You said you would stop them!"

The man laughed like a bull snorting, then he whistled again. His men looked over at him, he made a thumbs down signal. They stopped fighting Etam, he was on his knees. The man cutting the bridge stood back as it came apart vine by vine until in slow motion it sprung loose tumbling into the crevasse. The thugs cheered.

Several more men came out from the trees on horses to meet up with the huge man that had Tirsa. Owen hopped up on one of the rider-less horses they'd brought.

The leader man signaled for them to go. The horses broke through the trees, galloping across the volcanic rock and mud sounding like cannonballs crashing against the earth.

On the other side of the bridge, as soon as the thugs saw their boss leaving, they commenced to beating Etam again. He fought them valiantly until one ran up behind him and shoved him, he went flying, flailing over the edge of the steep chasm.

Bruno burst out of the temple running to help Etam. Jancarlo raced from the back of the temple, Johnson hurtled from one side and Knox tore out from the other, Stav and Lil Dam came from different directions. They ran to help Etam but saw him go over the edge and the thugs jumping up and down in glee.

As Jancarlo ran past one of the thugs- he swung his fist out plowing it like the speed of light into a man's jaw, the brute dropped like a sack of dirt. Jancarlo slid to his knees as he reached the cliff. Johnson and Knox did the same, knocking out mercenaries on their way following Jancarlo. Bruno was already there, lying on his stomach with his hands hanging over the edge.

Petrified of what he was going to see, Jancarlo dropped to his stomach next to Bruno and looked over. His relief at seeing Etam clinging to some roots turned to dread realizing the roots were plucking one-by-one out of the side of the bank. Frantic sweat pouring into his eyes, Bruno was holding onto one of Etam's wrists.

"My legs!" Jancarlo yelled reaching down to grab Etam's other wrist. Johnson and Stav fell to the ground and wrapped their arms around Jancarlo's legs. Knox dropped to his knees, rolling to his stomach he grasped Etam's collar. Lil Dam held onto Knox to anchor him.

The men grunted and groaned pulling with all their might, Etam scrabbled at the dirt with his boots climbing up the wall. Struggling with all the strength they had, they finally pulled Etam up and over, yanking him onto the flat land.

Etam didn't stop to talk, catch his breath, or tend to his wounds, scrambling unsteadily to his feet he sped to the temple to get his pack and his weapons. The thugs were trying to get up to flee but the team and Stav, Lil Dam and Bruno descended on them in fury. The ones that didn't go over the ravine were beaten then tied to trees.

"What's gonna happen to them?" Bruno asked, as he followed Johnson into the temple where the others were quickly gathering their belongings.

Tossing supplies and weapons into a backpack, Johnson replied noncommittally, "We might come back for them, more likely we will try to contact authorities to come and retrieve them."

Lindsey wandered out bleary-eyed appearing embarrassed at being caught in the middle of undressing to have sex. She asked, "What's going on?" but they all ignored her. She ran after Bruno catching his arm to stop him. "What's going on?" she repeated loudly, watching everyone scurrying about.

Bruno tersely shook off her hand, he didn't hide his fury at her. "While you were seducing me, Miss Tirsa was being kidnapped and the colonel was trounced and thrown off the cliff." He turned abruptly from her to hurry after the others that were already leaving to catch up with Etam.

Lindsey ran after him, grousing huffily, "Well he's obviously all right, I saw him run off into the woods."

Bruno didn't answer her, he raced to catch up with Etam. Not wanting to be left behind, and it appeared no one cared if she was, Lindsey sprinted trying to get to Johnson who she knew wouldn't be rude to her. They were all moving so fast she could only trail way behind them.

Out of breath, Bruno passed the men to reach Etam. Puffing, he tried to match his strides to Etam's longer, faster ones. He said between breaths, "Colonel, I…" he broke off not knowing what to say.

Louise Furley

Etam shot him a hard sidelong glance. "You were told to stay together. You were in the back having sex. What the hell was that, Soldier?" Etam kept moving, his brows slashed down over his eyes, mouth a pressed line. He had a rifle slung over his chest, and guns on his hips along with knives stashed around his body.

Dark color flushed Bruno's ashamed face as he kept pace with Etam. "Sir, Colonel, she- she- it was in my face sir, she like seduced me. She pulled her top off and stuck her nipples right in my face, I didn't, couldn't think..."

Etam nodded. He could understand. Whenever Tirsa was in sight, all rational thought left him as well, and although not that much older than Bruno himself, he had much more military training than the young OS had. However, right now he couldn't allow himself to react blindly, he had to think and plan and be cautious. He did not want to lead his team into ambush and certain death.

"Sir," Bruno asked, panting. "What about the bridge? How will we get across the ravine?"

The colonel kept his eyes trained ahead, sweeping the ground a few feet in front then to the sides, fanning out like windshield wipers. Remembering his map, he answered, "There is a shallow way across but it is a good day's travel and they are on horseback."

Bruno blanched at the dire concern the colonel was unable to keep off his face or out of his voice. Etam was so scared for Tirsa it was a struggle to gather his frenzied thoughts cohesively together so he could think of a strategy.

Jancarlo jogged up alongside, causing Bruno to move back a few feet.

Speaking through an expelled enraged breath, Etam said roughly, "It was Ziyad Rapha. That fucker has her." He gripped the butt of the Glock at his hip as if he could shoot the brutal mercenary right now. "The man is a no conscience feral beast. You know what he'll do to her," his voice broke.

The major had seen the kidnappers, he knew. Under his tan, his tough face paled. Jancarlo said to distract Etam from his gut-wrenching fears, "E, that Owen was a traitor, a goddamned confederate."

Etam nodded his concurrence. "*Ja*. It was probably Owen who had set the burros free as a diversion to nab Tirsa, and to ensure we had no animals to ride. I'm thinking he set up the rabbit too. He said he had good hunting experience and he could have done it while on guard patrol."

Jancarlo agreed. "*Ja*. I remember him asking about the horses in the beginning, if we had any."

"Me too. I'm thinking now he really wanted to know if we had any to see what kind of pursuit would we be able to achieve. That bastard has been with us from the start. He was one of the guards the day Adullam got into the yard and took Tirsa. We should have known it then. I racked it up to rookie mistakes. Knowing how we patrol also gave him a leg up to secrete cohorts in then and now. He suckered us, me."

"Betrayal. The worst kind of offense. We were all taken in," the major said toneless through grit teeth. "The death penalty kind of offense."

Etam nodded beside him. They stopped talking to conserve their energy for what lay ahead.

Chapter Thirty-Two

*T*ravelling through the woods wasn't that hard at this point as the trees were thin and sparse, the ground packed clay. They kept going until nightfall when it was no longer safe to travel. They chose a clearing off the animal path to bed down.

Etam peeled his pack off his back and tossed it on the ground. Untying the blanket, he spread it out, then threw himself down on the bag and dropped an arm over his eyes.

Johnson and Bruno were chatting quietly while positioning their blankets. Jancarlo was off to the side smoking a thin cigar and talking with Knox in low voices. Stav and Lil Dam were sitting on boulders taking their shoes off. They all watched as Lindsey, carrying her pack, started to walk past them heading towards Etam.

Blowing out smoke, Jancarlo's lids low over his eyes, his voice like coarse sand, he said mildly to her, "You would be best served to stay away from him, *sproeten.*"

Knox added, "In his mood, honey, he might hurt you, wouldn't mean to, but…"

A lurid gleam in her eyes, Lindsey's mouth turned up in carnal desire, the thought of the strong handsome colonel treating her roughly, she shivered, got hot thinking about it. She sneered at the two men, "Mind your own beeswax."

Her freckled nose in the air, she sniffed rudely then simpered over to where Etam was lying. Now was her chance with that blonde bitch out of the picture. She figured she could share the colonel's blanket, as dark as the forest was at night, the other men wouldn't be able to see them...play.

Knox stood with his hands in his pockets. Jancarlo leaned casually against a boulder, his ankles crossed, puffing on his cigar. The two majors watched Lindsey kneel down and roll her blanket out next to the colonel. Lying down, displaying herself in an openly wanton manner, she inched next to Etam then ran one finger sensuously down his arm then up his chest.

Bruno looked over with disgust. Not even half a day ago she was all hot and heavy with him. Guilt struck him. He didn't even like the girl. The colonel had entrusted him to stay with Tirsa and the group, and he had failed him because of a slut he had zero feelings for. She'd just come on so strong, he was male, his mind went blank while they- he shook his head in revulsion, more for himself than her.

He'd let down the man he respected most in the world, and now a young woman he liked a lot and the colonel was obviously crazy about, was in terrible trouble. Tears stung his eyes. He swiped furiously at them.

Johnson said kindly in almost a whisper, "He knows what happened, *broed*. He understands. You have exhibited your hard work and integrity in a hundred ways without complaint since we've been on this trip." He leaned over and patted the OS on the shoulder.

"We've all done things we've regretted. Including him." He motioned to Etam with his head. "Take my word for it, he doesn't think any less of you. All you can do now is man up and do your work the best you can. Okay?" He patted Bruno's shoulder again.

Rubbing his eyes, Bruno nodded, grateful to the major for his compassionate words. All four men watched Lindsey wriggle closer to the colonel, so close she was partially on top of him.

None of them could hear what Etam said, but suddenly Lindsey shot up looking like she'd been slapped, which she hadn't, they would have heard that. She jumped to her feet, grabbed up her blanket and stalked with a bright red face as far away as she could get from him, totally aware of the other men's mirth.

They all settled down to catch some z's. Etam was unable to sleep. He was thinking that it would take hours before they got around the ravine and back to where they could pick up the horses' hoof prints. In the meantime, it was pitch black, and Tirsa was in the clutches of Rapha and his band of cutthroats.

A single female sleeping on the ground with a group of hardened mercenaries, criminals, thugs. He shoved his fists in his eyes to wipe away the horrible picture his mind drew of the defenseless young girl trying to fight them off. Groaning his distress, he rubbed under his eyes then across his mouth. His hands on his unshaven face sounded like he was rubbing sandpaper.

Lying beside him, his voice husky, Jancarlo's said firmly, "E, we will get her back."

His words calmed Etam a fraction. *Ja*, he would get her back, but what could happen to her in the meantime? His brain roiled with the images of her torment.

"He must have been the one responsible for getting her on your ship. To take you out, and if not, get her here so he could snatch her, two birds with one stone." Jancarlo whispered, "E, it is their holy days, Rapha should be adhering to them, you think?"

Hearing his words, Etam allowed a pinch of hope to circulate in his head. "*Ja.* Maybe."

Lindsey had slipped her blanket between Johnson and Knox. When she tried to strike up a conversation they both turned away, shutting her down. The men believed if she hadn't enticed Bruno into having sex he would have been there to stop Owen from taking Tirsa.

"Well," she muttered audibly under her breath, "it wasn't my fault. It was so boring out there I had to do something to relieve the tedium."

None of them slept well. The howls and screeches in the night were jarring.

Everyone was ready to go when dawn approached. As soon as the night clouds started to break up, the group rose and wordlessly picked up their packs and started hiking.

Marching rapidly through the forest, no one said anything to Lindsey who was having a hard time keeping up, no one seemed to care whether she fell into a sinkhole or got eaten by a wild animal.

She was still steaming over the caustic, outrageously vitriolic way Etam had spoken to her. Actually, she trembled now recalling Etam's scathing words. She fled from him as fast as she could before he could make good on the vicious threat he gave her if she didn't get lost in one second. Gee, she was only trying to be nice, distract him from his concern over that stupid bitch.

It was three hours when they finally got around the ravine and near where the bridge was. They picked up Rapha's tracks right away and immediately followed them. It was no problem for miles because the tracks were deep in the clay and mud then started across a savanna they could follow where the horses had tromped down the grass. The deep mud would also slow the horses down.

The prints slowly disappeared when they entered a wide area of volcanic rock that was hard and slick like the black ice. The rock went on for miles. The only good thing was that it was slippery, the horses would have had to go very slowly.

Knox tramped beside Etam. "What about the map? You can figure where they're headed."

"*Ja*, I know the general direction, but," his mouth pulled in. "I don't have the map. Someone stole it. Likely Owen. I can find where we're going, but I can't be sure that's where she's going. Rapha is after the diamonds, we're after the book. Tirsa had told me she felt they were intertwined."

"The mission actually, E, is not the book or the gems, it's them. We were sent to arrest Rapha and his gang," Knox reminded him.

"I know. I figured we'd get the book then we'd be so entrenched in here we could track him without him knowing." Etam's shoulder twitched. "So, now we're after him first and then the book." He wiped a hand across his forehead. "Right now I don't even care about the fucking book."

Knox's brows rose in interest. "Really? You've spent a half a lifetime studying that book and planning to find it."

Etam glanced at Knox, his face set, his words drowned in suffering, he said, "Tirsa is the rest of my lifetime."

Trudging for hours with the sun beating on their backs, Etam was starting to panic that they'd totally lost their trail when Johnson called out.

He was crouched down, picking up something. He held his palm out to Etam.

Even through a day's growth of beard as he hadn't taken time to shave, when Etam saw what was in his hand his teeth glowed bright white against the black stubble.

"What is it?" Jancarlo asked, as the others came to see. Johnson held the shell in his hand for the others to view. Jancarlo gave Etam one of his rare smiles.

"*Ja.*" Still grinning, Etam said proudly, "She's a clever one, my girl. She knew I would come for her." He took the tiny shell Tirsa had been stringing on a necklace made of vines while sitting in front of the stone etchings.

He recognized the pearl one she had found so intriguing. A twinge of relief relaxed some of his stomach muscles as he squeezed it in his hand. Optimistic now, they forged ahead.

Every so often they would find another shell. In the distant trees, thick-furred spotted cuscuses, possums that resembled mini-bears awakened by their approach, some grey-white with splotches and others red, brown, black, observed the group moving closer to their perches. A vague rustle and they were gone.

Then darkness fell again. Discouraged that they hadn't found the pack of desperadoes, Etam dropped on his sleeping bag with eyes wide open. The longer it took to find her the more chances grew of her being hurt or killed. He couldn't even think about gang-rape because that would be worse than outright killing her. When they found the diamond mines, they would murder her anyway.

He scrunched his eyes, clenched his fists over them to push out the mental images.

Chapter Thirty-Three

*T*he man Rapha held an arm around Tirsa like a thick iron clamp. He was a very big man and he didn't care if he was hurting her.

When it grew dark, the mercenaries made camp. After he dismounted, Rapha pulled Tirsa down off his horse then left her, to speak with his gang.

The men made a small fire as they were settling for the night. The amount of males that were clomping around, it would be ludicrous for Tirsa to attempt to run. She sat in a ball on a log with her arms wrapped around her knees trying to make herself appear as small and as invisible as possible. Her body prickled with dread and terror seeing Rapha starting towards her, her skin shriveled, her heart sank, she couldn't think.

Dressed like a dirty pirate in a shirt missing buttons, black belt with a gold buckle, guns in harnesses crisscrossed over his chest, tight brown pants tucked into knee-high black boots that crunched the earth as he stomped up to her. "Get up. You will come with me," Rapha said with a smarmy smile, his enormous hands on his hips.

Knowing she had absolutely no choice, wishing deeply that she and Etam had made love before this animal… pushing down the queasy hysteria, her movements laggard and stiff, Tirsa climbed to her feet.

Rapha laughed crudely down at her obvious abject fear. "Don't worry, little girl. This is your lucky day. Due to our religious dictates we cannot have any form of sex or sexual contact with females during this holy weekend. It is believed that the sex act drains our energy like a vampire drains blood so…physical contact between the men and their women is not allowed. I'm pushing it by physically holding you on the horse, but that is necessary."

Her relief apparent in the color that flooded her ashen face wasn't lost on the barbarous man. Tall as a door, built like a heavy-weight wrestler with cords of muscles across his back, he had forearms like solid chiseled granite.

With brick-colored hair and mud brown eyes, the darkly tanned man had surprising patrician features, and a callous, yet attractive mouth. It was the savage delight that glinted in his merciless eyes that made Tirsa's heart thump and throat constrict so much she couldn't speak, could hardly draw a breath.

He bent at the waist until he looked her straight in her trembling eyes. "The holy days end on the 5th. Then, we will be able to make up for lost time, eh, *poquita chica*?" There was no mistake about the licentious gleam in his eyes as he grabbed the front of his trousers in a vulgar fashion and squeezed, laughing coarsely. "Baby," he slathered leering, "I'm gonna tear you up."

Tirsa crossed her arms tightly over her chest and gave him a haughty disdainful look, but could not get words past the lump in her throat.

"Aha, little girl, you are thinking he will come for you," he chortled at the look in her blue eyes confirming that was what she was thinking. His big head moved slowly, slinking from side to side. "Ah, but alas, I am the one who has to tell you," he sounded regretful but the tone didn't match the satisfaction in his voice. "Your colonel, Etam van Eleman, I'm afraid he didn't make it."

He had given the order to make sure the colonel was dead. Last thing he needed was a vengeful Etam van Eleman chasing after him, the highly skilled cop he remembered was relentless and vicious.

The colonel had caught him once and locked him up for illegal mining and Rapha knew he'd come after him again when he started pillaging the mines for the new diamonds, that's why he'd had his man in the states blackmail Tirsa into killing Etam. He should have known it would be a fruitless attempt. The colonel was too wily and a damned sick fighter, Rapha didn't relish having to deal with him in person again.

Forget even the mines, he'd taken his woman, the fearless colonel would ceaselessly, ruthlessly pursue him, and this time put Rapha in a grave. He hoped his men had done their job and *Kolonel* van Eleman was no longer a threat. Adullam had been the one to tell Rapha about Tirsa and her ancestry. They had been working together to find the mines. Eleman had easily, without hesitation taken out Adullam, Rapha had to watch his back. He hoped his men had completed the job and the *Kolonel* was dead, but, the man was what warrior stories were written about. If anyone could survive a 6-man killing unit it was Eleman.

He wished now he had told his men to shoot him with a gun. At the time he worried about gunfire drawing out the rest of Eleman's team so he'd ordered them to use the quiet

Taser. Oh well, can't unring the damned bell now, can he? He could only hope for the best.

Tirsa's mouth dropped, eyebrows disappeared in the furrows in her forehead, in disbelief she stuttered, "No...no...you said if I came without fighting you...that you wouldn't hurt him..." Her eyes pleaded with him to take back what he was implying.

His lips pulled in, he ponderously shook his head. "Oh well, it is the way in the jungle. Some things just...happen." Obscenely he palmed his crotch again, his gaze travelling the length of her. "Yes, when the holy days are over we will make up for lost time, you and I...my men can wait until I am finished."

Tirsa fisted her hands and shoved her knuckles in her mouth to keep from crying out. *There was no way, Etam can't be...oh my God...* tears sprung from her eyes like rain from the sky. *No*, she thought, *I have to be strong, I have to believe he is alive.* She couldn't bear it if he was...dead. She knew she could survive whatever horrors befell her out here, but if he was dead, she swallowed a sob, despair overwhelming her.

Rapha clutched her arm and dragged her over to where his bag was unrolled and threw her down. She fell to her hands and knees on the rocky ground. "Lay down," he barked.

She moved to lie on her side. With a grunt he lowered himself beside her. Tirsa started to inch away, he snapped out a huge arm and clasped his fingers around her throat pulling her back. When she shifted to where he wanted her, he took a rope off his belt and tied it around her wrists then tied the rope to the front of his belt.

He put his hand back around her neck. His massive body looming over her, his face an inch from hers, his voice guttural, eyes without mercy, the smell of alcohol and cigarettes intense, he said, "You only have one time. You try to escape only once and I will beat you to a bloody pulp, break all of your bones. I can still have you do the things I need even if you can't walk. You do believe me, don't you?"

She croaked out a tiny, "Yes."

Satisfied he had thoroughly cowed her, he dropped on his back and was snoring in minutes.

Tirsa lay staring at the same black sky, she hoped, as Etam, with diamond stars and the moon a bare sliver. Refusing to give in to tears and giving up, she told herself that he was alive. She remembered seeing Etam being battered by a group of men, but as they had left, Etam was still alive. So there was no way Rapha could know for sure that he was dead.

There was no satellite for phones out here, she hadn't seen or heard walkie-talkies or two-way radios or anything like that. There was still a chance he was alive, she had to believe it or…she might as well die now. She didn't want to live without him.

Chapter Thirty-four

*R*ising at daybreak, Rapha jerked Tirsa to her feet with the rope. He untied one of her wrists and led her from the camp to the thick bushes. Wondering what horrible fate awaited her now, Tirsa stumbled forward when he shoved her every few feet. He didn't push her hard, considering his size and hers, her hands and knees would be broken by now if he didn't hold back his strength.

"All right, that's far enough. I will hold this end of the rope, you can go over there. Here." He handed her some paper. When she just stared at the paper confused, he growled, "Go woman, relieve yourself. As I said, we cannot at this moment do anything sexual and that includes touching or viewing nude women or pornography. So have no fear, at least for now. Make it quick."

Before he changed his mind she stepped quickly into the bushes, slipping behind beautiful tasseled casuarina, sago and palm trees shading like fringe-topped poles. It was difficult doing her business with him lurking a mere ten feet away. She finished and grabbed up some bristle flowers growing amongst the creepers she spotted to use as a toothbrush.

Passing a Rainbow Gum, with its trunk green, blue, purple and orange, seeing some leaves on the ground she figured she could chew on them, poisonous to cats and dogs she should be okay if she doesn't swallow them. Basically a eucalyptus, the leaves had antibacterial, deodorant and other medicinal purposes. Stuffing them in her pocket she hurried back to where he impatiently waited.

Jerking the rope, Rapha said, "Let's go."

As they broke camp, Rapha spun Tirsa around facing west. "Owen said it was west you were heading, that's where the mines are. You will tell us which way to go. If you fail, the torture you will endure will rip away your mind. You will beg me to kill you to put you out of the agony." He poked a finger at her shoulder. "You savvy?"

Not sure what he meant by savvy, Tirsa figured it didn't matter, she got his point. Closing her eyes she stood still for a second. She could hear the rumblings of Rapha's men. As they continued on through the forest, more of them joined the group.

All told there now over thirty well-armed men. They were constantly bickering, occasionally breaking into fist and knife fights. Already they'd left one dead man behind who had stolen another's liquor.

Rapha had told her that's how it is with paid mercenaries that had no qualms about stealing, brawling, killing. He had shrugged with a rueful grin and told her, "You have to take the good with the bad."

The noise of the men didn't bother her, the louder they were the better chance of Etam finding them. She refused to give up hope that he would come for her. She was positive she would know, would feel it, if he was…gone.

"*Chica*," Rapha growled impatiently.

Opening her eyes she gave him another disdainful look. She felt she could act disparaging at the moment knowing he wasn't going to assault her- yet. However, he had no compunctions in hitting her, he raised a fist as big as her head. "All right," she said calmly, "I'm ready."

Rapha lifted Tirsa up on his horse and swung up behind her. He took his own hat off his head, dropped it on top of hers then untied a long sleeved shirt from his saddle and settled it over her shoulders.

He smirked at her bewildered look. "I like to take care of my possessions, I don't want you all peeling and sunburnt when we…" He let his words dangle knowing they would terrify her, thinking about it. "This is kind of fun, having to wait for our…pleasure, it's kind of like foreplay, huh? This is new for me, waiting," his breath blew hot on her neck.

Reaching both huge arms around her, he picked up her wrists and tied them together then tied the rope again to his belt. He chuckled in her ear, she could feel his breath misting her skin. "I heard what Eleman did to the last guy that tried to make off with you on horseback. A knife in the neck, eh? That fucker is fearless."

He laughed picturing the scene of Eleman like a gladiator galloping up, deliberately crashing against the other horse, stabbing the man in the neck and grabbing Tirsa off and onto his horse all in seconds. Owen had heard what happened and relayed it to one of Rapha's men he'd been meeting on the sly.

"I tell you, *chica*, we go way back, your colonel and me. I owe him for this," he said, pointing to a long nasty scar that ran the length of his arm. "As well as some others. When I get done with you we should be even. I might mail him what's left of your body." His laughter shouted out, echoing through the foothills they were approaching.

He said it to scare her but instead it gave her renewed hope that Etam was still alive if Rapha was seeking to harm him further. She tucked a tiny smile away in her heart.

The day and night was like the first one except now they were walking because there were a million hidden holes and loose rocks on the small hills they were ascending, too difficult for the horses to navigate so the men got off and walked them.

Telling her frequently that Etam was not, could not, be coming for her, Rapha kept Tirsa tied to him at all times and a few inches in front of him so she could lead the way. With all the scoundrels around them, Rapha needed to keep her tight to him anyway, or undoubtedly one of the lawless hotheads would snatch her and there'd be fighting over her, and then a big a bloody battle and time and more men would be lost.

The third day they were exhaustively hiking for hours when Tirsa slowed. Rapha dropped a heavy hand on her shoulder. "What is it, *chica*?"

They were in a field now just before the foothills. She stood still as a willow, the warmth enveloping her like a cozy blanket. She held her arms slightly out and up, her head tilted to the sun.

Not a patient man in the best of times, Rapha nonetheless held his tongue watching and waiting. Peering through narrowed lids he observed the beauty appearing to be veiled in a faint white haze. *Crazy.* He had lived off and on in these jungles and the strangest things have happened, this was nothing compared to sightings of the relic population of supposedly extinct Tasmanian tigers. Some tribes also talk of a local canine-like animal known locally as the also likely extinct 'dobsegna.'.

He could see why van Eleman fought so hard to keep this girl. She was exquisite, face and body, and with a sweet disposition, even when bravely fighting him. This only excited him more and made him more impatient to bed her. Rapha asked her questions just to hear her faintly accented lilting voice, it stirred him like catnap. The barbarian licked his lips.

Another day and she would be his to do with what he wanted. He could already tell one day with her was not nearly going to be enough, he knew he would be keeping her alive for a while for his pleasure.

His fingers curled next to his thighs, he was becoming aroused. He had prepared for it, knowing she would be sleeping beside him and riding with him on the horse. But this took him by surprise like a swift punch to the gut. He had to look away or he'd be shoving her on the ground and climbing on top of her-

"*Girl*," his snarl was sharp and grating, an onerous warning. He peered at her, squinting through tight eyes to distort his view of her beauty.

She turned brilliant shining blue eyes to him, her face a serene glow, lovely and sweet. "Yes, Mr. Rapha. We are here."

Frowning heavily, he glanced around. "Where? I see nothing. You'd better not-"

She started walking to the foothills. Snapping his mouth shut he strode behind her like the hulk following a child. His men followed with the horses in a crooked line tromping over tall grass and rocky mounds, the horses snorting, the men grumbling.

When Tirsa reached the rocky mountainside, she walked right through the solid rising earth wall like she was a ghost.

Rapha froze. "What the hell-" he stepped forward following where she had gone and saw, the hills and rocks curved in on themselves, a disguised illusion covering a hidden pathway.

When they stepped through the hills, the land beyond opened like a V into a valley in front of them. They walked on verdant grass that stretched like a rich green carpet. The border of hills widened and flattened until they came upon little wooden thatched buildings.

In minutes, people appeared slowly, speculatively. No one ever came into their valley.

The people had a unique appearance, like a cross of natives with European, and a vague Polynesian influence. Well under average height, most had dark hair and eyes, although some had lighter features.

When it seemed that the entire village had emerged and had gathered to view the strangers, Rapha stepped forward. "Who is your, uh, leader?" he asked in pidgin.

Tirsa stood a few feet away from him, she noticed the traitor Owen sidling up to Rapha's other side. He had the smirking gall to wink at her. She looked through him as if he didn't exist. Owen had stayed on the peripheral while traveling and sleeping. He was in cahoots with the mercenaries, but he wasn't actually one of them. Tirsa assumed he'd been recruited, bought off with money to betray the expedition.

A tiny wizened man spoke to Rapha in pidgin. That meant to Rapha that one or some or all of them had been out of the valley at some point. The man said politely, "We have no leader." He bowed respectfully. "We do not require one. We have elders for wisdom. We make decisions universally."

"What about you, why are you doing the talking?" Rapha asked amiably looking over the man's shoulder at the silent natives behind him. They weren't even talking to each other.

The wiry old man smiled with his lips pressed together. "There are many diverse indigenous people in this land speaking in 820 different languages. I speak the most variety of languages therefore I am merely the Speaker. I am the only one that ever leaves the valley to bring back some things occasionally such as the sheep and goats and try to teach the others some languages."

"I see. Is this everyone in the village?" Rapha asked the tiny man.

The man glanced around, there were at least 500 people, all ages, clustered behind him watching with intense interest and curiosity. Some were smiling a welcome, most were apprehensive. Turning back to Rapha he nodded serenely, replying, "Yes. All come every time something eventful occurs."

Rapha also smiled, but his was ugly. He pulled his gun out of his holster and aimed it at the man. At the same time the thirty or so mercenaries with him raised their weapons at the villagers.

No one spoke. The natives turned confused eyes from the men with guns to their Speaker.

His thin arms benignly at his side the Speaker said mildly, "Sir, there is no need for weapons here. We will be happy to accommodate you. Your men can stay in our meccthinji which is across to the side of the valley. It is a large structure we use for celebrations and such. We will gladly feed and house you for as long as you wish to stay."

Still holding his gun in a relaxed hand, Rapha said, "That's nice of you. What we want is you to show us where the mines are with the red diamonds and the wurtzites."

Hesitation crossed the gracious speaker's dark wrinkled face. "I do not under-"

BANG!

Rapha shot him right between the eyes. The old man didn't have time to blink, he just crumpled to the ground landing with his eyes wide open. The villagers let out a collective gasp of horror.

Red-face and raging, Tirsa launched herself at Rapha screaming, hitting him with her fists, "You didn't have to do that, why did you-"

Not fazed at all by her attack, her small fists more like moths batting against his huge chest, Rapha backhanded her, knocking her off her feet. She fell backwards landing beside the dead man. Rapha pointed the gun at her.

She was frightened but her rage was stronger, jumping up Tirsa started towards him again. One of Rapha's men grabbed her and held her immobile.

Sticking his huge face close to hers, Rapha smiled that ugly smile, tapped the barrel of the gun against her chin and said, "If we didn't have a date scheduled for tomorrow you would be lying next to that man bleeding out. But I have to say, *chica*, your ballsy wrath only makes you more interesting, and attractive to me."

Dismissing her, he aimed his weapon back at the villagers. He scanned their faces as he walked leisurely towards them. They were all rightly terrified, none moved, a baby was crying.

Rapha swaggered over to a young woman of around twenty and stuck the gun in her face. "You," he said reveling in the sheer terror that distorted her face. He could hear gasps and whimpering travel through the crowd.

A young man a few feet away, his voice unsteady, held his hands up in front of his stomach and said, "Please sir, she does not speak your language. I do."

Without moving his head, Rapha's eyes slanted thoughtfully to the man. He had already made his point, there wasn't any need to waste more bullets. "Come here," he commanded.

Nervously, with his hands still up, the young man who appeared to be in his late teens stepped charily towards Rapha. He had dark hair and grey eyes, was slim and toned, and dark-skinned from spending most of his time outside.

"I hear water, is there a waterfall or lake here?" Rapha asked the young man.

He nodded carefully. "Yes sir. Over there," he gestured to the east and told him, "is a deep abyss, at the bottom is roaring white water. A little ways down is a deadly whirlpool. We do not go near it, it is certain death if one were to fall in."

Rapha could see where the earth looked like it dropped right off. He walked backwards motioning with the gun for the man to follow him, he wanted to be a safe distance from the villagers, who knew if one would go nutso and attack him?

Nearer to his men, he ordered, "Surround them, you three stay with me." Rapha indicated three men directing with his gun. The men scattered, spreading around the villagers until they were evenly spaced out standing behind them.

Rapha asked the young man, "What's your name?"

The young man straightened his spine to stand taller in an attempt to hide his staggering fright of the giant brute who had just cold-bloodedly killed one of their own. "Sir, I am Majji, sir."

The natives wore pretty much the same things, men and women. Tan to beige loosely woven slacks and tops, sandals covered feet that were calloused from being barefoot a lot of the time. The women's hair ranged from short to long, the men all had long hair tied back in ponytails.

"Okay, Majji, this is what you're going to do. First, tell your people to go to the building you mentioned, the thinji-house," he pronounced it wrong but cared less. Majji waited for the rest. Rapha's brows arched in arrogance, he smiled his ugly cruel smile. "You would be doing that now. Everyone goes."

Immediately, Majji turned around to face his people. He took a shuddering breath fearing his voice would come out as an inaudible squeak. After a short cough, he said a string of words that Rapha didn't understand.

It worked whatever he said. The villagers without question or comment all turned en mass and started walking to the meccthinji building not knowing if they were going to salvation or execution. A few of the mercenaries stayed guarding the doors so the villagers could not leave, the rest rejoined Rapha.

"Very good, Majji, it's nice to see you value your life. Now, do what I tell you, and we will take what we want, and leave you all alone. Do you understand me?"

His voice failing him Majji gulped and nodded.

"Good. We know you are the guardians for what we want. Take us to the mines." Rapha waved the gun out towards the valley.

Without speaking, Majji rotated stiffly and headed down the mouth of the valley.

Chapter Thirty-five

*T*he man holding Tirsa dug his fingers into her arm and dragged her along next to Rapha as they followed Majji. The young native villager strode slowly yet purposefully on a dirt path that bordered the valley. Rapha's men trotted behind them.

Tirsa said to the man gripping her arm, "I will not try to run, you can let go of me."

He grinned at her then shoved her hard enough she tumbled to her hands and knees.

Rapha chastened him, "Tomlin, I don't want her bruised and broken when I…" he turned a sly eye to Tirsa on her knees glaring at him, "when we get to know each other better, tomorrow. Now, be a gentleman and help her up."

The man Tomlin, reached down and clutched her hair pulling her to her feet. She stood up and tried to kick him but he whipped out a knife and held it to her throat. "You must behave, little girl," he said cheerfully, breathing whiskey and cigarettes in her face, "or I will slice you into ribbons."

"Tomlin," Rapha made tsking sounds, "knock it off or you won't get a turn at her when I'm done."

With his hand still in her hair, Tomlin pulled her head back in an arch almost snapping her neck in two, so she had to look right up in his face. He jeered down at her, his mouth inches from hers. Scars like latticed fences crisscrossed his darky weathered face, under several days' growth of beard his wide mouth stretched from ear to ear with several gold teeth sparkling in it. Nasty filmy eyes burrowed into hers.

Licking his chops he said, "I can't wait," then he shook her loose and pushed her ahead.

Owen scuttled up next to her. Nudging her with his shoulder he mocked, "Hey sweetheart, not quite the little princess now are you?"

Unexpectedly, Tirsa swung in an arc and shoved him as hard as she could with both hands. Caught in the middle of taking a step, Owen couldn't keep his balance and toppled over sideways.

Tirsa stopped, with one hand on her hip she pointed a finger in his face, said cryptically, angrier than she had ever been in her life, "You *traitor*," she spat the word at him. "If I get my hands on a sword I will run you through myself." She snapped her head around and stalked off. All the other men were guffawing at Owen getting knocked on his butt by the wisp of a young woman.

"Ooo, bro, better not mess with that one, she'll eat you for breakfast!" one of the men chortled, the others laughed with him. His round face beet red with embarrassment and fury, Owen got to his feet and strode off muttering when they no longer had a use for her what he would do to her.

Travelling for less than ten minutes, Majji slowed then moved smoothly over to the side of the mountain. Rapha was right on his heels. Majji stood next to the rocky wall. "There." He motioned with his head, there was a large opening in the wall.

Greed written all over his face, Rapha eagerly shoved Majji aside and charged past him into the opening. His whoops of glee echoed out of the mountain. The other men rushed in all at once.

Forgotten, Tirsa caught Majji's hand and said urgently, "I didn't know there were people here, I thought I was only leading him to mines. We need to go while we can, free your people."

Majji fell back shaking his head. He was too afraid. Tirsa was going to argue with him but she could see he was firm.

Hurrying away from the mouth of the cave, Tirsa frantically searched for a place to hide, or run. The valley was wide open, there weren't any trees or foliage until at least a quarter mile out. The sun was setting so she might get a break and be able to hide in the dark. She headed for the trees but didn't take three steps when her hair was suddenly wrenched back.

"Where you goin' girl?" In desperate need of a bath, ranky Tomlin hitched his arm around her neck dragging her back to the cave. "Rapha says you need to see what you found for him."

Tirsa scraped at his arm with her nails trying to gouge him. He released her, she stumbled, he snagged her arm catching her up, and staked her against his side with a thick arm. He smelled like he'd fallen in a vat of stagnant whiskey.

Tomlin knew instantly it was a mistake to hold her to him, he couldn't stop his hands from roaming all over her body, he hadn't been around a woman for a while, not one like this one anyway. The ever-after punishment he would receive for sinning on the holy day cut into his frenzied mind, he suddenly roughly shoved her away.

"There you are, *chica*. Come see what you got me!" Rapha stepped out of the dark. Taking Tirsa's hand he tugged her into the cave. The narrow opening enlarged after a few feet in.

Rapha led her across the stone ground, then drew her into a cavern. Before she entered, Tirsa could see a bright colorful glow emanating from the cavern.

Her mouth dropped in awe. The cavern was filled with amazing streaming radiance. Standing in one spot, she slowly pirouetted to take it all in. It was like they'd stepped into a brilliant jewelry store. The glistening walls and ceiling sparkled with every color of the rainbow like a thousand lit Christmas trees.

"They're diamonds, girl, diamonds!" Rapha exclaimed in exhilaration, his own face reflected the colorful glow. His men were already chipping at the psychedelic walls with knives.

The problem was, they hadn't come prepared, their equipment was back on the horses and with the sun almost down, if the room wasn't so dazzling incandescent they wouldn't be able to see their hands in front of their faces.

"All right, men," Rapha boomed, "let's call it a night. We found the damned place, let's hit the sack and come back in the morning with the tools." So thrilled with the discovery that was long planned, and a rough journey to get to, he vigorously clapped his hand on Tirsa's arm guiding her back outside.

As soon as they emerged, Majji approached timidly, his arms rigidly at his sides, the dark hair was sliding out of the band, loose pieces drifted around his shoulders. "Sir. You must not take the crystal stones. They belong to the earth and to the Cormalia Goddess. It is a transgression that cannot be righted." His gaze dropped to the handful of diamonds gleaming in Rapha's hand, and his pockets stuffed with gems.

Majji's face screwed up as if he were in great pain. "No, sir, you must put them back, certain death will-"

"I got your certain death right here, boy." Rapha swung his gun up aimed it between Majji's eyes his finger on the trigger-

As soon as she saw the gun in Rapha's hand, Tirsa threw herself at him knocking the gun, a shot rang out, the bullet chipped off a piece of the mountain just missing Majji's head. Shock and fright slapped all the color from the young native's face.

"Run Majji!" Tirsa screamed, throwing herself at Rapha again grappling at his hand so he couldn't take aim at the teen who snapped out of his frozen terror and ran.

Rapha shook Tirsa off, grabbed her arms and hurtled her to the ground. Furious, he aimed the gun at her and cocked it. "You goddamned bitch," he barked, stepping closer to her.

Tirsa sat back with her hands braced on the ground behind her. The blonde curls a ruffled cloud around her. Saying a silent prayer, she stared defiantly at Rapha. She was damned if she was going to beg the ruffian for her life.

But, the big man laughed instead, he lowered his head bobbing it in disbelief. A huge grin covered his earthy face, shaking his head he wiped a sleeve across his mouth. His expression was pure admiration for the young woman sitting at his feet practically daring him to shoot her.

"You are one brave, insolent little bitch." He leaned over took her arm and yanked her to her feet. "I am looking forward to noon tomorrow more than I can remember anticipating anything ever before in my life. Except of course the diamonds." He grinned at her, held onto her arm and started walking.

Knowing if she dropped to the ground refusing to walk with him, he would just drag her by the hand, or throw her over his shoulder like Owen had done. So she went peacefully, biding her time until another opportunity to escape arrived. She deeply hoped he'd forgotten his threat of beating her to a pulp if she tried to escape. To distract him, she asked, "Noon?"

He nodded, traipsing across the dark green grass towing her along. "*Si.*" He grinned again, he had a handsome mouth but an ugly smile and a nasty grin. "Holy days end at noon." He leered at her, squeezed her wrist. "Don't you remember, girl, we have a date, tomorrow, at noon."

Her legs suddenly weakened, Tirsa could feel her entire body quaking. She only had the night to get away. Rapha moved faster, she had to walk quickly to keep up.

Tomlin came up alongside them. "We got all the villagers sequestered so we can take over their homes."

"*Si.* We'll take that one there, looks like each man can pretty much get a place to himself. I'm sure most of them will prefer to bunk together though. They won't be falling asleep early with the adrenalin from the find coursing through their veins. They will want to drink and gamble." Rapha let go of Tirsa's wrist and took her hand like they were lovers.

The houses were small wooden frames with thatched roofs made of woven palm fronds. Rapha threw the door open to one of the homes and ushered Tirsa inside. There was a main room and several bedrooms all very spartan. Plain wooden chairs and tables, homemade rugs made from goat fur softened the floors.

There was no electric, the natives made candles out of bee and palm wax and soap from vegetable oils. Rapha dragged Tirsa along as he checked out the rooms. In the kitchen were stores of jarred fresh vegetables, fruit, bread from their small wheat field, goat cheese and churned butter, and salted fish.

"You would think with all those jewels they could at least decorate a little. This is stark and boring," Tomlin grumped, lighting a cigarette. He opened cupboards. "I bet they don't even have liquor the queer little freaks."

"It's okay, I got plenty," Rapha grunted. Not missing the cagey light in Tirsa's eye, he headed towards the bedrooms. The doors to the rooms were all open and had no locks on them.

Rapha chose the one room in the middle that had no windows. "You're in here." He had picked up some candles on the way and handed her one and a pack of matches.

Tirsa subtly glanced in the room then looked around the big man down the hall searching for a weapon. She was also thinking when he'd mentioned the whiskey, the men would get drunk and pass out, Rapha would likely tie her up and she could use the candle to burn off the ropes.

Rapha roared with laughter, his hand on his belly he bent at the waist. "*Chica*, you got more balls than most men I know." Wiping a tear from his eye he said, "I can read you like a book. Still trying to find a way to make a run for it, huh?"

Tirsa frowned bewildered, she explained very seriously as if he was stupid, "I do not have testicles, Mr. Rapha, I am a female." Being in close proximity to men lately, she was picking up on slang, yet she still took things literally, such was her upbringing.

He barked out a crow of laughter at her innocence. "It must be true the way you grew up, Owen says you were raised in seclusion." Scratching his head then his big barreled chest, he set his beefy hands on his hips.

"Well, *chica*, I will be finding out tomorrow whether you are a male of female for sure. Although," his gaze went from her tiny waist to her full breasts, "I'm pretty sure I've already got it figured out. Riding on that horse with you bouncing against me, there's little doubt those are real feminine curves, baby."

Her skin crawling at his crudeness, she had been trying to sneak one imperceptible step at a time to the side to maybe suddenly dash away. He moved his arm setting his hand on the frame of the door next to her head, deliberately blocking her escape. She shrank away from him.

Grinning like a magpie he chuckled, "*Chica*, you make me laugh inside and out, I can't remember when I've had such fun with a female. Your courage astounds me." The grin widened, "I would like to spend some more time with you tonight," he sighed, the grin slipped, "however, I can't do another night with you next to me and not climb all over and inside you. I'm starting to feel like a pressure cooker as it is, so, in ya go."

He gave her a soft push then hovered in the doorway, sending her a snickering smirk. "I can read escape all over your face little girl. There's no window inside there, and there'll be a chair under the door knob. So don't waste your time plotting, get some sleep." He bent and before she could back away he grabbed her neck, kissed her hard on the lips then shut the door in her face.

Thinking he'll pay for that kiss in the afterlife, a tiny sin on the holy day, maybe only a tiny punishment. He grinned again, shoving a chair under the knob, it was worth it. He licked his lips tasting her. He couldn't remember tasting anything that damned sweet in his life. Tomorrow noon could not come fast enough.

Back in the main room, Rapha flopped down on what he would describe as a couch. It was a bunch of cushions stuffed with goat hair tied on top of one another. Tomlin handed him a bottle of whiskey then took his own and sat on a chair made the same as the couch.

"I see you found my booze." Rapha unscrewed the top and guzzled a long drink. "Ahh," he wiped his mouth with his hand.

A swinish glimmer in his eyes, Tomlin asked, "What are you going to do about her?" He gestured with his head towards the other room then bent his head back slugging down the fiery liquor.

Rapha drank some more. Settling back with a sigh and a belch, he wiped his mouth again with the back of his hand. "At first I thought I'd just do her and kill her, or give her to the guys, but," he hesitated, holding the bottle to his mouth without drinking, he tapped it against his lip.

"There's something…can't explain it…but I think it'll be a long while before I give her up." Tipping the bottle he drank thirstily like it was water.

"Uh huh. I can see it, feel it too." Tomlin leaned forward with his arms on his knees holding the whiskey bottle in both hands. "Of course you know van Eleman will come for her." His gaze slid sideways to Rapha.

Rapha's face stiffened. "He's dead, bro. I told the guys to make sure of it before they left the temple. I would have liked to get them all, that fuckin' Jancarlo Mercury and the rest, but it's highly doubtful our men are good enough to take them out. Using the girl to kill Eleman didn't work, but she was useful anyway as it turned out. We wouldn't have gotten

Eleman if we hadn't planned so well and got him separated from the others, and that was because he came after her.

"The ambush and using the Taser iced it. Couldn't use a gun it would have drawn the others or bring rangers down on us if there was any around. Jarlson said he saw Eleman go over the cliff. Anyway," he drained more of the alcohol then said with a slur, "his men will scatter without Eleman holding them together. He's the lynchpin."

"You better pray they did the job, took that cop out, because if not," Tomlin glanced at Rapha, "you're a dead man when he comes for her."

Lifting the whiskey, there was suddenly a slight tremor in his hand, the bottle hit Rapha's mouth cracking against his teeth.

Chapter Thirty-Six

*L*indsey could no longer keep up with the long fast strides of the men, she lagged behind further and further. Johnson went back to get her. "Hop up, hon, I'll carry you." He bent so she could climb up his back.

His hands under her knees, he jogged to catch up with the others. They hiked until they had to stop at the solid mountain wall that loomed dishearteningly impenetrable in front of them.

"There is nowhere else to go, E," Jancarlo said quietly, lighting a cigar. Musky wine-scented smoke trailed around and up.

Knox stood back surveying the massive stone wall looking for an opening, or trail, or hole, something.

Etam put his palms flat on the wall and walked back and forth feeling for, anything.

After a long search and finding nothing, the men stood in a line staring dejectedly at the mountain. Lindsey waited off to the side. "Dead end," she muttered with glee under her breath.

Seeing Etam's ears turn red, Johnson went over to her. "Honey, I swear if you open your mouth again the colonel is going to pitch you into the next ravine we come to." He sauntered back to stay with his mates. Lindsey crossed her arms and flattened her mouth into a hard line.

The men wandered around the mountain, pacing, studying, feeling the smooth and rocky protruding wall for another hour. The sun almost completely below the horizon, it grew dark quickly. Thick clouds stole in covering the moon and stars.

Jancarlo untied his blanket from his back and laid it out on the ground. Rolling into it he said, "We can keep looking in the morning." The rest followed suit.

Morning twilight lingered, the sky still hazy heavy with the night clouds, unable to sleep, one-by-one the group got up and wandered around just hoping to stumble across something.

Etam and Johnson were huddled in front of a crack in the mountain, everyone else was stretched along the wall still searching for an opening. Knox strolled over, spoke quietly, "I think-"

"Wait." Jancarlo flicked his second cigar of the morning away and crouched to the ground. Smiling, he stood up. He shined a tiny flashlight on his palm.

"A shell," Johnson murmured in wonderment. Relief swept over him. "Praise God." The four men hurried over, moving carefully in the dark to where Jancarlo picked up the shell.

Knox leaned a hand against the solid rock wall and fell over.

"Knox, what-" Etam reached a hand down and pulled the major to his feet. The two men put their hands against the mountain and were stunned when their hands appeared to disappear. Everyone gathered around and studied the wall's illusion.

"It's a pass-through," Knox said, blinking in disbelief. "We need to study it before we-"

Wasting no time, Etam moved right up to the opening. Not knowing what they were going to encounter on the other side, he said, "Lil Dam, you stay here with Lindsey, do not go through the opening until we return," then he stepped through the mountain. Knox went right behind him, Jancarlo and Johnson next, Stav and Bruno followed.

Stepping blindly through the illusional wall, Etam emerged slowly, his eyes adjusting to the dark. The clouds were breaking up, separating for the sun to rise. Dawn would be in less than an hour. The others coming to join Etam stood one-by-one in fascination. Spread in front of them was a bountiful valley.

In the low light facing north, they could see vegetable and wheat fields dotted with fruit trees way to the east, goats and sheep tethered nearby looked like sleeping fuzzy marshmallows. Wood huts clustered in loose knots mottled through the center of the rich green land.

The mountain wall bordered around the gardens and narrowed beyond, closing back into itself like a funnel. Flexible palms bending slightly in different directions sprinkled around the huts. They could hear the sound of muffled water splashing to the west, but couldn't see it.

Johnson whispered, "Kind of like a rustic Emerald City."

Knox's grin was a slash of white in the dark. "Hopefully without the flying monkeys."

Stav joined in, "What about Dorothy? She was a-"

"Really?" Etam cut in tersely.

The men shifted awkwardly, contrite at their foolish chatter. Etam said, "All right. Recon. I'll go-"

"*Neen*," Jancarlo stated flatly.

Etam turned to him with impatient objection in his raised brows.

The major said, "We will do the recon, you will stay here."

Shaking his head at his friend, Etam looked at Jancarlo like he'd lost his mind, he said resolutely, "No way Jan, I am not-"

"*Neen*," Jancarlo repeated impassively. "You go in, the second you see her you will recklessly go for her without thought, plan or care."

"Jan." Etam's brows now angry bars drawn over disputing eyes, he was ready to charge ahead without wasting time arguing.

"*Neen*," Jancarlo said again calmly, firmly, softly.

Etam stood with his hands on his hips glaring at the major. Then the tension drained from his shoulders. He knew Jancarlo was right. As soon as he laid eyes on Tirsa he would be killing anyone or anything between them then he would snatch her and run. Rash actions on his part could endanger them all. He dropped his head then looked up at his comrade.

The major set a hand on Etam's shoulder, they locked eyes. Etam's reluctant nod was short.

Jancarlo patted his shoulder then turned to the others. "All right. I will start to the east, Stav ten seconds behind me, Knox to the west, Bruno ten seconds behind him, Johnson, since you will blend in the dark the best, you take the middle."

A corner of Johnson's mouth pulled in, he said drily, "Humor, Jan? How unlike you."

"I was not being funny, merely utilizing all of our attributes to their best ability." Jancarlo turned but not quickly enough to hide a sage grin. His strong shoulders disappeared stealthily into the night.

Knox and Johnson silently bumped fists with Etam and they disappeared into the apocalyptic shadows. Stav and Bruno counted ten seconds and followed them.

A man of action the same as Jancarlo, it killed Etam to stand in the cover of the few trees near the mouth where they came through and wait. The woman he loved was out there, he peered into the dark trying to see something, anything, her, and here he stood uselessly, helplessly waiting. It seemed like hours to him but was really more like thirty minutes when first Johnson returned. They waited until everyone was back before debriefing.

His voice hushed, Jancarlo said, "There are villagers held captive in a sort of long house down past the huts. There are three men guarding them. Just past the gardens are the mines, I believe the ones in question. There are two guards there."

Next, Knox said, "There's a huge drop on the west, a steep abyss with whitewater. There was no one out and about. No other guards, Rapha must think he is safe from intruders. The horses are tied close to here, over by the start of the abyss. I tried to see into the huts along that side. In three huts I counted 4 men in one, 3 in the next, 5 in the third."

Johnson gave his report. "In the five huts I checked, there're at least 2-5 men in each." Bruno and Stav reported the same.

Contemplating their information, Etam crossed his arms crossed and said quietly, "So we're looking at, at least thirty men." The others nodded. He moved his hands to his hips. "Well," his patience frayed, he asked, "did anyone see her?"

He was met with Knox's and Jancarlo's shaking heads, holding his breath he looked at Johnson.

"E, I didn't see her, but Rapha and that screw Tomlin are in the middle hut. It's likely she's there," Johnson told him grimly, wishing he had better info to offer him.

Etam rubbed his hands over his eyes, scratched his fingertips down his face, down his neck. "He would keep her near," his voice cracked.

Clearing his throat, he continued more strongly, "All right. We will go back out in the same flanking formation, I'll go with Johnson. We will circle, wait for the sun to rise and wait for them to come out. I'd rather have the cover of night but it would be too difficult to rush all of the huts at the same time, there's not enough of us."

His team nodded in agreement. Etam instructed, "No guns unless absolutely necessary, we don't know if there are other natives, children, around in the line of fire. Use your knives, machetes." Although he was wired and could hardly hold himself back from rushing to the huts, he looked calmly at each of them. Then slashed out an arm and commanded, "Let's go."

They ran lightly, quickly but as quietly as possible, invisible in the cover of waning night. Before they reached the huts, some of the mercs were already out and heading to the mines.

Hiding behind the trees and huts, the team waited until it appeared all of the men had come outside. The mercenaries without hesitation went straight to the mines. Etam's team furtively followed them until the bulk of the thugs were in front of the mines.

His head swinging all around, Etam searched for that little blonde head that made his heart beat like crazy, but to no avail. She was nowhere to be seen. His stomach started jumping, *where the hell is she?*

Johnson whispered, "Maybe she isn't even here."

Etam shook his head. "*Neen*, the shell, she is here." They couldn't wait any longer, they would be spotted any second, he shouted, "Royal Netherlands Marechausse Military Police! You are all under arrest. Come peacefully or you will be shot!"

They had the element of surprise. Stunned, the mercenaries were slow to pull out their weapons. But they weren't called mercenaries for no reason, as they whipped out knives and guns moving aggressively to attack, Etam gave the order to charge, "*Go!*"

Etam's team and the mercenaries came together, screaming, bellowing, slashing and cutting.

Instantly surrounded, Etam thrust a dagger at the closest man, cut off the head of the next with his machete and kept moving. Attacking and being attacked from all sides, Etam, Jancarlo, Knox, Johnson, Stav and Bruno blocked and repulsed, thrusted and parried, deflecting and slaughtering their way through the bulk of the mercenaries.

Some more men poured out of huts with their butcher knives raised high in the air, screaming warrior yells, they rushed Etam's team. All fought valiantly, and dirty, some insane in frenzied bloodlust. The fighting moved away from the mines, across the valley to the west. Until-

"Van Eleman!"

The blood drained from his face, Etam knew the voice, knew what it meant. Lowering his weapon he turned. Everyone stopped fighting as if the movie scroll suddenly stopped rolling.

Rapha stood far enough away that Etam would be cut down before he got to them, but close enough he could see the terror, hope, and love in Tirsa's eyes. He could only wonder why she was wearing the cutthroat's hat.

Rapha laughed heartily, his arm long enough to cross Tirsa's chest to grip her opposite arm, he restrained her like a breath-choking seatbelt. He held his machete mockingly to his side knowing he could slice her head off before Etam could get halfway to him.

"Rapha," Etam said, walking towards them, struggling to keep his powerful legs from racing to the fiend and wiping the taunting smugness off his face.

The mercenary raised his knife to Tirsa's throat and warned, "That's far enough, Eleman."

Etam slowed, but kept moving. "Rapha, give her up and we will leave you in peace, for now. You will have a chance to-"

The man laughed again, not a pleasant sound. He lowered his arm from across Tirsa's chest to possessively splay his huge fingers covering her entire stomach with his burly hand. "I guess you don't know about our date today at noon." He rubbed circles around her abdomen to show his intent.

Grinning at Tirsa, he said, "I'm starting to picture her heavy with my child." Rapha wished he could run his hands all over her body in front of Etam, taunt him, but he had to wait until noon. He already had some digits in the punishment side of the afterlife.

Rapha's voice ringing victoriously, he crowed, "You are the one defeated, Eleman. I have the mines and I have your woman." Rapha gave her a rib breaking squeeze to emphasize his ownership.

Not moving his head, the colonel scanned the area with his eyes, counting men, trying to strategize a way to…

"It's been fun, Eleman, but enough for now. We are going to put you and your men into the building where we have the villagers sequestered. I'd like to say when we have what we want that you will all be set free, alas," he gave a big faux sigh, then grinned his ugly grin.

"It will take a long time to dig out those diamonds, even with the dynamite. I can't take the chance of any of you escaping, and to leave you all in there to starve to death would be…inhumane…" his bestial chuckle was completely compassionless. "So, I'm thinking we will burn you."

Etam, his face like cement, was not listening to the loud-mouthed criminal, he was busy trying to come up with a way out. He softened slightly when he saw Tirsa watching him, the bright blue eyes trusting him to get them all safe.

She struggled in Rapha's embrace knowing it was futile but she couldn't stand still while everyone else was putting their lives on the line to free her.

Seeing the lovers connecting, Rapha frowned, then nodded cheerfully. "Yes, that will be the easiest and quickest way to dispose of all of you. I can't let you go, Eleman, you would be relentless, never stop coming after me, even after I'm finished with…her. Which, I must say I unexpectedly plan on keeping her around for a while. Like I said, I'm gonna put my heir in her belly."

He licked the side of Tirsa's face thinking another small sin to do penance for in the afterlife, but again, worth it seeing Etam's furious face darken, the black eyes burning coals scorching across the green grass right at him.

A lesser man would have wilted into terror and run away as fast as they could. Rapha guffawed uproarishly, pleased with himself. The elbow Tirsa jammed in his side was nothing but a gnat against his muscled girth, it only made him laugh more. She was a feisty one!

"Rapha," Etam started, but the mercenary was done toying with him.

"Enough. We need to get to the mines, the sun is well up now and I have a date at noon to get ready for." Rapha motioned to Tomlin. "Take them to the longhouse." He turned to Owen who had slunk up next to him and ordered, "Get provisions to light the fire and go with him."

Own grinned hugely. "Yes sir." He couldn't resist, he reached out and like an adolescent, pulled Tirsa's hair, then, he dropped his hand to grope her breast but Rapha twisted her away.

"No, you fool, you break the holy days we're all cursed. Now go."

Owen could still reach her, he smacked Tirsa on the butt, thumbed his nose and started to swagger off. Rapha put his boot on Owen's butt and shoved him.

Owen staggered forward taking giant awkward stumbling steps, his arms swinging to catch his balance. Rapha's muddy eyes bored holes in the seaman's back as he skulked off to find lighter fluid. Rapha would have shot him right in the head if he didn't need every man he could get. Eleman had vastly diminished his troops.

When Owen passed Etam, he winked impudently and grinned in triumph at him. He said nastily, "I get her when he's done. Wanna watch, Colonel?" Seeing Etam's eyes burning promised retribution fiercely at him, Owen giggled, knowing the colonel was impotent to do anything to him. Still, he skipped quickly past the colonel who held himself in rigid control, other than his burning eyes, his expression was blank.

In fact, Owen didn't bother Etam as much as the power Rapha held over him, his team, and Tirsa. Etam's mind worked furiously trying to see, figure a way out. It looked like his only chance was to just charge Rapha and hope Rapha would push Tirsa aside to fight him. Rapha had made it clear he strongly desired her so it was unlikely he would kill her.

While Etam struggled to plan a way out of the mess, he saw Rapha drop a long sleeved shirt over Tirsa's shoulders and straightened his hat on her head. The burly man settled his meaty hands on her shoulders flaunting his ownership of her.

Rapha's sick smile spanned his face wide like batwings, teeth sharp and gleaming, he taunted, "You see, Eleman, I can take better care of her than you can, I won't let some dirtbag come along and easily take her from me." He gloated, knowing his digs struck Etam where it hurt. Rapha knew the colonel was the big saver and protector of women and children, but had failed in protecting his own woman.

Needling Etam further, he said, "Since I plan on keeping her for a while, I need to protect my investment. That lovely alabaster skin needs shielding from the severe sun, we can't have it turning rough from the UV rays, I want it to stay as soft as silk when I...touch it...lick it...everywhere."

His gaze swept her, his tongue rolled around his mouth. "I need her supple when she pushes out my...spawn." He burst into vile laughter.

Tirsa tried to shake away from his hands, but he just grinned and rubbed his chin against her face. He let Etam take a second to absorb the mental picture of Rapha's beefy calloused hands on Tirsa's naked body, then turned to his men and ordered, "All right, men, march them back to the

367

thinji-house where the natives are. As soon as they're inside tell Owen to fire it up."

Sliding his hands down from Tirsa's shoulders, Rapha wrapped his arms around her and near to Tirsa's ear he whispered, "We will wait safely here until the building is burning. Then it's off to the mines, *chica*." He gave her a hug.

"But only for a few hours, then, when the sun hits the high spot in the sky, its zenith, you know what happens then…" he loved it when she shuddered in his arms. It'll be a worse shudder in a couple of hours, when he strips her, he couldn't wait.

Rapha's men started moving towards Etam and his men, now with their guns trained on them, they were circling them, nudging at the men with the barrels of their weapons.

Etam was poised to make his run at Rapha when a shout and a blur burst behind the big mercenary. Etam's eyes popped but he leaped right into action.

Lil Dam held a pistol to Rapha's head, he shouted, "Let her go, asshole!"

Rapha froze. He hadn't thought to cover the entrance to the valley, he figured everyone was inside. His hands tightened around Tirsa, he was not giving her up. Lil Dam cocked the gun, Rapha let her go.

At that second all hell broke loose. Seeing Lil Dam had Rapha, Etam's men struck out fighting Rapha's mercenaries.

Etam ran to Tirsa, Tirsa ran from Rapha towards Etam but as he passed a small shed to get to her, Lindsey stepped out with a .357 Sig aimed at Etam's chest causing him to come to an abrupt stop.

"Hello there, Colonel, you are finally going to regret your boorish behavior towards me and nastily brushing me off." The redhead sneered at him, her pretty face was flushed with anger, the freckles blended together in her normally pasty but now ruddy petulant face.

"You know, scorned women and all that, and her," she said, nodding in Tirsa's direction. "The trouble that bitch has caused. You sent Dia away because of her, that was totally unfair. I'm going to shoot you first and make her watch then I will-"

Knowing the young seaman wouldn't chance the colonel's life, Rapha shoved Lil Dam hard to the ground now that Etam was under their power again. The gun hurtled out of Lil Dam's hand and one of Rapha's men grabbed it rushed off to join the other men fighting.

Rapha shouted belligerent yet nervous, "Shut up, Lindsey. Shoot the fucker before he does something." Last thing he needed was Eleman on the loose again. He turned and scuttled after Tirsa who had run but now stopped unsure of what to do.

Rapha wasn't carrying a gun, he'd thought the valley was impregnable, the opening virtually invisible. Regardless of the drama playing out there, further down the valley Etam's men and Rapha's mercenaries continued fighting for supremacy.

Lindsey shot Rapha a snooty glance while stepping closer to Etam and pendulating the gun from Tirsa to Etam and back. Over her shoulder she said to Rapha, "You've been doing things your way, now it's my turn to get it done right you fool." She grinned at Owen who had returned and was making his way to her.

"You too, Lindsey? You were a plant, a traitor too?" Etam asked, drawing her attention back to him.

Her disagreeable expression slid into a sly as a sneaky fox smile. She turned back to the colonel and said smugly, "Don't you remember the pirates told you redheaded women are bad luck?" She fluffed the strawberry locks which no longer tied in a braid, were a lot worse for wear from their journey.

"It was my job to keep Bruno occupied while Owen snatched the bitch. Clever, huh?" Her smutty grin sharpened with malicious cunning, she pushed her hair, heavy with dirt and fuzzy from humidity, off her bony shoulders. It flopped down her back like smushed springs.

Sneering arrogantly, her condescending eyes swept the length of Etam, the dirty hair swung back around covering her flat chest. "We couldn't believe you didn't see any of this coming, especially after the initial inept attack on you from that little blonde hoodlum." She shoved the kinky hair off her shoulders, sneering again at Etam.

"That was why you didn't catch on to us, your brain was clouded with…her." Tossing her high nose up at Tirsa, her words tapered off showing her hurt pride and irritation that Etam had chosen Tirsa over her.

"Lindsey," Tirsa called from a dozen yards away. The redhead swiveled slightly, taking a step to the side so she could see Tirsa and Etam at the same time. She leveled her vile gaze at the woman who in her mind was her rival.

"What do you want, you little bitch?" Lindsey snarled then turned her attention back to Etam.

"Your brother," Tirsa said in her sweet melodic voice, it hardened just a hair. "You know, the one you killed when you were 12."

Lindsey looked like she'd been smacked. Her mouth fell open, her eyes splat wide, the hazel irises splintered into alarm, then guilt, then disbelief. Blinking rapidly, dark red flooded her pasty skin as her defensive anger rebuilt. Her eyes narrowed at Tirsa, she hissed, "What are you talking about?"

Tirsa smiled grimly. "This isn't about you murdering him, God will deal with you on that. It's about what your brother, Sean, the one you hung in the tree because the ten-year-old had the gall to tell your parents, that jealous because your folks refused to let you have one, you cut up the neighbor's puppy and gleefully watched it die, slowly. It's about what he has to say to you."

Lindsey glared half in disbelief bordering on fearful belief, afraid of what her vengeful brother could do to her from the beyond, she stammered, "What...what did he...say?"

Rapha caught Tirsa's arm holding her from moving closer to Etam. Tirsa tried to shrug him off but it was like pulling away from a gigantic pit-bull. She said to Lindsey, "He said that he forgives you..."

What was left of color in Lindsey's face leeched out, leaving her skin like dried speckled paper. Her thoughts sailed back to when she and her brother-

"Dammit, shoot him!" Rapha hollered, jerking Lindsey back to the present. Etam had moved closer to her, his eyes on the gun.

Lindsey lifted the weapon back up. "Stop, Colonel." Infuriated with him, she still couldn't help admiring his rugged face, broad shoulders, remembering his strong, buff chest covered with dark hair, a cliché, she knew, but she undressed him with her eyes.

She had seen him before without his shirt. Picturing him bare-chested, it made her swoon even now, her gaze slid to his lean hips and what the tight jeans outlined. Hazel orbs bulging at *his* bulge, her sharp tongue swirled greedily around her thin lips.

Etam took another step towards her with his hands out, palms up nonthreatening, his head tilted to the side. With a slight sexy smile curving one side of his mouth, he said smoothly, "Linds, you read me wrong. I needed to keep Tirsa close to figure out her game. You know, keep your friends close and the unknown in front of you. Don't you think that you and I..." his eyes like sparking onyx discs blazed heatedly down her body then up to her vacillating, ambivalent face.

Uncertain, she felt herself start to melt. Really, how could she resist that body, those flaming eyes that obviously desired her, Lindsey lowered the gun slightly, "Maybe we-"

Etam exploded at her, throwing the entire weight of his body against her so fast she couldn't shoot the gun. Her bone-crushing fall to the ground knocked the wind out of her.

Lil Dam scurried over and snatched the gun she dropped while Etam bolted up the yard to Rapha who having captured Tirsa again was dragging her away. He lifted her off the ground to move more quickly, she punched and kicked and twisted but he carried her easily like an elephant holding a child curled in its trunk.

Etam raced after them, Jancarlo inches behind him.

When the men neared him, Rapha picked Tirsa up in his arms holding her high next to his chest as a shield. "Get back, Eleman, get back!" Rapha shouted, afraid of the fierce enraged colonel who never slowed just kept coming at them like a charging bull.

Etam was steps away when, panicked, Rapha lifted Tirsa higher, he moved closer to the edge of the steep ravine. Tirsa screamed and Etam ran faster, pumping his strong biceps as hard as he could, black hair streaming.

Rapha shrieked and threw Tirsa- over the cliff-

Etam roared, *"Neen!"* Never slowing he ran and sprung off the crest-

Right behind Etam, Jancarlo rushed up, stabbed his machete straight through Rapha's belly then kept going to the edge of the ravine. He dropped to his knees to look down the gorge.

Way down below, he could see rushing wild water. He searched, his eyes darting and dashing in all directions. He could see nothing but whitewater. He remembered the girl couldn't swim. "Go with God, *mijn broeder, blondine*," he murmured, making the sign of the cross over his huge chest.

Jancarlo didn't see Owen flying up behind him, he was just turning at the footsteps when the young seaman leapt in the air his intent to kick Jancarlo off the cliff.

While racing towards them, Johnson threw a knife, striking Owen in the shoulder while the beanpole was airborne- the force of it knocked him onto Jancarlo who blasted up with a primeval snarl and using his back shoved Owen right to the edge.

Screaming like a little girl, Owen's arms flailed, his eyes terrified, the moppy hair flying, he held his hands out to Jancarlo to grab him, save him. Jancarlo stood stock still, legs braced with his hands at his side and watched the seaman go over the edge.

"Jan!" Knox yelled, rushing in from the side. He skidded on his stomach to the precipice to catch Owen- but he only grasped air.

Crawling to the edge he peered over. He saw Owen's ochre hair flying all over and his arms flinging everywhere trying to fight the rushing current he had plunged into. Saying a quick prayer, Knox got to his feet as Johnson reached them.

The three mates stood heaving, panting, staring at the abyss. Knox said, "E's a damned strong swimmer, he'll be okay."

Jancarlo muttered, "Not if he does not get her."

"Let's go," Johnson said. "Bruno, Lil Dam and Stav are holding their own, we need to get back to them. Lil Dam said he had to come in against orders because Lindsey just ran through the opening into the valley, he was told to stay with her so he had to follow her. Rapha was more than twice his size, it took courage for the *luttel broed* to stick a gun to Rapha's head."

"He is a damned good man, make a fine soldier, could be a part of our team." Rare praise came from Jancarlo.

The majors nodded, agreeing with him. Jancarlo said, "The two others as well, good brave men. Like Etam." The three friends stood motionless for a moment, trying to get their focus off Etam and back to their adversaries.

Knox commented, "I saw five or six foul, scavenger merc's grab Lindsey and gallop off on their horses heading out of the valley, she was wailing like a screech owl screaming for help."

"Too bad." Jancarlo kicked at the dead Rapha as they ran back to finish the fight.

Chapter Thirty-Seven

Not knowing what was on the other side of the cliff, Etam leaped, he would either survive with Tirsa, or die with her, but he wasn't going on without her.

He flew in the air for a few feet then dropped like a rock, heading a long, long, long way down until he plunged head first into the roiling rushing rapids.

Thankfully it wasn't a shallow river or he would not have survived the collision. It seemed an eternity before his body slowed from boring down the deep water before he could slow, then roll and swim back up.

His lungs were bursting when he finally broke the surface. He popped out like a cork gasping for air, thinking how on earth could Tirsa who couldn't swim, have possibly survived the fall. Refusing to give in to his devastating thoughts, he shook the black hair out of his eyes, water sprayed around his head.

The powerful current was going south, but for a few moments it twirled him around and around, over his head he saw a figure bullet down into the water.

He could just make out that the figure missed the small whirlpool Etam was caught in and went shooting down the river. Etam fought the funnel to get in the middle of the current, once there the tumultuous water pushed him like he was a leaf.

He helped the current by swimming as fast and strong as he could, the ripping water so strong even his boots didn't weigh him down but they made kicking difficult, he wished he could get them off but they were tied. If Tirsa had been swept away like the other person, he would need to work fast to catch up to her, being lighter she would flow faster.

Plowing his arms through the surf like windmills and kicking for all he was worth, he only raised his head every few strokes to breathe and see if he could spot Tirsa. He swam on and on, his hope deteriorating when he saw Owen.

The seaman's arms flapped like a winded flag trying to swim the turbulent river. A water blitz attack from all directions, the riot of whitecaps pummeled, bludgeoning him, trying to pull him under. He bounced and rolled uncontrollably like a ball in a gale, yet somehow he had managed to stay in one area. He saw Etam.

Owen screamed, "Colonel! Help me! Help me!" His hands flagellating the water battling to stay afloat, he kept crying for help.

"I will come back for you, stay afloat!" Etam yelled, pulsing past the terrified traitor. He would, he knew he would try to help him, but he had to get Tirsa first.

"You bastard!" Owen screeched as Etam left him.

Etam fought on. It was far down the river from where he left Owen when he finally spotted the yellow hair tumbling and twirling in the clamorous torrent.

His heart beat even faster than it was from the exertion, she didn't look like she was...alive. Her arms weren't fighting, he saw her head go underwater, then she spiraled back up like a weightless doll, he surged into higher speed, spinning his arms manically and kicking his legs racing to her.

It seemed forever, he was almost to her when he saw her go under again. He dove down, saw the yellow hair like a diaphanous flowing net, and reached out and grabbed a handful. Pushing himself up, he yanked her with him until they both broke the surface. Her eyes were closed, mouth open, her head dangled back.

Etam wrapped his arm across her like a lifeguard, and swam as hard as he could to the shore. The current kept pulling him, he swam diagonally across the rapids until he got close enough to grab a rock.

Holding the rock, he pulled the two of them to the shallow shore, got a toehold and dragged them both up on the bank.

When they cleared the water, she was draped boneless over his arm. Shaking her, Etam yelled, "Tirsa! Tirsa!" He put his ear to her chest, she wasn't breathing. Laying her flat on her back he commenced CPR, 2 puffs of air into her mouth, pump pump on her chest. In seconds she jerked up and started coughing out water.

Etam rolled her on her side until she stopped coughing and choking then folded her over his shoulder, patting her back, speaking soothingly. So worried, he didn't realize he was speaking to her in Dutch, "*Liefje,* come back to me baby."

When she was breathing more easily, he put his hand at the back of her head, his long fingers holding her like a net, he gently pulled her to face him.

His heart skipped a beat. She was so wan, limbs like a ragdoll, her eyes still closed. He tenderly pressed his lips on hers then leaned back. Her eyes fluttered, then slowly opened. Etam smiled, just like Sleeping Beauty awakened by his kiss.

At first disoriented, she smiled weakly, murmured a throaty, "Etam," then she remembered, Rapha throwing her over the cliff- struggling in the rapids, she started screaming.

In alarm, Etam pulled her head to his shoulder, rocking her, he whispered softly in her ear, "It is okay, *liefje,* you are safe, it's over, I promise, baby, it's over. You're safe with me."

His hand under her chin he lifted her head, the frantic eyes jumped at his, then feeling the strength of his arms around her, the fright slipped out and love filled her adoring blue orbs. Her lips curved in a soft smile, she whispered, "Etam, you came for me."

"Always," he choked out then crushed her to his chest, one hand on her back the other cradling her head, his tears dropped on her hair.

Getting control of his emotions, he tilted her head back again, looked into her eyes and bore his lips down on hers. Her hands slid around weakly to clutch his shoulders. The passionate kiss filled with relief and longing and love lasted so long she finally had to tear away to catch her breath.

He brushed her wet hair back, touched her face with his palm. "I thought I'd lost you, first Rapha, then the fall, the water," his voice cracked. His hands shaking, he took her hands. Holding them, he just gazed at her, the woman he loved that he thought he'd never see again.

Her smile brave and tender, voice filled with despair, she told him, "He said you were dead, Etam." At his anguished look for the pain Rapha caused her, she quickly said, "I didn't believe him, I knew you would come for me. You had promised me you wouldn't let anyone ever hurt me again."

His eyes dropped from hers, his head hung. He looked up at her in misery through long spiky lashes wet with the river and his tears of relief. "But I didn't keep my promise, I let that bastard take you. I-"

She put her fingertips to his lips. "Hush." She said, "We were betrayed. You came, against all odds you found me and rescued me, risked your life for mine, that is all that matters."

Kissing her fingers, he stared at her earnest, sincere, beautiful face and crushed her to his chest again. "I don't know what I did to deserve you, *liefje*, but I will be eternally grateful." He found her lips and kissed her like he would never stop. But then, he remembered Owen.

He stood up and held a hand down to her. "Come on, I've got to go get Owen."

Bewildered, she allowed him to pull her after him. Etam hurried as fast and as safely as he could along the bank, running over rocks and mud. It took time before they got back to where he'd last seen Owen. He stopped, put his hand over his brow to cut the glare and scanned the rushing whitecaps.

"There," Tirsa said and pointed. Owen was still thrashing and bobbing in the water.

"Don't move from here, Tirsa." Etam kicked off his sodden boots and tore off his shirt then ran and dove into the water.

"No!" Tirsa screamed, running to the edge of the river. She couldn't believe he went back into the death trap he had just gotten them out of.

Etam had to work at going to where Owen struggled. Swimming diagonally again like in a riptide, Etam had to fight the magnetic push and pull of the powerful current.

"Owen!" he called to the seaman.

The exhausted young man thrashed helplessly in the powerful, surging water. "Help me!" Owen cried hoarsely over the roar of the water.

Etam worked harder to get to him. He was still quite far from the seaman when his blood curdled. He couldn't understand why Owen was being pulled away even as Etam kept coming. Now he knew why.

Owen hadn't moved from his position in the water because he was being dragged to an enormous whirlpool. The colonel and Tirsa had been fortunate to have been swept closer to the side of the river. He could hear Tirsa screaming for him to come back as he continued his trek to get to Owen.

Then the water seized the young traitor, twirling and swirling him in an endless circle, closer and closer to the vortex in the middle. Never relinquishing its hold on him, like a washing machine, the spiraling corkscrew sucked him around and around and down until Etam heard Owen's last cry for help before he disappeared.

Etam slowed, treading water, stared at the empty river. Owen had been a traitor and wanted to harm him and his beloved Tirsa, but like a mad dog, it's still hard to see it put down. It had been Owen or Tirsa, there was no contest, he had chosen to save Tirsa.

Nonetheless, the picture of the seaman being sucked into the bottomless water pit, and his last cries for help would never leave him the rest of his life.

He swam back to shore, back to Tirsa who was waiting with her arms out.

Chapter Thirty-Eight

*I*t took a few hours for Etam and Tirsa to get up the ravine. He found the lowest bank and they started climbing.

Taking a rest break, they sat with their arms around each other for a few moments, watching the water rush past. Weariness in his voice and residual terror of losing her, he said, "First thing, *liefje*, when we get home, I'm teaching you to swim." The blue eyes laughed up at him, he took the opportunity for a kiss to vanquish his lingering fear.

When they reached the top of the crest they had to hike back north to the mountain wall where they had first entered the valley. It was difficult to find because the opening had been an illusion and there was no shell to direct them.

Tirsa stood for a few minutes, her eyes closed, hands out. Then she opened her eyes and walked a few yards then disappeared.

"Hey," Etam called out and hurried after her. They passed through to the valley.

Stepping out onto the velvety grass they both breathed a sigh of relief. Etam was cautious though; he didn't know what they would find.

Another relieved sigh exhaled when he saw his men had released the villagers, and were dragging the dead mercenaries to a place away from the people. What they were going to do with them, Etam didn't know. The few mercs that survived had fled.

"E!" Johnson yelped, and ran to his comrade. Throwing his thick arms around him, he hugged the daylights out of the colonel.

The others heard him yell, they came running. Knox, Bruno, Stav, Lil Dam, all alive, all thrilled to see Etam and Tirsa, hugging them both. They had been preparing to hike the ravine in hopes of finding them alive.

Jancarlo was furthest away. He jogged to the group. He and Etam stood in front of each other. Jancarlo said, "*Mijn broeder*," then they wrapped their arms around one another.

Etam would never tell Jancarlo he saw the tears gleaming in the major's eyes, the stoic major would only deny it. When they separated, Jancarlo stepped to Tirsa who was unabashedly crying, so happy to be reunited with them all. Relieved none of them was seriously injured.

"Tirsa," Jancarlo said her name for the first time ever. "I am truly relieved and pleased that you survived. I regret the shameful way I have treated you. If E thinks you are a good person, and he loves you then that is good enough for me. He deserves a woman like you, strong and brave and kind." He hugged her, and awkwardly patted her back.

Etam stood watching them like a proud papa. Jancarlo released Tirsa and said, "Besides, if he had not gotten you back he would have been hell to live with." They all laughed at his flippancy, releasing the tension of the reunion and Jancarlo's heartfelt words.

"Come on, Colonel, you haven't seen the mines!" Bruno exclaimed and waved for them to follow him. They cheerfully trudged down the valley to the mines, smiling and waving at the happy villagers that were grateful for their rescue.

They entered the cavern, the brilliance of the resplendent, multi-faceted gems was blinding. Holding

Tirsa's hand, Etam looked around in awe. A kaleidoscope of dazzling color twinkled and sparkled like a rainbow of stars surrounded them.

The villager, Majji, timidly entered the cavern. He nervously asked Etam, "What are you going to do with the jewels? I do not mean you any disrespect, sir, but I must warn you, a curse will follow you if you try to take them. I tried to warn that man, Rapha, but he did not believe our lore."

Etam smiled at the young man. "No worries. We didn't come to New Guinea for the diamonds. We came for Rapha and for..." he wasn't sure how to approach the subject of the book he searched for.

Majji smiled serenely. "You desire the book of your ancestors and your God."

Etam's brows jumped at the teenager knowing about the book. He nodded slowly. "*Ja*, I mean yes, I search for the book of Jesus."

Majji grinned and said, "Come." He swiveled and started walking out of the cavern. Everyone followed him.

Lil Dam jogged to catch up with Etam who was holding Tirsa's hand as they walked beside the young villager.

The young seaman asked, "Colonel, you mean we can't have any of the diamonds?"

Jancarlo said, "The curse is real, when Rapha fell, diamonds rolled out of his pockets."

Etam added, "The diamonds belong to these people. We have no right to take them. If we bring any back, others will want to know where we got them and they will come and destroy this valley, and there will be even more destruction of New Guinea than already from the mine scarring, and sediment clogging the rivers."

383

Jancarlo said, "Plus, logging to make roads to get to the mines, devastating the habitat of fauna and flora. Be content you got to see them." He patted the young seaman's shoulder.

"It's okay, Major, it was fantastic, a dream come true, just coming here for this adventure." Lil Dam gave him a huge gold toothed smile. They all followed the villager back up the valley, light of foot they were so gratified.

Walking on springy botanical grass spritzed with wildflowers, Majji led them around past the vegetable gardens and fruit trees. On the other side of a small wheat field there was an ancient cemetery.

He threaded through the plaques on the ground until he got to an actual grave stone. It was a sculpture of the head and shoulders of a man.

Etam crouched in front of it. There was no name on the headstone. He stood up. "I guess I'm going to need a shovel."

Majji smiled impishly. "No sir." He put his hands on the stone and pulled it back. When it was lifted they could see a pocket in the ground under it.

Kneeling on the grass, Etam reached into the pocket. With both hands he pulled out a box and set it on the ground. Everyone moved in closer to see. He opened the box. Inside was a stack of sheaves of papyrus tied with a string made of straw.

Etam sat on the ground, crossed his legs, and with great humble care, his heart palpitating, he lifted the papers out setting them on his lap. Goosebumps on his arms, his face a mix of apprehension and excitement, he untied the string. He picked up a few of the papers and studied them.

On tenterhooks Johnson blurted, "Well?"

"Is it what we came for?" Knox asked.

"The second Bible, Jesus' own words, he wrote? Is it?" Bruno could hardly contain himself. His mother, a staunch Catholic would be out of her mind when he told her.

Etam grinned up at all of them but said ruefully, "I don't know, I think the writing is Aramaic. Maybe Hebrew, but probably Aramaic." He looked around. "Anybody speak…" They laughed at him. Etam said, "What about you, Majji? Master of all languages."

Majji shrugged, shaking his head, he smiled apologetically. "Sorry, sir."

"That's all right, my friend. Finding this, whether or not it's real is still incredible. I will always be grateful to you, Majji, for showing me where it was."

Tirsa hugged the young native to show her thanks.

He said, "You saved my life, Miss Tirsa, I owe you much." Majji wrapped his arms around her and held onto her.

"Uh," Etam said, pretending to be mad, "I'm grateful, Majji but I'm not giving you my girl, so take your hands off her."

Majji red-faced, immediately stepped away from Tirsa. The group laughed. Etam, tied the papers back up, put them back in the box, closed the lid and climbed to his feet.

The group stayed the night as guests of the villagers. They shared a big feast and got to learn a bit about each other. Etam's team was invited into various homes to sleep.

He and Tirsa were invited to a home but the occupants would not allow them to sleep in the same room as they weren't married or united as the tribe dictates.

Etam and Tirsa stood outside the door to the room she was to stay in. Aware the residents were blatantly and cheerfully watching them, Etam slipped his arms around her, pulling her against him. She looked up at him.

"I won't embarrass you," Etam said, "but I'm not leaving you without a kiss." He lowered his head and lightly brushed her lips, then he gently parted her lips with his to taste her sweetness.

Her hands wound around his neck then she knotted her fingers in his hair. Etam maneuvered them so he blocked the family from seeing, the kiss intensified. When he could hear them giggling he reluctantly drew away from her.

"*Liefje,*" Etam whispered, his fingers on her chin. He felt like he was being poured into her glowing eyes. "One last night apart, then I swear to God it will be the last. From now on you don't leave my side. Okay?"

Her response was to pull his head back down and seal his promise with their lips.

In the morning, the team gathered its meager belongings and prepared to leave. The good thing was they could take the horses. There would be enough to leave some with the villagers. The villagers said they didn't need them but you never know. Jancarlo told them how to care for the horses.

When they reached the entrance to the valley, the villagers and Etam's team said goodbye, and one by one they slipped through the illusional door.

As soon as everyone was through to the other side, they gathered to discuss their route back to Copestone.

Just as they started to leave, an immense explosion rattling the air and shaking the ground made them all jump in alarm.

Etam turned his horse back and rushed to the invisible doorway. He ordered, "Everyone stay here," then he stepped back through.

Galloping across the valley he could see fire and smoke billowing from the mines. He quickly found Majji.

"Majji, what the hell happened-"

The young native was upset but not frantic. He said, "That man, one of the men of Rapha's, Tomlin. He had snuck back into the valley and set off dynamite in the mines."

"Was anyone hurt?" Etam asked in concern.

"Just Mr. Tomlin, sir. He didn't get out of the mine in time before it exploded. Then-" the young man broke off as they heard a rumbling. He and Etam anxiously looked around.

The valley floor started to crack, then pull apart wider, the villagers came running out, boulders rolled down the mountains, then the mountains themselves started to crumble.

Majji yelled to Etam, "You need to go, go now or the exit will be sealed." He turned to run.

"But, Majji, what about you, the people-"

Majji hesitated, smiled warmly at Etam and said, "We will be fine, sir. It has happened before. Now go before you are trapped here with us."

He pivoted and with a wave, ran to join his people who were gathering the animals and disappearing past the mines. The center of the valley was splitting straight down the middle opening into a wicked widening crevasse.

Etam watched for a second, relieved that the people, their village and the mines would disappear and no one could come and destroy them, including the few mercenaries that had gotten away.

He kicked his horse to hurry back to the opening.

As he got to the hidden door, the mountain wall was coming down, rocks and boulders tumbled and rumbled, crashing around him, the horse leaped through the door.

Appearing on the other side, he saw his team waiting anxiously for him.

Louise Furley

"Go!" he shouted the order, all on horseback they fled from the collapsing, rapidly disintegrating mountain.

Epilogue

*T*he team was packed and ready, waiting for Bruno and Jancarlo to prepare the Zoeken for boarding. Etam and Tirsa were in the study. The day they had reached Copestone Lodge, Etam knelt on one knee and formally asked Tirsa to be his wife.

After a happy, "*Yes*!" She asked, "When?"

He had swung her up in his arms and groaned his words, "As soon as *bloedig* possible, *mijn liefje,* I can't wait to call you mine for real. And," his dark head had dropped to hers, "I can't wait to consummate our marriage."

Now, several days later, she sat on the couch watching him talking on the phone.

Etam was speaking in Dutch so she couldn't understand a thing he was saying. Saying goodbye, he disconnected the call and joined her on the couch. He took her hand, holding it with both of his.

"*Liefje,* it's done. Now that I know it was Rapha who gave the order to get you on board the Silenus and blackmailed you into killing me," he squeezed her hand, "which, by the way, you failed miserably at." He smiled lovingly at her as her cheeks reddened, mortified over the mission she was given, and thankfully was unable to carry out.

"I'm so glad I was a failure that day, Etam," she smiled, stroking her hand on his face.

He kissed the tip of her nose then continued, "I found out Rapha had recruited Owen while we were still onshore, before we had departed to New Guinea. Owen had a small criminal record that his father had paid big money to bury, but Rapha was able to dig up. He waved greenbacks in Owen's face and that was it."

"Oh, that's so sad," Tirsa said with real sorrow. "What about Lindsey?"

"Apparently, Owen and Lindsey had become buddies and he filled her in on the deal. She hated you so much she agreed to double deal with him. I'm sure the money was a draw as well," he added dryly.

Shaking her head sadly, Tirsa said solemnly, "And they both paid with their lives."

They were quiet for a moment. It was terrible that two young people with their whole lives in front of them had chosen to throw in with felons and had paid the biggest price.

"*Ja*, well, anyway," Etam squeezed Tirsa's hand. "The good news is, my people in the states were able to track down the thug that Rapha hired to conduct the kidnapping and make the arrangements to send you to off me. Personally, I'd like to thank him, because without him I wouldn't have met *mijn zeldzaam men*."

Seeing the lack of comprehension on her face, he leaned in giving her a tiny kiss, then told her, "It means 'my precious one.'" He pulled her onto his lap. She cuddled against him like she was made to fit right there.

"Anyway," he said, "they got the man and the other people that were involved. They are in custody, and your niece Meggie is back home safe and sound. We can call her as soon as you like."

Tirsa sat straight up, her mouth dropped. Tears rolling, she cupped his face and thanked him with the most passionate kiss Etam had ever experienced.

Just as he tightened his arms around her, she leaned back to gaze at his handsome face. It was glorious to finally be able to look at him as long as she desired.

She no longer had to struggle with her feelings, or worry what he or someone else would say about her staring at him. She could watch him at her leisure for as long as she wanted, free to drink in and appreciate every ounce, breadth and square inch of him.

She murmured, grateful and content, "Thank you, Etam."

"Ahh," he moaned, pulling her back into his embrace. Just as his lips fused to hers, he said, "You know how it gets me when you say my name…"

The End

Please look for Jancarlo Mercury's story next!

Gritty danger, suspense and hard won romance infuse this thrilling, passionate novel!

Tacienne Vinique is a young woman of extreme innocence. Brought up in strict isolation for her own protection, her mother has hidden her since she was a child from the deviant King Juvenet who planned to ravage the young girl then force her into marriage.

Everything in the world is new to Taci; airplanes, TV, phones, cars, men. Especially men.

Major Jancarlo Mercury is a hard-bitten, cold, harsh man with little patience for others than his own team. Women have one use, and he can barely tolerate them for that.

Taci has been found and captured. Tied to trees in the woods, she is about to be sacrificed to a savage warrior when Jancarlo charges in and saves her from imminent death.

Now, the major is tasked with keeping her prisoner, and safe from all those seeking to harm her, until he has to deliver her to the demented, sadistic monarch.

Jancarlo was chosen for the job because there is nothing but ice-water in his veins and he will be immune to Taci's haunting beauty.

Danger strikes at them from every corner.

Finally, it is time for Jancarlo to deliver Taci to her devastating future.

Except, he has been tamed by the flaming wraith's sweet, gentle ways, and it takes everything the iron major has in him to bring her to the king and leave her.

Will she survive the night?

www.ingramcontent.com/pod-product-compliance
Lightning Source LLC
Chambersburg PA
CBHW021426240626
47153CB00001B/48